About the Author

Celia Reynolds was born and raised in Wales and worked for almost twenty-five years in the film industry in London, and briefly Rome. In 2012, she left her job as European Marketing Director at Twentieth Century Fox to enrol in the Complete Creative Writing Course held at the Groucho Club in London's West End. Later that year, she was awarded Runner Up prize in the London Writers' Club/Hush Short Story Competition. She is now based on the Gower coast in South Wales.

@CeliaRWriter
@celiareynoldsauthor

Finding Henry Applebee

Celia Reynolds

OneMoreChapter

One More Chapter
A division of HarperCollins*Publishers* Ltd
1 London Bridge Street
London SE1 9GF

www.harpercollins.co.uk

This paperback edition 2019
4

First published in Great Britain in ebook format by
HarperCollins*Publishers* 2019

A catalogue record for this book
is available from the British Library

ISBN: 978-0-00-833632-5

This novel is entirely a work of fiction.
The names, characters and incidents portrayed in it are
the work of the author's imagination. Any resemblance to
actual persons, living or dead, events or localities is
entirely coincidental.

Set in Birka by
Palimpsest Book Production Limited, Falkirk, Stirlingshire

Printed and bound in the UK by CPI Group (UK) Ltd, Croydon
CR0 4YY

MIX
Paper from
responsible sources
FSC™ C007454
www.fsc.org

To my mother, Joy,
&
especially, gratefully, Caroline and Brian, wherever you are –
this is for you

'It's that—the *thought* of the few, simple things we want and the *knowledge* that we're going to get them in spite of you know Who and His spites and tempers—that keeps us living I think.'

Dylan Thomas, *The Collected Letters of Dylan Thomas*

'*Periissem ni periissem.*
I would have perished had I not persisted.'

Anstruther Clan Motto

Prologue

A Pollock on the Floor

Henry

What it all came down to, in the end, were the contents of a small brown suitcase, stored within stretching distance under the bed.

By Henry's own admission the case itself was unremarkable. Scuffed and shabby, it had mouldered, half-hidden in the semi-darkness on a slightly dusty, carpeted floor. The handle, which was made of a robust, finely crafted cowhide leather, had grown ragged, and the once shiny metal clasps designed to spring open with a conspicuously satisfying *click* were tarnished and dull. *And yet*, Henry reminded himself, *appearances can be deceptive*; what mattered to him lay meticulously preserved within.

He kept a firm grip on the suitcase's handle as he made his way onto the teeming concourse at King's Cross train station. It was still early, the air charged with a melee of arrival and departure announcements, the throb of engines, the irritable drone of traffic from the nearby Euston Road. Henry felt a carousel of emotion crank into gear inside him. *Focus!* he told himself. *Don't let yourself get distracted until you're seated on that train...*

He drew to a stop in the centre of the concourse and placed his suitcase at his feet. Overhead, an indistinct mass of words blurred and flickered on the electronic departure board. Henry rubbed his eyes and tried desperately to remember his Mantra of the Day:

'Applebee,' he mumbled under his breath. 'My name is Henry Applebee...'

Steadying himself with his walking stick, Henry lowered his gaze to the granite-grey concourse floor. Tiny spots of blood were raining down upon it, just inches from his black Derby shoes. It took him a moment to grasp where the blood was coming from, then he raised his hand to his face and realised with a start that it was trickling from his nose.

Henry's heart sank. The sharp slick of red struck a violent chord of colour amongst an uninspiring sea of grey and black, navy and taupe – flat, wintry hues which hovered like low-lying clouds around the shoulders of the commuters who stood transfixed before the overhead departure board, or scurried backwards and forwards, zigzagging continuously across his path.

'Whatever you do next,' he said in a valiant attempt at calm, 'DON'T PANIC!'

Henry's eyes darted to the dizzying conveyor belt of faces sailing past him. One or two of his fellow travellers turned and cast a cursory glance in his direction. The majority, he noted, barely seemed to register him at all. He wondered if they were repelled. Perhaps they were just far too absorbed in the busyness of their own lives to notice an old man with a bloody nose?

He teetered, incredulous, as blood continued to gush in slow motion from his body and began to form an expanding pool of crimson on the floor.

It was out of his peripheral vision, as he detected the ferrous taste of metal trickling down the back of his throat, that he suddenly saw the figure of a girl running towards him. Henry scanned the outline of her face, caught the lightness and the ease with which she moved. For one brief instant, he debated whether she might be an angel. But then, as she drew closer, he saw to his relief that she was just a girl, an ordinary teenager like any other, probably seventeen or eighteen at most. Besides – now that he came to think of it – wasn't an angel supposed to materialise in a nimbus of white light? Not arrive sprinting, dragging a wheelie bag behind her and spilling milky coffee from a paper cup onto the floor...

As she approached the centre of the ever-widening circle in which he now found himself, the frothy liquid splattered left and right, merging with the bloodstains on the ground.

Henry and the teenager stared in unison at what they had done.

'It looks like a Jackson Pollock,' he said, marvelling, despite himself, at the effect. He pointed at the evolving creation with his stick. 'I think the technical term is "*drip painting*".'

The girl scraped her long, mousey hair behind her back and tilted her head to one side. She was standing right next to him now, eyes narrowed, lips pursed in contemplation.

'Looks to me like the inside of my head,' she replied in a lightly accented voice. 'When I'm having a bad day. A day full of demons.'

Henry thought this was an interesting analogy, but he was too distracted searching for something to stem the blood flow to express the fact out loud. He patted the pockets of his overcoat and noticed that the fringes of the girl's multicoloured scarf were stained with thick, wet splashes of coffee.

Silently, he berated himself.

'It's dramatic, though,' the girl continued. Her tone was attentive, her pale eyes keen, unwavering. 'Like an explosion of light and dark.'

Turning at last to face him, she pressed a pocket-sized packet of tissues into Henry's palm.

Henry fumbled, his stiff, papery fingers tugging clumsily at the slippery semicircle of perforated plastic.

The girl edged closer and cupped her hand around his arm. 'Are you okay?'

Henry nodded. Instinctively, he felt that he should ask her name, discover the identity of this troubled, angelic stranger who had rushed, unbidden, to his aid, but his heart was still jackhammering beneath his ribs.

It was the damnedest thing... Half of him had expected to see his life flash before his eyes, and yet *surely* this wasn't his time? Not *here*. Not *now*. Not when his journey was only just starting to unfold?

He blinked several times in succession in an effort to ground himself more fully in his surroundings.

The irony of the situation weighed on him like sin.

Here he was, once again in a bustling train station (albeit one on a much grander scale), ready to resume where he had left off all those years ago, the night of a snowstorm, and of a slow-curling flame...

Henry raised his head. Fixed his gaze on the soaring lattice-work of white metal girders which strained and arced, crisscrossing like a giant sugar cage high above the station concourse. He felt the girl take the tissues from his hand. There was a moment's hesitation, and she began to wipe the trails of blood from his chin.

Henry kept his head held high and inched his foot discreetly along the ground, searching for his suitcase. He found its flat, armoured surface with his heel and gave an inner sigh of relief. *It was still there. Everything was fine. His plan was all on track!*

In the expectant space before him, Henry sensed the Pollock seeping into the concrete, morphing like a kaleidoscope and creating wondrous new forms, until the blood slowed into droplets, and finally into nothing at all, so that all that remained were shiny swirls of milk-white and scarlet and caramel-brown; a promising – if unexpected – explosion of light and dark on a once empty floor.

Part One

ENCOUNTERS

1

The Notebook

KENTISH TOWN, LONDON, DECEMBER 5: *JOURNEY EVE*

Henry

My name is Henry Arthur Applebee. I'm eighty-five and counting, with an arthritic knee, a healthy head of hair and all my faculties, though not all my own teeth. I've had a pretty good life, but I'd be lying if I said I didn't have any regrets. Anyone who gets to my age and says they have no regrets is either deluded, or senile, or both. When all's said and done, the facts remain as follows:

I may be old, but it doesn't mean I don't still have any dreams.

Who's to say there's an expiry date on achieving your goals?

Is it ever too late to right a wrong?

Celia Reynolds

Now that Devlin's gone, I've learned that establishing a focused and precise daily mantra can be a very effective way of ensuring your marbles are still intact. 'Stay engaged in life!' – that's what they say when you retire. Then, as time hurtles by and everyone you know starts dropping around you like flies, it's: 'Keep your mind active. Cultivate a hobby. Join a community group!'

But for me, it all comes down to my notebook. The Revealer of Secrets. The Holder of Truths. The place where those I've loved reach out – right from between these very pages – and, grinning, take me by the hand and say, 'Come in! Don't be shy. You want us to show you something marvellous?'

It began, somewhat prosaically, with Adam Donnelly, a young man from Wyedean who called in to see me at the start of July. Banjo and I had been managing just fine on our own up until then. But visitors have an annoying knack of stirring things up; of reminding you there's a whole sprawling world beyond the confines of the one you've learned to inhabit by yourself.

'We'd like you to write an article for the Wyedean quarterly magazine,' Adam D. said. 'It's for a retrospective we're running on former members of the teaching faculty, and as our most senior contributor, we'll be featuring you in our cover story. You'll be the poster boy for excellence! For a life well and truly lived.'

A small weight snowballed inside me. 'Will anyone still be interested?' I asked. This was not false modesty; on the

10

contrary, I was positively taken aback. The corners of Adam D.'s mouth veered upwards. 'You're one of Wyedean's most esteemed former language teachers, Mr Applebee. The board thinks a self-penned profile will be illuminating not just for the current staff and pupils, but also for your peers.' 'Oh,' I said, 'I see. Are any of them still alive?'

I hadn't heard from Wyedean in a long while and the request puzzled me. 'What kind of illuminations are you looking for?' I asked. 'Anything uplifting,' he replied. 'Anecdotes, observations, greatest achievements. That kind of thing. It's a tough world our pupils are facing. Hugely competitive. Our aim is to buoy them up with as much support and inspiration as we can.' Adam Doolally drummed his fingers on the arm of my wing-back chair and smiled encouragingly once again.

Doubtful as to my ability to either illuminate or inspire, I nodded. Signed on the dotted line, as they say. It was only after he'd gone that the full magnitude of the task hit me: academic career aside, I couldn't think of a single event in my life which might reasonably qualify as a 'greatest achievement'. Nothing worthy of the inspiration-hungry readers of the Wyedean quarterly magazine, at any rate.

How in the name of all that's holy does a senior citizen, occasional UFO spotter and Francophile reduce eight-and-a-half decades (and counting) of life to a fifteen-hundred-word article? It felt remarkably as though I were being called to account. 'Impress us!' Wyedean seemed to be saying. 'Tell us what you know. What you've learned. Show us who you are.'

Bells of panic filled my chest. (Never a good sign at my age.) What Wyedean wanted was insights, the Happy Ever After. But what about the areas of my life where I'd failed so spectacularly? What on earth was I supposed to say about those?

I decided to narrow my focus and stick to the long, seamlessly interchangeable years spent teaching hormonally fuelled adolescents to conjugate French verbs. It was quite staggering, when I came to think about it. Entire decades had slipped by. Decades filled with page after page of Verlaine, Gide, Maupassant, Baudelaire. It was extraordinary, the degree to which I'd buried myself in those pages. Revelled in their majesty. Wallowed – privately – in their pain.

To Wyedean, I was still Mr Applebee: devoted (and, it would seem, fondly remembered!) former Head of French; but to me I was just Henry, the gauche, skinny teenager running around the streets of Chalk Farm with Devlin, yet to put on the uniform, yet to meet the girl.

When the article was finished, I dropped it, shamefaced, into the post box and tried desperately not to think of it as a lie. An evasion, maybe, but then how could they know it was the things I didn't put in – the personal things, the things buried at the bottom of a dusty suitcase – which had defined me?

Changi… Sunburn so bad the skin peeled away from my chest in sheets. Everyone told me to keep quiet about that. It was a punishable offence. The officers would scrub the blisters with salt water if they got wind of it. I grew up so fast, I barely recognised myself when I arrived back home.

And then, when I did so, I climbed a staircase and there she was. The very last thing I was ever expecting to happen to me, Fra—

Henry's hand jerked abruptly from the page. A noise (a grunt? A cough? A chuckle?) filtered through the wall from the spare room.

'Devlin?' he whispered. 'Devlin, is that you?'

Henry cocked his good ear to one side, but all he could make out was the steady *ticktock ticktock* of the carriage clock on the mantelpiece. He held his breath, the curvature of his spine straightening by degrees until finally, he felt it: his brother's voice, brushing like dew against his skin.

Evening, Henry. How're things?

Henry wiggled his finger in his ear. *Devlin*. Where does one begin to capture the essence of a man whose character had been so large, so utterly irrepressible that even in death his exuberance couldn't be contained?

Don't keep me guessing, Devlin continued. *How's tricks? What's going on?*

Henry settled back into his chair and attuned himself to the frequency, as though he'd stumbled across some strange, transcontinental broadcast on the radio. 'I'm fine,' he replied to the room at large. 'Fine, that is, aside from the fact I'm sitting here, in my living room, talking to you.'

He stared into the flat, empty space ahead of him and beamed.

Following up his Wyedean article with a notebook of 'recollections' (*memoirs* seemed too worthy a concept, too weighty, too proud) had been the result of an overwhelming urge to continue writing, only *this* time Henry was determined to do it for himself alone – no expectations, no limitations, no holds barred. What he hadn't bargained on was the way the focused bursts of concentrated silence gave rise to many strange and wonderful occurrences, not least of all these fleeting, otherworldly conversations with Devlin, two years gone.

Occasionally, like today, Henry answered him out loud, but he didn't like to make a habit of it in case he forgot himself and did it in public. Next thing you knew, if anyone saw him chuckling or talking to his dead brother while he was queuing for his pension at the post office, they'd be carting him off to the funny farm.

'I'm going away,' Henry ventured with a faint whiff of heroism. 'And the truth is, I don't think I've ever felt so simultaneously terrified and exhilarated at the prospect of anything in my entire life. I leave for Scotland tomorrow morning on the nine o'clock train.'

He lowered his gaze. Deep inside his chest, his heart began to quiver.

Away? Devlin's voice, bolder now, slipped a little further beneath Henry's skin. *It's her, isn't it? The girl? Don't tell me you've actually gone and found her after all this time?*

Henry bristled. 'She has a name, Devlin. And as to finding her, yes, it would seem to be the case.'

There was a momentary pause.

Hellfire. So what's the problem?

Henry shifted in his seat. 'Well – if you must know – I've had a premonition. But I won't be stopped,' he added in a tremulous voice. 'Not by you. Not by anyone.'

Have you finally gone loco? Devlin shot back. *When have I ever discouraged you from doing anything? The way I remember it, it was always you who'd be running after me! Ah Jesus, Hen, what's with the premonition, anyway? I leave you alone for two minutes and you're moonlighting as some kind of oracle? Sounds to me like someone's got way too much free time on their hands!*

There was another brief pause. *Well go on. Let's have it then.*

Just the tiniest bit miffed, Henry cleared his throat. 'That despite all my hopes and prayers for the contrary, nothing at all is going to go to plan.'

He sucked in his cheeks and waited for Devlin's disembodied response. When it didn't come he shook his head, waited, shook it again, but the signal – for want of a better word – was gone.

Alone once again, Henry slipped off his tortoiseshell glasses, rubbed his eyes with the heels of his hands and rose stiffly from his chair. He carried his notebook into his bedroom and placed it next to a jar of Vicks VapoRub on the bedside table. Banjo, his Parson Russell Terrier, padded into the room behind him and hovered at his side, his ears drawn back, his face full of mistrust.

'Banjo, come on now, get out from under my feet,' Henry said gently.

On the eiderdown, his small brown suitcase lay open and ready, the air around it lightly tinged with must. A faint tremor rippled upwards from Henry's fingertips as he stepped towards it, and with painstaking care and attention proceeded to remove a series of bundles from the elasticated pocket running along its side:

1. a silver hair-slide, a pearl and diamanté butterfly perched on its tip, wings spread;
2. a uniform cap, field service, blue-grey;
3. a paper napkin the colour of turned cream, bearing the faintest imprint of coral lipstick;
4. a picture postcard, the back of which was filled with a seemingly random miscellany of words and phrases, each forward-sloping letter jostling against its neighbour like links in a tightly woven chain;
5. a jagged strip of dark red velour.

Henry unwrapped each item individually and turned it over in his hand. Raising his gaze, he cast a surreptitious glance at the alarm clock by his bed.

Twelve hours exactly to departure.

One memory at a time, Henry placed his past back in his case. His preparations complete, he made his way back to the living room and lowered himself into his wing-back chair with a cup of Ceylon Orange Pekoe and three custard creams.

'Amended Mantra of the Day,' he said, turning to Banjo's upturned face. 'No matter what age we reach, or however much our lives may settle beneath the inevitable cloak of familiarity, it is never, ever too late to be amazed.'

Henry wondered what the people from Wyedean would say if they knew the context behind his words. That he was a fool, probably. That after a lifetime of so-called academic excellence, how banal, how *unoriginal* of him to admit that what mattered to him most now was love.

He shifted his gaze to the antiquated furniture and mountains of yellowing books as though viewing everything for the first, or last, time. He would not return. The world could mock him all it liked, he wouldn't give up until he'd said the words he needed to say to the only person alive who mattered to him now.

Henry's hand drifted to an envelope peeking out from his cardigan pocket. Inside it: pre-purchased train tickets for Edinburgh. First Class. *Two*.

'Perhaps it'll be fine after all,' he said, his spirits revived by a resurgent ray of optimism. He leaned over and rubbed the back of Banjo's head. 'And if it's not fine, then stone me, at least it'll be illuminating...'

2

Wide Awake

FINSBURY PARK, LONDON, DECEMBER 5: *JOURNEY EVE*

Ariel

Somewhere along a dusky stretch of track, Ariel felt her nerve waver. She drew her face back from the window as the train decelerated, leaving the grainy, urban blackness behind and easing its way beneath the vast, multi-arched roof of Paddington Station.

A stranger standing in the aisle purred into her phone: 'We're pulling in now... I'll meet you in the usual place... Yes... Yes, me too.'

Ariel lowered her eyes and picked at a hangnail embedded in her thumb. If anything should happen to her over the next few days – some random accident, some freakish act of nature, or God, or destiny, or whatever – Linus would be the one to get a phone call. It could come from London, Edinburgh, or just about anywhere in between; the point was that a police officer would call with the news, and none of it would make any sense because she hadn't told him the truth about where she was going. It would be a disaster. The worst possible way for him to find out she'd lied.

Actually, that she'd been lying to him for days.

She squeezed her eyes shut and tugged. A quick, sharp flare of pain and the hangnail came away in her fingers, a tiny droplet of blood mushrooming upwards and outwards over the rosy surface of her skin. *Don't be a wuss*, she told herself. *It's two days! Forty-eight hours from now it'll all be over.*

At 20:37, Ariel stepped down onto a freezing cold platform, her wheelie bag in her hand. She pulled her multicoloured scarf tighter around her neck and joined a fast-moving line of passengers heading towards the ticket barriers. On instinct, she tilted her face upwards and breathed in the thick, metallic air. A faint murmur of danger (unspecified, intangible, largely cinematic in origin) caught at her chest. *The pull of the city,* she thought, her spirits lifting. *A promise of adventure. Thank you, God! Now I remember.*

The descent to the Underground led her into a frenzied warren of escalators and tunnels. Ariel negotiated her route to Finsbury Park with relative ease, surfaced at ground level and walked down a long, starkly lit passageway until she reached a busy sleeve of London high street. She emerged onto Seven Sisters Road and faltered. A dense knot of pedestrians scurried past her, snatching her breath away, their faces armed with hard-edged confidence – the kind of attitude, she decided, that only a city as awesome as London could produce.

She stepped to one side, flipped open the canvas bag slung over her shoulder and searched for Tumbleweed's email on her phone. *Mags is cool with you staying the night,* he'd written. *You'll like her. Just don't call her Magdalena. Crazy girl thinks it makes her sound like a disciple.*

She memorised his directions, crossed over the road and set off to her right. A zigzag of turns, and she arrived at last at a steep run of concrete steps leading to a side-street basement.

Ariel lingered for a moment on the pavement and peered into the milky darkness. 'Mag-da-le-na,' she intoned, airing the word out, freeing it so it wouldn't sneak up on her later and catch her unawares.

She dragged her wheelie bag to the bottom of the stairs and pressed her finger to a bronze buzzer. A light snapped on beyond the window, and a wiry cat, perched territorially on the windowsill, glowered at her with bilious green eyes.

'Hi there,' she said, backing carefully away from it.

Behind her, the door swung open. 'You must be Ariel,' said a girl with violet, asymmetric hair. 'I'm Mags. Come in!'

The first thing Ariel felt was the music, slipping inside her, squeezing the air from her lungs like a vice. '*Aladdin Sane,*' she said, dropping her shoulder bag to the floor. 'Ziggy goes to America. 1973.'

Mags raised her eyebrows. 'Yeah, it is! You a Bowie-head?'

Ariel tilted her hand from side to side. 'Kind of, I suppose. I used to think I was the only person on the planet who thought it was called *A Lad Insane* until I found out the pun was intentional. Estelle – my mother – was a massive Bowie fan. It's weird to hear it here. Reminds me of home.'

'Shit. Sorry.' Mags took an aborted step towards an old-school iPod and seemed to be weighing up whether or not to turn it off. 'Tumbleweed told me what happened, I'm –'

'It's okay. It's fine, don't worry.'

Ariel smiled awkwardly and looked away, her throat thickening, an icy, sinking sensation billowing through her insides. She tried to distract herself by focusing on her surroundings: low ceiling; a lumpy sofa; floorboards bare apart from a shabby, oversized Persian rug; cheap lamps and mirrored cushions and a half-eaten pizza scattered at random intervals around the room.

The back wall was covered with what she assumed must be Mags's artwork. Sketch after sketch of semi-naked, contorted torsos which somehow managed to look both fragile and disarmingly self-possessed.

'Are those yours?' she asked, moving closer. The hand-drawn charcoal figures were softer close up; less physically arresting. 'They're amazing! Seriously, I wish I could do that.'

Mags threw her an appreciative smile. '*Gracias*. They're part of my coursework. I'm still working on my technique, but honestly, I'd rather look at those than at that hideous woodchip wallpaper underneath.'

Ariel pulled off her gloves and ran a finger over the pock-marked surface of the wall. She'd grown up in a house full of woodchip wallpaper, but this stuff looked original, like it had actually been there since the '70s, long before she was born.

She took a step back and inhaled. The air smelled damp and faintly aromatic, an oddly comforting blend of the rundown and the exotic.

'You're a lifesaver for putting me up,' she said, turning back to Mags. 'Linus thinks I'm in Oxford with Tumbleweed, so at least being here with you makes me feel less guilty.' She caught the look of curiosity on Mags's face and shrugged. 'It was a necessary lie. Given the circumstances.'

'No worries. Any friend of my cousin's. Who's Linus, anyway? Your boyfriend?'

Ariel smiled. 'No, he's my dad.'

'You call your dad by his first name? *Wow*. Progressive.'

Ariel rolled her eyes. '*Trust* me, you wouldn't say that if you met him. The name thing's just something I've done for a while. It's no big deal, really.'

Her gaze drifted to the sofa.

'That's where you'll be crashing, I'm afraid,' Mags said. 'Or if that doesn't grab you, my boyfriend and I are going to a party in Kensal Rise. It might even turn into an all-nighter if the booze holds out, so don't be surprised if we don't come back...' She paused. 'You know, you're welcome to come with us if you like?'

As she spoke, a tall, monobrowed guy in a donkey jacket slunk into view in the bedroom doorway. He looked over at Ariel and grinned. 'Alright?'

Ariel held up her palm in greeting. She opened her mouth to answer Mags's question, then faltered. *A student party. In London. Cool, arty, interesting people her own age. No one to answer to but herself. Wasn't that what eighteen-year-olds were supposed to do? Let their hair down and have some fun?*

22

She took a breath, felt the sharp thud of a door slamming shut somewhere deep inside her, and slowly shook her head. 'Thanks, Mags, but I have to leave early in the morning to get to King's Cross. I can't risk missing my train.'

When they'd gone it felt as though they'd taken every trace of oxygen from the room.

Ariel laid her coat and scarf on the arm of the sofa. She stood tugging at the sleeves of her jumper, trying to adjust to the stillness. In Oystermouth, she was used to it. At night, once the bay had grown cool and dark and secretive, not even the low roll of the waves carried to her bedroom at the back of the house. But here – *in the city* – it was unexpected. Unsettling, even.

She turned and searched for the iPod before remembering that it, too, was gone; swept into Mags's pocket along with a packet of Rizlas and some gum. The only sounds now came from the street: the swoosh of passing traffic; the truncated slamming of car doors; the dull scrape of anonymous, torso-less feet on the pavement beyond the railings; low voices, muffled voices, distant, unintelligible all.

Alone in the city's alien underbelly, Ariel watched the pulsing of her heart through her clothes, the first leg of her journey begun.

She settled herself cross-legged on the floor and unzipped her wheelie bag on the Persian rug. Her hands slid beneath the hastily packed layers of clothing until they found the large, padded envelope at the bottom. She lifted it out and placed it in her lap, contemplating, as she had done so many times before, the startling immediacy of Estelle's handwriting etched across its front.

Ariel read the words out loud: *'For E.M.H.'*

Secured with a strip of Sellotape beneath it was a Post-it Note containing a phone number and an address on the outskirts of Edinburgh – some far-off village she'd never even heard her mother mention before. And below that, five words, their lettering markedly less defined: ARIEL, PLEASE DELIVER BY HAND.

Ariel ran her fingers over the words, held the package to her chest, closed her eyes. It was bad enough not knowing what was inside it, but now she'd had to lie through her teeth, too. 'Promise me you won't tell him,' Estelle had asked her. 'You must promise me you won't tell Dad anything about this at all.'

Why???

'Fuck.' Ariel glanced at the low-rent transience of her surroundings. Here, in this abandoned basement, the package had mysteriously transformed itself into the most intimate object in the room...

She lowered it to her lap and slid it back inside her case.

The second envelope – the much smaller one containing a letter 'inviting' her to begin her journey – had arrived by post the previous week, addressed in an unfamiliar hand to *Miss Ariel Bliss*. It remained tucked away where she'd hidden it, in the inside pocket of her canvas shoulder bag.

Remained, as it turned out, an enigma, even after reading.

* * *

The bathroom, Mags had told her, could only be accessed by walking through the bedroom. ('Cracks me up,' she'd called as she headed out the door. 'Whenever I want to blow people's minds, I tell them my shitty rental has an underground *en suite!*')

Ariel pushed open the bedroom door and switched on the light. Immediately to her right was a desk weighed down by a large pile of books on art and design. Alongside them were a couple of well-thumbed Ursula Le Guin novels. Half a dozen by Stephen King. She reached out her hand and touched the woody texture of their spines with her fingertips. *Home*, she mused, with an unexpected smile.

The bathroom itself, tucked away in the far corner of the room, was narrow, windowless, white; surely, she thought later, the least likely location on earth for what was to happen next. And yet it was right here, as she was bending over the sink – one hand drawing her hair back from her face, the other holding her toothbrush – that she suddenly felt a pair of hands brush against her shoulders from behind.

Ariel dropped her toothbrush into the basin and spun round. Every cheesy horror movie she'd ever seen flashed before her eyes. Slowly, she turned once more to face the mirror. The reflection staring back at her was her own, the backdrop nothing more than a plain, ceramic tile.

'Holy shit,' she said in a horrified voice. 'Get a grip! *Idiot.*'

A shiver of recognition rippled along her spine. Ariel gasped, her eyes open wide. What she'd felt had been cold, fragile, and something else – something she almost didn't dare artic-ulate – something *familiar*. The invisible hands had lain on her body for the briefest of seconds, but they had been there, she was certain of it.

Just before dawn, a pair of car headlights sliced through the living room darkness with two exploratory beams of light. Ariel stirred and raised her head from the sofa. She listened for the sound of Mags's key scraping against the door, the drunken rapping of knuckles on the window pane, but none came.

A shadow flitted briefly past the window. *Bollocks. She hated being scared!*

She stared up at the ceiling, her heart thundering in her chest, then reached her hand to the floor and fumbled for her phone. At her touch, the screen sprang to life, illuminating her face with a bright, neon glow. She tapped on the email icon and opened a new message. LONDON CALLING, she wrote in the subject line, then backed up and changed it to LONDON, WIDE AWAKE!

Hey Tee, it's me. I'm at Mags's place and I can't sleep. Confession 1: I've been thinking about Estelle and wondering if she can see me. If she thinks I'm doing a good job. If I said the right thing when I told Isaac she left us to become a star in heaven and light up the sky over Oystermouth Bay. He started looking for her every single night, and when he couldn't see any stars he asked if she'd forgotten to shine for us. I panicked and told him Estelle's star was so beautiful and bright, she was probably needed some-where else...

Confession 2: My head's been full of demons again. It's kind of intense. There's just so much pressure to be a fully formed person, straight out the gate. Maybe I'm losing it. Maybe it's just me?
Confession 3: A secret scares the crap out of me. Do you think my promise to Estelle will make everything come right?

Ariel lifted her thumbs from the keypad. She entered Tumbleweed's name in the To box. Scanned over what she'd written. Faltered.

Tapped Delete.

In the distance a car alarm began to wail.

She slid her legs from her sleeping bag and carried her phone to the woodchip wall of artwork. Shivering in the half-light, she ran her eyes over the shadowy rows of pictures until she settled upon a sketch of a woman, her arms loosely folded over her small, bare chest. The woman's face was in profile, her expression hard to read. Ariel leaned her head to one side. From one angle, she thought she saw rapture; from another, grief.

'What are you looking at?' she whispered.

A thin wedge of light from the window shimmied across the floorboards. London was lonely at night, she decided. It wasn't the great big adventure she'd been expecting.

'Loneliness is nothing more than an illusion,' she reminded herself. 'Just like Frank said.'

She accessed the camera function on her phone and held it up in front of her. 'Anyway, I'm not here for an adventure,' she added in a purposeful voice. 'I'm here because of a promise.'

Ariel stared at the wall ahead. *Then again, what if her cross-country mission brought her closer, somehow, to Estelle?*

She snapped a photo of the woman in the picture and sent it to Tumbleweed.

Somewhere nearby, in the city of shadows, a clock struck five.

Her train to Edinburgh was at eight...

She made her way back to the sofa, zipped herself inside her sleeping bag and dropped her gaze to her canvas bag lying nearby. The person who'd sent her the letter – summoning her to Scotland in such a polite, cryptic way – had no idea Ariel would be arriving early. *And that was just the way she liked it.*

In fact, it was about the only part of this entire weird undertaking that was perfectly fine with her.

3

The Tower

BLACKPOOL, FEBRUARY 1948

Henry

Henry's jaw drops. The moment he steps inside, he can smell it: something raw; and electric; and alive.

The entrance hall at street level is bigger, grander than he'd imagined; high-ceilinged, ablaze with light, fizzing with expectation. He joins the queue behind a man in a flamboyant silk tie and gazes overhead, cap raked at an angle, hands resting casually in the trouser pockets of his uniform. The new year is six weeks old. He's back in Britain at last. He is almost, but not quite, home.

Henry roots his feet to the floor, his grey eyes drinking in the wonderment of it all. Lined up ahead is a medley of earnest faces, young men and women like himself, each more dedicated than the next to the business of having a good time.

His thoughts flit impatiently to the music, to the chance to finally kick back and relax. He sucks in his cheeks and whistles, long and low. *This is it,* he thinks. *This is something marvellous indeed!*

In the shelter of the foyer it's warm, too. Outside, a blistering wind tears along the promenade, snapping at the skirts of a group of girls who bustle through the open doorway behind him, giggling, a saucy glint in their eyes, their cheeks rouged raw by the chill. He reaches inside his jacket for a cigarette and pulls his hand out empty. *Damn it. He gave his last one to Davy Hardcastle.* 'Good luck!' they'd called out to him. 'See you back at the billet! Don't do anything I wouldn't do.'

Henry smiles to himself. *The Tower Ballroom.* It had been his idea to come here all along, but the others had their own plans. O'Malley (it was always O'Malley; was there any place on earth the guy didn't know?) had heard of a bar where the girls kicked up their heels, danced a merry jig on the tables, and if you were lucky, let you run the tips of your fingers up and down the finely stitched seams of their stockings, all the way to no-man's-land where the gossamer silk ended, and a narrow strip of quivering bare flesh lay waiting to lead you all the way to heaven...

Henry pays his entrance fee and makes his way up a vast staircase, two steps at a time, all the way to the top floor. The dull *click* of his right knee as he climbs. The heavy drag of his boots. He tries not to think about how disorientated he feels, how the heft of his body would fall slack and clumsy from lack of sleep if he let it. As he rounds a bend, the muscles in his calves protest and contract beneath his skin. He keeps his eyes fixed on the turn ahead. Pushes on.

The scent of perfume, of anticipation, clouds the air. He wishes his uniform didn't hang so loosely on his diminished frame, but there's not much he can do about that now. Back at the billet he'd stumbled upon a hollow-eyed stranger in the mirror – a human coat-hanger – no body inside to speak of, just his air force blues suspended like a phantom before him. Henry tugs at the hem of his jacket and pulls himself upright. It's an automatic movement, ingrained by now. But there are no commanding officers here. No roll call awaits. Just soaring melodies, couples whirling like spinning tops on the dance floor, and eight shimmering glitter balls rotating overhead.

He reaches the top floor, passes through a pair of double doors and enters the ballroom at balcony level. A blast of music rains against Henry's skin, and a sweet, invigorating rush of adrenaline surges like nectar through his limbs. To his left, row upon row of plush, upholstered seats fan out vertiginously one behind the other, each arranged to afford the best possible view of the dance floor. It takes a moment for his eyes to adjust to the low-level lighting, but he can tell at once that he made the right decision to come upstairs – there are far fewer people up here, and the spectacle is magnificent, like a view from Mount Olympus itself.

'Bet you any money the Café de Paris never had anything on *this*.'

Henry turns, sees the man in the silk tie standing in the shadows to his right.

'The place in London,' he continues. 'Piccadilly. Got bombed in the Blitz?'

'I never went there,' Henry replies. He shrugs, his mouth curling into a smile. 'I wasn't old enough to get in at the time.'

'Wouldn't have stopped *me*,' the man says with a wink. He leans in. '*You're* a Londoner, aren't you?'

Henry, unsure where this is leading, smiles again. 'I am.'

'Thought so. I hear the London girls can give guys like you and me the runaround. They can be – you know, standoffish. *Stuck-up*. But let me tell you something, my friend, they go stark raving mad for it here. It's the electromagnetism. A couple of spins on the dance floor, and the music releases all their inhibitions. Know what I mean?'

His breath smells faintly sour, and, Henry detects, there's an unnatural glassiness to his eyes. 'Hey, fella,' he says, nudging Henry's arm, 'I can spot a rookie a mile off. It's your first time here, am I right?'

Henry concedes a grin. 'Maybe. Or then again, maybe I've just got a rookie kind of face.'

The man sidles closer. 'Well, Rookie, take it from me... if you're looking for a pretty girl to dance with, you're wasting your time up here. I suggest you follow my lead and make your way downstairs.'

Henry takes a discreet step backwards. 'Thanks for the tip,' he says lightly. 'I'll bear it in mind.'

He waits for the man to leave and looks around for a place to sit. Immediately ahead of him the first half-dozen rows are almost entirely empty, with the notable exception of one young woman seated alone in the front row. At first, all Henry can make out is the hazy outline of her silhouette. Her bird-like frame is perfectly still, her back draped in shadow, her head tilted forwards over the shiny gold barrier towards the dance floor below. He slips his hands into his pockets and waits to see if anyone joins her, but there are only a handful of spectators milling around, and behind him, two or three couples, lost in their own private dominions, quietly ensconced in the upper rows.

Henry glances towards the staircase. He wonders if perhaps he should go downstairs and get something to drink, when some force – some strange, visceral, magnetic pull – draws his attention back to the young woman. Henry trains his eyes on the back of her neck. And yet she herself doesn't look round once... She must be totally engrossed; he's never seen such powers of concentration in a dance hall!

Go over to her, he tells himself. *Introduce yourself. Find out who she is.*

He takes a step and falters as the light from a glitter ball sweeps firstly over him, then over the girl. He can see her more clearly now: the lush India green of her dress, cinched at the waist; narrow shoulders; soft waves of sandy brown hair swept up in a bun and held in place by an array of decorative clips which glint and sparkle in the beam of light circling above. them. Henry counts ten seconds exactly until the glitter ball completes its circuit of the room. The association is inevitable, instantaneous. *Like a spotlight in a POW camp,* he thinks. *Thank Christ I never had to see the inside of one of those.*

Slowly, he makes his way along the second row until he's no more than a foot or two away from her. As he nears the back of her seat, Henry flicks his eyes in her direction. A fine layer of down curves upwards from the nape of her neck, as though reaching for the light. And, he realises with delight, she's not sitting still after all – she's moving! Both hands tapping out the rhythm of the music against her thighs.

Henry continues to the end of the row and glances behind him. The girl tips her head further over the barrier and a strand of waved hair slips loose from her bun and bounces against her cheek. He watches, transfixed, as with an almost hypnotic display of ease, she raises both arms to her head and clips it casually back into place.

'Who *is* this girl?' he mumbles under his breath.

He can't understand it. He hasn't even seen her face, and yet all he can think about is how intoxicating it must feel to be on the receiving end of such an intense gaze. *Like looking into a lighthouse. Like dancing a waltz with the sun!*

He doubles back along the front row until finally, somewhere between taking off his cap and smoothing down his hair, he comes to a stop beside her.

'Wait!' she cries, holding up her palm.

Henry freezes.

'This is the *absolute* best bit! See the couple in the centre of the dance floor? They come here all the time. They dance for half an hour like they own the place, then they're gone. I thought they might be partners in the romantic sense, too, but Daisy downstairs in the cloakroom said someone told *her* they're twins. It's all just rumours, though. Either way, they're definitely professionals. Look how perfectly they're holding each other! No one else can *touch* them!'

Henry turns and sees a handsome, dark-haired woman staring with queenly confidence into the fiery eyes of a swarthy, Mediterranean-looking male. Their bodies are pressed so closely together, you could barely thread a shoelace between them. As a couple, they're flawless, incandescent. Henry hates them already.

'Oh yes,' he says, as the pair smoulder their way provocatively across the dance floor. 'Not bad. Absolutely nothing intimidating about them at all.'

To his surprise, the girl responds with a hearty laugh.

'I'm sorry to disturb you,' he continues, cursing himself – inwardly – for his inopportune timing, 'but is this seat taken?'

She turns her head and extends him an appraising gaze. She's about his age – nineteen or twenty, twenty-one at most – with a peaches and cream complexion, a lively expression, and the most extraordinary liquid blue eyes he's ever seen. Henry freezes a second time. *Oh God*, he thinks, *she's beautiful. What now?*

She scans his eyes and casts a brief, sideways glance over his shoulder. In the interminable moment it takes for her to respond, Henry manages to convince himself that all she wants is a little peace and quiet to enjoy the dancing. *Why else would she be sitting up here all alone?*

Who or what, if anything, she sees or doesn't see, he can't be sure, but gradually her mouth softens into an irresistible smile.

'The seat's free,' she replies. 'Sit down. It's so quiet up here today we've got the entire row to ourselves.'

Henry grins and lowers himself beside her. The second his buttocks hit the chair he's overcome by a violent urge to face her, to win her over before he's even learned her name. Instead, he does as she does, only with considerably less grace – pinioning his eyes to the dynamos on the dance floor, his hands clamped like barnacles to his knees.

'*Venus and Adonis*,' she says, after a beat.

Henry stares into the gaping void before him. He didn't think it was possible he could feel any more affronted by this unbearably slick, depressingly accomplished couple if he tried.

'You've *got* to be kidding me,' he replies. He turns mechanically to meet her gaze.

'What?'

'You're not seriously telling me they're called Venus and Adonis? If they *are* professionals – and with names like that, I pray to God for their sakes that they are – then Venus and Adonis *have* to be stage names. I mean, it's a bit over the top, isn't it? You do realise their real names are probably Shirley and Ken?'

The girl stares at him for a stunned five seconds, then bursts into a helpless fit of giggles. Her laughter is so infectious that soon Henry is laughing, too. In fact, the suppressed nervous tension that's been building inside him from the moment he sat down quickly runs riot, and before long they're both laughing so hard, they're practically doubled over.

She leans towards him and, still giggling, holds up a thin, pink hand. '*No!* I'm not talking about the *dancers*. I'm talking about that... right there... the inscription engraved in the stonework above the stage. Can't you see it?'

Instantly sobering, Henry follows her gaze. 'Sorry?'

She leans a fraction closer. 'Straight ahead of you... I asked Jimmy the doorman where it comes from and he told me it's from Shakespeare's *Venus and Adonis*. I'd never heard of it, much less read it, but it made me laugh how it's wound up here, in a dance hall. Must be a reference to the music, don't you think?'

Henry sees it now; frankly, it's impossible to miss when she's pointing at it so prettily, the graze of her voice just inches from his face. He clears his throat and reads the quote out loud:

'"BID ME DISCOURSE, I WILL ENCHANT THINE EAR..." Yes,' he says, trying his utmost to compose himself, 'I'd say it is. It might refer to the music, or maybe to a fellow music lover, like you?'

He peels his hand from his knee and holds it out towards her. 'I'm sorry – you had me distracted there for a moment – I should have introduced myself. I'm Henry Applebee. It's a pleasure to meet you.'

'You don't need to apologise.' She gives him a dizzying smile. 'Honestly, I haven't laughed so much in ages.'

Henry casts an anxious glance at Shirley and Ken, who (to his immense annoyance) are still lording it over the dance floor. If *that's* what he's up against, then what he's about to say next could quite possibly result in the most mortifying ten or fifteen minutes of his life...

'Would you like to dance?' he ventures, regardless. 'I must warn you, though, I'm not much of a dancer. It's the music I enjoy most of all.'

'Oh, I wouldn't let *them* put you off,' she replies. Her expression, her voice, are utterly forgiving, wholly kind. 'Music lovers make the best dancers of all. My nan told me that. She had polio when she was a lass and she's been weak in her legs all her life, but no one loves a tune more than she does. It's worth dropping by for tea just to see her doing the rumba around her kitchen.'

Henry laughs, then remembers she hasn't yet accepted his invitation.

She holds his gaze, her blue eyes appraising him once again. 'I haven't seen you here before. Are you stationed at Kirkham?'

His hand, still reaching towards her, starts to shake. 'I am, yes. Actually, I just arrived today. From the Far East.'

'You arrived today and you're already at the Tower Ballroom? You really *are* a music fan, Henry!'

Henry grins. 'Certified. Have been my whole life.'

'Me too. Hook, line and sinker!'

She smoothes down the skirt of her dress. 'How long are you here for?'

'Forty-eight hours,' he replies. 'Then it's demob for me.'

'Oh.' Her voice gives nothing away. 'In that case, we'd better get moving.'

Henry glances back over the barrier. 'There's just one thing… If you expect me to share a dance floor with Venus and Adonis down there, could you at least tell me your name?'

'Of course! But we have to be quick if we want to get downstairs before this song finishes. Come on, I'll tell you my name on the way.'

She rises from her seat, and as she edges past him, the hem

Finding Henry Applebee

of her dress brushes against his knees. All at once, the possibility of holding her in his arms on the dance floor scatters Henry's thoughts like bowling pins. His heart batters furiously against his ribs.

It is then, without warning, that it begins...

She takes his hand and everything around him starts to disintegrate. Henry feels his feet slide from under him as a sharp, violent jolt yanks him against his will by an invisible chain, back, far back along a dark, dank tunnel. The swell of music fades, and as the light from the glitter balls begins to dim, Henry finds himself struggling to retain the receding image of her face. He strains, forcing himself to stay present, but while sound and vision distort, the warmth of her hand and the touch of her skin remain both elusive, and at once, agonisingly real.

Henry's body jerks and tenses. He's in Kentish Town, in his bedroom, the only sounds the contented sighs and snuffles of Banjo's nocturnal breath.

Willing himself back along the thin, dark tunnel, Henry silently repeats the words over and over:

Don't wake up. Don't wake up. Don't wake up.

He keeps his eyes firmly closed. There is a moment's grace, a final glimpse beyond the velvet darkness, and then, from far away, her voice:

'Don't worry, I'm not much of a dancer either, but I could happily watch everyone else dancing all day long. It's nice to meet you, Henry. I'm Francine, by the way.'

39

4

The Glass Wall

KING'S CROSS STATION, LONDON, DECEMBER 6:
DEPARTURE

Ariel

A riel closed the basement door behind her and dragged her wheelie bag back up the concrete steps. She followed the zigzag of turns in reverse and retraced her steps to Finsbury Park tube station. As she neared the entrance, a crowd of commuters with misery splattered across their faces came pouring towards her.

'Has something happened?' she asked a woman in a camouflage parka and bright orange boots.

The woman sighed. 'There's a security alert at Victoria. The entire line's been closed. Don't even bother trying to get on the Piccadilly Line... the platform's rammed. It's total chaos down there.'

Ariel's heart sank. 'Are there any buses? I have to get to King's Cross.'

'Sure, if you're willing to spend the rest of the day getting pushed around in a queue with everyone else here.' She flicked her eyes to Ariel's wheelie bag. 'It'll be a bun fight to get on them, though, especially with that. Personally, I'm calling it quits and going home.'

Ariel looked up and down the length of Seven Sisters Road. If taxis ever drove along it, they weren't doing so today.

She checked the time on her phone. If she didn't get to King's Cross in the next thirty minutes, she wouldn't have a snowball's chance in hell of catching her train.

She stared back at the entrance to the tube station. 'Sod it,' she said, to anyone who cared to listen. 'I'm going in.'

Tightening her grip on her wheelie bag, Ariel threw herself into the fray – one more nameless face (or so it seemed to her), caught up in the slipstream of the day, the rush hour crush eventually propelling her onto a heaving Piccadilly Line platform, its force pressing in around her, relentless, immense.

Five trains came and went before she finally managed to squeeze herself through the doors of a carriage which was already bursting at the seams. Her wheelie bag dug into her legs, as well as those of the strangers squashed up close and personal against her. 'Sorry,' she kept saying, over and over. 'God, I'm so sorry.'

''S'alright, love,' one man replied with a resigned grimace. 'This is London. We can take it.'

Ariel gave him a nervous smile. All she could think about

as the tunnel closed around them was that she wasn't going to make it. No way was she going to make her train.

At King's Cross, she spilled out of the tube train door and jostled her way through a scrum of commuters funnelling upwards into the mainline railway station.

The time on her phone showed 8:26.

'*Shit.*'

She stepped off the escalator and paused to orient herself. A young boy with a freckled face and a mop of unruly hair crossed in front of her, tripping over his shoelaces, shooting her a curious stare. *Hey, you look just like my brother, Isaac!* she almost called out to him. But the crowd swept them onwards, the momentum carrying her all the way to the central concourse, where the boy disappeared from view.

Positioned high against the back wall, the electronic departure board displayed running updates on an array of trains bound for the north. Ariel scanned the screen until she found the one she was looking for:

Destination: Edinburgh. *Departure*: 9a.m. *Status*: On Time. *Platform:* Not Yet Allocated.

She glanced over her shoulder and spotted a Starbucks to her right. Weaving her way towards it, she placed her order at the till and moved to the end of the counter to collect her drink. Her hand slipped inside her canvas bag while she waited and wrapped itself around her phone. She toyed with it in the palm of her hand, then fished it out and saw that a message from Tumbleweed had just that second come in.

Ariel opened it. A close-up shot of a pair of bright purple running shoes – primed and ready for action in the middle of a sun-drenched field – filled the screen. As usual, there was no message; the rule was they always let the pictures do the talking. ('Sounds like a cop-out to me,' Linus liked to tease her, but then in her humble opinion, her father had always been overly fixated on words.)

'Grande cappuccino for Ariel?' A dough-faced barista slid her cup across the counter and winked. 'Is that Ariel as in *"brilliant cleaning every time"*?'

'Yes,' she replied with a well-practised smile. 'That's me. I haven't heard the washing powder reference in a while, actually. Lately, it's either been Sylvia Plath or *The Little Mermaid*.'

A large, floor-to-ceiling window separated the interior of the coffee shop from the station concourse beyond. She dragged her wheelie bag towards it and turned her attention back to her phone. The implication of Tumbleweed's message seemed to be that someone – *she* – was running.

But in which direction? she wondered. *And towards, or away from, what?*

'So what are you going to do?' he asked her.

'What am I going to do about what?'

For the past quarter of an hour, Ariel and Tumbleweed had been sitting on a stretch of gorse-covered cliff top; a long, rugged cummerbund of land which leaned, and eventually fell in jagged increments, to the sea. Behind them lay the billowy green contours of the Langland Bay Golf Course. Ahead, the bay itself, languid, flecked intermittently with wispy bursts of spray.

'The package Estelle gave you,' he replied. 'Don't you want to know what's in it?'

Ariel shrugged. 'Yes. No. I don't know. Not really.'

She clamped her arms across her chest and reminded herself to breathe. It was the previous November, two days since Estelle's funeral, and all she felt was numb. *Was this normal?* she asked herself. Everyone had told her it would bring closure. *Relief.* It was, she'd discovered, a lie. To her, it felt more like the ceremony's solemn finality had brought with it a kind of shutting down – a formal sealing in, in a way – of everything that was ransacked, and empty, and broken.

Linus, Ariel, Isaac: they were three now. It didn't fit, *would never* fit, she was sure of it. The void in her heart was indescribable. The last thing she wanted to think about was the package when it was as much as she could do to reorient herself on solid ground.

'You're still in shock,' Tumbleweed said. He leaned his long, rangy body against his elbows. Tossed a hank of straw-coloured hair from his eyes. 'My bad. I shouldn't have brought it up.'

'This sucks,' Ariel replied. She gave him a placatory smile. 'Sorry.'

She hadn't been out on the cliffs in weeks. Once, when she was small, Linus had brought her not far from where they were sitting now in search of lost golf balls. He told her he'd be able to sell them on for extra cash, though as it turned out, the payout was barely more than negligible. She'd trailed along behind him, stopping every few paces to gaze at the mountains of bright yellow gorse. It was only when she felt a familiar pressure building between her legs that she remembered where she was.

'Daddy, wait!' she'd cried. 'I need the toilet!'

Linus turned and gave a carefree wave of his hand. 'Hurry up, then! We'll stop off at the loos by the tennis courts on the way home!'

Ariel peered to her right. The gorse was almost as tall as she was, its prickly fronds rising just inches from her chin. Beyond it, she knew the earth sloped away to the edge of the cliff and a dense outcrop of rocks below.

Her legs froze.

'Daddy, please come back and get me! I'm scared!'

Linus's reply, breezy as the air itself, floated backwards on the wind. 'What's got into you? Come on, pet. I'll wait for you on the path.'

She watched him plough ahead, hands on hips; his easy Sunday stride. Ariel lowered herself to her knees and began to crawl through the thick, briery grass. Overhead, a scalding sun beat down onto her shoulders as a warm trickle of urine seeped between her thighs. She dug her fingernails into the earth, determined not to cry. When she finally reached the path, Linus (who was oblivious still) caught her by the waist and swept her playfully into his arms.

'I wish it could change things,' she said. She turned back to Tumbleweed and brushed the memory aside. 'But whatever the envelope contains, it's not going to bring back Estelle.'

Ariel felt a tear forming in the corner of her eye. 'And there's something else... I don't understand why she'd ask for pen and paper and then not write a single word to Linus. Or Isaac. Or – or me.'

Tumbleweed draped his arm around her shoulders. 'Oh,' he said gently, 'that's what's bothering you.'

She shifted her gaze to the distant demarcation where the sky dripped down to meet the sea. 'None of it makes any sense. Freaks me out when people find stuff out after someone dies.'

'Seriously?' Tumbleweed raised his eyebrows. 'Like what?'

Ariel shrugged. 'I don't know... Affairs. Secret lives. Debts. Stuff like that.'

She saw him suppress a smile.

'Come on, that's not who Estelle was. And anyway, if you want to get to the bottom of *that* enigma, all you have to do is deliver the package like she asked. Either that, or open it yourself.'

'No way, Tee!' Ariel recoiled so fast, Tumbleweed's arm plummeted like a dead weight to the ground. 'I'm not going to open it when she specifically asked me *not* to. It would be –' she paused, searching for the right word – '*disrespectful.*'

'Fair enough. So then you know what to do. You'll deal with it when you're ready, right?'

'Right.'

She watched the setting sun burn a hole in the sky, the dying embers of a red-hot fire which sparked and flared, and eventually extinguished itself as it slipped, still smouldering, into the bay.

'Aw sod it,' Tumbleweed cried. He raised himself up off the ground and pulled Ariel to her feet. 'In *my* experience, things rarely turn out the way we think, anyway. *Sometimes*, my friend, they actually turn out *better*.'

Ariel tossed the plastic lid from her cappuccino into the waste bin and stared through the glass wall. The commuters who up until now had been congregated in a dense mass beneath the overhead departure board appeared to be mysteriously drifting apart. There was no pushing or shoving; no obvious threat, whispered or otherwise, of genuine alarm. Instead, what she was witnessing was far more subtle; more like a slow, insidious peeling away...

She moved closer to the window and followed the rift to its natural conclusion. Hovering at the end of it, about halfway between the coffee shop and the electronic screen, was a well-dressed elderly gentleman, a small brown suitcase at his feet. Judging from the empty space around him, he was alone, and to her horror, he was bleeding profusely.

'Oh my God!' she cried. 'That man needs help!'

A handful of customers standing alongside her raised their heads, stared for a moment or two, looked away.

The man was leaning heavily on his walking stick, his expression dazed. The collar of his shirt and the cuffs peeking out of his coat sleeves were a brilliant white. His shoes glistened. Everything about him – from his elegant woollen coat, to his smart grey suit, pale blue shirt and tie – was immaculate; everything apart from the jarring sight of blood pouring from his nose.

'What's *wrong* with everyone? Why doesn't anyone help?' she muttered under her breath.

Tear-shaped droplets of blood were now running down the man's neck and seeping into the edges of his shirt collar. Several splashes landed on his shoes. On the ground immediately before him, a widening circle of liquid was slowly beginning to pool.

Suddenly, Ariel started.

Frank...

A revolving zoetrope of images began to rotate in rapid-fire flashes to her brain:

The wound – jagged, gaping – running along the back of Frank's head...

The blood – creeping like a scarlet inkblot between his shoulder blades, trickling along the crease of his trousers, all the way to the shards of broken glass at his feet...

The child's face – her own face – streaked with tears, a protective grip on her arm warning her there was no permissible way to intervene...

Grabbing the handle of her wheelie bag with one hand, her cappuccino with the other, Ariel pushed her way through the door of the café and ran. Directly ahead of her, the old man lurched from side to side, as though on the brink of falling down. Ariel sped through the crowd towards him, hot coffee sloshing over the edge of her cup as she moved, burning her fingers, staining her clothes, splashing messily to the ground.

When she reached him, the old man's eyes – a pale, muddled grey – met hers and widened in surprise.

Instinctively, they both looked down.

'It looks like a Jackson Pollock. I think the technical term is "*drip painting*"' he said, pointing at the pooling canvas with his stick.

His voice was warm, and, Ariel noted with surprise, unexpectedly calm.

She turned the name over in her mind. *Pollock*. Linus would know him, she was sure; and yet ironically, during her most memorable visit to a gallery – the National Gallery, as it happened – Linus hadn't been with them.

She thought back to the endless rows of paintings and the cathedral-like dimensions of the rooms. Now, so many years later, her most vivid recollection was of Estelle's disappointment at finding Van Gogh's vase of yellow sunflowers permanently obstructed by the shoulders, heads and hats of tourists conspiring to keep it hidden, on one side or another, from their view.

'Looks to me like the inside of my head,' she replied. 'When I'm having a bad day. A day full of demons.' She drew her hair back from her face and leaned her head to one side. 'It's dramatic, though. Like an explosion of light and dark.'

She pulled an unopened packet of Kleenex from her canvas bag and pressed it between the old man's fingers. He was a full head taller than she was, and, she couldn't help noticing, impressively upright for someone who was obviously more than a little reliant on his stick.

Ariel placed her hand behind his elbow and did her best to reassure him with a smile. 'Are you okay?'

The old man nodded and tilted his head to the ceiling.

'That's it, keep your head back. Don't look down.' She slipped a tissue from its packet and began to wipe the smears of partially dried blood from his face. 'Is there someone I can call for you? A friend or relative, maybe?'

'No,' he said quickly, 'there's no one to call. No one I want to bother, at any rate.'

His face was waxen and drawn, but his eyes seemed more focused close up – sharper, and somehow more determined.

He shifted his gaze an inch or two to the right, in the direction of the electronic screen. 'I can't understand what happened. It just –' he paused, clicked his fingers – 'came on like that! Right out of nowhere!'

Ariel guided his hand to his face and encouraged him to pinch the bridge of his nose between his thumb and forefinger. She noticed he wasn't wearing a wedding band, but then she wasn't sure she'd ever seen a man as old as he was wearing a ring. She tried to imagine what it must feel like not to have an '*in case of emergency*' person to call. And yet he was on his way somewhere; there must be *someone* who cared enough to know if anything happened to him, surely?

'Are you all right, sir? There's an awful lot of blood. I'll call an ambulance and have someone take a look at you.'

Ariel tightened her grip on the old man's elbow. Standing alongside them was a middle-aged man with a *Station Supervisor* badge pinned to his lapel. He'd come armed with a folding plastic chair which he was already in the process of opening.

'There's no need for an ambulance,' the old man said. He squeezed out a narrow smile. 'It's nothing serious, and the bleeding's stopped now, as you can see.'

He took a concerted step *away* from the chair and lowered his gaze to the floor. He seemed far more interested in the whereabouts of his suitcase, which was still lying next to the Pollock at their feet. Bending very gently forwards, he caught hold of the handle and moved it an inch closer to his heel.

'With respect, sir,' the Station Supervisor resumed, 'it's my responsibility to ensure the safety and well-being of all incoming and outgoing visitors to the station. I'd be a great deal happier knowing someone had checked you over.'

The old man's eyes darted once again to the electronic screen. Ariel followed his gaze and saw that the Edinburgh train was now ready for boarding on Platform 6.

'Thank you,' he replied, 'but I'm afraid I have a train to catch. In fact, I really should be on my way...'

'Sir, under the circumstances I'm not sure continuing with your journey would be wise.' The Station Supervisor slipped a pen and notepad from his jacket pocket and gestured to the circle of blood glistening at their feet. 'There's clearly some sort of medical issue here... I'll need to compile an incident report at least. May I take your name, please?'

'You have to file a report?' the old man cried. 'For a *nosebleed*?'

Ariel gave him a discreet look of solidarity.

His arm tensed lightly beneath her hand.

'I don't have much time, but of course – if you need it – my name is Henry Applebee. From Kentish Town.'

'Mr Applebee, are you travelling alone today? If so, I think it would be best if I alerted a relative before you board your train. You really should have someone meet you at your final destination.'

Ariel threw Henry another sidelong glance and saw that the first real flicker of alarm was now flashing across his face. His eyes flew from the darkening smears of blood on his clothes, to the thick, liver-coloured streaks on the backs of his hands and nails. He rubbed distractedly at a stain on the lapel of his coat, his chin sinking to his chest, his posture drooping, as though his entire being were buckling beneath the force of an impossible weight. The change was so pronounced, she wondered if he might be suffering from some sort of delayed shock.

'What must I look like?' he mumbled, seemingly to the ground.

And suddenly, she understood. What Henry was experiencing wasn't shock, after all. *It was shame.*

Sliding her hand upwards from his elbow, Ariel squeezed the back of Henry's arm.

'Henry isn't travelling alone. He's with me,' she said, looking the Station Supervisor squarely in the eye. 'My name is Ariel Bliss. From South Wales. Thank you for your help, but we really have to get going.' She turned to Henry and smiled. 'We'll be fine once we're settled on the train.'

'Absolutely!' Henry said brightly. 'We'll be right as rain!'

The Supervisor gave her a hard stare. He seemed to be acknowledging her presence for the very first time, and didn't appear overly impressed with what he was seeing. 'I see.' He made a low grunting sound at the back of his throat and bent over to retrieve his folding chair. 'One last question,' he said, pulling himself upright once again. 'Could I just verify where you're both travelling to today?'

'Edinburgh,' Henry replied at once. 'We're on the nine o'clock train.'

'Edinburgh?' The Supervisor raised his eyebrows. 'That's quite a journey!'

'Oh yes,' Henry said, reaching for his suitcase. 'You have no idea.'

Neither of them uttered a word as they set off towards the ticket barrier, their suitcases at their sides. Ariel could feel the Station Supervisor's eyes boring into the backs of their heads as they walked, tracking their progress through the crowd. She was sure Henry could sense it too, because the moment they were through the barrier he began to move more quickly, the acceleration of his footsteps accompanied by the heightened *tap-tap-tap* of his stick on the granite floor.

She glanced at the train, eager to depart, before them.

Promise me, a voice rang out in her head.

I promise, Mam.

Ariel tightened her hold on her wheelie bag. She focused on the soft, rhythmic rattle of its wheels, and kept one eye trained on the mysterious stranger at her side. She wondered who he was, where he was going. Most of all, she found herself wondering who or what could be so important to him that he was prepared to lie to catch his train...

Finally, as Henry leaned in and whispered the words, 'Thank you,' under his breath, she stopped wondering altogether, and knew only that she had done the right thing.

5

The Promise

BLACKPOOL, FEBRUARY 1948

Henry

The North Pier is almost deserted apart from Henry and Francine, who stand at its furthermost tip, four-penny bags of cod and chips in their hands, a crisp wind whipping about their ears. The sky is leaden and eerily still, while below them waves slosh and break repeatedly against the pier's wooden ballasts. The water is washday grey, streaked with menace. Henry is aware it's a testament to their desire to see each other again that they find themselves here at all, blown about like sea-drift, when most people have retreated indoors to the comfort of a cosy tearoom, a favourite armchair, a lover's tender embrace.

Francine's presence beside him feels rare, disarming. She's wrapped in a powder-blue coat a shade or two lighter than her eyes. Her cheeks glow with a wintry flush, and a dab of soft-hued coral-coloured lipstick enhances the natural lustre of her mouth. Henry thinks she looks gorgeous. She took his arm when she met him at the station, and he – unsure whether she would be there or not, but hoping for the best – offered to take her to a restaurant for lunch, so they could chat and get to know one another better, but she said no, not to worry, fish and chips would do just fine.

'I know a good place down by the pier,' she said, a faint, nervous breathlessness to her voice. 'You'd never find it without me. Come on, I'll show you the way.'

They talk in quick, excited bursts. Like the day before, the conversation flows in an effortless current between them. It is, Henry thinks, a tacit commitment on both their parts to share as much of themselves as possible, conscious that they only have today before he has to return home to London and face the responsibilities of a brand-new civilian life.

Around them the wind thickens and roils in great swirling eddies, whisking the waves to a pearly-white froth. Between the cold and the lingering spectre of disorientation, Henry's hunger is acute. He wolfs down the last of his chips, pausing only to steal shy, sideways glances at Francine. Lying on his bunk in Kirkham the previous evening, he was certain he'd be able to visualise every contour, every quirk and subtle complexity of her face. But it was her eyes – her fearless, wild, liquid blue eyes – which had branded themselves so indelibly on his brain.

'I'm glad you came back today. I had a nice time yesterday,' she says, squeezing in close against his arm.

At the gentle pressure of her body, Henry feels the gravitational pull between them intensify. His stomach flips, and a jolt of electricity sparks like tinder along his spine. He takes a breath. Reins it in.

'I was looking forward to seeing you again,' he replies. 'In fact, I was afraid you might not be able to get the day off.'

When she told him what she did for a living she'd seemed almost apologetic at first. But then, in the delicate arching of her neck, in the involuntary upwards tilt of her perfectly formed chin, he'd seen a flash of defiance, of self-preservation. Being a waitress wasn't something she'd aspired to, she told him, but it paid the rent, and it was better than doing the exact same thing for less in Sheffield where she grew up.

'I always knew I'd like to try my luck somewhere new,' she said matter-of-factly. 'And Blackpool seemed as good a place to me as any. *Plus* –' she added with well-appointed irony – 'at least here I can get a bit of sea air.'

The wind whistles through the railings and flies under the skirt of her coat, sending swathes of powder-blue fabric fanning like an accordion around her legs. Francine screams and grabs hold of Henry's arm with one hand, while with the other she tries frantically to preserve her modesty by wedging a fistful of pleats between her knees.

'Anyhow, you needn't have worried,' she says when she's composed herself. 'Getting time off wasn't a problem. February's off season. If it weren't for the Americans and the lads like you visiting from Kirkham, Blackpool would be a ghost town at this time of year.'

Henry scrunches his empty chip paper into a ball and looks

around for a waste bin. On the roof of the Pavilion Theatre immediately behind them, a turbo-sized gull stretches its wings and follows his movements with immense, twitching eyes. Henry slips a protective arm around Francine's shoulders, and with a forced air of nonchalance says, 'The Americans have always had more money to throw around than we have. I suppose here's the obvious place for them to spend it.'

Francine stares evenly at the horizon. In the daylight, away from the twilight shadows of the Tower Ballroom, her skin appears even more radiant, even smoother and more unblemished than he'd recalled. And there's a freckle, he sees now; a small brown beauty spot nestled just below her jawline at the side of her neck. Henry manages to stop himself from leaning in and kissing it. Instead, he tries to intuit what she's thinking, what unknown visions are unfolding behind her eyes. He doesn't want to think about all the other servicemen who've passed through the town as he is doing, least of all now, when his own uniform is due to be handed back in in just twenty-four hours' time.

He leans his torso against the railings, swivels his head to catch her eye. 'You look very pretty today, by the way.'

'Thank you! It's a new coat.' She smoothes the fine, woollen fabric over her hips and smiles. 'I've been saving up for it for ages. Mam says I like to kid myself I'm Rita Hayworth.'

'Oh, Rita's a bombshell all right,' Henry shoots back, 'but she doesn't have your eyes.' He sees the look of delight on her face and laughs. 'I'm not sure where *that* came from... I mean I meant it, obviously – but I've never said anything smooth before in my life.'

'Come on, I don't believe it!' she cries. 'I've never met an airman yet who didn't have a ready line, though that was a particularly flattering one, I'll be honest.'

Henry shakes his head. 'I'm serious! Despite all my brother's efforts to educate me, I can guarantee that any smooth-talking genes in our family went exclusively to him.'

A small wound, calloused over the years, briefly makes its presence felt in Henry's chest. It's ingrained in him by now – this terrible ache of being in thrall to someone he looks up to so much, and yet can never match, never live up to, no matter how hard he tries. Devlin has always had such a seductive charm about him. Obstacles – be they romantic or otherwise – just seem to disintegrate in his path. Never in a million years could he know the agony, or inevitability, of always feeling second-best.

'Well,' Francine assures him with a smile, 'I think you're sweet.' She throws him a long, penetrating gaze. 'Henry? Can I ask you something?'

'Of course.'

'What time do you have to be back at your billet?'

All at once, her smile wavers. Henry catches her by the hand and pulls her towards him. 'Not for hours and hours yet. Let's not worry about that now. But we should get inside out of the cold. Your hands are freezing.'

They walk arm-in-arm along the pier towards the promenade, the pleats of Francine's coat brushing against the side of Henry's leg as she moves. On the beach below them a cocker spaniel races along the shoreline, pawing at the water, sending flecks of surf cartwheeling into the air. Francine turns to watch it, and the same lock of hair which slipped loose from her bun the day before tumbles against her cheek. It flutters momentarily in the breeze before whipping round and catching on her lipstick.

Henry grins.

'Hey! What's so funny?' She digs him in the ribs, plucks the strand of hair from her mouth, and with the same relaxed ease clips it back behind her ear.

'Have you ever had your tea leaves read?' she asks, as they approach the entrance to the pier. Directly ahead of them is an elaborately painted sign advertising the clairvoyant skills of a woman with the rather dubious name of Madame Futuro. 'A girl at work read mine the other day – just for fun. I didn't believe what she told me, though.'

'Why not?' Henry replies. 'Did she tell you that you were going to meet a handsome stranger?'

Francine draws to a stop. 'Yes. One who would change my life. How did you know that?'

'I don't know...' He clears his throat. 'I mean, honestly, I was just kidding. Isn't that what they tell everyone?'

'Probably.' Francine rolls her eyes. 'She said I was going to meet a man in uniform. Which in this part of the world doesn't exactly narrow it down... And then she said something about a farm, and that part made no sense to me at all. I just kept nodding. No way was I going to let on what I was thinking, and then –' She breaks off, squeezes Henry's arm.

'And then what?'

'Nothing I choose to believe in. I'm sure she was making it all up as she went along. Anyway, you're from London, aren't you?'

'Yes,' he replies. *I've lived my entire life in a neighbourhood called Chalk Farm.*

'So I was right! It was all nonsense.'

'Why?' Henry asks, his curiosity getting the better of him. 'What else did she say?'

For a second, the light in Francine's eyes dims. She steps towards him and kisses him on the cheek. 'I'm just really happy to see you.' Her voice is so unexpectedly tender, it sends shivers along Henry's spine. 'Forget I mentioned it. It was silly of me to bring it up.'

They pull away from each other, and holding hands, leave the entrance to the pier. Henry weighs the silence – the first one he's been conscious of since they met. He glances sidelong at Francine. Her gaze is fixed straight in front of her, her features composed, but Henry senses that whatever she's left unsaid is lingering, still, between them.

'Million-dollar question,' he says, in an effort to lighten the mood. 'You find a pot of gold at the end of the rainbow. There's a card attached with your name on it. What do you do?'

'*Anything?*' Francine says at once.

'Anything.'

'That's easy. I'd open a dance school. I'd hire someone to teach me, then I'd run classes of my own. I'd be the Ginger Rogers of the North. I'd be in *heaven*, Henry! No one would even recognise me back home. Either that, or I'd give it all away and join the circus.'

Her delivery is so deadpan that Henry doesn't dare ask her if she's being serious.

'I don't see either one happening, though,' she adds with a touch of sadness. 'But the dreams themselves cost nothing, do they? What about you? What will you do when you leave the RAF?'

Her question, natural as it is, catches Henry off-guard. 'I haven't decided yet,' he replies. He raises his hand to his neck and fiddles needlessly with his tie. 'My father died not long after I volunteered, and my brother, Devlin, saw active duty in the end, though it was only for a few months. Thank God he made it back in one piece, his ego fully intact...' He smiles, a rush of anticipation seizing hold of him. 'So much has changed since I've been away. It's the oldest cliché in the book, but whatever I end up doing, I'd like to make a difference if I can.'

The second the words are out of his mouth he fears he's said too much, when in reality, he knows perfectly well he hasn't said enough. He lowers his eyes and stares with studied intensity at the tips of his boots. *Tell her. Tell her, you idiot. You know she'll understand.*

'What is it, Henry?'

He lifts his head and smiles. 'Before I volunteered I was doing pretty well with my studies. Devlin never showed much interest in school, but he's always been charisma on a stick, so somehow it didn't seem to matter.'

'Charisma on a stick?' Francine cuts in. 'Are you sure you two are related?'

Henry bursts out laughing. 'Yes – although Devlin was first in line when they were handing *that* out, too.' A flicker of insecurity flares inside him all over again. 'Trust me, I speak from experience when I say you'd understand if you met him.'

'But I haven't met him,' she says. Her gaze zeroes in on him with laser-sharp focus. 'I'm right here – with *you*. Anyway, I think charisma is for film stars, and highly overrated for everyone else.'

Henry realises he's beaming like a prize fool.

'Stop trying to distract me,' she says, smiling back at him. 'Go on, tell me what you were going to say about your studies.'

'You really want to know?'

'Yes!'

'Okay, well, discovering I had a gift for languages was a revelation, almost like acting in a way – a chance to reinvent myself and shine. So I've been thinking I might go in for a career in teaching. Maybe then I can inspire others the way my teachers inspired me.' He pauses. 'I didn't *actually* say that out loud, did I? God, the clichés are just pouring out of me today.'

'No they're not!' Francine replies. 'I think it's *wonderful*.' She steps towards him and presses her hands against his chest. 'You have to promise me you won't let anyone tell you otherwise. You've got that look about you, Henry! You might even be one of the greatest teachers London's ever seen!'

She slips away and runs along the promenade. Henry chases after her, catches her by the waist and lifts her into the air. As he swings her round, her face, the pier, the sky, the Tower, blur and merge before him. Francine screams, and with a lightning swipe, she grabs hold of his cap and brandishes it like a trophy above her head.

'Come on,' he says, lowering her to the ground, 'let's go

inside somewhere and have a cup of tea to warm up. What about over there?'

Henry motions towards an imposing building with an elegant red-brick façade on the opposite side of the road. The Shore Hotel looks decidedly grand, a watering hole for the privileged no doubt, a whiff of the silver spoon about them, but Henry doesn't care – right now he'd be happy to go just about anywhere as long as he's with Francine.

She follows his gaze and quickly shakes her head. 'No, Henry, we can't go there. That's where I work. I don't want my colleagues waiting on us. It wouldn't feel right on my day off.'

'Of course, how stupid of me. A film, then? Some place warm and cheery?'

'Yes. The Winter Gardens! If we're quick, we'll be just in time for the matinee.'

She waits for a Fleetwood-bound tram to rattle past them, then she takes Henry's hand and leads him in the opposite direction from the hotel. When they reach the other side of the road she comes to an abrupt stop and looks at him with an expression of such startling gravity, he wonders what can possibly have transpired to unsettle her in that briefest of journeys from one side of the promenade to the other.

'What's wrong, Francine? Have you changed your mind? We could always do something else if you prefer?'

Her arms fall like a rag doll's to her sides. 'Nothing's wrong,' she replies.

'Then what is it?'

Henry scans her face. Her eyes are laced with such intricacy of emotion that every attempt he makes to interpret them proves utterly beyond him.

Francine glances at the pier, at the Shore Hotel rising large and grandiose behind them. Turning slowly to face him, she floors him with the most ingenuous of smiles.

'Okay, Henry, here it is: I've never met a boy like you before. I'm just a regular Yorkshire lass, not like the London girls you're used to. I don't have fancy tastes. I'm smart, and I'm passionate about the things I like, but I'm not cultured or clever like you.'

She holds her palms out from her sides and shrugs. 'I'm a waitress who scrubs up well and only owns one good coat, and this is it. But I wear my heart on my sleeve, and I swear it's every bit as hopeful and fragile as the next girl's.

'You won't break it, will you?'

6

The Return

KING'S CROSS STATION, LONDON, DECEMBER 6:
DEPARTURE, 8:47 A.M.

Henry

The hairy trek between concourse and train with an unknown, if kindly, teenager was rapidly turning into the longest walk of Henry's life. But then so far, nothing at all was going the way he had expected.

He moved steadily forwards, his vision trained in missile lock-on with the carriage door ahead. An *invalid*! He'd been made to feel like an *invalid*! And all he'd done was tell a little white lie about the fact he wasn't travelling alone, and even that wasn't an *entire* fabrication.

In Henry's inside coat pocket a Basildon Bond envelope grazed lightly against his chest. Two tickets had been purchased at his niece, Amy's, insistence, and yet barely ninety minutes had passed since she'd telephoned to say that she wouldn't be able to accompany him after all:

'I'm so sorry, Uncle Henry, but the twins woke up with chickenpox and Dan's renovation job in Berkshire has overrun. I feel terrible about letting you down, but I'm going to have to stay home and take care of the girls. Will you be all right on your own?'

This, in a way, had been Spanner Number One, though Henry wasted no time at all in assuring her that he was more than capable of making the journey by himself. The point was, her *intention* to go with him had been there, so what difference did it ultimately make if instead of being here by his side, she was trapped at home in Ladbroke Grove?

As he manoeuvred himself one footstep at a time towards the waiting train, Henry briefly entertained the possibility that somehow, via a perverse twist of fate, he'd inadvertently *willed* the morning's events into being. In truth, not once during the course of the last few tumultuous days had he considered it necessary for Amy to escort him – like some glorified minder! – on his trip. And yet, he acknowledged with a faint twinge of guilt, there was no denying that if it hadn't been for her chance discovery, he wouldn't now find himself at the epicentre of one of London's busiest train terminals at all.

Henry brushed the thought from his head and reminded himself that he didn't need a babysitter; his destination was Scotland, not the moon. And he wasn't *that* incapacitated! Just because he was eighty-five (and counting) didn't mean he couldn't make it halfway across the country in one piece. Plenty of people his age would have driven!

He squeezed the handle of his suitcase and listened for the reassuring sound of the aged leather creaking beneath his fingers. His joints ached. His mouth, which still tasted ominously of blood, felt stale and dry.

If he could just get himself into his seat... If the guard would only blow his whistle and send the train wheezing and grunting out of the station... If he could put some distance at last between himself and the weary, winter-tide streets of cold, old, lonely London... Then and only then could he be certain that nothing and no one might prevent him from reaching his destination on time.

There had been all of eight days to digest the news, which in Henry's world was less time than it took for the bulletproof avocados from his local corner shop to embrace their natural-born destiny and ripen. One minute he was pottering on the patio, mimicking the sound of the Papadopouloses' chickens clucking in their homemade coop next door; the next, he was engaged in the most surreal telephone conversation of his life.

'Uncle Henry, it's Amy. I'm calling to say that I've found her. I think I've found the woman you've been searching for all these years.'

Henry pressed a finger to his ear and waited for the punch-line, the *dénouement*, the inevitable *Candid Camera* reveal.

He stared at the framed reproduction of Monet's sublime water lilies floating serenely on the hall wall. His instinct, once he'd had a second or two to process Amy's words, was to gasp, but his jaw fell slack and all he could muster was an acute, ear-splitting silence.

He wrapped his hand around the empty glass vase on the bureau, moving it an inch this way, that way, keeping the pads of his fingers pressed to its cool, hard surface for no other reason than because it was the only object in his immediate line of vision that was solid, and tangible, and real.

A wave of longing rolled through his body. The sensation came close to overwhelming him until it was matched, molecule by molecule, by a slow-moving river of fear in his veins. *What if there'd been a mix-up? What if this was all just another terrible mistake?*

'Uncle Henry, are you there?'

'Yes, Amy,' he replied. 'I'm here.'

'Good, because I need you to listen to this – it's from an article in last night's *Evening Standard*: "*The inspiration for the novel came from the author's mother, Yorkshire girl Francine Keeley, who in the aftermath of the Second World War worked as a waitress at Blackpool's Shore Hotel.*" Did you hear that? It's her name. Her hotel. *Same town.* From everything you've told me, I don't think there can be any mistake.'

Slowly, Henry let the vase go. Amy was right. *The match was nothing short of perfect.*

'I'm sorry, Amy,' he managed at last. 'What exactly is this article about?'

There was a momentary pause.

'Oh. Sorry, I should have said... It's a spotlight on a new wave of debut authors, one of whom has written some sort of mystery-thriller set on the Lancashire coast in the 1940s.

She credits her mother – *"Francine Keeley"* – and the Shore Hotel as the jumping-off points for her story. Honestly, you should thank the customer who left the paper behind in the café this morning, because otherwise I would never have seen it. I'll drop it over to you after work and you can read it for yourself. In the meantime, I think it's probably safe to assume that according to this, Francine is – or at one point *was* – married. Either way, the one thing we know for sure is that she has a daughter.'

Henry felt as though he were floating out of his shoes. He reached out his hand and grabbed the edge of the bureau before sinking in a state of burgeoning delirium onto the hallway chair.

Banjo raced in from the patio and began to paw frantically at Henry's shins. Henry's body slumped forwards, his elbows skidding to his knees. He was trying his damnedest to formulate a response, but his powers of expression were scrambled, his train of thought unclear.

'I wouldn't blame you for thinking it's too late,' Amy continued on the other end of the line. 'It was practically a lifetime ago, after all. Then again – if she really is that important to you – if you make contact with her daughter, you'll find Francine. The ball's in your court, Uncle Henry. What do you want to do?'

|||||||||||||

Henry gripped the handle of his walking stick and pressed ahead. Determination coursed through every muscle of his body. He'd seen Francine in his dreams again last night, only this one was more real to him than most; so real he was sure he could even smell her perfume.

Her words haunted him still:

Francine.

Always and forever, Francine.

Even now, the memory cleaved Henry's heart in two. Time, it seemed, had been cruel, and capricious. It had healed nothing.

One thing he'd learned for sure: digging around in his memories as he sat, pen in hand, bent over his notebook, was like sifting for gold; he never quite knew when the most precious nuggets of all – the ones with the power to steal his breath away – were going to filter up to the surface.

Catch me, Henry! – her arms beating wildly against her sides – *Catch me if you can!*

Her smile was electric. Sometimes it was a transitory feeling, gentle as a whisper, as intangible as a baby's breath; at other times it was a profound ache that grabbed hold of Henry's heart and tightened its grip like an iron fist. It astounded him how the human heart could remain so vital and complex with the passing of the years; an organ so unwaveringly loyal and pure and constant on the inside, while the outer body bowed to its inevitable decline.

And yet...

Henry glanced in renewed horror at his blood-splattered clothes. He'd experienced spontaneous nosebleeds once or twice before, but never like this. He wondered if it were a side effect of the medicine he'd been prescribed (but so rarely succumbed to taking) for one of his various ailments. He'd never placed much stock in doctors' pills and potions; they handed them out far too readily for his liking, when mostly – just like every other lonely pensioner he knew – all he wanted was a chat and the opportunity for a bit of social interaction in the waiting room. And *now* look at him! A disgrace in his dove-grey suit! He wasn't sure things could be going any worse. He must look like a decrepit Sweeney Todd!

Henry came to a stop alongside the train and placed his suitcase at the platform's edge. Thank heavens for the girl: *Ariel*. Here she was standing right next to him telling him that she was travelling to Edinburgh, too:

'I was supposed to be on the one that left at eight,' she said, a little disconsolately. 'But I had a total nightmare getting here on the Tube. I'm sure it'll be fine if I just get on this one. I don't suppose it's full.'

As she spoke, a horde of passengers swarmed onto the platform behind them, and jostled past in a shamelessly undignified scramble to board the train.

'Well, not *completely* full, anyway,' Ariel added with a frown.

She turned and peered briefly through the First Class window. 'Is this your carriage? It looks nice. Would you like me to see you to your seat?'

Henry smiled, partly at her kindness, but mainly at the expression of wonder on her face. He cast a discreet glance at the holes in her jeans, at her faded black plimsolls (just like the ones he and Devlin had worn in school!). At her side was what he assumed must be the hand-me-down exterior of her rather tired-looking suitcase on wheels. He didn't want to jump to conclusions, but at her age he could never have afforded the luxury of first-class travel. More to the point, if it hadn't been for her helpful intervention, in all likelihood he might not have been allowed to board the train at all...

'My niece was supposed to be travelling with me today,' he said in answer to her question. 'But she's been otherwise detained. Could I offer you her seat as a token of my thanks? Unless –' he added somewhat doubtfully – 'you already have a first-class ticket?'

He slipped the Basildon Bond envelope from his pocket and held out the tickets for Ariel to see. She looked down and regarded them with what appeared to be an expression of mild apprehension; or perhaps, it occurred to him with dismay, it was just sheer disbelief.

A violent rush of heat rose beneath his collar. 'Of course,' he muttered quickly, 'if you'd rather not spend the entire journey in the company of an old man, and a bloody one at that, then I completely –'

'Thank you, Henry.' Ariel raised her head and gave him a shy, but none the less winning smile. 'If you're sure it wouldn't be a problem, then yes, actually, that would be great.'

Relief flooded Henry's face. 'That's settled then!' he cried. 'No sense in a perfectly good ticket going to waste!'

Ariel's gaze shifted to the carriage steps, to his white-knuckled fingers curled around the handle of his stick. 'Here, let me help you.' Moving nimbly alongside him, she slipped her hand once more behind his arm.

Henry picked up his suitcase and stepped onto the train. The engine was already turning over, the microcosmic glow of the sleek, purring carriage firmly in his sights. The carriage door swung to behind him, gathering him up, buffering him in its steely embrace. He made his way inside, his heart pounding at the realisation that here, at last, was his return.

To his past...

And to the mistake that he'd give anything in the world to change.

Part Two

CONFESSIONS

7

Train Hopping

DECEMBER 6: *EN ROUTE*

Ariel

A riel slid her wheelie bag into the luggage area just inside the carriage door. As she released the handle, three words popped into her brain, imprinting themselves like a trail of skywriting on the inner trajectory of her gaze: embrace the unforeseen.

What, she asked herself, *was that supposed to mean?*

She repeated the phrase under her breath. It wasn't exactly unfamiliar, but then neither could she remember where she might have picked it up. Maybe it meant she wasn't supposed to be running after all? Maybe what she actually needed to do was surrender, and trust that what was meant to unfold would do so naturally, of its own accord?

Immediately ahead of her, Henry drew to a stop, double-checked his reservation, and with a contented, 'Ah, here we are,' placed his suitcase on his seat.

Ariel followed behind him and walked into the carriage's immaculate interior.

'Holy shit.'

Her eyes made a rapid tour of her surroundings. The lighting was calm and muted. The seats were spacious and spotlessly clean. Even the air seemed less dense. She glanced to her right and saw that her seat was opposite Henry's at the carriage's near end. Their seating area (a table for two designated for herself and Henry, and a table for four with an aisle in between) was quasi-separated from the remainder of the passengers by a dusky glass panel which stretched all the way to the ceiling. She wondered if it had been tacked on as an afterthought, or whether it had been purposely designed to offer a small corner of additional exclusivity. Either way, she liked the subtle degree of privacy it provided. *Seems like the perfect refuge*, she mused, *for anyone with something to hide.*

'That's you,' Henry said. He gestured amiably to her seat. 'Make yourself at home!'

'Thanks, Henry,' she replied.

She slipped off her coat. Her mohair jumper – which had long seen better days – wilted under her gaze. *Shit*, she said again – silently, this time. She could just see Linus shaking his head in horror, then covering it up with a smile. She – like the rest of her family as far as she was aware – had never had the pleasure of travelling anywhere First Class.

She tucked her canvas shoulder bag under the table and sat down. 'It's another world in here,' she said, her voice shot with awe. 'Lots of leg room. Actual metal cutlery. Nice.'

An invisible steward had laid the table with white china mugs, place mats, svelte silver spoons – all much too smart for a girl from Oystermouth wearing ripped jeans and a charity-shop jumper. Her fingers sought the ends of her sleeves and curled around them into a protective ball.

'My niece persuaded me to treat myself,' Henry replied. 'Of course, that was when she thought she'd be travelling with me. It'll be one less thing for the bucket list, I suppose!'

Ariel smiled, then glanced over her shoulder and furtively eyed the door. She wondered if Henry would be offended if she made an excuse and slipped back to her rightful place in Standard Class, where she belonged.

Something moved in the corner of her eye, a quick flash of blue. A guy in his mid-twenties was lounging behind the table for four across the aisle. He was dressed in a woollen beanie, faded black jeans, and an electric-blue fisherman's jumper almost as threadbare as her own. A tangle of rope and leather cords snaked around his wrist. His dark hair was splayed out in a casual mess beneath his hat, and from the dusting of stubble on his chin, it was obvious he hadn't seen a razor in days.

He looked over and met her gaze.

Ariel gave him a self-conscious smile and deflected her attention further down the carriage. A group of businessmen were staking out their terrain, visibly assessing the available table space between themselves and their neighbours. She stared at them in disbelief. It was like laptops at dawn! Did they *seriously* not have enough room?

'Well, there's plenty of room here!' Henry said in a cheerful voice.

He removed his coat, folded it into a rectangle and placed it next to his walking stick in the luggage rack overhead. 'How the other half lives! It'll be walk-in closets for everyone next!'

He bent over and rummaged in his suitcase, which was now lying open on his seat. Ariel tilted her head and discreetly peeped inside. His belongings were arranged in neat piles and held in place by four crisscrossing elasticated straps which snapped together in the middle like a pair of gentlemen's braces. The case's lining – a soft, fuzzy turmeric – was patchy and worn, its edges stained with rusty blooms of ochre and brown. Overall, she got the impression the suitcase must be almost as old as he was.

'Back in a jiffy,' Henry said. He pulled himself upright, tucked a bundle of fresh clothing under his arm and retraced his steps through the sliding door.

A palpable air of mystery lingered in his wake, absorbing Ariel's thoughts entirely before curling around her shoulders and settling on the now closed, tight-lipped surface of his suitcase.

'Excuse me? If you don't mind me asking, is the gentleman okay?'

Her neighbour in the woollen beanie was staring at her over a copy of the *Time Out Guide to Edinburgh*. His question – along with his American accent – caught her momentarily off-guard.

'Oh. Yes, he's fine, thanks. He had a nosebleed. A pretty bad one, but it seems to be under control now.'

'Nosebleed, huh? That's a relief. I thought maybe he'd been in a fight.' Beanie Guy's deadpan demeanour segued into a broad, easy smile.

She waited for him to return to his book, but he held her gaze, his inquisitive brown eyes watching her closely, like someone examining something curious, something foreign or unfamiliar under a microscopic lens. A moment later he shifted forwards in his seat, his palm pressed to his chest.

'Hi, I'm Travis Farlan. I'm guessing we're going to be sitting across the aisle from one another for the next four and a half hours, so I thought I may as well live up to the cultural cliché of the gregarious American and introduce myself.'

As he spoke, Ariel noticed a battered music case lying on the window seat beside him. The case was liberally plastered with a ragtag collection of stickers, the majority of which were scuffed and fraying at the edges. She caught the word '*Chicago*' emblazoned across one; '*Monterey*' on another. A couple of friends from school had wandered the hallways with stickered cases like that. Violins and flutes, mainly. The odd French horn. Every once in a while one or other of them would get pounced on in the schoolyard. One boy even had his viola tossed into the recycling bin. She never understood why they were targeted like that. She always thought they were cool.

'If you're the gregarious American, does that make me a classically reserved Brit?' she countered with a smile.

Travis held up his hands and laughed. 'Touché!'

Ariel leaned her elbows on the table, taking care not to

disturb the precise alignment of the crockery any more than was absolutely necessary. 'I'm Ariel Bliss, and he's –' she pointed vaguely towards Henry's empty seat – 'Henry.'

She hesitated, unsure what more to add, then decided the truth was as good as anything under the circumstances. 'Henry and I met in the station this morning. I went over to make sure he was okay, and when he found out we were both travelling to Edinburgh he offered me his spare first-class ticket as a thank you.'

'For real? That's awesome! You and I are kindred spirits. My first-class ticket was a gift, too.' He uttered a low chuckle. 'We're like a pair of high-class railroad bums. I guess both of us landed on our feet.'

'Sorry?'

'It's a train-hopping reference. Or don't you guys have that over here?'

Ariel gave him a blank stare.

'Maybe not...'

She raised her eyebrows. 'So...'

Travis seized his cue. 'So basically, there's this whole subculture of homeless people who ride freight trains all over the U.S. – illegally, obviously. They're like modern-day hobos. They haven't got any place to live, so they use the rolling stock as a means of putting a temporary roof over their heads. Some of them cover hundreds and thousands of miles a year hopping from one freight carrier to another. Some even travel with families, kids as young as five or six.'

'Sounds dangerous.'

'Uh-huh. Imagine risking your life every time you jumped!

They'd argue it's worth it just to have the chance to kick back in one of those old, open boxcar carriages and watch the world fly by. You need some balls to do it, though.'

Ariel nestled deeper into the folds of her multicoloured scarf. 'Can't say I'd be up for it on a freezing cold day like today.'

Travis rubbed the back of his neck and shrugged. 'They stuff their clothes with newspaper to keep warm. Apparently.'

She shot him a questioning glance, but Travis just smiled and shook his head. 'It's not what you're thinking... I'm a New Yorker, born and bred. I've done my fair share of cross-country travelling, but never like that. I'm a professional musician. There's no way I could jump on and off moving trains and risk injuring my hands. I wouldn't be much of a sax player without fully functioning fingers.'

He draped his arm affectionately over the top of his saxophone case and gave it a gentle pat. 'Train hoppers have to contend with a shower of loose ballast if they fall between cars. They can lose limbs. Wind up dead. I like to think of myself as a free spirit, but those guys are fearless. I'm way too attached to life to risk it all for a cinema-screen view of the American landscape, no matter how awe-inspiring it might be.'

Their conversation was interrupted by the slamming of carriage doors and the piercing trill of the guard's whistle. Ariel stared out of the window as the train began its slow, steady advance from the station.

'Right on time,' a voice announced at her side.

She turned to see Henry looking a million times better. 'Hi, Henry. That was quick!'

Beneath his jacket he was now wearing a plain white shirt and light green tie. He'd washed his face and neck. Even wiped the specks of blood from his shoes. His complexion was still a little drawn, but overall she thought he looked pretty relaxed, considering.

He dropped his soiled clothing into a Tesco carrier bag which he flattened and slipped inside his suitcase, immediately above the elasticated straps. He clicked the case shut and bent over to lift it onto the luggage rack.

Travis sprang to his feet. 'Can I help you with that?'

'Oh, not to worry, I can manage. Thank you,' Henry replied.

The loose, crêpey folds of skin on his neck stretched and tautened as he arched his back, and with quivering arms slid his case overhead. Lowering himself at last into his seat, he cast a final glance through the metal bars running above him.

'We made it!' he said to Ariel. 'I don't know why there's always such a tangible sense of achievement about boarding a train. It almost makes you feel worthy of a medal just for negotiating your way to your seat.'

He clasped his hands in his lap, leaned his head against the back of his seat and closed his eyes.

Elsewhere throughout the carriage passengers shifted and settled; announcements were made over the loudspeaker; newspapers, books and laptops were opened; tablets switched on; earphones wedged in ears. Seduced by the rhythmic rocking of the train, a sea of heads lolled left and right.

Ariel gazed out of the window at the flat, industrial grey of the urban cityscape whizzing by. They were picking up speed now: ca-choo ca-*choo*, ca-choo ca-*choo*, ca-choo ca-*choo*.

Before long they slithered through a tunnel, and then, not even twenty minutes from King's Cross, the train was flanked by a retinue of fields, and a bank of leafless trees rose to attention like balding consorts on either side of the track. The train barrelled onwards, the sun scrambling from behind a cloud to shine upon the trees' outstretched branches, infusing them with an oddly mystical glow.

Exactly twenty-three minutes from London, the first cow lumbered into sight.

Ariel sank back into her seat.

The long journey north had begun.

It was dull and stuffy inside the shop, and she'd grown tired of sitting curled up in the window, her finger tracing the underside of the green and gold lettering on the far side of the glass.

Bliss Books – *Est. 1988*

Specialists in Mind, Body, Spirit

New and Second-hand Esoterica and

Rare Volumes Available

Please come inside and browse!

She lifted the back of her hair and fanned her neck with her hand. Estelle was busy serving a woman with a sleeping baby strapped to her chest. Linus, huddled deep in concentration in the corner, was adding the finishing touches to a homemade display case for a brand-new delivery of dowsing pendulums. Of the handful of regular customers swaying like reeds among the shelves, all Ariel could see were their arched, round backs.

She blew a damp strand of hair out of her eyes and searched for Linus's ancient Olympus behind the counter. The camera (*her* camera to be exact, now that she'd persuaded him to give it to her for her eighth birthday a few months earlier) was poised for action exactly where she'd left it the day before, on a concealed shelf below the till. She wanted to feel its sleek, black casing beneath her fingers and crouch down low like a photojournalist, whiling away the afternoon taking pictures of the tourists as they browsed, unsuspecting, among the stacks. White as death and slippery with factor fifty at the start of their holidays, by the end they'd be golden-fried and half a stone heavier from all the 99s, and the cockles and chips, and the drink.

But today, nothing.

Ariel trailed through the shop, along the cool, shady passageway leading to the back garden, and settled into a deckchair with a copy of *The Adventures of the Wishing-Chair*.

'Hey, mind if I bring my coffee and join you?' Frank shouted from the attic window. 'It's hotter than a Texan barbecue up here!'

She looked up, saw a smiling face, a crisp white T-shirt, a

swirl of glossy, jet-black hair, and waved to Frank to come down. She hoped he might be wearing his stage clothes, but so far he hadn't worn them once during the day, not in the whole two weeks he'd been lodging with them, not unless he was on his way out to do a show. And yet Frank managed to look like Elvis no matter what he wore, with his jutting cheekbones, his immaculately sculpted sideburns, his perfect, china-white teeth. According to Estelle, Frank wasn't far off Linus's age, but Ariel thought he looked *years* younger. Linus was in his early fifties and already had grey hair.

'The mercury's gotta be well up over eighty today,' Frank said as he launched his six-foot frame through the back door. He ran a hand through his quiff and reached for a pair of aviator sunglasses in his back pocket. 'At least out here there's a trickle of fresh air!'

He crossed the lawn in four easy strides and lowered himself onto the grass next to Ariel's chair. The turn-ups of his jeans rose to reveal a tattoo of an eagle on the inside of his left ankle. 'I got that in Philly when I was eighteen,' he said, rubbing his finger over the dull, black ink. 'Thankfully, it's pretty hidden away down there. I don't like it so much any more.'

Ariel smiled and stared at her reflection in the mirrored lenses of Frank's sunglasses. Her face looked small and oddly distorted beneath the sunhat Estelle insisted she wore to keep the heat off the top of her head. Whenever she became too hot, her head began to pound and she broke out in a prickly red rash on her chest and arms. She wasn't supposed to be sitting out here at all at this time of day, but she liked slipping on her yellow Woolworth's sunnies and gazing up at the cloud formations sailing overhead. She was convinced there must be other people like her somewhere on the planet, daydreaming beneath the rolling, marshmallow sky. Sometimes she invented stories about who they were and where they were living. Sometimes she imagined them inventing stories of their own about her.

Frank took a sip of his coffee and pointed a suntanned finger at her book. 'Any good?'

Ariel's smile widened so much, her cheeks began to hurt. 'It's brilliant! Do you read, Frank? I do it all the time. It's one of my favourite things to do, but I don't think it's because we own a bookshop that I like books, because the books we sell aren't really storybooks at all. I think it's because when you're reading it doesn't matter where you are or what else is happening around you, it's impossible to feel alone. Do you think that too?'

She was vaguely aware that her words had spilled out of her mouth in one long, breathless rush, but she hoped they made her sound smart all the same. She searched Frank's face for a reaction, but it was difficult to tell what he was thinking without seeing his eyes.

'Sure, I like reading!' he replied. 'But not as much as singing. That's when I feel least alone in the world, when I'm singing and performing. Nothing can touch me then.'

'What's it like travelling around all the time? Don't you miss home?'

Frank took another sip of his coffee and cocked his head to one side. 'Being on the road can be lonely, I guess. But like I said, singing and performing is what I do. Sometimes you get lucky and make a new friend or two along the way. Cyn is with me most of the time, though, so it's not very often I'm completely on my own.'

Frank's girlfriend, Cynthia, was a Priscilla Presley lookalike. She may not have been American like Frank, but she was a living, breathing, raven-haired Barbie doll; the prettiest girl Ariel had ever seen. She still couldn't believe they'd be renting their attic room for an entire month while they did their *It's Now or Never* summer roadshow. It was the most exciting news she'd heard since Estelle and Linus told her they were at last expecting Baby Number Two.

'I'm glad you've got Cynthia,' Ariel said. 'It must be nice to have a friend like that.'

Frank smiled. 'Well, sure! But you have friends too, don't you?'

Ariel pointed at her book. 'Of course. My friends are in there. That's why I'm not lonely.'

Frank looked from her face, to the book, then back again. 'That's cool, Ariel. But I was thinking more about *real* friends,' he said gently. 'The kind you can call up and invite round to play?'

Ariel shrugged. 'They *are* my real friends. They're always there for me when I need them and they never call me names.'

'Why d'you say that?' Frank's voice tightened. 'Has someone been calling you names?'

Ariel gave a slow nod. 'Just some of the children in school. They call me a weirdo.'

'A *weirdo*?' Frank cried. 'Why?'

'I don't know... because of the shop and stuff. They say my gym things smell of incense. Mam says I should ignore them, but one or two are really mean.' She sighed. '*They're* the ones living in fantasyland. I'm sure they think we sit around all day staring into crystal balls and talking to pixies.'

Frank ripped off his sunglasses and hurled them onto the lawn. 'WHAT?! You mean the little fella with the pointed ears and the wings at the breakfast table this morning wasn't *real*?'

Ariel burst out laughing. 'See, that's why I like you, Frank! You're a weirdo like me!'

Frank held up his palm and high-fived her. 'Loneliness is just an illusion, kid. Don't let anyone dim your light! It takes an awful lot more courage to stand out than it does to blend in. When you're older, you'll understand. Anyway, where's the fun in being *ordinary*?'

He shifted his attention to a giddy chorus line of geraniums soaking up the sunlight in the border along the side wall. He'd put his sunglasses back on, but Ariel could tell he'd adopted that far-off look that grown-ups got whenever they were trying to solve a problem in their heads.

'Hey,' he said, turning back to face her, 'are you excited you're going to have a baby brother or sister?'

Ariel almost squealed. 'I'm nearly eight and a quarter! I thought it was *never* going to happen. A real-life brother or sister is going to be the best early Christmas present ever!'

Frank gave her one of his megawatt smiles, then dropped his gaze to the grass between his feet. He was still ruminating over something, she could tell by the way he was chewing on the side of his lip. She had a pack of cards under her deckchair and was about to ask him if he'd like to play a game of rummy, when he said, 'Is your mom in the store today?'

Ariel nodded.

'I'm just going to go inside and ask her something, okay?'

Frank pushed himself up off the ground and walked back to the house, his chest thrown out like a soldier on parade, his shoulders kneading the air. The grass where he'd been sitting looked flat and lifeless, as though some spectral hand had slipped, unnoticed, over the garden wall and combed it flush against the earth.

Ariel groped for her pack of cards and placed them alongside her chair where she could see them. She laid her book face down on her lap, made two circles with her thumbs and forefingers and held them up like binoculars to her face. She swivelled left and right, scanning the periphery of the garden from her seat.

It was quiet and empty as a church.

The only movement came from the plants, metronoming in the breeze, and her heart, which began to sink, gradually by degrees, when she realised Frank wasn't coming back outside.

She pulled her hat over her forehead and watched a ladybird zigzag its way across the shiny turquoise cover of her book.

At its edge it tumbled, spread its wings, and flew away into the hot, yellow air.

The train let out a low, mechanical rumble, quietened, rumbled again.

Ariel extended her foot under the table and patted the carriage floor, searching for her canvas bag with her toes.

Henry's slumbering body jerked and resettled, his eyes quivering beneath shuttered lids, his expression placid and immutable as stone.

Gently, she withdrew her foot. Across the aisle, Travis was scribbling something in the margin of his guidebook. He'd raised his feet and legs onto the empty seat opposite and looked so damn chilled; like he didn't have a care in the world.

She tried to look away, but her eyes kept returning.

She wondered if he knew she was looking at him.

His head bobbed back and forth, as though a private soundtrack was playing inside his brain. God, she wanted to speak to him.

She decided to wait until he'd finished writing and then ask him where he'd been to, where he was headed. What it felt like to be free.

Travis flicked his eyes to the window. When he turned and glanced expectantly in her direction, Ariel opened her mouth to speak, but her words lost their foothold and slipped back inside her, free-falling, like coins into a dusky well.

'Ariel!' Frank came bursting back through the garden door. 'Your mom's agreed to bring you along to the show today, kiddo! I told her the fresh air'll do her good, what with her expecting and all. We'll be leaving here together at three.'

Ariel stared open-mouthed as Frank disappeared inside the house to get changed. 'I'm going to a concert,' she said slowly. 'Mam's agreed to take me. Frank didn't let me down after all!'

They set off in a cloud of hairspray, chugging along in Estelle's second-hand Fiesta up the hilly Newton Road. Ariel wrapped her fingers around the Olympus and cradled it next to a bottle of orange Fanta, already turning tepid in the heat.

'Frank says we can stand right down the front, Mam, near the stage. He says we can have free Mr Whippys on the way in.'

She looked at Frank over her shoulder and grinned.

'Hey, it's the least we can do!' He tapped Cynthia on the arm. 'Right, Cyn? It'll be nice to see a couple of familiar faces cheering us on.'

Cynthia smiled. 'You bet, babe.'

Frank's hair was shiny and sleek, the sequins on his jumpsuit shimmering in a wide belt of sunlight streaming in through the rear window. Cynthia looked stunning as ever in a fitted lace dress and towering heels. She was holding on to the back of Ariel's seat, her body bent forwards at the waist so that her hair – backcombed into oblivion – wouldn't chafe on the Fiesta's roof.

'It feels so good to be out,' Estelle said into the rear-view mirror. 'Such amazing weather! I bet there'll be an enormous crowd.'

Ariel looked at her mother sitting serenely behind the wheel. She smelled of something darkly sweet – a heady mix of fresh mint, patchouli and honeydew melon. Ariel breathed it in and stared at Estelle's blossoming silhouette. Her mother was swollen-bellied and glowing in a loose cotton top and harem pants. An orange tie-dyed headband held her shoulder-length hair from her face, and a golden amber pendant dangled

93

like a rising sun at her throat. She wanted to reach out and touch it, to feel the silky warmth of the stone between her fingers, but she was afraid she'd distract her mother from the road.

'What's up, poppet?' Estelle flicked her eyes to meet hers. 'Do I look all right?' She lifted a hand from the steering wheel and smoothed it over the sweet, round spill of her stomach. 'I think they call this *hippo chic*.'

'You don't look like a hippo!' Ariel protested. She leaned in and smiled. 'You look like an undercover angel.'

The first half of the show went off like a dream. But then, as Frank neared the mid-point of his set, Ariel heard a series of wolf-whistles and garbled shouts directed at Cynthia, who was perched on a stool at the side of the stage.

'Who is it, Mam? What are they saying? I can't see.'

Estelle scanned her eyes over the back of the audience enclosure. 'It's nothing. Just some boys being stupid, that's all. Ignore them, poppet. Keep your eyes on the stage.'

The pungent tang of hot dogs, seaweed, and suntan oil hung heavy in the air. Ariel felt a flare of heat from the press of families packed in behind her. *There'll be plenty of kids in the audience*, Frank had told her. *Vacationers – here for a good time. I thought it might be nice for you to hang out with some of them. And a day away from the store with your mom will be cool, no?*

Frank was serenading a woman in a giant straw hat standing a few feet away. Cynthia was beating one hand against her side in time to the music. In the other, she held a glass of iced water which she sipped at intervals through a red and white striped straw. *She looks incredible!* Ariel thought. *Untouchable...*

'Hey! I'll give you something to suck on, darlin'!'

Furious, Ariel spun round. The shout, like the others that had preceded it, had come from somewhere in the back row.

'Oi!' a man's voice bellowed. 'Watch your language, will you? The place is full of kids, for fuck's sake! Let's just take it easy and enjoy the show!'

Ariel raised herself up onto her tiptoes, but she was too short to see over the tops of the adults' heads. 'Why can't you be quiet?' she muttered under her breath. 'Whoever you are, please stop shouting or go away.'

As she turned back to face the stage, a plastic water bottle sailed over the barrier and hit Frank in the centre of his chest. He stared at it for a moment in confusion, then picked it up and tossed it to one side.

'Why would anyone do that, Mam?' she asked. 'Frank hasn't hurt anybody.'

Before Estelle could reply, the crowd surged and Ariel felt herself being shoved up against the metal barrier separating the audience and the front of the stage.

'What the –?' Estelle cried. She reached down and caught hold of Ariel's hand. 'Okay, that's it. Time for us to go.'

Ariel dropped to her knees and fumbled on the ground for the Olympus. 'I don't want to go, Mam. We can't leave. We need to stay and wait for Frank and Cynthia.'

She clambered back to her feet and managed to pull her hand free of Estelle's grip, but her mother caught her by the arm and began to manoeuvre her towards the exit at the side of the stage.

By now a full-blown scuffle had broken out behind them, and the troublemakers – whose faces Ariel still couldn't see – were starting to hurl other objects into the air. Empty food packaging. Leftover scraps of food. It was disgusting. She saw Cynthia hovering warily in the wings. Frank's backing music was still playing, but Frank wasn't singing; he was striding towards Cynthia, motioning to her to leave the stage.

'*Please* let me go,' Ariel shouted. 'I want to go and help!'

Estelle pulled her closer. 'Listen to me – Frank will be fine. The event security team will make sure nothing happens to him or Cynthia, but we need to go back to the car now. Do you hear me?'

Ariel's eyes filled with tears. 'You're just jealous! You're jealous because Frank's my friend and he arranged this treat for me, but you don't care! You don't care about anyone except yourself!'

She twisted away and stared over her shoulder at the stage.

'Ariel,' Estelle cried, 'that's *enough*!'

And that's when it happened. Ariel called Frank's name at the exact same moment a glass bottle, its edges serrated where it had already been smashed in two, shot through the air like a rocket and caught him squarely on the crown of his head. She stood and watched in horror as it pierced Frank's scalp before tumbling, shattering into a million glittering pieces at his feet. For one agonising second nothing happened, then a stream of the brightest red she'd ever seen began to pour down the surface of his jumpsuit.

On it ran, over his collar, between his shoulder blades, trickling to the ground along the curve of his back and legs.

'I'm sorry, Frank,' she said when he arrived home from the hospital, his face drained, a bloodstained towel draped around his neck. 'It was all my fault. You wouldn't have been hit if I hadn't called out to you.'

Frank tossed a painkiller into his mouth and knocked it back dry. 'Hey, kiddo, there's only one person to blame for what happened, and that's the birdbrain who threw the bottle. You have nothing to apologise for. You're my wing girl, you know that, right?'

Ariel stared miserably at the conspicuous expanse of bandage running across the top of Frank's skull. The backs of her eyes began to prickle.

Frank placed his hand on her shoulder, then pulled it away again when he saw it was still smudged with blood. 'Listen, when you work in this business as long as I have, you see it all sooner or later. I've had people throwing themselves at me in adoration, and other times, I've been called everything under the sun. Those teenagers today were high. A couple of bad apples from out-of-town, the police said. Don't you give it another thought, okay?'

Ariel nodded. SHE WOULD. NOT. CRY.

'Thank you for arranging it so I could come and watch you sing,' she said in a muffled voice. 'I really loved it. Maybe one day you'll come back and visit us again?'

Frank brushed his quiff – which was now hanging lank and lifeless over his forehead – out of his eyes. 'Sure! Why not? Never say never, that's what I always say.'

Ten days later, he and Cynthia were gone. Ariel stood on the pavement and took a photo of them waving goodbye.

The taxi beeped its horn and sped off to join a hazy stream of traffic snaking its way along the Mumbles Road. She lowered her hand and felt something sharp in the pit of her stomach; something wild and mournful, like a howl.

The following weekend, a postcard arrived for her from Blackpool. On the front was a cartoon image of a grinning donkey trotting along the beach dressed in high-tops, top hat and tails.

Ariel smiled and flipped it over:

Hello Ariel!
The fella on the front has the right idea – life's too short to blend in! Don't be lonely. And BOO to anyone who calls you a weirdo!
Chin up, and show 'em some razzle-dazzle!
Love from your wing man,
Frank x (and Cyn too x)

Ariel nearly screamed with happiness. She placed the razzle-dazzle donkey next to the lamp on her bedside table.

'See you in the future, Frank,' she said.

Which surprised her, given that she couldn't have imagined – even for a second – the where, when, or why.

8

Snowfall

BLACKPOOL, FEBRUARY 1948

Henry

By the time Henry and Francine emerge from the Winter Gardens, only the coat tails of the afternoon remain. The sky shivers as rowdy swirls of snow begin to fall in dense, persistent flurries. Flakes gather in the grooves of Henry's cap and along the shoulders of his uniform jacket. They nestle deep in the folds of Francine's coat, and dust her hair with a riot of glistening white. She pulls a flimsy scarf edged with cornflowers from her handbag, and with fingers red-tipped and stiff with cold, she secures it in a casual loop around her head.

Henry gazes up and down the pavement, unsure what to do. The last train back to his billet doesn't leave until just before midnight. They have hours together yet, and they can't keep wandering around in this; they need shelter, or a temporary stopgap at least.

Directly ahead, the Tower recedes from view, renouncing all judgement, its rust-coloured spire bowing out beneath a baldachin of drifting snow.

'We could go to my flat, if you like?' Francine says. Her tone is airy, unselfconscious. 'It's only about a fifteen-minute walk from here.'

Henry turns to her and nods. Keeps his expression neutral. *So,* he thinks, *this is it.*

Francine continues, 'My flatmate, Jenny, has gone back to Sheffield for a couple of days, so we'll have the place to ourselves.'

She takes his arm and they turn inland, their eyes pinned like lamplight to the road ahead. The touch of her hand and the brush of her shoulder against his arm almost send Henry reeling. He sucks in his cheeks. Feels the blue-white air vibrate with the weight of all the words that go unsaid, but he holds them in, willing Francine to keep the conversation rolling until he can centre himself once again.

'The flat'll be nice and warm once it's heated up,' she says, as though reading his mind. 'I'll put the electric fire on and make some tea.'

Henry marvels at her naturalness, her lightness, her poise. A snowflake lands on her silver hair clip, right at the tip where an ornate butterfly emerges from the edge of her scarf with outstretched wings. The delicate snow crystals graze the fusion of metal and diamanté and pearl before dissolving into nothingness, only to be replaced by more, and more again. Francine laughs and shakes her head as feathery flakes break their fall against her eyelashes, then tumble onwards, sweeping like powdered sunlight across her skin.

'You never expect it to snow by the sea, do you?' She glances upwards at the clouds. 'Before I moved here I'd never have thought it was possible to build a sandcastle out of snow or a snowman out of sand.'

Guiding him gently by the arm, she leads him down a long, anonymous road away from the promenade. A group of Boy Scouts jostle past them, catching slivers of snow in upturned caps, trails of warm air rising from their mouths with each new exclamation of delight.

A few yards behind them a dapper young man with a pencil moustache whistles his way along the kerb. 'Afternoon,' he says chirpily. He gives Francine an admiring glance. Catches Henry's eye and grins. (If he'd winked, Henry would have sworn it was Devlin.)

Francine barely seems to notice. *She must be used to it,* Henry thinks. A smile of wonderment inches across his face. *Or maybe she couldn't care less about another man's attention now she's walking home with me...*

Francine rests her head against his shoulder. Henry nods at the young man as he passes by and finds to his surprise that his nervousness has been tempered by a brand-new sensation: *pride*.

'What does Jenny do?' he asks. Relaxing into his stride, he tries not to let his mind jump ahead to how it will end – how it *could* end, if they let it – later that day when they're alone in Francine's flat.

'Jenny works as a coat-check girl on the weekends, and she's a waitress like me during the week,' Francine replies. 'We moved here together from home last spring. She told her mam we were going to be secretaries, but I couldn't lie to mine – she knows that given half the chance, all I'd do is dance.' She looks up at Henry and smiles. 'I read that Rita Hayworth started dance classes as soon as she could stand. Imagine that! Some girls have all the luck.'

Henry grins. 'I don't know about *luck*. Sounds like an awful lot of work for such a small child.'

Francine is undeterred: 'I'm not afraid of hard work. I think it's inspiring. Waitressing is just temporary. Everyone has to start somewhere, don't they, Henry?'

Her voice is bright and weightless, and there's a rosy flush of colour to her cheeks. Henry knows it's just the wind pawing at her skin, but he can't help wondering if there's a trace of heightened emotion too.

He draws her closer towards him and pays little attention to the direction they take as they walk. Francine guides him through a maze of cookie-cutter residential side roads, their similarity rendered all the more pronounced by the unifying mantle of still falling snow. By the time she comes to a stop, he's lost his bearings entirely; even the ubiquitous Tower has been fully erased from view.

'Well, this is me.'

She lingers on the pavement in front of a narrow, terraced house. Henry glances over his shoulder while she fumbles in her handbag for her key. The street is deserted save for a solitary housewife pushing a pram, her face laid low by exhaustion, her eyes staring blankly at the road ahead. There is, he senses, a surreal quality to this unfolding. The scene before him illusory. Evanescent. And yet the pounding in his chest is mountainous, and utterly, utterly real.

'After you, Henry.'

The key clicks in the lock and a pencil of light catches the hollow of Francine's cheek as she speaks. Henry hovers for a moment in its reflection. *Christ*, he thinks for the hundredth time, *this girl's a dream.*

She holds out her hand and smiles. 'Come in.'

Beaming from ear to ear, he steps inside. Francine follows behind him and directs him along a dimly lit hallway, up a staircase to an unassuming doorway on the first floor.

She sidles past him and unlocks the door. 'It had better not look like a pigsty. It was fine when I left, but Jenny's a whirlwind, especially when she's packing a bag for home.'

She leads him into a modest sitting room presided over by an unwieldy sideboard, a rickety dining table, an unlikely menagerie of chairs. The room is sparse but homely, and, Henry notices with surprise, there's a refreshing hint of disorderliness about the place, as though a group of children had been playing tag there just moments before.

'I'm going to bloody kill her.'

'Oh, I wouldn't worry,' Henry says gamely. 'If you think *this* is untidy, you should try living with a bunch of airmen for two years. They don't call it a "mess" hall for nothing, you know.'

Francine tilts her head back and laughs. She plugs in the electric fire and sweeps up an armful of laundry from a wooden clothes horse which stands before it on three sides:

stockings, slips and assorted items of underwear, mainly. Presumably not the sort of stuff she wants Henry to see.

'They're Jenny's,' she says, blushing. 'Not that it makes a difference. She must have done the washing before she left.'

She disappears with the clothes through a half-open door.

'It must be nice to live with someone you know so well,' Henry calls out. 'Like being with family, only without all the squabbling.'

'Sometimes we squabble,' Francine replies. 'Jenny isn't the tidiest person in the world, and she can be infuriatingly unpredictable, but she's fantastic fun. And having her here makes me feel so much less homesick –'

She walks back into the room, gives Henry a guilty stare. 'Oh. Sorry, Henry.'

'What for?'

'For complaining about homesickness to someone who's been stationed abroad for so long.'

Henry stands, his back to the fire, and tells her not to worry, that yes, there were times when he missed being home in London, but he'd never been away before, so he tried to look on it all – good and bad – as an adventure. 'I wouldn't change it for the world,' he says brightly. 'Not the majority of it, anyway, though I'm glad to be back now.'

Francine makes her way to a tiny kitchen leading off from the sitting room and puts the kettle on to boil. Henry leans against the doorframe, his gaze following the milk-white underside of her wrist as she warms the teapot, fills it to the top, lets the tea brew for exactly three and a half minutes before pouring it out into two china cups.

The teacup nearest to him is cracked, a spidery black line trailing perilously close to the handle join. Francine flicks her eyes to him and smiles. 'If this were work, and you were Mr *"High and Mighty"* Sinclair, he'd make me throw that out.' Casually, before he can tell her otherwise, she swaps them over. 'Luckily for me, I have an untarnished reputation for never letting anyone's order end up in their lap.'

Henry laughs and walks to a faded armchair by the fire. He's never had his own place and is amazed at how natural it feels to be here in Francine's world, surrounded by the intimacy of Francine's things. He stares in awe at the easy mundanity of it all: the ironing board propped against the wall; the remains of a plate of Marmite and crackers on the dining table; a pair of slingback shoes tossed beneath the sideboard.

His eyes come to rest on a stack of fashion and movie magazines piled up in a wooden crate by the window.

'I get those from Housekeeping,' Francine says. She carries the tea things into the room and hands Henry his cup. 'Once a month, after the new ones come in. It's either that, or they end up in the bin.'

'Very enterprising,' he replies. He twists round in his chair and grins. 'What about those?'

Huddled to one side, in a corridor he assumes leads to Francine's bedroom, are three dressmakers' dummies. Their headless bodies stand shoulder to shoulder, their torsos draped in an eclectic array of female apparel: a plastic raincoat; a waitress's uniform; a colourful collection of scarves and pins.

'Oh, you mean The Girls? They used to belong to the dressmaker who lived in the flat before us. Our landlady, Mrs Adkins, told us that one day she just disappeared owing three months' rent. But those she left behind. Jenny and I keep them as a badge of honour, just in case she returns.'

She bites her lip, glances up at an oval of damp in the corner of the ceiling. 'It's not exactly Buckingham Palace, and the pipes knock and hiss something terrible, but –'

'It's perfect,' Henry interjects.

The corners of Francine's mouth rise. 'It's *passable* more like, but I'll take the compliment anyway. Thank you, Henry. Like I said, you're very sweet.'

She walks to the sofa opposite him and sits down. Henry turns to place his cup on a small side table next to his chair. His hand begins to shake, causing the spoon to clatter noisily against the saucer and a good half-inch of tea to spill over the side of his cup. *Oh God*, he thinks. *Please. Not now.*

He dabs at the spilt tea with the end of his sleeve. 'I'm sorry,' he says quickly, 'that was clumsy of me. And as for trying to clean it up with my sleeve –' his face falls – '*very* sophisticated.'

He buries his hand between his knees. 'The shaking... it's a kind of tic, I suppose. They used to tease me about it at Changi. No one said as much, but I'm pretty sure it was the reason I was assigned to clerical duty in the end.'

'You don't need to apologise.' Francine glances towards the kitchen. 'If this were a fancier restaurant, I'd have given you a serviette... Anyway, it probably doesn't happen half as often as you think.'

'No. Well... every now and then. When I'm nervous.' Henry covers his embarrassment with a smile. 'I'd never really noticed it before, but in service it's not so easy to blend in. I wouldn't make much of a waiter, would I? Or a surgeon.'

'I'd *never* tease you, Henry.' The look in Francine's eyes is suddenly fierce, resolute. 'I don't understand why servicemen have to be so cruel – or some of them, at any rate. I don't care if you were flying planes, manning a watchtower, or sharpening pencils, I'm sure most of them don't have a brain *half* as clever as yours!'

The elements in the two-bar electric fire spark, rending the air with soft cracks of electricity.

'It's nice of you to say so,' Henry replies. He looks Francine in the eye and grins. 'Anyway – on a practical level – at least sharpening pencils will come in handy when I'm a teacher.'

He shifts his weight to the edge of his seat and holds his palms to the fire. He wants desperately to get up. He wants to sit next to Francine, feel the proximity of her body just inches away from his, but he doesn't want to crowd her. He doesn't want her to think it's the only reason he came.

'It'll warm up soon,' she says, leaning in to meet him. 'At least I hope it does, otherwise you'll never want to come back to the North West again.'

Suddenly she gets up, skitters towards the Bush Bakelite wireless on the sideboard. ('A Christmas present to Jenny,' she tells him, 'from her fiancé, Tom.') She switches it on and fiddles with the dial until the big band melody *Chattanooga Choo Choo* pours out over the airwaves.

'Glenn Miller!' she cries. 'Don't you just love him, Henry?'

Henry nods. 'The best. Forty was way too young for him to go.'

'It was! By about fifty years!' She taps her hands against her thighs. 'This song has such a great opening. It makes me want to pack a suitcase and jump on a train right now!'

The room reverberates with the brassy, tromboned cry of a train rolling out of a station. Henry watches, mesmerised, as Francine kicks off her shoes, twirls, floats breathlessly back to her seat. She sings along to the lyrics as naturally as though she'd written them herself. Her exuberance is infectious, intoxicating in the extreme. He lays his cap on the arm of his chair, and in one fluid movement rises to his feet.

Don't mess up, he tells himself. *Don't mess up. Don't mess up.*

Outside, an anarchy of snowflakes flutter past the window, forming singular patterns on the glass. A crystal veil, or so it seems to him, safeguarding their seclusion, obscuring the world beyond from view.

Henry walks to the sofa, sits down next to Francine and slides his hands around her waist.

For a moment she doesn't move, doesn't blink.

'You're beautiful,' he says with a small laugh of incredulity. 'I can't believe I haven't told you that until now.'

'Thank you.' Her face softens into a smile. 'So are you.'

Henry leans in and kisses the freckle sitting below her jawline at the side of her neck.

Still, she doesn't move.

He pulls back, meets her gaze. 'Is this –?'

'Yes,' she says, her eyes locked on his. *'Yes.'*

Finding Henry Applebee

Henry nods. He inches closer, feels the subtle flow of her body beneath his fingertips as she yields to his embrace. And just like that, he's gone. Lost to a place of refuge. A place of completeness. A place of unaccustomed bliss.

9

The Sax Man

DECEMBER 6: *EN ROUTE*

Travis

Travis figured she must be lost (emotionally? Spiritually?),
but then what was she, eighteen? Nineteen, tops? Wasn't
that her prerogative? Her rite of passage? Fuck, not so long
ago he'd been that age himself. And what a freakin' battle of
wills *that* turned out to be!

When Ariel and the old man first walked through the
carriage door the first thing he noticed was the ethereal, almost
otherworldly expression on her face. Like someone who wasn't
entirely *present*.

A few days earlier, he'd spent an afternoon wandering in a
state of awe around the *Pre-Raphaelites: Victorian Avant-Garde*
exhibition at Tate Britain. He sat on a bench at the centre of
a vast, cavernous room, a slalom of tourists, art aficionados

and students buzzing around him, a rich thrust of colour on the walls, and waited for the crush to settle. Ariel, with her long, wavy hair parted down the middle, translucent skin and pale, haunted eyes, looked to him like she'd sailed fresh out of a Rossetti or a Millais and wound up here, like a twenty-first-century *Lady of Shalott* on a London to Edinburgh train.

Travis hummed a riff in his head. Kept his eyes on his book. Across the aisle he could sense Ariel's gaze honing in on him. He didn't want to flatter himself by assuming she was interested. Probably she was just bored... Distracted, maybe? He couldn't get a read on her at all, but he was pretty certain she had something she wanted to say.

He picked up his pen, circled a handful of Edinburgh music venues in his guidebook and scribbled the words *Worth checking out?* in the margin.

Then, immediately alongside them, he added, *Ask Uncle Frank.*

As the train rumbled northwards, a haze of thin, wintry light filtered through the carriage window, teasing the edges of the stickers on Travis's sax case. He leaned his head against the back of his seat and tuned his body to the gentle rock 'n' roll of the train. Let himself be transported. Breathed it in...

The acrid aroma of mildew and cheap perfume permeating the underground dive bars. The crawl of the overhead spot-lights on his skin. Cities seeped in history, musical and otherwise. New York. Boston. Philadelphia. Chicago. New Orleans. Monterey. Montreal. Toronto. Copenhagen. Amsterdam. London. Each one a glittering memento of his own private battle scars. A geographical tattoo. Each with its own unique story to tell.

If you want my advice, kiddo, Uncle Frank once told him, *you'll do as I do and think of the past as a casual acquaintance: warmly, but not to the point you want to invite it over for a beer every other night of the week.*

Travis loved that! He was young. And *alive!* His life was way too full of promise to get caught up in the nostalgic, dreamlike spell of what had gone before. And yet if anyone ever questioned him, his passion would come bursting to the surface all over again.

Because he'd learned by now that some moments in life are pivotal.

And when they happen, you know things are never going to be the same again.

'Tell me about it,' she said.

The time: eight days earlier. *The girl:* Barbara, a bubbly German vlogger. *The place:* her friend's apartment somewhere off Portobello Road.

Travis shifted his head on the pillow. 'What do you wanna know?'

'Tell me what it's like to be a musician, stupid.'

He ruffled his hair and smiled. 'You're *still* asking me questions?'

'I'm a vlogger,' Barbara replied demurely. 'It's what I do.'

Travis slid his naked body out of the side of the bed into

a room mired in the afterglow of perpetual impermanence: bland, blond, Ikea furniture; the printout of a Lufthansa e-ticket on the bedside table; her backpack packed and ready on a single, upright chair. He wanted to answer her, but the truth was he had to go. *She* had to go. Didn't she tell him she had a plane to catch back to Berlin?

They exchanged email addresses on the tacit (he assumed) understanding that it was unlikely, though not impossible, that their paths would cross again. Back home in New York he'd probably have received a slap on the back from his friends. But here, in a chilled, stark, post-dawn London, his exuberance was beginning to pall beneath the hollow spectre of emptiness that so often follows a transitory exchange of sex.

Travis gave her a warm hug goodbye, said it had been great to meet her, when what he really wanted to assure her was that he wasn't, by nature, a player. He wasn't *that guy.*

'Have a safe trip home,' he said, shrugging his coat around his shoulders. 'I'd better be on my way.'

Jazz. The electrifying, soul-elevating, mind-bending buck and throw of it. His all-consuming passion wasn't something he could easily sum up standing with his balls to the wind in the bedroom of a girl he'd known for less than a day.

He'd discovered it during Easter break, the year he turned ten. His father, Travis Sr., had employed a local carpenter to remodel the garage of their home in Oceanside, Long Island, with floor-to-ceiling shelving and a worktop area to accommodate his growing collection of model planes.

Marv Lamott – the man hired for the job – was a thick-set, six-foot-five African-American with a smile as wide as the Hudson River, and – somewhat improbably given his gargantuan frame – a jaunty, almost musical gait. For three days straight, Marv pulled up in his Ford Ranger pickup truck, laid out his tools on the garage floor and plugged in a portable CD player which he carried inside under one arm, his toolbox cradled in the other.

The music Marv played was jazz.

Its effect on Travis, mesmerising.

It began with the strange, soaring, syncopated rhythms drifting into the front yard. Travis could hardly believe what he was hearing. The free-floating melodies lit a fire in his brain, while each new explosion of sound burrowed deeper and deeper into his chest, breathing his breath, flirting with the very beat of his heart.

He spent two whole days peeking around the garage door, watching, listening. He figured Marv knew full well he was there, but if the carpenter happened to glance over his shoulder, Travis immediately pulled himself back out of sight.

It wasn't until day three that Marv finally called his bluff. Rising up from the CD player was a sweet lament, rich and dark as buckwheat honey. (Later, Marv told him it was a Ben Webster ballad: four-and-a-half minutes of such profound sensuality, Travis's love affair with the tenor sax was sealed right there and then.) Marv's toolbox was lying open amongst a tumble of wood shavings, but the man himself was nowhere to be seen. Travis braced himself, took two steps inside the garage door and 'BOO!' – three taps on his left shoulder blade and there was Marv standing right behind him, hands on hips, laughing like crazy.

'Hey there!' he boomed. 'You lookin' for me?'

Travis stared at the grinning giant towering above him. 'Hi. I guess I was, yeah.' He wiped his hand on the back of his sweatpants and held it out towards him. 'I'm Travis. Like my dad.'

Marv wiped his own enormous hand on a strip of yellow cloth hanging from his waistband and thrust it towards Travis's chest. 'Marv Lamott. Nice to meet you, Travis my man. So tell me, is it the carpentry you're interested in? Or is it the jazz?'

Travis told him he didn't know the first thing about it, but he liked the way it didn't have any rules.

'Oh, it's got rules all right,' Marv assured him. 'Though you wouldn't know what to look out for unless you knew what they were.'

Travis followed the carpenter into the garage and lowered himself onto the edge of his father's bench press. He glanced guiltily at the meticulous rows of newly constructed shelves running up and down the walls. His dad would crucify him if he thought he was getting in Marv's way, but Travis Sr. was at work, buried behind his voluminous steel desk at the Long Island Rail Road Company. He'd never know a thing...

'Could you teach me?' Travis said. It surprised him, how easily the question rolled off his tongue. He looked over at Marv and grinned. 'As long as I'm not bothering you or anything?'

115

'You wouldn't be botherin' me at all!' Marv replied. 'I've nearly finished up here anyways.'

As Marv put the finishing touches to Travis Sr.'s new oak worktop, he told Travis that people often struggled with the complex language of jazz; no matter how hard they tried, they just couldn't understand its nuances. And while it might sound on the surface like it had no real structure, the secret to jazz was improvisation. *Creative intuition.* Composing on the spot and inventing brand-new melodies right off the top of your head.

'Wait, so you're saying it's possible to play *and* compose at the same time?' Travis asked, incredulous.

'Heck, yeah! This is jazz we're talkin' about, Travis. Not *pop*.'

According to Marv, the melody and harmony could be endlessly reworked and embellished. Jazz artists didn't just play the exact same notes over and over, they changed them up. Added their own flavour to make them more personal and unique. Constantly defying expectations, they soared to whole new realms of musical possibility, all the while remaining loyal to the original essence of the tune. *The returning melody*, Marv called it.

'Sure, it's free in its expression,' he added with a shrug, 'but that don't mean it's disorganised.'

Travis eyed the stack of CDs lying next to Marv's toolbox. Marv followed his gaze, reached across the table for a slip of paper, and began to write.

'Here,' he said when he'd finished. 'These guys are all world-class saxophonists. There's plenty more where they came from, but if you're interested in delving deeper, I'd say they'd be a pretty good place to start.'

Travis ran his eyes over the names: *Charlie Parker, Sonny Rollins, Joe Henderson, Jimmy Giuffre, Paul Desmond, Dexter Gordon, Coleman Hawks* –

He hadn't yet reached the end when Marv asked for the piece of paper back, and with a flick of his wrist added *Miles Davis (trumpet!), Bill Evans (piano!)* and *Charles Mingus (double bass!)* to the list.

'Just to make sure you get a fully rounded education,' Marv said with a wink. 'Remember, Travis, jazz is collaborative. It's never only about the horn.'

Travis turned to thank him, but Marv was already halfway out the garage door. 'Hey, Marv!' he called out. 'You forgot these!'

On the worktop table were two CDs, their plastic covers chipped and worn. Travis picked them up. Tried their titles on for size: '*Speak No Evil* by Wayne Shorter. *A Love Supreme* by John Coltrane.'

'Just somethin' to kick-start your collection,' Marv responded with a grin. 'Check out Coltrane's entry on the track called *Resolution*. There's a Jimmy Garrison bass solo up front, then Coltrane comes in with Elvin Jones on drums and McCoy Tyner on keys. Those names might not mean much to you right now, lil' man, but trust me, that shit'll kill ya every time.'

At some point, Barbara had completely cracked Travis up by asking him if his father was in the music business too.

'My *dad*?' he replied. 'You gotta be kidding me! He's retired now, but when he was working his high-powered job in payroll, a creative day for him was loosening his tie.'

He chuckled and looked away. If they had more time – if he thought Barbara's interest in discovering who it was who'd inspired him was personal as well as professional – he'd have told her:

'I was thirteen. His name was the Sax Man. Meeting him was one of the single greatest moments of my life.'

Uncle Frank had a view on that, too: *I'm telling you, Travis, no one is entirely powerless in the face of their own destiny. But if you ask me, some things are just fated. Sometimes, The Powers That Be toss us a ball that's so obviously heading in our direction, the only logical response is to reach up and grab it.*

And grab it was exactly what Travis did.

Enter Pivotal Moment #2.

The summer it happened, Travis's mom took on a part-time job managing a friend's vintage tearoom on the Upper West Side. On Saturdays, they caught the Long Island Rail Road train at East Rockaway and travelled into the city together. While she worked her shift, Travis embarked on a meandering trail that covered the Museum of Natural History on Seventy-Ninth Street, and extended east through the park to the Metropolitan Museum at Eighty-Second, and the Guggenheim a few blocks north on Fifth.

Travis knew his mom assumed he spent most of his time hanging out at the museums, but on days when the sun streamed down in brilliant pools of light, the only place calling to him was the sprawling urban landscape of Central Park.

In hindsight, he never could decide whether it was the Bethesda Fountain angel that first led him to the Sax Man, or the euphoric tones of the Sax Man's tenor horn that first led him to the angel. In any event, the two became inextricably intertwined.

He'd entered the park at Strawberry Fields, and had been wandering from west to east when he first glimpsed the tips of the angel's magnificent bronze wings rising upwards through the trees. He curved round to his right and wove his way along the path to Bethesda Terrace. As he drew nearer, the angel began to grow in stature, and the soaring strains of a velvety smooth saxophone riff became increasingly more audible on the breeze.

At the lower terrace's outer edge, Travis stopped in awesome contemplation of both the music, and the ethereal *Angel of the Waters* silhouetted against a flawless July sky. Wings spread high and wide to the heavens, the angel was poised mid-stride, head gently inclined, the folds of its tunic rippling behind it, propelled by the driving forward motion of its legs.

Inspired by the angel's sense of purpose, Travis climbed one of the two stone staircases leading to the upper terrace. At its summit, a group of rollerbladers in cut-off tops and sweatpants glided in dizzying circles around a wide, open concourse. And beyond them, standing off to one side, were a disparate cluster of onlookers listening to a man Travis couldn't yet see, playing a sax.

Travis made his way to a nearby bench and sat down. Observing intently through a constantly shifting break in the crowd, he watched the musician tip forwards and backwards at the waist in time with the music, his fingers flying with mind-blowing dexterity over the keys, barely lifting off the sax at all.

The man was dark-skinned like Marv, and almost as tall, though older; Travis guessed mid-forties, but he could have been older still. A sprinkling of white hair was just visible beneath a trilby hat worn deep and low, the brim skimming the right-hand lens of a pair of circular sunglasses. At his feet was an open saxophone case. Every now and then onlookers tossed in coins or dollar bills as a token of their appreciation, and when they did so, he nodded, tipped his hat and said, 'Why thank you! Thank you very much!'

An hour passed, maybe two, before Travis finally rose to his feet, determined to drop into the waiting case all that remained of his weekly allowance. As he made his approach, he didn't lift his eyes for a second from the gleaming horn and the dark, nimble fingers running up and down the keys.

He was too shy, too electrified to look into the man's face.

For the remainder of the summer, he went back every weekend to hear the Sax Man blow his horn. Once, he took along his mom during one of her rare breaks, promising to show her something incredible. Travis extolled the agility of the man's finger work. The fluidity of his range. The silky soulfulness of his tone. Above all, he marvelled at the way man and horn melted into one. And all the while the *Angel of the Waters* was urging forwards, in Travis's eyes at least, so it, too, could enjoy the show.

He was hooked.

Travis begged his parents for sax lessons.

When they finally consented, he practised until his fingers were raw.

Three years passed, and by his sixteenth birthday, *he was ready*. It was time to go back to the park and approach the Sax Man about his craft...

He'd been dreaming of it for months. And yet not once – not in the entire time he'd lain on his bed in Oceanside rehearsing all the questions he was planning to ask – did it occur to him that his hero might no longer be there. The very idea of not finding him on the terrace was inconceivable; as flat-out crazy as the notion of Bethesda Fountain without its angel.

But the very first day Travis went looking for him, the Sax Man was nowhere to be found. He scoured the park from Wollman Rink to Harlem, just in case the musician had relocated to a different spot. A week later, he searched for him again; and the next four weeks after that. But the Sax Man was gone. *Sparito*. He couldn't believe it! *Why had he never had the foresight to approach him before?*

Fast-forward another four years, when Travis was a budding college student of twenty, and just when he'd convinced his dad he was knuckling down for good – that's when it happened for real...

The location was an apartment building downtown, just

east of the Bowery. Around one-thirty in the morning, Travis and a bunch of his friends spilled out of a party into a torrential downpour of such spectacular intensity, even the bouncer checking IDs outside CBGB raised his eyes to the skies in disbelief.

Travis's group pulled up their hoods and headed for the busy intersection where the Bowery meets E. Houston. As they neared the crossing, Travis spotted the figure of a man standing on the edge of the sidewalk. His shoulders were hunched over, the cold, hard rain ricocheting off his umbrella like water off a steel drum. Eyes to the ground, the man stepped into the road, straight into the path of a delivery truck which came hurtling around the corner through a dense curtain of rain.

'Hey!' Travis screamed.

He leaped forwards, clamped his hands around the man's shoulders and yanked him back to safety. The truck roared past, showering them both with a chest-high spray of rain-water. Seconds later it was gone, speeding towards the East River, its chassis lurching from side to side, tail lights blazing.

'*Sweet Je-sus!*' the man cried. He curled his free hand around Travis's forearm and dragged him beneath the glistening dome of his umbrella. 'D'you realise you just saved my *life*?'

His face was partially in shadow, his heavy features rigid with shock, but Travis recognised him at once. 'I know you!' he said in amazement. 'You're the Sax Man from Central Park!'

The man's eyes widened. 'Yes,' he replied. 'You bet I am!'

'I used to listen to you play when I was a kid,' Travis gushed. 'The first time I ever laid eyes on you I went home and asked my parents to sign me up for sax lessons!'

'Is that right? Well that's something, I gotta say. What's your name?'

'Travis. Travis Farlan.' Travis held out his hand and pumped the older man's palm up and down. 'You have no idea how psyched I am to finally meet you!'

The deep grooves running along the man's brow relaxed and softened. 'Travis, it's good to meet you, too. I'm Curtis Walker III, but Curtis'll do just fine. Hey listen, I owe you. How 'bout we grab a coffee? Get outta this crazy rain for a while?'

Travis grinned and suggested a place he knew in the West Village – an all-night diner where they ate blueberry pancakes, drank coffee and talked until the storm began to subside. Curtis told him he was still blowing his horn. He'd been filling in in a friend's jazz quintet, playing gigs in a little old town called London, England...

'I'd forgotten how good it feels to get out on the road. There's something about being away from home that brings out all the blue notes, y'know? Then other times I'll see a pretty face, or an inspiring vista, and I'll write something real joyful. You read music, don't you, Travis?'

Travis nodded. 'When I watched you play I could never tell where you ended and the sax began. You made it all look so freakin' easy.'

Curtis leaned his head against the back of the booth and laughed. 'The secret is to breathe as one with your sax. Feel the notes deep in the marrow of your bones. That's when it starts to flow for real.'

Travis felt his heart lunge. 'Could you show me?'

The words slipped from his lips with such artlessness, such ease. He hoped he wasn't being presumptuous, but this was the second time in his life that fate had – quite literally, in this instance – thrown someone into his path capable of teaching him exactly what he needed to know. He'd missed his chance to speak with Curtis the first time around; it would be a crime to let the opportunity pass him by again, surely?

Curtis used the flat end of his spoon to nudge his trilby hat an inch or two higher on his forehead, then he spread out his palms and grinned: 'For the guy who saved my life? *Hell*, yeah!'

And that was it: *the game-changer*. He withdrew from Columbia Law School during the second semester of his first year. Caught the train back to Oceanside. Broke the news to Travis Sr. while he was working in the garage on a new model plane.

'I'm sorry, Dad, but getting a law degree was your dream, not mine.'

'*My* dream?'

Travis Sr. stared at him as though he were some sort of imposter; a street kid who'd wandered through the door by accident looking for a place to sleep. 'Have you completely lost your *mind*? What kind of weak-minded individual walks away from the most prestigious law school in the city? From everything he's been working towards? From his goddamned *life*? A *quitter*, that's who!'

Travis took a step backwards. Lowered his eyes to the floor. 'Please, Dad, I meant what I said. I'm sorry. You just need to

have a little faith in me. That's all I ask. Just a little faith.'
The silence that followed was deafening.

Travis closed the door to Barbara's building, squinted up at
the fickle London sky, and walked the short distance to
Portobello Road. When he reached the junction with Elgin
Crescent he paused, turned to his left and continued on in
the direction of the railway bridge at the far end of the road.

Milling behind two long, parallel rows of fruit and veg
stalls, stallholders stamped their feet, their breath mingling
with the steam from takeaway cups of tea and coffee held in
rough, fingerless-gloved hands. He surveyed the colourful,
eclectic parade of shops, bars and restaurants vying for space
on either side of the road. There seemed to be a café or juice
bar of one kind or another on every corner. He scanned over
each one in turn, mentally eliminating them one by one.

A little way ahead, squeezed rather optimistically between
a line-up of big name conglomerates, was a fifties-style, char-
acterful café with a wooden bench and a purple and white
awning outside. Travis made his way towards it. Spotting an
empty table in the corner, he placed his hand on the door
and walked inside.

'Morning.' The woman behind the café counter greeted
him warmly with a smile. 'What can I get you?'

Travis skimmed the menu board on the wall behind her
head. After a moment's indecision, he opted for a double
espresso, orange juice, and something called a *'Love Bagel'* –

the house speciality packed full of healthy fats and fibre, a sprinkling of flax seeds, an optional (yes please) dollop of cream cheese.

'Excellent choice! Is that to have in or to go?'

'Uh, to have in, please.'

She nodded and told him to take a seat. She was middle-aged – older than the other two, a quiet air of authority about her – with cropped, ash blonde hair and a smart cotton apron with the words *Amy's Place* printed in cursive purple lettering across her chest.

Travis thanked her, edged his way to the empty corner table and sat down. When his food arrived, he demolished it in an instant. Knocking back the last of his espresso, he opened his leather bag and dug his hand inside. Wedged side by side were his laptop, a half-eaten packet of protein bars, and a dog-eared copy of the previous day's *Evening Standard*, its cover torn, its breaking news stories already outdated, its edges curling quietly like kale.

Travis pulled them out one by one and piled them onto the café table. His wash bag was lying squashed at the bottom. He pulled that out, too, balanced it on his laptop and ran his hand over the prickly contours of his cheeks. His meeting with a booker friend of Curtis's wasn't for another hour yet. Maybe he'd skip going back to Uncle Frank's beforehand and just clean himself up at the venue. Wing it. Hope his night on the tiles wasn't written like a big fat neon sign all over his face.

He took some money out of his wallet to cover the check, returned his laptop, wash bag and protein bars to his bag, and left the cash and the *Evening Standard* on the table.

The woman in the *Amy's Place* apron glanced over as he got up to leave.

'Thanks!' he called out to her. 'That was awesome! The best breakfast I've had since I arrived!'

'Great to know,' she replied. 'Spread the word!' She cupped her hand conspiratorially around her mouth. 'Trip Advisor would be fantastic!'

She slipped from her post behind the counter, passed by him with a mug of tea and sat down at his now empty table. 'Two minutes' break,' she said with a guilty smile. 'It makes my day to see customers walking through the door, but it's been like Clapham Junction in here all morning.'

She dropped Travis's money into her apron pocket and took up his discarded *Evening Standard* in her hand.

Travis hiked his leather bag over his shoulder and stepped outside into the crisp London air. All at once, with minimum effort, he fell in step with the neighbourhood locals filing past the colourful smorgasbord of market stalls, and continued on his way, his face turned to the future, never looking back once.

10

The Letter

DECEMBER 6: *EN ROUTE*

Ariel

A riel peeled her gaze from the carriage window. The train whipped along the tracks, rocking her body with unexpected violence as she leaned to one side and retrieved her canvas shoulder bag from the floor.

She slid the letter from the inside pocket. The stationery was pale cream and weighty, yet understated. The ink – a brilliant iridescent shade of indigo-blue – changed colour according to the light, like an oil spill, or a newly formed bruise.

She cradled the letter in her lap, holding it low beneath the overhang of the table where neither Henry nor Travis could see it. Since its arrival the week before, she'd read it a hundred times over, but now she examined it again, scouring the neatly flowing handwriting for clues:

Dear Ariel,

I expect the contents of this letter, written by someone you think of as a stranger, will come as quite a surprise. Let me start by explaining that I am an old friend of your mother's, although, given that our contact over the years was fairly sporadic, it was only recently that I learned of her passing. I was so sorry to hear the news. Please know that my heart goes out to you all for the enormous gulf she must have left behind.

I should mention that we have, in fact, met once before, several years ago in London. We had tea with Estelle and Isaac down by the river, at the National Film Theatre café. You were almost ten at the time, and so full of wonder. Estelle introduced me to you as Mia. Perhaps you remember?

There's so much I'd like to tell you, but in this rather unique instance I'm afraid a letter would fall short of what I have to say. I'm writing, therefore, to ask if it would be possible for us to meet again, at my home in Cramond, just outside Edinburgh? You're probably wondering at the location, but I'm hoping you'll be willing to place your trust in me. All I ask for is one day.

Work commitments have been keeping me busy of late, but <u>Friday, 7th December </u>is currently a completely free day. If you're available, could you come to Scotland then?

I've taken the liberty of enclosing a cheque which should cover your travel and accommodation expenses. I thought you might decide to stay the weekend – given that it's quite a way for you to come – so hopefully this amount will be sufficient. I would be very happy, of course, for you to stay with my husband and me, though I realise you might prefer the freedom of one of the hotels in the city. Whatever you're more comfortable with is fine by me.

My card with my contact details is enclosed. I'd be grateful if you could get in touch as soon as possible to confirm if you can make it.

One last request: it would be best if you didn't mention any of this to Linus until after you and I have met. I'll explain all when I see you. I know Estelle would have wanted it to be so.

With warmest wishes,
EVE MARIE HOPE

Eve Marie Hope… E.M.H… Mia… Ariel turned her face back to the window. It was still doing her head in to think that she and *E.M.H.* had already met.

On the back of the envelope she'd scribbled down the questions that had been bugging her for days:

1. *Why's it so important to both Estelle and Eve Marie that Eve Marie and I meet again?*
2. *If they were friends, how come Estelle never mentioned Eve Marie/Mia's name before or after our trip to London?*
3. *What's Eve Marie so desperate to tell me? And why in person???*

Then there was the package. Ariel still had no idea what Estelle was so determined to bequeath – or return? – to Eve Marie. And WHY had they both insisted that Linus be kept in the dark – a man from whom (as far as she was aware) Estelle was incapable of keeping a secret?

Ariel stared at the ghostly palette of her reflection embedded in the carriage window, the scud of clouds – as nebulous and mercurial as her memories themselves – floating overhead. She tried to paint a mental picture of the woman she'd met eight and a half years earlier, but all she could conjure up were dreamlike fragments of an indistinct whole. A faint Scottish accent (or was that just something she was projecting onto her now?). A quiet, reserved manner. A figure (tall? Blonde?) who'd sat chatting with Estelle while she and Isaac amused themselves nearby.

What she remembered most of all: the silkiness of the frosting on the chocolate cake served on a plate decorated with cherries; the rainbow-coloured spines of the books stacked side by side on trestle tables outside the café window; the buses – iconic, red as ripe tomatoes – pressed nose to tail along the Embankment; the thick, oily odour of the Thames, rich with industry, flowing under Waterloo Bridge.

And then, after Mia had gone, there was what happened back at their hotel, when Ariel had made Estelle cry.

All of this was so much clearer in her mind than the nondescript woman she never imagined for a second might come into her life again.

⸻

'You've taken so many photographs of Isaac in his buggy,' Estelle said. 'Don't you want any pictures of anything else?'

'It's not just Isaac in his buggy. It's Isaac tugging on a balloon at the Tower of London and the London Eye and London Zoo,' Ariel replied. 'The background's different every time. I'm doing what I always do. I'm collecting memories.'

The whole point, she explained, was that she'd be able to show Linus the places they'd been visiting while he was stuck in the shop back home. 'And they're for Isaac, for when he's older, so he can see that he was here and that he had a grand time.'

She finished her cake and wondered how much longer she'd have to stay trapped in her seat before she could be excused from the table. Estelle's friend, Mia, was pouring them both another cup of tea. Isaac was strapped into a booster chair and chewing on a half-eaten gingerbread man, a spray of crumbs accumulating like specks of gold dust on the floor beneath his feet. Ariel wanted to explore the open-air book market on the pedestrian boulevard outside. Already in the short space of time they'd been sitting there, it was obvious it was miles busier than the modest flow of traffic which trickled through the doors of *Bliss Books*.

She turned impatiently to observe it. On the far side of the stalls flowed the Thames itself, wider, murkier, more muscular, somehow, than she'd imagined. She was dying to get up and have a look at it.

'Mam, please can I go outside and look at the stalls? They might have something we can take home for the shop?'

Estelle glanced over at Mia and smiled.

'Can I, Mam? I won't be long.' She pressed her hands against the edge of the table and pushed back her chair.

'Poppet, I don't think you'll find the kind of books we sell in Oystermouth, but you can go and have a look as long as you promise to stay close by where I can see you. No wandering off, okay?'

Ariel nodded, looped the toggles on her duffel coat and disappeared through the café exit before Estelle changed her mind. The January air blew cool and brisk along the boulevard, carrying with it the clatter and scrape of board on concrete from the skateboard park nearby. She waved at her mother through the window and set off down the long, symmetrical rows of display tables loaded with paperback novels, autobiographies, reference guides on art, music and film. She ran her hand over their multicoloured spines, pausing every so often to leaf through the pages of anything bright or unusual that caught her eye.

When she arrived at the end she stopped and spun her gaze upwards. Arcing overhead was the stone-girdered underside of Waterloo Bridge. Linus had told her there were people living under the arches of the bridges in London, but with so much toing and froing on all sides she couldn't see how that could be possible here.

She peered over the railings and wondered if anyone was spying on her from their hiding place nearby. Most likely, she decided, they preferred to live further down the river, tucked away in alcoves, safe from prying eyes and the winter chill, only coming out at night when it was quiet and calm, when they could be kings and queens of all they could see, with only the moon and stars to judge them...

'Ariel!'

Ariel turned, saw Estelle smiling and waving at her from the entrance to the café.

'It'll be time to go soon! Come back inside and say goodbye to Mia before we leave!'

Ariel raised her hand. 'Okay!'

She threw an urgent glance of longing at her surroundings. 'I'm not ready to go home yet,' she whispered. 'I want to stay here. I want to have an adventure.'

'Mam, I've got a funny feeling in my stomach. Like we've stepped into another world and everything's different. And now that we've seen it, we can never go back to how it was before. My heart's beating really fast. Feel it.'

Estelle leaned over the half-filled wheelie bag on the bed and placed her hand on Ariel's chest. 'What's wrong, love? You're not anxious because I pulled you out of school to come to London, are you? You've only missed a day. Most kids would be thrilled to have a day off school.'

Ariel shook her head.

'Then what is it?'

Estelle ran her eyes over the bland eggshell interior of their hotel room. Spotting one of Isaac's toy trucks on the floor, she bent down and tossed it into the case. 'The energy's a lot different in cities. It's more frenetic. I think maybe you're tuning into it. Perhaps we packed too much in over the last couple of days. There was just so much I wanted you to see.'

A trio of muffled sounds wafted in from the corridor: the soft thud of a door closing; a medley of high-pitched voices; the melodic *ping!* of the lift door.

Ariel pulled her knees in under her chin. 'But that's just it. I don't know how I'm ever going to see it all. The world's so big, even if I set off today it would take me *years* to see everything. I'd be travelling forever and a day!'

She was sure Estelle would understand. Once, her mother had told her that they had traveller's blood running through their veins; adventurers – ancestors forever on the move, the only constant roof over their heads a tinfoil sprinkling of stars. But Estelle's expression was one of sheer incomprehension. Worse still, she actually seemed amused. She didn't even try to disguise it! She was laughing right in Ariel's face!

'Come on, poppet, you're just overtired. You've got plenty of time to see the world when you're older. You don't need to be worrying about that now.'

Ariel felt a well of indignation bubbling beneath her skin. Some nerve, some deep, emotional ligament suddenly stretched and snapped inside her. 'It's not funny!' she cried. 'You *know* we never go anywhere! You don't care less about Isaac and me. All you care about is the business. You're always in the shop!'

Her words echoed plaintively around the room. It was as though a rampaging ogre had come charging out of her, determined not to be ignored. She bit her lip, but the more she tried to stop herself from crying, the more she thought she might actually implode.

'Well, that's just not true, is it?' Estelle countered. 'We're away now in London, aren't we?'

She wasn't smiling any more. She turned to Isaac, who was tugging on the telephone cord so hard, he was in danger of pulling the whole thing down on top of him. 'Let go, Isaac, you're going to break it. Give it to Mam, there's a good boy.'

She prised the cord from between his fingers and tucked it behind the desk out of sight. Isaac's eyes widened in confusion. He stretched out his hands in search of his plaything, then crumpled, furious, to the floor. Two seconds later, he started to wail.

Ariel sat motionless on the bed and tried to remember how happy they'd all been just a couple of hours earlier. A thin stream of snot dribbled from Isaac's nose. Estelle scooped him up off the carpet, carried him to the bed and bounced him softly on her knee.

'You might not think it now, but it won't always be this way,' she said. 'If Dad and I are always working, it's for you and Isaac, no one else. We want things to be stable... for the future... but perhaps you're right. Perhaps we should be paying more attention to right now. To collecting memories as a family, all of us together.'

To Ariel's horror, a tear began to trickle from the corner of Estelle's eye. She walked to her mother's side of the bed and kissed her cheek. 'I'm sorry, Mam. I didn't mean to sound so spoilt. Please say you forgive me?'

Estelle's eyes glistened in the shallow light. 'It's all right, poppet. Everything's going to be fine. Let's finish packing. It's time to go home.'

illlllllllliiiii

Ariel folded Eve Marie's letter, slipped it back into its envelope and placed it in her canvas bag at her feet. As she righted herself, a Highland Terrier poked its face around the back of the chair a few seats ahead of her. Its fluffy white head was cocked to one side, its almond-shaped eyes trained with great intensity on the sliding door through which its owner had temporarily disappeared. It didn't move a muscle, not even when a steward came bustling down the carriage aisle bearing two large containers of tea and coffee.

'Sir? Miss? Can I offer you something to drink?'

Henry stirred and slowly opened his eyes. He'd been dozing the entire time since they'd left King's Cross and looked a little disorientated – as though he'd woken from a distant dream – but he smiled when Ariel caught his eye. He opened and closed his mouth, his lips dry, his face glazed with sleep, and asked the steward if he could pour him a cup of tea.

'Certainly, sir. Miss? Anything for you?'

'Could I have a coffee, please?' Ariel wrapped her hand around her mug and flashed a surreptitious glance in Travis's direction. *Can you believe it?* she wanted to say to him. *All of this is free!*

'We're in the countryside already,' Henry said as the steward moved away.

She followed his gaze and stared at the variegated fields billowing off into the distance, the grassland all puffed up and preened like a plump, green cushion as far as the eye could see. Giant thimbles of hay crenellated the horizon. Closer in, isolated farm holdings stood neat and square as toy houses, while droves of horses huddled together in twos and threes, flicking their tails, tossing their heads, gazing quietly about them.

'It's as green as Wales,' she said.

'Green as the Heath in bloom,' Henry chimed. He slid his hand into his jacket pocket and scattered a handful of black and white striped sweets onto the table. 'Everton mint?'

Ariel looked down at them and smiled. They seemed a little past their sell-by date – the sticky glucose veneer had lost its sheen, the plastic wrappers starting to droop at either end – but she didn't want to offend him by saying no.

'Thanks, Henry.' She picked up the mint nearest to her and slipped it into the pocket of her jeans.

'Which part of Wales do you come from?' he asked, sweeping the remainder of the sweets to one side.

'Oystermouth. It's on the western end of Swansea Bay.'

Henry furrowed his brow and pressed his lips so tightly together, they momentarily disappeared from view. 'I can't say I've ever been there,' he said with a shake of his head. 'But I did know a boy from Fishguard once, a long time ago when I was stationed in the Far East. His name was Freddie Farnborough – which couldn't have sounded less Welsh – but everyone called him Taff all the same.

'Taff was the only person I've ever met who could play any tune under the sun by tapping it out on his front teeth with his fingernails. His *real* talent, though, was for practical jokes. One time, he threw a flare into the open stove in our billet while a crowd of us were gathered round it, having a smoke. Taff shovelled it in with the coal without a single one of us noticing. You wouldn't believe the bang it made when it caught alight. I've never seen grown men move so fast in my life! There were sparks flying all over the place, and so much red smoke, you couldn't see a hand in front of your face. Nearly frightened us to death, not to mention almost burning down our billet! Taff was laughing so hard, he fell over during the scramble, banged his head on his bunk and knocked himself out cold.'

Ariel laughed and stared once again at the wintry landscape whizzing by. 'When I was younger my mother and my brother, Isaac, and I once took the train up from Swansea to London. I pressed my nose against the window and spent half the journey in a dream. If I saw horses, I pretended they were being ridden by imaginary cowboys and Indians galloping alongside the train. When the horses disappeared I'd think up something else, like a giant hot-air balloon, or a glider racing overhead. But none of them could catch the train. The train was a Welsh dragon flying down the tracks, with glass windows for eyes and electric-blue sparks for fire power. I wish I'd thought of flares. All it was missing was smoke pouring out of its nostrils.'

'How wonderful!' Henry cried. 'Did it have a name?'

'Not that I remember, no.' She smiled sheepishly. 'I think I was a little in awe of it at the time.'

Henry shrugged. 'Well, there's nothing wrong with an active imagination. These days, people don't daydream enough. And there are few better opportunities for doing so than when you're travelling on a train.'

There was a gradual deceleration, and then, like steam releasing from a pressure cooker, the train shuddered to a halt.

Henry twisted round in his seat.

'Must be Peterborough,' Ariel said. She peered ahead through the window. 'Looks like we're just outside the station, waiting to pull in.'

When they arrived a group of Japanese tourists boarded their carriage, several of whom were trailing expensive-looking golf clubs in their wake. One couple gestured to the reserved seats across the table from Travis and waited patiently in the aisle for him to move his feet. Travis mumbled an apology and scrambled to rearrange his things. The couple stored their golf clubs in the luggage rack by the door, but Travis kept his saxophone case on the empty seat beside him, slumped against the window like a tipsy friend.

Ariel looked over at him and smiled. Thin wisps of light slanted in through the window, illuminating the colours of the stickers on the case's exterior, picking out their nuances like gems. 'Do you mind if I take a picture of your sax case?' she asked.

Travis grinned. 'You want a picture of *this*?'

Her smile widened. 'Yes. But you don't need to move it,' she added quickly. 'The lighting's perfect right there where it is, on the seat.'

Travis appeared genuinely thrilled at the request. 'Be my guest! As long as you let me have a copy if it comes out well.'

Ariel reached under the table for her canvas bag and groped inside for her phone. When she sat up she saw that Henry was staring at his suitcase in the luggage rack above his head. He kept his gaze glued to it for some minutes; looked almost as though he might reach out a crooked finger and touch it, to reassure himself, perhaps, that it was still there.

Peterborough to York. The stretch of land that followed distinguished itself by half a dozen concrete towers belching great plumes of smoke into the sky. Trackside, train engineers huddled together in bright orange reflective overalls, and hard hats, white as bone. Like the horses they'd passed earlier, the men showed little interest in the tubular blur of metal and glass flying by, immune by now, Ariel presumed, to its thunderous roar, the smell of burning rubber in its wake.

She accessed the camera function on her phone and held it up to the window. The train stopped briefly to let another locomotive pass. Stationary, it made it harder to ignore the debris tossed at intervals onto the neighbouring tracks: empty drinks cartons; crisp and sweet wrappers; a soiled nappy.

On a sloping bank lay a child's dilapidated pedal car, visibly weathered from alternate beatings by sun and rain. The car had come to rest awkwardly on its side, as though the child or parent had grown bored of it and pushed it, driverless, down the bank for fun.

On the same slope a few feet beyond it there was a discarded front door, its number peeled away, its surface iron-flat and solemn as a tomb.

At Doncaster, an announcement rang out that they would be making an unscheduled stop to pick up a fitting for the train. Ariel watched a sea of blank faces look up from the opposite platform as the carriages limped in. After a brief interlude, they set off again, an oncoming train zooming past on the adjacent track, swift as a bullet from a smoking gun.

An enormous field sparsely populated with sheep, black heads bowed, followed. And then the return of the concrete towers, six or eight pairs dominated by a huge, spindly mast. Together they soared skywards, vast tendrils of smoke sputtering from their gaping mouths.

Through it all the quiet *click, click, click* of Ariel's camera, collecting memories through the glass.

'What are you going to do with all those pictures?' Henry asked. 'They must be very out of focus.'

'Some more than others,' she replied. 'The important thing is to be able to see the subject. Any peripheral blurring just adds texture, and an element of mystery.' She smiled. 'I actually think it's kind of cool when the background is partly disguised.'

'It sounds almost as though you use them for a game.'

She leaned her head to one side. 'Um... sort of, I suppose. A friend and I send them to each other when we've got something we want to say.'

Henry frowned, causing the liver-spotted skin on his forehead to wrinkle even more prominently than it had done already. 'You only send pictures? No words?'

'Yep. Just pictures.' She rolled her eyes. 'My dad thinks it's lazy. He doesn't understand that an image can do the talking by itself.'

Henry's frown deepened. 'I think I'd have to agree with your father on that. It sounds very precarious to me, with rather a wide margin for error. Wouldn't it be easier to just pick up the phone and speak to each other directly?'

'But that would defeat the point,' she said flatly. 'Everyone uses words, but sometimes, words can be a lie.'

Henry ran his finger along the collar of his shirt and gave

it a quick, sharp tug. A band of colour began to spread over his neck and jawline. Ariel wondered if perhaps he needed some air.

She scrolled through her picture gallery until she found the photo of the dilapidated pedal car. 'Take this one, for example,' she said, holding it up for Henry to see. 'Should I ever need it, this one has a very clear message.'

'That you're going for a drive?' he suggested. 'To a toy shop? Or a garage?'

Ariel smiled once again. 'No. That whatever it is I'm going through or working on has crashed and burned. There's a clear sense of abandonment surrounding the car. It's no longer a plaything; someone's favourite toy. It's been shunted onto an unofficial dumping ground on the side of a railway track and left there to rot. It's pretty unequivocal, I think.'

Henry's eyes narrowed, his face shrouded in a thick veil of doubt. 'Does this person mean a lot to you? The person you send the photos to?'

Ariel shifted in her seat. 'He's my best friend. Why?'

'Well, it's just that people can make mistakes. Someone could get hurt. It would be a terrible shame for something to be misinterpreted by either one of you, when perhaps whatever was misconstrued was not at all what the other one was trying to say...'

She lowered her eyes and swiped distractedly through the latest batch of photos on her phone. She wasn't sure Henry had understood. It was just a laugh, just a bit of harmless fun, but before she could reply he addressed her again, more brightly this time:

'Is that why you're going to Edinburgh? To visit your friend? If you don't mind me asking, of course. If you think I'm being indiscreet then I'll pop another Everton mint in my mouth and be quiet.'

Ariel laid her phone face down on the table. 'No. My friend's in Oxford at the moment, studying for his degree.'

She looked away, ashamed of her evasiveness, but Henry merely nodded and made no attempt to press her further. Her eyes drifted to her first-class ticket tucked into a metal holder by the window. Henry had been so kind... *Why did she have to go and be so damn defensive?*

His hands were loosely clasped before him, a stray smudge of blood still clinging to his wrist where he'd failed to rub the soap. Ariel stole a fresh, sidelong glance at his face. There was a whole lifetime's worth of experience buried behind his watery grey eyes, and maybe, she saw now, just maybe the faintest suggestion of pain...

'Actually,' she said, holding herself a little straighter in her seat, 'I'm on a kind of mission. I was given something by Estelle, my mother, before she died – a package she asked me to deliver by hand to someone she knew in Edinburgh. It was very important to her for some reason, though she didn't tell me what was inside.'

Henry's expression crumpled, his features rearranging themselves into what looked like a genuine portrait of dismay. 'Oh, I'm so sorry! Your mother must have passed away very recently?'

Ariel shifted in her seat a second time. 'It was a year ago... There were some things I had to take care of at home. I wasn't

144

really in a position to deal with it until now.' A flush of discomfort swept across her face. 'Rosemary...' She stopped, edited herself. 'We have someone helping out now. It felt like the right time.'

She clamped her mouth shut and avoided any mention of Eve Marie's letter.

Henry reached his hand across the table and gave her forearm a tender pat. 'Well, *that* your mother would quite understand, I'm sure. She trusted you to do it, and you're doing it. She couldn't expect any more from you than that. And just *think* how much better you'll feel when it's behind you!'

He re-clasped his hands in front of him and settled back into his seat. The train rattled along the tracks, the view from the window casting an increasingly somnolent spell over the occupants of their carriage.

Ariel wondered whether it would be polite to ask Henry the reason for his own trip to Scotland. *Was it her imagination, or had he deliberately not mentioned it?*

Her gaze drifted upwards to his suitcase. Maybe she wasn't the only one keeping something secret?

Henry glanced at his watch, tapped its face a few times with his forefinger, and muttered something inaudible under his breath.

'Sorry, Henry?' she said.

'Late,' he replied, fixing her with his glassy eyes. 'I can't understand it! We're already running late!'

11

Awakening

BLACKPOOL, FEBRUARY 1948

Henry

'Henry?' Francine nuzzles her face against his. 'It's late. You should get going. You don't want to miss your train.'

In the colluding darkness Henry peers at his watch and groans. It's past eleven already. What felt like hours and hours ahead of them have all but vanished, spirited away in a ticking time bomb of rapidly diminishing moments. Somehow, entire legions of time have marched by.

'Go on, try me,' he says. 'Give me sixty seconds, and I'll come up with every reason under the sun for not getting on that train.'

Francine's forehead crinkles into a frown. 'Now you're just teasing me. What about that clean record of yours? You can't mess it up on my account, not when you have such great plans.'

'A minor, insignificant detail,' Henry replies. 'My C.O. told me my conduct has been exemplary. What can he do to me now? Discharge me?'

He kisses her shoulder, levers himself up from the bed and reaches for his shirt, his socks, his tie. A heaviness overcomes him, dragging at his limbs. He doesn't want to leave, could quite happily stay here all night in these anonymous streets made soft and silent and perfect by snowfall, as though the benevolent sky itself had pulled a silvery-white membrane over their world and whispered *shhh,* take your time. Enjoy this moment.

No one will disturb you.

No one will know.

Slowly, his muscles spent, he tugs on his boots. When they'd tumbled through the door together, pulling awkwardly at each other's clothes, the only thing he'd registered of his surroundings was the pristine island of the bed. Now, as he looks around him he sees that Francine's bedroom is dotted with mysterious trinkets. Small china jars and intricate wooden boxes lie grouped together, forming miniature cityscapes in front of the dressing-table mirror. Alongside them, a powder compact and lipstick. A half-empty bottle of perfume. A matching hairbrush and comb.

On the windowsill sits a silver paperweight shaped like a woman's shoe. Even from a distance, he can tell it's been beautifully crafted. He studies them all – these strange, mute inhabitants of Francine's world – in the thin chink of light from the hallway, and tries to guess what's inside them, what hidden, private pieces of her they might contain.

Francine follows his gaze. 'Most of the things here are from my nan. She was left them by a neighbour she used to read to when she was younger. She calls them her *curiosities*. I always liked that name.' She slides her feet to the floor and gasps. 'Henry! Let's go back to the sitting room. It's absolutely *freezing* in here!'

In one seamless movement she scurries from the room, a long, oriental-style gown fluttering up behind her, a sweet note of jasmine on her skin. Henry remains where he is a moment longer, but she's gone; out of sight in the room beyond. He listens, hears her turn on the wireless, switch it off again. Then, the sound of running water from the kitchen sink.

'Francine?'

A sadness – fleeting, delicate as a dream – creeps over him. Lifting himself up from the bed, he makes his way along the corridor to join her. In the enveloping stillness of the hour, he crouches down low in front of the fire, his eyes blinking steadily in the pearly light.

'Henry,' she murmurs behind him, 'I'm coming with you.'

Henry swivels on his heel and rises to his feet. In Francine's hand is a tumbler of water. A single drop slides down the surface of the glass and falls, glistening, along the arch of her foot. She stares at it for a second in surprise.

'You're coming with me?' he asks in a puzzled voice. 'To Kirkham?'

'*Kirkham?*' A playful smile, winning in every way, spreads across her face. 'No, not to your billet! I mean to the station. You'll find it much more easily if I'm with you, and I thought at least then we could have a moonlit walk through the snow?'

'Oh,' he says, laughing, 'right!'

He slides his hands around her hips and pulls her towards him. Building behind her eyes, Henry sees the same flare of sadness he'd felt himself just minutes ago.

'This is entirely workable, you know.' His voice rings out with deliberate optimism. 'There must be hundreds of trains from London to Blackpool. All you have to do is say the word, and I'll meet you in the Tower Ballroom.'

The corners of Francine's mouth rise. 'On the balcony?'

'Absolutely! Or even on the dance floor. We'll be the new Venus and Adonis, only you and I will be having far too much fun to worry about being perfect.'

'Yes!' she cries. 'I'll look forward to it!'

'And then when I'm a teacher, I can take advantage of all those school holidays. It must be at least six weeks over the summer.'

'Oh.' Momentarily, her enthusiasm falters. 'The summer's the busiest time at the hotel. Mr Sinclair usually has to take extra staff on to cope with all the tourists. He'd rather work me to the bone than risk losing any of his precious customers.'

Henry is resolute. 'We'll manage. Even if I have to book into the hotel myself.'

Francine stares at him. 'You'd do that for me?'

'In a heartbeat.'

She gives him a dizzying smile. 'Then it's a deal! In the meantime, don't move a muscle, will you? Just give me two minutes and I'll be ready.'

Francine plants a long, lingering kiss on his lips. The imprint of her gaze is so strong, so enduring, that for a second

Henry can barely breathe. He glances down and sees her half-empty teacup on the floor next to the sofa. 'Don't worry, I'm not going anywhere, I promise.' He masks his giddiness with a grin. 'I'll sit right here by the fire. I can always read your tea leaves while I wait.'

The effect of his words is instantaneous.

Francine's elation evaporates before his eyes. 'That's not funny.' She pulls away from him, and turns quickly to leave.

'Francine?'

'I'm sorry, Henry.'

'Hey, wait!' he says, catching her gently by the arm. 'Talk to me! What's wrong? What did I say?'

Francine lowers her eyes to the floor. To his alarm, her arm beneath his hand is trembling.

'I told you,' she replies in a quiet voice, 'I don't believe in it. You said yourself they tell everyone exactly the same thing. Good, bad, indifferent, it doesn't matter... it's all just make-believe.' She lifts her chin and shoots him a defiant gaze. 'I may be young, but I'm not stupid.'

Henry grapples for a response, but the only thing he's capable of is a stunned silence. 'Francine,' he manages at last, 'I'm not going to pretend I understand the first thing about what just happened. All I know for sure is that the only thing that's real to *me* right now is this – you and me together.' He swallows. 'I'm crazy about you, I have been from the second I saw you. And there's nothing make-believe about that.'

Francine stares at him once again. Slowly, the tension slips from her face. 'You see!' she cries. '*That's* why I don't believe in tea leaves! People can tell me what they want. You'll always be the finest person I've ever met!'

She slides her arms around his neck and holds him so close, and with such tenderness, she doesn't see that Henry's hands have once more begun to shake.

'Wait for me,' she whispers in his ear. 'Wait for me here, will you? I'll be right back.'

She lowers her arms and runs to the bedroom to get changed. Henry buttons up his jacket. Smoothes back his hair. Places his cap at a downwards-sloping angle on his head. Resting a buttock on the arm of the chair, he fixes his gaze on the three headless dummies in the corridor. Nothing could have prepared him for this... Less than forty-eight hours earlier, he'd been cooped up at sea aboard a sweltering aircraft carrier bound for England. Now, he's in a nameless northern street, a world away from where he's headed, from where he's been, his heart and mind in a spin.

He adjusts the knot of his tie, pulls his jacket flat against his chest. From the bedroom he hears the sound of drawers opening and closing. Elsewhere in the building a floorboard coughs, a window rattles in its frame, the pipes splutter and hiss.

In the vast, speculative future that lies before him, Henry is suddenly aware that nothing in life is certain. In fact, for all his youthful optimism – for all his lofty ambitions for what he one day hopes to achieve – in reality he can predict nothing at all of what might, or might not be. He is simply waiting, the starting gun cocked and ready, the chrysalis poised to break.

So much lies ahead of him. He's *sure* of it.

'Anything could happen,' he mutters under his breath. 'Anything at all. But this –'

Henry lifts his head.

Francine emerges, breathless, along the corridor in her powder-blue coat, her hair tumbling around her shoulders, her eyes shimmering in the cool evening light.

'Here I am, Henry.'

She holds out her hand and smiles. 'Are you ready?'

12

The Room

DECEMBER 6: *EN ROUTE*

Ariel

Winter was approaching. So rapidly, in fact, it was hard to believe it was nearly a year since Estelle was gone.

Ariel cleared the dinner plates from the table and stood washing a mound of dishes at the kitchen sink. Linus – heavily distracted, even by his standards – was lost in thought beside her.

'Is he ever coming back to us?' Isaac had asked the previous evening.

'Dad's right here, Isaac. He hasn't gone anywhere. He's just missing Mam, that's all. Keep telling him how much you love him. It'll pass, I promise.'

Her father scooped a tea towel and a pile of freshly washed cutlery from the draining board. 'How is it possible that three people can create so many dirty dishes?' he groaned. His face was almost comically aghast. 'You'd swear we'd been feeding a family of ten!'

'Is there something else I can do?' Ariel replied. She kept her eyes trained on the sauce-splattered frying pan in her hand. 'I mean it. Just tell me when things are getting too much for you and I'll do whatever I can to help out.'

Linus dropped the tea towel onto the counter. 'Ariel.'

She scrubbed the pan harder.

'Put the pan down.'

Mechanically, Ariel did as he asked.

'Darling girl,' Linus said gently, 'you're doing more than enough already. It's not right that you should be taking so many things on board. Not when you've already given up so much.'

'I haven't —'

'*Yes*,' he said with a wave of his hand. 'You *have*.'

He reached for the tea towel and a plate. 'The thing is, pet, I've made a decision.'

Ariel's stomach dropped. 'A decision? About what?'

Her father's eyes rose prophetically to the ceiling.

She followed his gaze and prayed that after eleven months of grieving, he hadn't finally cracked and lost the plot.

'It's the attic!' he cried. 'You and I can fine-tune the details together, but this afternoon I received an offer.'

'An offer?' she echoed warily. 'Who from?'

'A customer... someone who's going through a tough time. Her name's Rosemary and she needs a place to stay.' He placed his hands on his hips, and for the first time in weeks, he dazzled her with a full-on smile. 'She's interested in a short-term let and says she'll help us out any other way she can. It's just what we need, pet, I truly believe it.'

Twelve days later, Ariel was sitting on a bench overlooking the gnarled expanse of Bracelet Bay, Estelle's copy of *Birdy* lying open in her lap.

'Could I join you? Is that all right with you, my love?'

At the sound of Rosemary's voice, she started. 'Oh.' Ariel's face was limp with disappointment. 'It's you. Hello.'

November 5. Guy Fawkes Night. That evening, she was taking Isaac to watch the fireworks display at St Helen's Ground. Rosemary had suggested it over breakfast, as though Ariel were incapable of coming up with the idea herself. And now here she was again, tracking her down like a homing missile; an over-zealous sniffer dog forever on her trail.

The skin beneath her shirt started to bristle. Bollocks. *Why was the woman always in her face?*

It was starting to feel like an invasion. The day Rosemary moved in, she'd climbed onto a chair and hung Native American wind chimes above the attic door. It made no sense to Ariel whatsoever; the door to the attic was halfway down a windowless stretch of landing where not even a token breeze was likely to blow. She wondered if they were intended as some sort of New Age alarm system to deter anyone else from entering. (Though why anyone would want to do so, Ariel couldn't imagine. Besides, the room had its own lock and key.)

And Rosemary sang. *Constantly.* She steeped vats of hideous *Sencha* green tea in the kitchen, and zoomed around the house in a pair of calf-strengthening FitFlop sandals which slapped incessantly against her pedicured, doll-like feet.

But that wasn't the worst of it. Rosemary – an energetic, forty-one-year-old soon-to-be-divorcée – had taken over all but one of Ariel's shifts in the shop in exchange for a modest reduction in rent. Which meant what, exactly? *Ariel was now surplus to requirements?*

'It's just temporary,' Linus insisted. 'It'll probably only be for six months at most. Just until Rosie gets herself sorted and we get ourselves back on our feet.'

Ariel rolled her eyes.

So how's it going with the new girl? ☺ Tumbleweed messaged her. Maybe u should make the most of her? For all u know she might blow away again as quickly as she blew in?

I wish! Ariel replied. Only problem is, Linus and Isaac seem happier. The only person who isn't is me.

With more free time on his hands, Linus had resumed his walks along the cliffs from Mumbles Hill to Caswell Bay, occasionally deviating from the path to search for golf balls like he'd done when she was a child. He'd stop for tea and a slice of bara brith in the beachfront café, then return home calmer and more grounded, a splash of colour in his cheeks, a sweep of sea salt in his hair.

But it wasn't over.

One night, Ariel woke to find him hunched over the kitchen table, tears streaming down his face. 'What are you doing down here?' she cried. 'It's the middle of the night!'

'Hello, pet,' he replied. 'You know, I could ask the exact same question of you.'

In his hand was a resplendent photograph of Estelle, a

ribbon of frilly-edged seaweed strung like a beauty queen's sash across her chest. And the room – Ariel would never, ever forget it – the room was full to bursting with the excruciating absence of everything that had once been.

'Your mother was fifteen years younger than me,' he stammered through his tears. 'She wasn't meant to go first.'

'Don't,' Ariel begged. 'Please don't think about it any more tonight.' She slipped her arm around his back and led him towards the stairs. 'You'll feel better in the morning. Remember what she used to tell us? Everything will look brighter once the sun pulls out its ray gun and scatters the howling moon.'

Ariel was jolted back to reality by the sound of a woman clearing her throat.

Oh God. *Rosemary*. She'd almost forgotten about her.

Rosemary took a tentative step closer to Ariel's bench. Her fiery mass of long, auburn hair swirled around her shoulders in the wind. Her eyes – an undeniably striking shade of green – stared hopefully into Ariel's face.

'I didn't mean to disturb you. I just thought maybe we could have a little chat now that we have a minute away from the shop?'

Ariel nodded and gestured to Rosemary to sit down. Behind them, on the far side of Mumbles pier, the tide had retreated so far out, it was difficult to imagine it might ever return. The beige silt left in its wake stretched for miles; a vast, muddy moonscape which yielded like blocks of fudge beneath the feet of the dog walkers who picked their way across it. Ariel always thought it looked more like freshly laid cement than sand.

'What did you want to talk to me about?' she said.

'Estelle,' Rosemary replied. 'I wanted to tell you that I knew her a little, that's all.'

Ariel's throat thickened. 'You did? I didn't know that.'

A smile, far softer than Ariel had ever noticed before, lit up Rosemary's face. 'I guessed as much. I used to pass by the shop from time to time, and whenever I went in she was always there, sitting behind the counter, cheerful as a field of daisies.'

'Yes,' she said in a quiet voice. 'That sounds like Estelle.'

Rosemary's smile faded. 'I think she must have heard – I mean about my ex-husband and his playing around. He's always been such a high-profile character. But I felt like such a fool.

'The last time I saw Estelle she gave me a clear quartz bracelet and told me it would help clear negative energy from my life. Honestly, I already had quite a collection of healing gem bracelets at home – one for every emotion under the sun – but none of them had ever been given to me like that. Your mum was quite a woman, may she rest.'

Rosemary paused. Crossed herself.

'I know it must be a bit of an upheaval for everyone, having me around, but it's going to take a while for the divorce to come through. I won't be renting your attic room forever, but while I am, I hope you and I can be friends?'

'Of course,' Ariel replied. She squeezed out a smile. 'Why wouldn't we be?'

Rosemary clapped her hands. 'That's *wonderful*! Because I thought that with me helping out in the shop, it might free you up to focus on you, and what you want out of life?'

Ariel spun her head to one side, and in a renewed surge of annoyance, prayed the wind would blow Rosemarysodding-Poppins and her FitFlop sandals back down the promenade where they belonged. 'You don't need to worry about me,' she said coolly. 'Everything's fine. I'm just working things out, that's all.'

Rosemary made a shuffling movement beside her and got up to leave. 'Okay. Well, there was just one other thing I wanted to say.'

Ariel turned and saw that Rosemary's face was almost the same shade of crimson as her hair.

'I don't want you to worry that anything's going to happen between your dad and me. I can imagine what it must look like... a widower opening up his home to a budding divorcée... but it honestly couldn't be further from the truth. Don't get me wrong, Linus is a lovely man, but I'm done with men for the foreseeable future.'

'God, no,' Ariel replied with far more vehemence than she'd intended. 'I never thought that for a minute!'

She picked up her book and searched frantically for her page. She'd rather chew sand than admit to Rosemary that the possibility *had* – in a fleeting moment of insanity – occurred to her, though somehow she didn't think Linus would have either the energy or the inclination to keep up with *Little Miss Perky*.

Rosemary beamed. 'I'm so pleased we've had this conversation. Talking helps everything! It's such a massive relief.'

York to Darlington. As the train pulled into York, Ariel spotted a coal locomotive, wrapped from tip to tail in a gaudy bandanna of graffiti, snaking its way slowly, and incongruously, along a parallel track, just beyond the station's impressive glass and iron roof.

She stared at the sharply angled lettering and cartoon-like images (mainly octopuses with huge, bulbous eyes and tentacles the size of sycamore branches). Its appearance here, in this most stately of English cities, struck her as both exhilarating and vaguely subversive. She took a series of photographs with her phone and turned to show Travis, but his seat was empty, his book lying face down on the table.

'It looks like a New York City subway train,' Henry said. He gestured out of the window, then dropped his gaze to her phone. 'How are you going to caption your photographs? *"York, New York"*?'

'Maybe,' she replied, laughing. 'You're getting the hang of it already, Henry.'

The train made a rough, lurching movement, and an unexpected waft of cold air swept over the back of her neck and shoulders. She peered through the glass and saw a brooding pocket of clouds gathering overhead. The sky was growing increasingly metallic, its molten surface streaked with rivulets of grey, the sun – for the brief period of time it had been with them – suddenly lost from view.

She closed her eyes and shuddered.

In a different place, a different time, she'd been here once before.

'It's time, pet. Mam wants to see you. She's asked for you to go along alone.'

'Alone? Why?'

Linus shrugged. 'I need a break – or so she tells me. There's no arguing with her as you know. Between you and me, there never was.'

Estelle's hospital room, he assured her, was light and airy, filled with late autumn sunshine. Ariel paused to gather herself at the door. When she stepped inside she saw that the room had been kissed by winter. The walls, drained of colour, drew in on themselves, sliding downwards like a Salvador Dalí clock face, dragging with them whatever precious units of earthly time remained.

'Mam?'

The word caught on her lips. She never called her that any more. It was Estelle, always Estelle, ever since her sixteenth birthday when she'd started using her parents' Christian names as a joke. It surprised even her how the habit had stuck. But today it was the only word that came when she opened her mouth to speak.

'Mam – it's Ariel. Can you hear me?'

She walked to the side of the bed and pulled up the plastic visitor chair angled nearby. Her mother's emaciated body lay tucked in like a bird's wing beneath the cover, her hair dark, defiant still, curling against the pillow.

Ariel scanned the hollows of her mother's face. How could she even hope to hold on to someone who couldn't be kept? There was so much she wanted to say. A million things she'd never get the chance to tell her if she didn't do it now, but the same one word kept bubbling up inside her, as though it sensed the truth even before she did; as though it knew her window of opportunity for using it was rapidly running out.

'*Mam.*'

Estelle opened her eyes. 'Hello, lovely. You look tired. Are you eating?'

Ariel smiled. 'Yes, I've been eating. So has Isaac. Vegetarians are paler, you know that.'

The corners of Estelle's mouth rose. 'Still stubborn as a mule.' Her eyes, clouded with morphine, moved slowly. Her voice was thick and faintly slurred. 'I never could convince you to eat meat.'

Ariel glanced at an unopened carton of apple juice on the tray table near the bed. 'Can I get you anything? Do you want some water? Or some juice?'

Estelle shook her head. She gestured to her bedside cupboard. 'Open it, poppet.'

Ariel did as she asked. Found the large, padded envelope. Pulled it out and laid it on the bed next to Estelle. 'Is this what you want? Is this why you asked to see me?'

Estelle nodded and explained what she wanted her to do.

Ariel stared at the envelope in confusion, its contents jealously hidden from view. 'Please, Mam,' she whispered. 'Please don't go.'

She stared at the tubes protruding from Estelle's body. She hadn't even realised her mother was ill at first.

'Why won't you say it?' Ariel had asked her. 'Why can't you say its name?'

162

'Because if you name it, you empower it,' Estelle had replied calmly. *Calmly*, when all Ariel had felt was rage.

The word rebounded inside her like a scream: *cancer*. Why? Why couldn't she just rip back the bedclothes, make her mother get out of bed and rise up, Lazarus-like, and be well again?

Estelle nudged her hand. 'Promise me.'

Ariel turned her face to the window. She could feel the heat building behind her eyes, her vision furring as hot, angry tears began to tumble down her cheeks. She tried in vain to stop them. She tried to brush them away with the back of her thumb so Estelle wouldn't see.

'I promise, Mam,' she replied.

Estelle smiled, and with a shallow rise and fall of her chest, she drifted to a fitful sleep. Ariel kissed her forehead, her cheek, her hand, and with the envelope tucked beneath her arm, she retreated slowly towards the door.

Outside the window, David Bowie's *Let's Dance* spiralled upwards from the car park, its famous bassline shattering the silence of the room. Ariel glanced towards the bed. Estelle's body shifted and settled. She waited a moment longer to watch her sleep. Everything she wanted to remember, everything she still wanted to know about the woman whose heart continued to beat before her would have to wait.

She didn't want a brown paper package. She didn't want a secret. She didn't want the responsibility of any of it.

She wanted Estelle. She wanted her mam. That was all.

Ariel excused herself, slipped out of her seat, and walked through the sliding carriage door.

She found Travis chatting with one of the stewards in the vestibule area. As she approached, the moon-faced man slapped Travis jovially on the arm and disappeared into the adjoining carriage.

'It's Andy's Silver Wedding Anniversary this weekend,' Travis said, his back pressed to the wall, one foot crossed casually over the other. 'He and his wife are catching a plane from Edinburgh in the morning. Two nights at Claridges. He's been saving up for it for months. I asked him why they don't just travel back by train and he said she wouldn't give thank you for it. He knows too many people. Staff and customers are always stopping him to say hello. So I told him they should have done the whole thing in disguise. He said he wished he'd thought of that. They've got matching Sonny and Cher outfits at home.'

He cracked open the train door window, lowered his head, and peered out at the rugged swathes of countryside rolling by. A blast of near arctic air whistled ominously past his shoulders. 'I think it might snow, don't you? Sky looks like it's ready to burst. My guess is we're heading straight for it.'

Ariel tapped her hand against her thigh, her legs tensed, her feet planted hip-width apart to stop herself from toppling over.

'Travis? Can I ask you something?'

He turned back to face her and smiled. 'Sure. Ask away!'

'When did you know you wanted to be a musician?'

Travis's eyes narrowed, his expression suddenly turning way more serious than Ariel had been expecting. 'Uh, well, I pretty much knew for certain when I was thirteen. That's when I started taking sax lessons. But it wasn't until I was in my early twenties that I made the decision to pursue music as a full-time career. Why d'you ask?'

'I just... I think it's cool that you knew what you wanted to do. And that you made it happen.'

Travis chuckled, a low, playful rumble that harmonised perfectly with the bassline rhythm of the train. 'Actually, it wasn't quite as cut and dried as all that. Music may have been my passion, but my parents had other ideas. They – my dad, especially – wanted me to be an attorney. And for a while I worked my butt off to achieve it, though I can't see that my dedication would have lasted. My heart just wasn't in it.'

'What happened?'

'Let's just say we agreed to differ.'

'Do you regret your choice?'

'What, and miss all this? The thrill of an open road – or an open railroad, even? The chance to play sax for my supper? No, I don't regret my choice. No way.'

Ariel watched his face – the carefree upwards tilt of his mouth, the laughter lines rippling outwards from his eyes when he smiled. His sense of ease – of surety in his own skin – was mesmerising.

'You're really lucky.'

'Lucky? Nah, I don't think it's that. I think it's just *cojones*.'

A second passed, and they both burst out laughing.

'Look,' he continued, 'I'd be lying if I told you I didn't care about not having my dad's buy-in. I'm only human. I still want to make him proud.'

'You really don't think he is?'

Travis shrugged. 'Passive acceptance is one thing. Actively getting behind my achievements and attributing any kind of meaningful value to them, *that's* something else entirely...'

He raised his hands and rubbed them over his face, as though washing away an invisible stain. 'If you're asking if my life's perfect just because I followed my dream, the answer's no. There's always going to be something else to strive for, something that remains just beyond our reach, because that's the way it works. It's what drives us to be better. Nobody gets everything. I just happen to believe that the best chance we have in life is to start by being truthful with ourselves about who we really are. It was my dad's dream that I pursue a career in law, not mine.'

'Thank you,' she said.

'For what?'

'For being honest. For not bullshitting someone you only just met.'

Travis smiled. 'Hey, I told you, we wound up here against the odds. We're on the same side, you and I.'

'Which side is that?'

'The lucky bastards' side,' he replied.

'Right,' she said, laughing, 'I forgot.'

Travis hooked his hand through a narrow gap at the top of the window. With a flick of his head, he turned and gazed intently at her once again. 'Stop me if I'm stepping out of line here, but I heard what you were saying to Henry about why you're going to Edinburgh. I wasn't eavesdropping or anything, it's just, you know, you're sitting right across the aisle from me...

Whatever's going on for you right now, it'll sort itself out. It might not seem like it now, but it will. I guarantee it.'

Ariel let out a slow exhalation of breath. 'I don't know... I'm eighteen. I thought I'd have everything sorted out in my head by now. Half the time, it's full of demons. I think it's getting worse. I question everything.'

Travis grinned. 'Asking questions is good! Anyway, it's a universal complaint. Worst thing you can do is to convince yourself you're the only one who feels that way. Believe me, there are plenty of lost souls floating around, searching for an anchor. You just didn't bump into one yet. Are you in college?'

She lowered her eyes. 'No, I left school just after my mother died. I didn't finish my exams.'

Travis was undeterred: 'Well college isn't necessarily the answer for everyone. Plenty of kids go because it buys them a few years. And that's fine, if you can afford it. I mean, at least it puts you in a supportive environment where you can broaden your horizons. If you're lucky, meet some pretty inspirational teachers. It's tough to argue against it, because at the time you have to commit to it, you're still figuring out who you are.'

'The only person *I* argued with was myself.' Ariel tugged at the ends of her sleeves. 'I think I may have made a mistake. I don't know any more.'

Travis's face lit up with a rapturous smile – as though the door to some glittering magic castle had just opened behind his eyes. The effect was so infectious, and so completely unexpected, it almost knocked her sideways.

It was physically impossible not to smile back.

'Are you *always* this optimistic?' she asked.

'I am with you.'

She guessed he'd been shooting for deadpan, but his laughter soon burst through.

'So maybe you messed up,' he said. 'Big deal! Charlie Parker said that music is your own experience, your thoughts, your wisdom... In other words, if you don't live it, it won't come out your horn. You're still going to get where you're going, just maybe via a different route.'

'Nice analogy.'

Travis ruffled his hair and smiled. 'Sorry – I don't mean to sound like a smart ass. It's just, you're *obviously* crazy about taking pictures. And you seem pretty switched on to me. My guess is you'll figure it out.'

Ariel slipped her hands into her pockets and tapped her head against the carriage wall. 'Thank you,' she replied. 'I wish my teacher, Mr Deacons, could hear you say that.'

His actual words were: 'It's a question of potential, Ariel. It's a question of making the right *choice*.'

Trevor Deacons: mild-mannered, balding; the hair from his head all seemingly migrated southwards to a thick biker's moustache which arched over his upper lip like the curve of a badger's tail.

She stared at the classroom wall, terrified she was going to faint. If she could just tell him the truth... How Linus had been forgetting things; important things like bill payments, and policy renewals, and random household repairs. How the roof was leaking. How the hem of Isaac's trousers needed letting out. How she'd found a colony of maggots squirming in the outside bin.

Just that week she'd discovered that their electricity supply was on the verge of being cut off until she swept the final reminder letter – written in the blazing red ink of shame – off the doormat and swiftly arranged for it to be paid.

It sucked.

'I understand things are difficult for you right now,' he said in an achingly patient voice. 'Just think carefully before you make a decision you might regret. It's less than a year until your exams. After that you'll be free to make your own choice about what you want to do. At least then you'll have the qualifications under your belt. If you leave now, you'll have nothing.'

'I know that, sir. I'm sorry.'

In her pocket was a bespoke *Bliss Books* bookmark, still ingrained with the scents of petitgrain, may chang, patchouli and sweet orange – Estelle's favourite aromatherapy oils.

She pressed the strip of cardboard between her fingers.

Mr Deacons uttered a sigh of defeat. 'If you change your mind you must let us know, Ariel, okay? It's never too late for a bright girl like you.'

'Yes, sir,' she replied. 'I understand. Thank you.'

Her brain was swimming. Deep pools of doubt swirled inside her head.

She turned and waded from the classroom through her underwater world.

Along the corridor, down the steps, through the schoolyard, out of the gate.

One step at a time, Ariel kept walking.

Darlington to Newcastle. Ariel returned to her seat just as the Victorian station at Darlington slid gracefully into view. Broad and ornate, it was characterised by a magnificent cast-iron clock jutting outwards from the platform wall.

The train pulled away, passing a large, weather-beaten metal sign by the side of the track. *London 250 Miles* it announced, with an arrow pointing back the way they'd come.

They continued on through Durham, its historic cathedral cutting an impressive figure, soaring – holy, majestic – above the River Wear.

The camera on Ariel's phone clicked. Clicked again.

Further ahead, a cemetery, deserted apart from a solitary gardener, bent at the waist, pulling weeds from between the flagstones.

'You know who *you* should talk to?' Travis said.

He was half leaning into the aisle, his gaze honing in on her with such razor-sharp focus, they could easily have been the only two people on the train. 'My Uncle Frank. He gives the best career advice of anyone I know. The man's spent his entire life going against the grain, and it hasn't worked out too badly for *him*.'

Ariel pressed her head against the back of her chair. She

was worried about Henry. When she'd returned to her seat she'd found him sitting with a crossword puzzle open on the table in front of him. His gaze was fixed directionally onto the page, but his pen was lying off to one side, his overall expression glazed.

'Been to stretch your legs?' He looked up from his crossword and smiled. 'I used to do that all the time on train journeys when I was younger. Now, I'm afraid, I wouldn't trust myself to stay upright for very long without my stick.'

She glanced at the few simple items Henry had laid out on the table. 'Can I get you anything? Or can I walk with you to the end of the carriage if you'd like to get out of your seat for a bit?'

'Thank you,' he replied. 'That's very kind of you, but I'm all right for now. As long as we stay on schedule, I'll be right as rain.'

A bottle of mineral water had materialised on the table in Ariel's absence. She unscrewed the lid, poured one half into a glass for Henry, the other for herself, then she turned and asked Travis what it was his uncle did for a living.

'Uncle Frank's a lounge singer, though he gets kind of bummed if you call him that to his face.'

'Really? Why?'

'He doesn't like being pigeonholed. He says it curbs his style... *Any*how, if nothing else, it proves that there were pre-existing musical genes *somewhere* in my family. All on my mom's side, of course.'

'I can think of worse things to do for a living than singing to a roomful of people sipping expensive cocktails all night,'

Ariel said. 'At least they're not going to chuck beer cans in his face.'

Travis rolled his eyes. 'Yeah, well, some of the venues he performs in are a little rougher around the edges than you'd expect.'

'What sort of stuff does he sing?'

'Jazz standards, mainly. Berlin. Porter. Gershwin. The usuals. He's also started writing his own material, but he says the bookers aren't so keen on him basing his set around songs the audience can't sing along to. Doesn't stop Uncle Frank from trying to slip a couple into his repertoire every now and then, though.'

Ariel smiled. 'Has he always performed that style of music?'

Travis shook his head. 'Uncle Frank was a leading Elvis impersonator until he threw in his jumpsuit a few years back. He used to make for great conversation around the dinner table, though his work was almost exclusively over here. I always used to wonder what it must be like for him travelling to gigs around the UK while the rest of us were living a regular life back on Long Island.' He laughed. 'You look surprised. I'm used to that. Telling people about Uncle Frank gets a reaction every time.'

Ariel was suddenly aware that her mouth had fallen open.

'Travis –' She stopped, weighed the unlikelihood of what she was about to say next, then decided to say it anyway: 'By any chance, does your uncle have a tattoo of an eagle on his left ankle? He got it in Philadelphia when he was eighteen.' She paused, her voice rising a notch in anticipation. 'His name's Frank Carmichael?'

This time, it was Travis's jaw that nearly hit the floor. 'Are you *shitting* me?' he cried when she told him how she and Frank had met; how sad she'd been when it was time for him and Cynthia to pack their bags and leave.

'Small world, I guess.' Ariel laughed. 'What did you think? That I was picturing some sort of glitzy showman dripping in rhinestones and pomade?'

'Well yeah!' he replied. 'In my experience, that's usually the assumption!'

'Not me. I was just a kid, but Frank really paid attention, you know? He was kind to me.'

Travis nodded. 'That's Uncle Frank all right.'

'How is he?' Ariel asked. 'Is he back living in America now?'

For the first time since they'd met, she thought she saw Travis hesitate. He rubbed his hand along the side of his neck and gave a quick, businesslike nod.

'He's good. Uncle Frank's good. He still lives in London. The past few weeks I've been using his apartment in Stoke Newington as a base while I've been in Europe. His work schedule has slowed down quite a bit, but he's got a couple of pre-Christmas gigs up north. Tonight he's doing a show in Edinburgh. I've never been to Scotland, so when he invited me along as his guest I leaped at the chance. I thought it would be the perfect way to support him and round off my visit to the UK.

'Hey,' he cried, 'why don't you come with me? Why not come along tonight and watch Uncle Frank perform?'

Ariel suddenly remembered her childhood conviction that she and Frank would one day meet again. 'Oh, I don't know,' she said quickly. 'I think it might be weird after all these years. I doubt he'd even remember me.'

Travis waved his hand. '*Trust* me, if he spent a month with you – even if it was a decade ago – he's going to remember. Uncle Frank never forgets a face.' He paused, his expression turning serious once again. 'Honestly, I think he'd really appreciate it if you came.'

Across the table, Henry gave a loud, emphatic cough.

'I'm sure it'll be an awesome show,' Travis continued. 'Assuming your meeting's not until tomorrow, what else do you have to do tonight?'

Ariel turned her head and briefly met Henry's gaze. The words 'embrace the unforeseen' came sailing back into her brain. Behind her, the sliding door to their carriage opened and closed, sending another waft of icy cold air swirling around her shoulders. She glanced through the window at the pewter-coloured sky. The snowstorm Travis had predicted looked like it might be about to descend upon them after all.

'Okay,' she said, turning back to him with a smile, 'if you're sure Frank won't mind me showing up unannounced, then yes. Thank you! I'd love to.'

Travis gave her an enthusiastic thumbs-up, and grinning, looked away.

The train continued its thunderous path, pushing northwards, testing the mettle of its wheels. Ariel sank back into her seat. Until now, her only plan for the evening had been to explore her surroundings; immerse herself – on her own terms – in the city that seemed to hold the answer to so much.

All I ask for is one day, Eve Marie had written in her letter. *One day.*

But for what?

13

Impasse

DECEMBER 6: *EN ROUTE*

Henry

Physically, Henry had to admit that the similarities were few and far between. The young American sitting across the aisle was dark-haired and brown eyed (and how could one put it, just a touch *unkempt?*).

Devlin, on the other hand, had had a thatch of honey blonde hair and sharp, mischievous blue eyes. Always scrubbed up a treat. Still, there was something about Travis's easy affability and bright openness of expression that reminded Henry so strikingly of his brother. He supposed it must be that they each appeared to possess that same, most elusive of qualities: an engaging – and often bewildering – lightness of being. Travis's conversation with Ariel was filling him with a warm zephyr of nostalgia. If only Devlin were here, too; the two men would have hit it off big time, that was for sure!

He made a mental note to jot down his observations in his notebook later that evening. (He didn't trust the legibility of his handwriting on a moving train.) *Pharoah's*. The joke had merit even today. Henry – with his respectable teaching position, his structured, thoroughly conventional life (one which thanks to his Wyedean article he'd been forced to admit had failed to reach the heights of '*illuminating*') – had ended up with a brother in the nightclub business.

The premises had been set back beneath a row of cast-iron railings on a quiet turning just off Charlotte Street. Henry always considered Ancient Egypt to be an unlikely concept for a jazz club, but Devlin insisted it gave the place an edge. The hostesses wore thick black eyeliner and sculpted, Cleopatra wigs. Mock obelisks lined the entryway. They even had miniature gilt pyramids built out of plasterboard on either side of the stage. As a destination for discerning connoisseurs of late-night music, *Pharoah's* may have lacked the understated class and kudos of *Ronnie Scott's*, but Devlin was never happier than when he was standing at the bar, all suited and booted, with a Black Russian cocktail in his hand and a pretty girl on his arm, acting like he owned the place. ('Manager, owner, what's the difference? Call it what you will, Hen, I'm the one with the keys in my hand at the end of the night.')

Amy always said that growing up watching her father work so tirelessly to ensure the business ran like clockwork had taught her everything she ever needed to know about customer service. Professionally, it was Devlin's pride and joy. The last thing anyone ever expected was for the entire place to go up in flames...

Henry's eyes grew moist as he remembered the words Devlin had used that August bank holiday, way back at the end of the '80s, when his dream palace came tumbling down: 'It's gone, Henry —' his voice cracking over the phone — 'Razed to the ground, every last inch of it.'

He said the building had been completely gutted; nothing but a few scorched light fittings, the crumbling remains of an obelisk, and a warped music stand left smouldering amongst the ashes. His only solace was that no one had been inside at the time.

'I still can't believe it,' he sobbed. His sorrow (the free and candid expression of which, Devlin always insisted, was the mark of a true man) poured like cigar smoke down the line. 'But damn it, Henry, it *was* pretty fantastic while it lasted, wasn't it? Didn't it shimmer? Didn't it *shine*? Final outcome aside, I'd do it all again in a heartbeat. No hesitation. No regrets.'

As the train crossed over the River Tyne, Henry noticed that the unruffled aura of quietude which earlier that morning had descended upon him like a beneficent cloud was rapidly beginning to subside.

Something was wrong. For one thing, he had the disconcerting sensation that his head was floating off his shoulders like a balloon, while the rest of his body was stuck like tar to his seat. He prayed it was just a temporary attack of nerves.

Then again, maybe it was high blood pressure. Or was it low?

He refused to believe it might be anything more sinister. (And frankly, after his performance at King's Cross, the last thing he wanted was to draw any more attention to himself; he'd already caught Ariel throwing him a glance or two of concern every now and then.)

No, Henry told himself, *whatever malady was troubling him could be traced back to his elevated emotions. Of that, he was in little doubt.*

He focused on his breath and turned to regard the tranquil, ever-evolving countryside scrolling past the window. He'd always found the unbroken spells of time spent in transition between one station and another to be quite magical. That sense of knowing and yet not quite knowing where you were... It was like travelling through a twilight zone. A vast, impenetrable no-man's-land. Occasionally, people popped into view, shuffling their feet from side to side to keep warm, or tramping red-cheeked and mud-splattered over fields. A few stood stiff as scarecrows and stared at the train with a cool mien of defiance, as if to say, *We belong here, but you are only passing through. It is you who are a momentary smudge on the landscape. It is you who are anonymous, insubstantial, unidentifiable. Not us.*

Below the carriage window a parallel set of coppery-black railway tracks lay like fat ropes of liquorice, interweaving and merging before once again pairing off. *Where did they end?* he wondered. He envisaged them circling the globe like ribbons of steel, uniting the world, always stretching further and further into the unknown...

Henry was roused from his reverie by the train grunting to a standstill somewhere in the deserted hinterlands between Newcastle and Berwick-upon-Tweed. There was no discordant screech of metal on metal. The train simply slowed, shuddered with the force of a lethargic lawn mower, and then cut its engine entirely.

'That's strange,' he said, turning to Ariel. His forehead concertinaed into a frown. 'I wonder what's happened now?'

Ariel leaned in close against the window and peered towards the front end of the train. 'I can't see anything out of the ordinary. Maybe we're just waiting for another train to pass by?'

A prong of anxiety jabbed at Henry's chest. There had been no announcement – a fact which he hoped might signify that the train's stationary interlude would be of a couple of minutes' duration at most. But no sooner had the thought occurred to him, than a suspiciously buoyant voice boomed loud and prophetic over the carriage intercom:

'Ladies and gentlemen, this is your train guard speaking. As you'll have noticed, we've come to a temporary stop. This is owing to an electrical fault on the line. On behalf of North South Railways, please accept my apologies for any inconvenience this may cause to your journey. We're working to rectify the situation as quickly as possible. I'll come back to you with a further update in due course...'

An audible grumble of discontent ricocheted up and down the carriage. Henry glanced over his shoulder and saw that one or two of the more visibly aggrieved passengers had taken mobile phones out of their pockets and were already tapping furiously on the screens. Elsewhere, there was much concentrated checking of watches and wrinkling of brows. *Surely,* he thought, *it couldn't be anything very serious? At this point, they didn't even know for certain how long they might be delayed.*

It was then, as he turned once more to face the window, that Henry saw the snow.

The prodigious grey clouds which had been shadowing their course with ominous persistence for the last hour or so were evidently incapable of withholding their wintry load a moment longer. Thick, cottony flakes were already starting to graze the carriage windows. As though preparing itself for the worst, the disgruntled landscape on either side of the train seemed to withdraw before his very eyes, battening down, becoming mournfully still.

Henry felt his body yield to a fresh wave of paralysis. *It was beyond all reason.* Once again, here he was sitting on a stationary train in the snow, just as he had been all those years ago with Francine...

'Henry? Is everything all right?'

Henry started. Ariel was leaning forwards in her seat, her hand reaching tentatively for his forearm. She was wearing the same expression of concern that she'd displayed when she first approached him on the concourse at King's Cross Station. He couldn't imagine what might have prompted her to regard him in such a manner now... He dug around in his pocket for his tissues. Raising his hands to his face, he dabbed his eyes and blew his nose very, very gently.

'Henry,' Ariel said again in a low voice, 'I hope you don't mind me asking, but who's Francine?'

'Francine?'

'Yes. You said her name out loud. A minute ago, when you were looking out of the window.'

Henry dropped his hands to the table. 'I did?'

Across the aisle he could see Travis looking over at him now, too. No doubt they'd both begun to suspect that they had a classic case of senile dementia in their midst...

Oh, what joy to be young and bright and strong, and in abundant possession of that most vital of youthful qualities, curiosity! Henry felt his heart bleed at the very thought of it. When he and Devlin were kids their father often took them on secret UFO spotting excursions to Parliament Hill. As they lay flat on their backs on the summit, a flask of hot tea at their sides, a wide tarpaulin of night sky stretching overhead, he told them that curiosity was the fuel that powered the world, and that without it, we would all simply be standing still...

'I'm sorry,' Ariel said quickly. She drew back into her seat. 'It's none of my business. I just wanted to make sure everything was okay, especially if we're going to be stuck here for a while.'

Henry managed to harness the wherewithal to conjure up a smile. 'Thank you, that's very kind of you, but there's no need to worry. Everything's fine, I promise. I'm a little concerned about the delay, that's all.'

He turned to assess the steady drift of snow tumbling against the carriage window. *What had Ariel meant by 'stuck here for a while'?* He cast a doubtful glance at his gold watch, a retirement gift from Wyedean, practically an antique by now. The clasp was a little loose and needed fixing, but it still kept time beautifully. And the engraving on the back meant as much to him today as it had then: *"Un Grand Merci pour Le Grand Henri"* – a touching reference to *Le Grand Meaulnes*, one of his all-time favourite books.

Henry tapped the watch face three times with the tip of his forefinger, as though performing a covert spell. He knew he should stay centred and calm, but with each passing moment he was beginning to feel increasingly discombobulated, and, as the reality of the situation struck home, more than a little alarmed...

What if they couldn't continue with their journey? What if they all had to march off the train in single file, in the freezing cold, and be ferried up an icy motorway on one of those dreadful replacement bus services? The driver would take his suitcase and store it in the hold at the bottom of the coach, and someone might take it by accident, or it might get left behind, and then what would he do?

What if they shut the motorways due to the adverse weather conditions and there were none of those dreadful replacement bus services at all? Not until tomorrow? They'd end up in some depressing roadside hotel called *The Travellers' Grudge*, or wherever it was people stayed these days when they were stranded, their lives disrupted for reasons entirely beyond their control. He'd wake up in a tired, soulless room reeking of pine air freshener and rampant disenchantment, and he'd know, right then, that it was over. That everything he was hoping for had been in vain. And that by the time they were finally on the move again, it would all be too late...

'Did you know that the back of a woman's neck can tell a

man everything he needs to know?' Henry cried, his eyes blazing. 'That's the way it was for me with Francine. I knew. I knew the moment I laid eyes on her.'

Ariel and Travis stared first at each other, then at Henry. This time, Henry felt certain, he'd gone and done it. This time, his young companions would realise beyond any reasonable doubt that they had a stark raving lunatic on their hands, but it was too late to worry about that now.

'I'm sorry if I startled you,' he continued, 'but the fact is I absolutely, categorically *must* get to Edinburgh tonight. Do you think we'll make it?'

Henry's heart was hammering like a tom-tom in his chest. He willed Ariel and Travis to give him a positive reply. He would not be stopped now. Not when he had waited so very, very long...

'*Yes*,' Ariel replied with thrilling conviction, 'I *do*. Whatever the reason you need to be in Edinburgh tonight, we'll get there, Henry. It's only snow.'

'And an electrical fault,' Travis added rather unhelpfully. 'Which I'm sure is being fixed as we speak.'

Henry was so overcome with relief that he almost reached out and shook his companions' hands. He wished he were a nimble young man again. He'd grab hold of his suitcase, hop down onto the tracks and *walk* the remainder of the way to Scotland if he thought it were the fastest way of getting there. And (wheels notwithstanding), he'd willingly carry Ariel's suitcase as well, balanced on his shoulder like a builder's hod. After all, she had her own reasons for needing to get to her destination in a timely manner. And from what he'd understood from their conversation, the American did too.

'Thank you!' he replied. 'Thank you both!'

Henry relaxed once more into his seat. As his head grazed the soft leather curve of the headrest, a familiar voice began to whisper with some urgency in his ear:

Hen. HEN! Can you hear me?

Henry cleared his throat.

Listen to me, why don't you just tell them? Let someone else in? You're all in the same boat (or train... whatever...). What have you got to lose?

Henry turned his face to the window and gave a discreet shake of his head. *No, Devlin. They wouldn't understand. It was too long ago.*

Too long ago? What are you banging on about? It wasn't the Stone Age! You think nobody falls in love any more?

Henry pinned his gaze to the snow. It was truly astounding. Even now, arguing from the Great Unknown, Devlin still managed to be right.

It was easy for you, he replied. *Love just fell into your hands, over and over again. It had never been that way for me, remember? You never knew the meaning of the word heartache. Then I met Francine and it seemed like everything was finally going to go right. But I messed it all up, Devlin, and the only person at fault was me. If I open up now, it'll all come pouring out of me. And they'll see me as a failure. What's to be gained from that?*

Devlin's reply was so forceful, so flagrantly commanding that Henry was convinced it must be loud enough for the entire carriage to hear:

Celia Reynolds

First off, when are you going to get it into your head that YOU ARE NOT A FAILURE? You have to stop being so hard on yourself, Hen. You'll do yourself an injury! Even if everything DOES come pouring out of you, SO WHAT?! For once in your life, JUST GIVE SOMEONE ELSE SOME CREDIT! What in HELL'S name are you waiting for? GO ON!!!

Henry opened his mouth. Blurted the words to Ariel before he even had a chance to dispute them: 'Would you mind if I told you about her?' He turned quickly to Travis. 'It's just that I've kept it inside for so long, I thought perhaps it might be helpful in some way if I spoke about Francine?'

To his surprise, Ariel gave a spontaneous cry of delight. 'She's why you're going to Edinburgh, isn't she? I *knew* there must be a reason why you had to be on this train!'

Henry blinked. He hoped he hadn't come across from the outset as some sort of eccentric old fool.

He took a breath. Felt the words gathering inside him. 'Yes,' he replied, 'it's all part of the story. A small story, perhaps, but it's my story. One that's shaped my world for the last sixty-five years.'

14

This is Where it Begins

DECEMBER 6: *EN ROUTE*

Henry

Henry intertwined his fingers, one forearm resting parallel to the edge of the table, the other hanging at his side. Now that he'd been given the green light to continue, he found himself wondering where to begin; wondering, indeed, whether it had been hasty of him to suggest telling them his story at all.

Changi. 1948.

His lips parted.

These bright, young people, their entire futures spread out before them. What in heaven's name had possessed him? Could they really be interested in anything an old man like him had to say?

'Curiosity,' he began, 'I joined up for no better reason than because I was curious to see the world. On New Year's Day, 1948, when my return orders came through, I was five months past my twentieth birthday and had been stationed in and around RAF Changi in Singapore for two years.

'I hadn't been on so much as a boat trip to Calais before that. All I knew were the streets of Chalk Farm in London where I grew up. I studied. I enjoyed cricket, listening to music on the radio and watching films at the local picture house every Saturday night. If asked, I'd say that if I had a talent for anything, it was for languages, and for helping my older brother, Devlin, out of scrapes. As for girls, there'd only been one or two to speak of. Usually, they were far more interested in Devlin, and I understood why; he played life by his own rules, always, and like most of the kids in the neighbourhood, I idolised him, too.'

Henry paused a moment before continuing: 'I volunteered as soon as I was able. Less than six months' training and I was stationed abroad. Sweltering temperatures. Rivers of sweat. Thick layers of dust under our fingernails for months on end. A likely dose of syphilis for anyone who was reckless enough to get too friendly with any of the local prostitutes. Our days were punctuated by sunburn and thunderstorms, then we'd face humid, mosquito-infested nights.' Henry looked at Ariel and Travis and smiled. 'At least we had tinned peaches as a treat on Sundays. I grew up so fast, I scarcely recognised myself when the time came to go back home.

'I packed my kit bag and arranged to leave on an aircraft carrier called HMS Vengeance. Most of my fellow volunteers chose to come back by plane – no unnecessary delays, back in a jiffy, their suntans still intact. But there were others like myself who preferred the idea of spending five or six weeks on a ship, stopping off at different countries along the way. I made no secret of the fact that taking the slow route home was a deferral mechanism of sorts; a kind of self-enforced decompression zone between two distinct phases of my life: one known, the other yet to be written.

'Whichever way you looked at it, travelling by sea at least gave us a chance to acclimatise. In Malta we changed from our khaki drill uniforms into our air force blues, though by now, so many of us had lost weight while we'd been away, we had difficulty accepting our regulation uniforms as our own.

'My pal, Davy Hardcastle, and I joked about how lean and sinewy we'd become, like the black panther we once saw prowling over the rafters of our billet roof. As we neared Plymouth harbour, we stood on deck smoking and congratulating each other on our transformation.

'Dawn was just breaking as we approached the shore.

'"Captain's havin' a laugh!" Davy cried. He kicked his feet against the railings. "This can't be England?"

'Thick black clouds were swirling over our heads. The temperature was close to freezing, and before long a blizzard – the likes of which neither of us had ever seen before – engulfed the ship entirely. I stared at Davy in amazement. After two years in the tropics, we were sailing back into the bitterest winter either of us had ever known.

'We pulled on our greatcoats and prepared to disembark. Our orders were to report immediately to the receiving camp at RAF Kirkham in Lancashire. The troop train was already waiting for us at Plymouth Station, and from there we began the long journey north. Some of us managed to doze on the train, but by the time we arrived in Kirkham, close on lunchtime, we were completely wired. We filed into camp and were told that with the exception of the clothes we were standing in, our entire RAF kit would have to be handed over.

'*This is it,* I thought. *This is where it begins.*

'It was a uniform, that's all. Nothing more than fabric and fasteners, a cap and a sturdy pair of shoes. But it was only then that the reality of the situation hit me: surrendering it and everything it had come to represent would be tantamount to the stripping away of an era, a ritual shedding of skin. They may as well have told me I'd be walking out of there naked. It was a new start – for all of us – and with our life as servicemen behind us, we'd be once more on our own.

'In the hour or so that followed, a sergeant took our particulars; we were given food, a medical, the chance to clean up. Finally, we learned we'd have the rest of the day and the following day to ourselves. We could hardly believe it – a full forty-eight hours of freedom before we made our individual journeys home!

'Myself and Davy and the others raced out of camp and retraced our steps to Kirkham train station. As far as I was concerned, there was only one possible destination given how close we were to the coast. Back then, Blackpool was in its heyday; a larger-than-life entertainment capital overflowing with dance halls and fortune-tellers, pubs and amusements and theatres featuring all the biggest stars of the day. We bought our tickets and jumped on the first available train.

Thirty minutes later, we found ourselves in an iconic seaside resort, so different from everything we'd become accustomed to in the Far East that even in winter, with its looming Pleasure Beach and sweeping promenade almost entirely devoid of holidaymakers, our presence there felt nothing short of surreal.'

Henry felt his heart beat faster. 'I spotted the famous Blackpool Tower at once. I stood staring up at its russet-brown spire, a giant monolith of cast-iron and concrete and steel, rising like a bayonet into the sky. Davy and the others started tossing ideas around about where to go, but I left them to it and headed straight for the Tower.

'By the time they caught up with me I was already outside, scanning the playbill.

'"It's Reg Dixon!" I cried. "The man's a living legend! You coming with me?"

'"Nah, mate," Davy replied. "You go for it. Knock yourself out. Me and the boys've got somewhere else in mind."

'Another of our group, O'Malley, wished me luck and started doubling back along the promenade.

'"See you back at the billet," Davy added with a grin. "Don't do anything... you know the rest."

'Alone in the entranceway, I opened the door and stepped into the foyer. I paid my entrance fee and headed upstairs. As I made my way onto the ballroom balcony, I turned to look for a place to sit, and that's when I saw her...

'Francine was sitting in the front row, her hair swept up in a bun, her gaze fixed onto the dance floor below. I stood a short distance away and waited for her to look at me, but she was so engrossed in her surroundings, she didn't even register my presence.

'My eyes sought the back of her neck and stayed there. I was afraid if I went over I'd disturb her, but when I asked her later if that was the case, she just smiled:

'"Don't worry, this place is usually stuffed to the *gills* with airmen, and I promise you most of them aren't half as polite as you."

'I sat down beside her, unable to believe my luck at finding her there alone. We must have talked for hours – it was hard to tell in the semi-darkness in the middle of the afternoon. Finally, I plucked up the courage to ask her if she'd like to go on somewhere else.

'"We could go to Fortescue's?" she replied. "It's a little café around the corner. The tourists who stay at the fancy hotels think they're getting the best Blackpool has to offer, but Fortescue's does the best cakes in the North West, and the tea's fantastic, too. Wait for me, will you, Henry, while I get my coat?"

'The café wasn't far from the front, and every time the door opened the smell of seawater wafted in and mingled with the aroma of freshly baked dough from the kitchen. A woman with heavily painted eyebrows led us to the last empty table in the window. The café only had room for about a dozen people, and Francine and I were squashed so closely together, our knees were bumping under the table. I tried to shift myself backwards, but in the limited space available there was nowhere for me to go.

'My chair scraped noisily against the floorboards.

'"At that rate, you'll end up on the pavement." Francine was looking at me with an enormous smile on her face. She pressed a paper napkin to her mouth, imprinting it, as she did so, with the outline of her lipstick. "Here," she said when she caught me staring at it, "a little kiss from Blackpool. Think of it as a memento from one music lover to another. See, it even has an *F* for Francine in the corner; that way you won't forget me."

'I laughed and slipped the napkin into my pocket. I knew exactly what I wanted to say next; it was the one thing that had been foremost on my mind since we'd met earlier that afternoon, but it was Francine who asked the question first:

'"Henry? Do you have someone waiting for you? You know, someone special, back home?"

'I stared at her for a second in surprise. "No," I replied, "there's no one. To be honest, it's been a while since I've had female company to talk to."

'"Was that why you came to the Tower Ballroom?"

'There was an edge to her voice, a subtle inflection, nothing more, but noticeable none the less.

'"Actually," I replied, "it was Reg Dixon who drew me in. But then I saw you. You looked so caught up in the music, I thought it would be nice to talk to someone who's as crazy about it as I am." I shifted in my chair and felt my knees bump against hers once again. "Are you glad I came over?"

'Francine gave me an appraising gaze. She seemed to take forever to answer my question, and then, just as my confidence began to waver, her eyes filled with laughter and she smiled. "Like I said, most of the lads around here are not exactly dependable, and getting involved with anyone at the hotel where I work is... complicated. So yes, I'm happy to have met you. I think we make a fine couple, Henry Applebee, don't you?"

'She pointed to our reflections neatly framed in the café window: her head bent in ever so slightly towards mine; my hand inching towards hers across the chequered tablecloth. From the corner of my eye I caught a glimmer of light from the ornate butterfly perched on the end of her silver hair clip. The delicate moulding of diamanté and pearl shimmered in the cone of light from the electric lamp immediately above us. The butterfly seemed so vibrant and alive, for a second I thought it might actually beat its wings and take flight.

'That night, I barely slept a wink. Davy Hardcastle and the others arrived back at the billet like marauding giants, loud-mouthed and clumsy, reeking of cheap booze and even cheaper perfume. They passed out on their bunks almost immediately, but I lay awake in the darkness listening to their snores and the sound of the wind howling through the trees. All I could think about was the following day when Francine and I had agreed to meet again.

'I caught the train at Kirkham Station and found her waiting for me at the other end in a gorgeous new coat. We ate fish and chips on the pier and bought tickets to see Vivien Leigh in *Anna Karenina*, though I was so conscious of Francine's presence beside me, I didn't exactly pay much attention to the drama unfolding on screen. My mind was still reeling from something she'd said earlier that afternoon. Francine had stood on the promenade and offered me her heart, and I was so stunned – and so happy – I looked her in the eye and promised not to break it –'

Henry came to a sudden and unexpected stop. 'I'm sorry,' he mumbled. He pressed his palm to his forehead. The words *promised not to break it* were rattling like a death knell in his ears. 'I seem to have lost my thread there for a moment.'

'It's all right,' Ariel said kindly. 'My dad trails off midsentence all the time.'

Henry lowered his hand to the table. 'He does?'

'Absolutely. And I don't even mean when he's telling a story. He could literally just be talking about the weather or what we're having for tea. He's been like that for months.'

Travis rolled his eyes. 'Wish I could say the same about mine.'

Ariel flicked her eyes in his direction. Some brief, wordless communication – entirely unfathomable to Henry – passed between them.

'My dad's never lost for words where I'm concerned,' Travis added by way of explanation. 'Although these days, he doesn't say half of it to me directly – I just get it all second-hand from my mom.' He shrugged. 'Maybe it's better that way.'

Henry detected an underlying tone of regret in Travis's voice. Clearly, he was carrying some sort of wound, though he was doing his very best to disguise it. 'I'm sorry to hear that,' he said. 'Did the two of you have a falling out?'

'You could say that,' Travis replied. His eyes held a complicated mix of nonchalance, hurt, and resignation. 'He's just not exactly a fan of music. Or not of *my* kind of music, anyway.

195

Especially not when I'm the one who's playing it.' He glanced sidelong at Ariel, as though what he was about to say next was intended solely for her. 'There isn't really a whole lot I can do about it. Jazz is the essence of me. I pick up my sax, and it just comes flying out of me.'

'I understand,' Henry said with a nod. 'When I was your age, it was Glenn Miller and Duke Ellington that did it for me – plus all the other big bands of the 1940s. I thought the way their music made me feel was the greatest thing ever. When you have a passion inside you like that, it's contagious. You can't just repress it.'

Travis stared at him in surprise. 'You're dead right! Do you think maybe you could give my dad a call and explain that to him?'

Henry's heart soared at the mere prospect of it. 'I'm afraid it's not my place to do so, Travis. But if I *did*, I'd tell him that a passion that powerful doesn't fade, either. Just because you're as old as the hills, doesn't mean you feel things any less deeply. It's like everything else, as far as I can tell: the trivial falls away, but the extraordinary stays with you forever.'

'I like that,' Ariel said slowly. 'It reminds me of something someone once said to me about there being no fun at all in always being ordinary.'

Henry nodded. 'Anyway, Travis, I hope you and your father can patch things up. It might just be a classic case of him being frustrated in his own dreams, perhaps? Though it would be a pity for him to take it out on you. Not that I'm passing judgement, of course.'

Travis took a moment to contemplate this. 'Do you think

maybe there's some kind of secret club for people who feel things more intensely than other people? If there is, my dad sure as hell isn't a member of it.'

Henry smiled. 'Oh, I'm sure if you scraped beneath the surface, you'd find a subject he's passionate about.'

Travis mumbled something under his breath. 'Model planes,' he said, looking up. 'He keeps them in the man cave he's built for himself out in the garage. No one else is allowed to go near them.'

'There you go!' Henry replied. 'Each to his own! But he's not going to talk to you about it if he thinks you're not interested. Anyway, some people are just naturally less effusive. Not everyone's comfortable expressing their emotions, powerful or otherwise.'

Ariel tugged at the ends of her sleeves. 'My dad's the complete opposite. If anything, he's *over*emotional. He cries a lot. But then he has just lost his wife, so I think it's understandable.'

Henry's face fell. He tried to think of something to say that was both tactful *and* uplifting, but all he could come up with was a painfully inadequate, 'Oh! I expect it's a question of just being patient with him.'

'Yes,' she replied in a stoic voice. 'Better out than in, I suppose.'

Henry snapped his mouth shut. He needed to refocus; he was getting way off track already, and he'd only just started.

'I think,' he ventured, 'that if it's okay with you, I should continue with my story. I'm worried I might lose my nerve if I don't keep going.'

'Of course, Henry,' Ariel said. 'Tell us everything.'

Travis gave them both a distracted nod. He still appeared lost in contemplation about something. 'I'm pretty sure my dad's a lost cause,' he said a moment later. His gaze drifted across the aisle to Henry. 'But Francine was like you, wasn't she? She had the same passion inside her, and she wasn't afraid to express it.'

Ariel glanced from Travis to Henry and smiled. '*Yes*. And it's stayed with you all this time.'

Henry's eyes widened. Evidently, he'd underestimated them. 'You're right,' he replied. 'On all counts!'

He turned his attention inwards. In the reflection in the carriage window he saw the moonlit streets of Blackpool, and the snow, slanting in silver filaments around him. He pressed his feet to the carriage floor and felt snow particles crunch beneath his shoes. He wasn't marooned in a first-class carriage any more. He was back, innocent and oblivious; hurtling towards the chain of events that in just a few short hours would derail everything.

15

Three Little Words

DECEMBER 6: *EN ROUTE*

Henry

Henry cleared his throat.

The snowstorm. The walk to Francine's flat.

Resuming his account, he quickly set the scene, determined to tell Ariel and Travis everything.

'I'm sure you can guess what happened next,' he said. 'Francine and I knew we'd be alone, and it went the way we both wanted in the end. It was as though we had an invisible gold thread running between us after that.'

Henry swallowed, his focus not wavering for an instant: 'As the evening drew to a close, Francine insisted on accompanying me to the station. The last train back to the billet didn't leave until just before midnight, but I agreed on condition she let me pay for a return taxi home. It was far too late for her to be wandering about by herself, and there was already a good inch or two of snow on the ground when we set off. We made our way through an endless labyrinth of side streets, conscious that with each successive step our time together was rapidly running out.'

A palpable sense of unease began to creep into Henry's voice: 'We weren't the only people hurrying towards the station that night. If anything, it was where the evening's partygoers had, by necessity, relocated. Once inside, we were greeted by a cacophonous riot of activity. The platform was spilling over with airmen in various states of excitement and inebriation, all awaiting the last train back to camp. Some still had girls hanging on their arms. Others clutched half-empty bottles of liquor between their fingers. The noise of their banter was overwhelming, the circumstances hardly conducive to a private farewell. I was beginning to fear that our final moments together might be ruined, when I turned and saw the Kirkham train was just that instant pulling in.

'"Look, Francine! That's my train! It's not due to leave for another ten minutes. Let's go inside and find a quiet place where we can talk."

'We wove our way to the end of the platform, boarded the train and entered an empty compartment where we could be alone at last. I closed the door behind us and sat next to Francine under a muted yellow light.

'She'd worn her hair loose to walk me to the station, with only the butterfly slide holding it in place behind her ear. As I leaned in to kiss her, she slid the clip casually from her hair.

'"Henry, I want you to take this and keep it until I see you next."

'I stared down at the union of metal and pearl and diamanté which she pressed now into my palm.

'"It's not valuable – at least, not to anyone but me – but I like the idea of it all the same."

'"The butterfly?" I said, closing my hand around it and realising with a start that I had nothing to give her in return.

'Francine smiled. "My nan says you need the patience of a saint to catch one, but butterflies are so beautiful and free, *I* don't think they should be caught at all."

'I told her I'd treasure it and keep it safe, that it was only on loan until we saw each other again, then I pulled her close and kissed her. As we drew apart, I asked for her address and promised to write the minute I was back in London. She took a pen and a piece of notepaper from her handbag, scribbled down her details and slipped them into my top left jacket pocket.

'By now the train was starting to fill up, and as we stood to take our leave, the door to our compartment was flung open by a group of airmen visibly the worse for wear. I recognised one of them immediately – a known troublemaker called Sturridge who'd been stationed with me at Changi. Sturridge had been one of the first of my division to arrive back in Britain by plane, though evidently, he'd decided to extend his service and stay on at Kirkham a little while longer.

'My jaw tensed. Sturridge was the worst kind of smart-arse: volatile, and impossibly full of himself. A few months earlier, O'Malley and I had found him taunting one of the Chinese girls who did all the sewing and darning in the camp. Sturridge laughed the incident off, swearing blind that nothing had happened, but O'Malley had a score of his own to settle and reported Sturridge to our C.O. Sturridge was temporarily deployed to Tengah – a transit camp, and a much less coveted post. By the time he returned to Changi he had a chip on his shoulder the size of an ocean liner, and was ten times more belligerent than before.

'He stared at me now with disgust, a poisonous smirk spreading over his face when he realised who I was. "Well, if it isn't *Aircraftman Applebee*. And with a bit of skirt in tow, too. You weren't planning on bringing her back to the billet for an undercover tour, were you? Or has she already had the pleasure of your airman's salute?"

'"I see you haven't lost your charm, Sturridge," I replied. I drew Francine closer and led her towards the door. "Let us through, will you? We haven't got much time."

'"Oh come on, Applebee. *Relax*. Seems a shame to break up a party, don't you think?"

'Sturridge lurched to one side as Francine and I edged past him. "Hey, stand back, boys! We don't want our dicks to get in the way of a *lady*!"

'Sturridge's friends let out a chorus of jeers and proceeded to enact every obscene gesture imaginable. I ignored them as best I could and led Francine out into the corridor. It was uncomfortably full, and I had to struggle against an oncoming flow of boisterous, drunken servicemen in order to help her off the train.

'"Are you all right?" I asked when she'd succeeded at last in climbing down onto the platform.

'Francine was silent. In fact, from the moment Sturridge

launched himself into our compartment, she hadn't said so much as a single word. I closed the carriage door and took hold of her hands through the open window.

'"I'm sorry you had to experience that," I said with genuine embarrassment. "They're a bunch of idiots who've had way too much to drink."

'Francine turned her head to one side and seemed miles away, as though she hadn't even registered what I was saying.

'"Francine?"

'"I know him," she said quietly.

'"Know who?" I was so caught off-guard by her response that I honestly didn't understand to whom she was referring.

'Halfway down the platform a whistle shrieked, and the train responded with a rough, uneasy lurch.

'"Never mind," she said, turning back to face me. "It's not important now."

'The train was already moving, but she stood up on her tiptoes and kissed me. "I'll miss you, Henry. I'll miss you so much! Don't forget to write, will you?"

'"Of course not," I replied. "I'll write the moment I'm home, I promise!"

'Francine let go of my hands and gave me a heart-stopping smile. "Bye, then!"

'"Bye, Francine!"

'She blew me a final kiss and stepped out from the shelter of the platform roof to wave me down the tracks. A shower of snowflakes fluttered across her face. She wrinkled her nose and laughed, then lifted her hands and cupped them around her mouth.

'"I LOVE YOU, HENRY!"

'"I LOVE YOU TOO, FRANCINE!"

'She waved until her arms grew fainter and fainter, until her entire frame receded into little more than a blur. All too quickly a thick veil of darkness and drifting snow swept in to fill the expanding space between us.

'I lowered my hand, pulled myself back into the belly of the train, and felt instantly deflated and alone.

'I made my way back through the carriage, searching in vain for a temporary refuge where I might have a moment or two to myself. As I passed by the compartment where Francine and I had been sitting, I heard a voice call out to me through the open door:

'"Hey, Applebee! Her name's Francine, isn't it?"

'My body jerked sideways and froze. Sturridge was leaning forwards in his seat, his elbows needling his thighs, a cigarette smouldering between his fingers. He seemed more alert than he'd been when he burst in on us earlier, and his eyes – colder, steelier than I'd remembered – were watching me closely.

'"What did you say?"

'As I spoke, the train jolted, knocking me forwards into the open doorway. I steadied myself against the doorframe and returned Sturridge's stare.

'"You heard me. I was referring to your lady friend, if that's the right terminology."

'The words spewed like venom from Sturridge's mouth. One of his bleary-eyed companions sniggered. Another kept his gaze trained on both Sturridge and myself, his eyes darting eagerly back and forth between us.

'Before I could respond, Sturridge took a drag on his cigarette and spoke again, this time enunciating his words with knife-like precision:

'"I'll say it one more time, dumb fuck. *Her name's Francine.*"

'My throat constricted, my entire body bristling as he uttered her name a second time.

'"And how would a scumbag like you know that?"

'My voice was thin as a shadow, and I didn't have to look at my reflection in the mirror above Sturridge's head to know that in the space of one brief exchange, every last drop of blood had drained from my face.

'"How d'you *think*?" He let out a scornful laugh. "What are you going to do now, Applebee? Start *shaking*?"

'My stomach pitched and rolled, and for a second I was convinced I was going to throw up. I knew right then that there was only one way this was going to end. I clenched my fists and took two determined steps towards him.

'"Pretty little thing for a common waitress, isn't she?" he went on. "Or should I say, *for a whore?*"

'The words were barely out of Sturridge's mouth before I'd leaped towards him and punched him in the face. "BASTARD!" I screamed. "You filthy, disgusting BASTARD!"

'A thick rope of muscle flexed along the side of Sturridge's neck. I reached out and grabbed him by the collar of his jacket. He wasn't an especially tall man, but he was broad-shouldered and solidly built. Temporarily, I had the advantage of surprise, but once he'd gathered his wits about him, he wasted no time at all in rising to his feet and driving a heavy punch deep into my abdomen. I groaned, my body doubling in two, then I felt a second punch land on the side of my face, followed soon after by a third above my left eye.

'"Easy, Sturridge, easy!" The airman who'd been watching us with such rabid intensity from his seat tried to pull his friend away from me, but by now Sturridge was in full flow, raining down punches on my head and upper body.

'By sheer force of will I managed to haul myself upright. When I was once again at full height, I drew back my arm and landed a final blow on Sturridge's cheekbone. It was then, as Sturridge spun sideways and spiralled backwards against the seat, that I felt a pair of arms wrap themselves around me from behind.

'"Leave it, Henry! He's a piece of shit! Whatever he said to you, he's not worth it!"

'Davy Hardcastle had pushed his way through from the corridor, the very same corridor where he now tried to drag me, despite the fact it was teeming with a rowdy group of airmen, all jostling to witness the action for themselves.

'"Come on, mate," Davy growled in my ear. "We're hours away from demob. Don't blow it all now, for Christ's sake!"

'I glowered at Sturridge, who was sitting slumped to one side and bleeding from an open gash below his right eye. "I don't believe a word you said!" I yelled at him. "You're nothing but a filthy liar!"

'Sturridge raised his head and cut me a sardonic smile. "Is that right? Then ask yourself this, *fuckwit*: how come I have such vivid memories of a flat with an army of dressmakers' dummies standing to attention outside a girl's bedroom? A room with a rose-covered eiderdown on the bed and the smell of jasmine in the air? If you thought for one second that you were the first guy to see them, you're even stupider than I thought. Tarts like her are two a penny."

'He spat into his hand and wiped a trail of blood from his cheek. "I bet she saw you coming a mile off. She probably told you she loved you, right? And you were gullible enough to believe her. It's a fucking *act,* Applebee, and if you weren't so pathetic, you'd have realised it for yourself."

'Sturridge turned to his friends and winked. "You know what they say about whores: easy come, easy go, right boys?"

'I roared like a wounded animal and made a final aborted lunge in his direction, but Davy had already anticipated my reaction and tightened his grip on my arms. As I felt the last of my strength give way, he turned me around and frogmarched me down the corridor as far away from my tormentor as he could get me.

'Davy bundled me into a compartment at the opposite end of the train to Sturridge's. He shut the sliding door behind him and stood with his back pressed against it, just in case I might be harbouring any ideas of trying to push past.

'"What the FUCK, Henry? It's not like you to get into a fight, least of all with a nutjob like Sturridge! If this is about that girl you met, then you're better off forgetting all about her. We're going home tomorrow, remember? It's what we've been dreaming of for months. Now's not the time to invite trouble to hop on board for the ride."

'I stared at the floor, shell-shocked, numb, my head in a

daze. A tremor of pain rippled through my arm. The knuckles of my right hand were bloody and bruised, though whether the blood was mine or Sturridge's, I couldn't tell.

'"He's full of crap, you know." Davy pulled a packet of Camels from his pocket and tapped it against his palm. "You don't want to go listening to anything that comes out of *his* stinking mouth."

'He offered me a cigarette, but I waved it away. I was beside myself with anger. Humiliated beyond belief. I couldn't understand how one interaction with Sturridge could turn the happiest day of my life into something so squalid. So commonplace. So base.

'"Thanks for stepping in," I managed at last. "I'm not sure what would have happened if you hadn't."

'My body sank back against the seat. A secondary wave of nausea was rising ominously in my throat. I could feel Davy's brain whirring away beside me, but the last thing I was in the mood for was explanations.

'"Let's just forget it," I said cheerlessly. "I don't have the stomach to talk about it right now."

'Davy lit a cigarette and gave me one of his customary grunts. "Fine, but I suggest you clean yourself up before we get back to the billet. Your face looks like a smacked arse. And *that*, sonny boy," he said, pointing his finger at my eye, "is going to be one hell of a shiner by sun-up."'

Henry briefly touched his hands to his face, as though the bruising and the shame were visible all over again. He lowered them to his lap, his cheeks flaming.

'Davy and I kept our distance from the others once we arrived back at camp. He scooped up a handful of snow and, as we passed through the gates, smeared it over my face in a gesture of mock playfulness. He thought it might disguise the unholy mess brewing underneath, but we managed to get inside without anyone giving us any bother.

'We saw Sturridge making his way towards one of the huts furthest away from ours, which was probably just as well. I trudged into our sleeping quarters and lowered myself onto my bunk. A nightmarish loop of words and images kept churning over and over in my mind.

'Finally, in the uncomfortable stillness that followed, I remembered. Francine had told me herself, after all:

"I know him."

'Three little words uttered so casually on a station platform.

'Three little words I knew would haunt me forever more.

'Why she'd admitted it, I couldn't imagine. It hardly made a difference. I'd actually allowed myself to believe that what had happened between us had been real – that I was special – and that Francine's feelings for me were sincere. But now I saw it for what it was: a sham. I honestly couldn't believe it was happening to me again... A few months before Devlin joined up, I saw him walking through Chalk Farm with his arm around the shoulders of a girl I thought might actually be falling for me. But Devlin hadn't known my feelings, and they both looked so happy – I just didn't have the heart, or the courage, to tell him. Anyway, the truth was, what I'd felt for her didn't even come close to the way I felt about Francine.

'I tugged at the collar of my shirt. I couldn't breathe. For an

209

hour or more I'd been lying on my bunk fully clothed, my mind racing, a voice whispering obscenities in my ear until I was half demented. I needed to rouse myself fast and get some air.

'I got up and crept towards the door. I pulled my boots on in the hallway and quietly stepped outside.

'The snow was still falling, the camp infused with a deathly hush save for an owl hooting in the shadows on the far side of the boundary fence. I didn't know where I was going. I didn't care as long as I was moving. Nothing felt worse than lying or standing still, tormented by my thoughts and the graphic visualisation of Francine and Sturridge, their bodies entwined together.

'I quickened my pace, finally breaking into a run. Anything to shake that image from my mind. Anything to obliterate the pain of the word *whore* beating like a bludgeon against my brain.

'The camp was bordered on one side by a dense bank of trees, and without any conscious plan, I found myself heading towards it. I kept in close to the hangar walls, afraid that someone might see me running at such an ungodly hour and assume I was making a break for the perimeter fence. When there was nowhere further to go, I came to an abrupt stop and stared out into the darkness.

'The wood's uniform blackness was alleviated only by a ghostly dusting of snow which was already weighing down some of the younger, less robust branches. I began to shiver uncontrollably. Somewhere on my person I had a pack of cigarettes, but my hands knew where to go; they knew what they were looking for even before I did.

'I unbuttoned my top left jacket pocket, slipped my fingers inside, and came upon the piece of notepaper Francine had placed there just a few hours earlier. I pulled it out. Looked at it almost with surprise. The paper was small and rectangular, folded neatly in two. I turned it round in my fingers. There wasn't enough light to read by, so I searched for the box of matches I always carried in my trouser pocket. Holding the notepaper between my thumb and forefinger, I lit a match and held it up in front of me.

'My eyes skimmed past the address and settled on the parting salutation:

Always and forever,

Francine

'A violent spasm shook me.

'*Always and forever...*

'Three more words which rose up to mock me.

'The match was almost spent, but before the flame was extinguished entirely I moved it an inch closer to Francine's note. I held my breath as it caught against the paper, licking the edges of the words before setting them alight.

'The flame spread quickly, consuming each letter in turn until only cinders and dust remained. I stood and watched in silence as the disintegrating particles joined with the still falling snowflakes, pirouetting to the ground.

'The following morning, dressed in strangely alien, civilian clothing, I presented myself at the appointed hut to hand in my uniform. I had decided to give them everything except my cap, which I was determined to hold on to as a keepsake of my service. They weren't too happy when I reported it lost, but then neither were they happy at the sight of my conspic- uously raw black eye. As Davy had predicted, I did indeed have a real shiner, though the purplish, liver-coloured bruising was nothing compared to how I was feeling on the inside, sobered somewhat, by the cold light of day.

'I passed my belongings over the counter and was inches from the door when the sergeant who had received my kit called out to me:

'"Oi! There's something in here, mate!"

'I turned and saw him pulling his hand out of the bottom right-hand pocket of my uniform jacket.

'"You lot would forget your bleedin' heads if you didn't have me to double-check you still had them screwed on! Here you go. Looks like it might belong to your sweetheart. I doubt she'd be very happy if she thought you'd left it behind."

'I hurried back towards him. I'd been so distracted when I'd finally undressed during the early hours of the morning that it hadn't occurred to me to check the remaining pockets of my uniform. I approached the counter and held out my hand. There was a brief glint of silver as the sergeant dropped Francine's butterfly hair clip into my palm.

'I muttered my thanks and made my way back to the exit. The clip felt so light and innocent beneath my fingers, I could barely bring myself to look at it. When I was through the door, I wrapped it in a handkerchief and slipped it into the small brown suitcase I'd purchased in Kirkham the day before.

'The London train was scheduled to leave within the hour.

I took a final stroll around the camp, said my goodbyes to army life and turned my thoughts to the future.'

Henry paused and let out a deep exhalation. 'I thought I could control my feelings. That I could put what I felt for Francine behind me. But as I soon discovered, that one critical decision to walk away from a promise would mark me out forever.'

16

An Unexpected Meeting

DECEMBER 6: *EN ROUTE*

Henry

Henry stared at the hypnotic gusts of snow drifting resolutely past the window. Words, it seemed, had temporarily failed him.

A subdued hush had fallen over the carriage, the remainder of the passengers lost in thought in their own private daydreams. Henry felt a stirring in his brain, his heart, his abdomen.

You can't stop now, Henry.

Henry kept his eyes trained on his reflection.

Just take a breath, Devlin continued. *And keep going.*

'Henry?' Ariel said.

Henry turned his head.

'Would you like some more water?'

'Yes. Thank you.' He gave her a grateful smile. 'I was just taking a moment.'

Ariel refilled his glass and pushed it towards him.

A moment's fine, Hen. Just DON'T LEAVE THEM HANGING!

'OKAY!' Henry blurted out. His hand shot to his mouth. 'I'm so sorry,' he said, glancing quickly from Ariel to Travis.

Travis appeared entirely nonplussed by Henry's outburst. 'No worries. As long as everything's good.'

'He's fine,' Ariel interjected. 'Aren't you, Henry?'

Henry nodded. He wondered if what he'd just recounted had shocked them. It had all come flooding back so forcefully, perhaps he'd let his passions get the better of him. But no... There was nothing at all to be gained from any kind of *half* telling. Evasions could be just as deceitful as lies. He'd go on exactly as he'd started. *It was all or nothing.*

Ariel and Travis looked over at him, waiting. Evidently, they'd decided to reserve judgement for now – at least until they'd heard the rest of what he had to tell them.

Henry tapped the side of his head, but even Devlin had fallen silent.

'So you went back to London,' Ariel said, with a gentle prompt.

'Yes,' Henry replied.

Travis raised his eyebrows. 'I bet that was a shock! London must have needed so much rebuilding?'

Henry nodded. 'Parts of it had been truly decimated. Everything from the transport system to the hospitals needed fixing, but it was still my home, and I was grateful to be there. I started looking for work right away. I knew my strengths by now, and had set my heart on teaching. I got lucky – in September, I was accepted onto a reputable training course, and not long after I'd completed it, I was taken on as teaching assistant to the French master in a small north London school.'

Henry smiled. 'It turned out I derived genuine pleasure from filling young minds with facts and seeing them thrive. But it was also a much more demanding role than I'd ever imagined as a schoolboy myself. In addition to taking classes, there were hours of preparation, endless marking, and occasional private tutoring. Needless to say, it was the perfect way to lose myself; time passed very quickly.

'Even so, I was still too inexperienced to understand that what I felt for Francine could not be quite so easily pushed aside. Our encounter had been a *coup de foudre* and it had struck deep. In moments of weakness, I tortured myself by replaying every second of our time together. Insecurity had long been second nature to me, but as time passed, my doubts multiplied, and I began to believe with increasing certainty that something wasn't right.

'In the end, I sought solace elsewhere. Not with anything like the regularity or success, I might add, of my brother – it would have required a seismic shift in my character, self-confidence and looks to achieve that. But I told myself that there were plenty more fish in the sea, and if I had fallen in love once, I could fall in love again.

'The remainder of my twenties passed with all the usual distractions. I was young, and by nature, optimistic. It's possible that I might have succeeded in forgetting Francine after all had fate not intervened. But fate *did* intervene. And it came in the guise of an unexpected meeting, in London, two days before my thirtieth birthday...'

Henry took a sip of water and pressed his hands to his knees: 'It was August 1957 and I was enjoying the long, lazy summer holidays that members of the teaching profession look forward to with such relish.

'Once or twice a week, I'd got into the habit of taking a bus into the West End and strolling along Regent Street, down past Trafalgar Square to the Lyons Corner House on the Strand. Lyons Corner House was a favourite hangout of mine – a vast, hugely popular meeting spot, so much more than a regular café. They even had live music playing almost continually in the themed restaurants on the upper floors, which for a music nut like me was irresistible.

'I'd just had a bite to eat upstairs, and was making my way back out onto the street when I collided with a young man walking briskly in the opposite direction. I apologised for my clumsiness, but the man insisted the mistake was all his:

'"No need to apologise. The fault was mine entirely."

'He bent down to retrieve his newspaper. When he righted himself, I found myself staring into a familiar pair of piercing, close-set eyes. The man's hair was coiffed and oiled, and he was smartly dressed in a linen suit and fashionable oxblood brogues. His build was stocky – the brawn all packed like casting clay about his chest and upper arms – and while I could tell he'd gained a pound or two in weight since last we'd met, there was no mistaking it was Dean Sturridge standing before me.

217

'"My God. Henry Applebee?" he cried. "Well, this is a surprise!"

'To his credit, Sturridge spoke without a trace of rancour or irony in his voice. He took a step backwards, his eyes scanning over me the way mine had over him, a companionable smile lighting up his face when he realised who I was.

'"Hello, Dean," I replied. "It's been a while. How are you?"

'I'd never truly appreciated until then just how fickle the passing of time can be. A balm, on occasion. A convenient dulling of events we might otherwise choose to forget.

'Sturridge and I had hardly left each other on good terms, but by now almost ten years had passed since our altercation on the Kirkham train. Despite the overwhelming hostility my younger self had felt towards him, I found to my surprise that what I saw when I looked at the respectable man standing before me was not an adversary, but merely a former serviceman like myself – someone with whom I'd shared such an unforgettable and formative period of my life. That there had been unpleasantness between us was undeniable. And yet somehow, nearly a full decade later, the integrity of our RAF bond was still intact.

'As we stood outside that crowded doorway on the Strand, I recognised in Sturridge's eyes the same warm familiarity that I knew was present in mine. We shook hands, and by mutual agreement decided to step back into the café together and catch up over a drink.

'We addressed the usual preliminaries first. I told him about my job as a French teacher, and how in recent years I'd begun to spend a portion of my holidays travelling around the cultural capitals of Europe. We both laughed at the irony of us having left the RAF with a far greater practical knowledge of the Far East than of the wealth of countries closer to home. I admitted, then, how privileged I felt to now have some limited resources at my disposal with which to explore them.

'For his part, Sturridge told me how a few years after demob he'd secured a lucrative position with a London based telecommunications company, assuring me that wonderful developments were to come in the world of television broadcasting. He'd also got married some years earlier and had one small child, with a second on the way. Things were good, he told me:

'"Better than I'd have ever thought possible when I left the RAF a cocky, self-absorbed s.o.b. with no concept whatsoever of how to navigate my way through real life."

'After complementing each other on how well our lives on Civvy Street had progressed, it was I who decided to bring up the circumstances of the last time we'd met. Our conversation was beginning to draw to a close by then, and I felt sure we were comfortable enough in each other's company to reflect on the past with maturity and poise.

'Nevertheless, the moment I broached the subject of Francine, the skin on the back of my neck started to prickle. My jaw tightened. Worse still, as I struggled to preserve my equanimity, the relaxed and perfectly amiable man sitting across from me began to morph – in my mind, at least – into the brutish, irascible Sturridge of almost a decade earlier.

'I edged forwards in my seat and looked Sturridge square in the eye. "Do you remember the last time we spoke, Dean?

Do you remember what we were fighting about on the Kirkham train?"

'Sturridge made a soft clicking sound on the roof of his mouth. He met my gaze head on and answered almost immediately. "Actually, I do. Weren't we arguing over some girl you had with you on the train?"

'"Francine," I replied in a strangulated voice. "Her name was Francine."

'"Right. I doubt I'd have remembered it myself, but yes, that sounds vaguely familiar."

'The easy nonchalance of his tone riled me, but I forced myself to keep my emotions in check and pressed ahead: "Something happened that night which I've thought a lot about over the years. It was something you said – "

'"Look, Henry," Sturridge interjected, "I'm sure I don't need to remind you that I was a prick back then."

'In a pre-emptive gesture of conciliation, he held his palms up towards me. "Whatever I said, we should probably just forget it. It was nearly ten years ago, after all. Water under the bridge and all that."

'I shook my head, and in the same strangulated voice said: "Yes, but that's just it, Dean. After all this time, against all the odds, here you are sitting right across from me and the simple fact is I *can't* forget it. I'm not going to fly off the handle, I promise, but for old times' sake, would you just tell me if you were being straight with me about having been in Francine's flat? About having been in her bedroom? About –" the lining of my stomach coiled and twisted – "about having been intimate with Francine herself?"

'Sturridge's eyes slowly glazed over. He looked as though he were delving back into a quagmire of long-forgotten memories, searching for the answer to some elusively cryptic clue. My blood began to boil as I waited, willing him to say something – *anything* – that might bring closure at last to my growing ambiguity over what had transpired all those years ago.

'"Jenny," he said suddenly. "You mean Jenny, don't you? She was the waitress I had a, let's say *interaction* with. The girl with you on the train was her flatmate. I'd met her when Jenny took me back to the place they shared together. It was a bit awkward, as I remember. Your girl – Francine – could see that Jenny and I wanted to have some time alone, so she made some excuse about having to go into town to meet a friend. And she did, though she didn't look too happy about me being there. I don't know why, it wasn't really any of her business.

'"I never laid eyes on Francine again until the night on the train. My *relationship* – if you can call it that – with Jenny was somewhat fleeting. I think I saw her a couple of times at most, you know how it goes. I dare say she was mad as hell with me for not staying in touch, but that's how I was back then. She was a bundle of laughs, though. Cracking pair of legs. Probably married with a couple of kids of her own by now."

'I stared at Sturridge in astonishment, my mouth ajar. *Jenny?* The girl he'd been involved with was *Jenny?* Why hadn't I thought of that possibility myself? Was I so blinded by jealousy that I'd failed to even consider it an option? Or was it because

Francine had told me that Jenny was engaged, and by assumption, off the market and unlikely to be playing around?

'My relief at finally uncovering the truth was marred only by the devastating realisation that I'd chosen – without question – to believe Sturridge's version of events. I'd been so sure that I was the victim in all this, I'd never even given Francine the opportunity to explain things for herself.

'I took a large swig of water from a glass on the table before me and spoke to my companion in a slow and deliberate voice: "So, Dean, you're telling me that nothing happened between you and Francine?"

'Sturridge nodded. "Correct."

'"But then... how did you know so much about her bedroom? You even commented on her perfume." I paused, the muscles in my face tensing once again. "You told me she was a *whore*, Dean. If I remember correctly, you said tarts like her were two a penny."

'Sturridge let out a short, exasperated laugh. "Jesus wept, Henry, have you been lugging this around like a dead weight all this time? Christ, I'd have called the girl anything under the sun if I thought it would get a rise out of you, you know what I was like! I'm sure I went snooping around the flat, poking my head around doors while Jenny was in the bathroom or doing God knows what. As for the perfume, I hate to disappoint you, but plenty of girls wore the same fragrance back then. I either recognised the smell of it in her bedroom, or it was a lucky guess. At this point, I really couldn't say."

'Despite Sturridge's frustration, I thought I detected a hint of genuine remorse in his face. He ran his hand over his forehead, and with an almost disarming degree of earnestness said:

'"Look, I'm sorry if I buggered things up for you, but the fact is, even if there *had* been something between your girl and me, you do realise it would have been before the two of you even *met*?"

'And there it was: he'd said it. Though Sturridge couldn't know the ramifications of our argument, there was no getting around the fact that I'd been completely in the wrong to over-react the way I had. He knew it, and so did I. The only person who didn't know the truth was the one true victim in all of it: Francine.

'"Anyway," Sturridge went on, "it just wasn't true. Sounds to me like what you had with Francine was the real deal. Whatever I said on that train, I was an arse, and I'm sorry, Henry, I really am. I just wanted to mess with your head. She'd probably have had way too much sense to get mixed up with the likes of me anyway, even if I was a bit of a looker in my air force blues."

'Sturridge's words, heartfelt as they were, cut me to my core. There was nothing more to say. We shook hands and got up to take our leave.

'Before we parted we exchanged contact details and made polite, well-meaning promises to meet up for drinks one evening after work; maybe even have dinner at his house in Putney so I could meet his wife and child.

'We never actually did, though. Still, I kept his address and phone number in my desk drawer at home for many, many years afterwards. That was one mistake, at least, I was deter-mined never to make again.'

17

The Search

DECEMBER 6: *EN ROUTE*

Henry

Ariel and Travis had scarcely moved a muscle while Henry was talking, but as he finished the account of his meeting with Sturridge, the train jerked briefly to attention before shuddering to an abrupt halt once more.

Henry peered out at the bleary expanse of snow-swept countryside which rose and fell like reams of muslin beyond the window. The flurries were coming down thicker and faster, creating a hoary snow globe vista on either side of the train. He moved his face closer to the glass and watched a flock of starlings soar upwards from a field, wheeling, swooping theatrically, smearing the sky black in a perfectly synchronised aerial ballet.

'I don't know what to say, Henry,' Ariel said as he turned

back to face her. 'You must have been absolutely gutted when you found out Sturridge had deliberately lied to you on the train.'

Travis had propped his body sideways in his seat, his attention fully focused on Henry, a keen drift of sadness etched across his face. 'What did you do? I mean, *c'mon*… what *could* you do, under the circumstances? If it'd been me, the first thing I'd have wanted to do was go find her, only I wouldn't have had the first idea where to begin.'

Ariel stared at him across the aisle.

'What?' Travis asked with a shrug. 'It's not like anyone had access to Facebook or Twitter in 1948. Man, the whole thing sucks. It must've felt like she'd disappeared into the abyss.'

Ariel leaned across the table and gave Henry a sympathetic smile. 'Just so you know, even if social media *had* existed in the 1940s, it might not have made a difference even then.'

She turned patiently back to Travis. 'It was never going to be as simple as just jumping on a train... Think of it from *her* perspective – she must have been heartbroken! Social media couldn't have fixed that. And anyway, even today the entire planet isn't on Facebook. Even if they have access to it, the fact is not everyone *wants* to be.'

'Well yeah!' Travis shot back. 'Not those who don't want to be found! Being a ghost online is the easiest thing in the world for someone who wants to hide.'

Henry watched their conversation unfold. (Or perhaps *unravel* might be the more accurate way of putting it.) In the loaded silence that followed, he sensed that some sort of line – invisible or otherwise – had just been crossed. Not that it mattered; considering he only had the vaguest idea of what Ariel and Travis were talking about, the fact was, if either one of them had inadvertently said something to offend him, they need hardly have worried.

'Yes, well, as you say, things were different then,' he said with as much levity as he could muster. 'Either way, my chance meeting with Sturridge was the turning point that changed everything. Sturridge didn't know it, but his words had once again had a dramatic impact on my life, this time setting me off on a lifelong mission to seek amends for breaking my promise to Francine.'

'You see!' Travis cried. He threw Ariel a distinct look of triumph. '*Obviously*, Henry is a man after my own heart!'

Ariel responded with a sweet, philosophical smile. 'Well *obviously* Henry made a commitment to go and find her, otherwise he wouldn't be sitting here with us today.'

Henry cleared his throat. 'The *truth*,' he said quickly, 'is that I realised it would be easier to just let things be. Even if I saw Francine again, I knew there might be little I stood to gain. If life had been kind to her, she would have long since forgotten the young airman who sat next to her in the Tower Ballroom. She would have moved on, and found happiness elsewhere.'

'Yes, but you couldn't just give up,' Travis cut in. 'From everything you've told us, she's clearly the love of your life.' He flicked his gaze to Ariel. 'If *you* were Francine, wouldn't you want to know the truth about what happened?'

An entire melting pot of emotions seemed to pass over Ariel's face, but somehow she managed to wrangle them into a concise and diplomatic, 'Yes. I would.

'Sorry, Henry,' she said, turning back to face him. 'We didn't mean to interrupt.'

'No,' Travis echoed, 'we didn't mean to do that at all.' He shifted forwards in his seat. 'But you did search for her? Like you said, you wanted to try and put things right?'

'Yes,' Henry replied. 'To both of your questions.' He waited a beat before continuing. 'My biggest fear was that I'd irreversibly messed things up. Even if by some miracle Francine were still free, I couldn't imagine her feeling anything for me now apart from reproach – or worse: ice-cold indifference.

'I was so ashamed of myself. How long had she waited for me to write? What must she have thought when the realisation dawned that my letter was never going to come? That I'd lied? That I'd gone and done exactly what she asked me *not* to do, and deliberately broken her heart?

'My naivety had long since faded, and I knew my chances of winning her back were slim, but my mind was made up: *I had to find her.*

'The question was how? I had destroyed her address in a jealous rage in Kirkham. And I knew I'd never be able to retrace my steps to her flat from memory – the night Francine took me home I was far too distracted to pay attention to where she was leading me. Besides, it was highly unlikely that she would still be living in the same rented accommodation ten years on.

'I knew her family came from Sheffield, but Francine had told me almost nothing about them other than a few fleeting allusions to her mother and grandmother. She'd never mentioned brothers or sisters. She'd spoken of her flatmate,

Jenny, but I didn't know her surname or her current whereabouts, and Sturridge hadn't indicated that he knew them either.

'There was only one thing I knew for certain: when we met, Francine was working as a waitress at the Shore Hotel.

'It was a long shot, of course, but I found the telephone number and called, requesting that I be put through to the restaurant manager. I even remembered Francine referring to him as Mr "*High and Mighty*" Sinclair. But the person who answered the phone was new. After something of a delay, I was transferred to the general manager's secretary, a Miss Wilson, who had access to the hotel's personnel records. After a brief discussion, during which I explained my wish to locate an old friend and former (or perhaps, existing?) employee of theirs, all Miss Wilson could confirm was that a waitress by the name of Francine Keeley had terminated her employment during the summer of '48, the same year we met. There was no indication about where Francine may have gone next, and regrettably, Miss Wilson made it clear that she was not at liberty to provide me with any further particulars – staff personnel records were strictly confidential, she was sure I understood.

'My decision to place a personal ad in *The Star* newspaper in Sheffield was something I thought long and hard about before finally moving ahead. Even if Francine hadn't returned home, there was always a chance that friends or relatives might see the advertisement in her absence and pass the message on. However, I was wary of burdening her with any unwanted intrigue, especially if she might now be in a committed relationship with someone else. As much as the thought pained me, the fact remained that I could very well be the last person on earth she might ever wish to hear from again.

'In the end, I opted to place an ad, just once, in which I mentioned that a former airman and fellow music lover from the Tower Ballroom was sorry to have lost contact with her over the years, and was hoping to get in touch.

'It was signed "*H.A.*".'

'Oh my God, Henry.' Ariel broke her own rule and interrupted Henry once again. 'Did she see it?'

Henry rubbed his eyes. 'Honestly, I have no idea. Maybe I was just unlucky. Or maybe she did see it and chose to ignore it... In any event, I lost my nerve after that. I just couldn't bear the thought of causing her any undue embarrassment if she genuinely had no wish to see me again.

'That September, school started back under the leadership of a radical new headmaster who swooped in like a bird of prey, hungry for the school to reach new heights of success, and giddy with seemingly limitless ideas for reform. He kept us all – teachers and students alike – on our toes, and once again I found myself caught up in a never-ending spiral of class preparation, extracurricular tutoring, exam prep, and the organisation of the yearly school trip abroad. By now, I was no longer a teaching assistant, but a fully-fledged French master in my own right, and my responsibilities had increased accordingly.

'As the months flew by, I prepared to accept the possibility of defeat. My only solace was to convince myself that wherever she was, whatever she was doing, in all likelihood she was with a better man than me.

Celia Reynolds

'But I was wrong,' Henry said slowly. 'It wasn't over – not for her, not for me. The gold thread was pulling taut between us, and just when I thought all hope was gone, Francine and I were drawn into each other's orbit once again.'

18

Synchronicity

BLACKPOOL, MARCH 1968

Henry

Henry pays the driver his fare and steps out of the taxi onto the pavement.

He breathes in the brawny, sun-whipped air, his blood pumping with a genuine mix of curiosity and nostalgia. He hasn't been back to Blackpool for twenty years, not since the night he and Francine parted. In his hand is a small overnight bag. He's alone, standing on the threshold of one of the plethora of Bed and Breakfasts leading off from the front – in this instance, a sprawling, family-run affair about halfway between the South Pier and the town's bright, bawdy centre.

'Henry Applebee,' he says to a young gentleman manning the reception area. 'I'm checking in. I think my friend booked four rooms in total?'

The young man nods, tells him he's in luck, one of the larger twin rooms has been cleaned already. He hands him his key. The groom-to-be and the rest of Henry's colleagues aren't arriving until later in the day, but Henry was quick to explain to them that he had a long-standing attachment to Blackpool from his time in service: 'I'll go on ahead on an early morning train,' he said casually. 'It would be nice to revisit a few old haunts before the celebrations begin in earnest.'

By 'celebrations', he means 'stag do', their seaside destination widely hailed as cheap, chipper and cheerful – or as the groom-to-be put it: *perfect for a group of largely single men who don't spend enough time letting go.*

Henry tosses his bag onto the bed nearest the window and leaves again almost at once. In contrast to his previous visit, the weather this time around is glorious. He steps out into a beautiful spring morning, not a cloud in the sky, and heads for the promenade. Rising tall and imperious in the distance, the Tower dominates his eyeline, its steely silhouette as bold and commanding as ever.

He walks shoreside, past the Central Pier and the amusement arcades, all the way to the North Pier and the majestic Shore Hotel. Henry stands and stares for some moments at its striking red-brick façade.

No Henry, we can't go there. That's where I work...

A surge of longing engulfs him. He feels it in his gut, in the tight, hollow cradle of his abdomen. He knew it would happen, he just hadn't expected it to be so quickly. He catches his breath, wonders if he should go inside and steal a glimpse of the world Francine once inhabited, but his plans are set, the Tower already calling to him.

He doubles back and turns down a nearby side road. To his surprise, he stumbles upon the little café, Fortescue's, looking for all the world exactly the way he left it. Henry stops and lingers at the door. By now, Blackpool is deep in the throes of the Swinging Sixties – all joss sticks, flower power and cheesecloth shirts. Record shops have sprung up around every corner. The big band music he'd been so crazy about in his youth has long been relegated to specialist programmes on the radio. Now, it's the Beatles and the Rolling Stones who rule the airwaves, their songs pouring out of boutique doorways and blaring from car radios up and down the promenade.

Fortescue's, on the other hand, looks like it's been preserved in some sort of mystical time warp, its clientele merely updated versions of those who'd frequented it twenty years before. Henry slides his hands into his pockets and steps towards the window. A pair of young lovebirds sit drinking bottles of Coca Cola and holding hands across the chequered table cloth. They barely notice the forty-year-old man peering through the glass, but Henry is mindful of intruding, and quickly walks away.

At last, he arrives at the entrance to the Tower. This too, from the outside at least, seems to be little changed. Henry smoothes back his hair and steps inside. Perched behind the counter is a peroxide blonde – in her mid-fifties, he'd say – lost to the world in a copy of *Woman's Weekly*.

'Hello?' Henry says in a hopeful voice.

The woman raises her head. 'Sorry, darling, if it's the ball-room you're after, we're not open for another thirty minutes.'

Henry stands his ground and makes a deliberate show of checking his watch. 'Oh, it's just that I'm passing through, you see, and I only have a short amount of time before I leave. I came here many years ago when I was stationed in Kirkham, and well – if it's not too much trouble – I was wondering if I might just pop upstairs and see if it's all still the same?'

He throws his entire weight behind his smile, the way Devlin always does to such electrifying effect.

To Henry's amazement, it works.

''Course you can, duckie.' The woman winks, and with a heavily bejewelled hand she waves him past. 'Go on. Up you go! You know the way.'

Henry thanks her and begins to make his way up the familiar staircase, all the way to the top floor. There'd been a fire in the ballroom in 1956, and he heard they'd had to close the whole place down for a couple of years in order to carry out extensive renovations. He pushes open the doors to the upper tier, afraid he might find it changed beyond all recognition. But the moment he steps inside, he sees that everything's the same, exactly the way he remembers it.

He makes his way to the balcony and sits down in the same seat he'd sat in two decades earlier, Francine by his side. The entire place is empty. No music is playing, and the glitter balls hang dormant overhead. And yet even in the midst of such towering stillness, a glimmer of magic floats seductively in the air.

Henry peers over the barrier onto the dance floor – oceanic now, without its dancers – the polished wood all magnificently restored with a glorious inlay of mahogany, walnut and oak. Something moves in the corner of his eye, and a cleaning lady in a bright, floral pinafore materialises like a pantomime character out of the gloom. Henry watches as she crosses beneath him, a trail of soap suds dripping from the mop and bucket in her hand. He opens his mouth to say something, but she continues on her way, her hips swaying heavily from side to side, a net of weariness cast about her neck and shoulders until finally, she's swallowed up by the shadows in the far reaches of the room.

Alone in this cavernous dance hall, so evocative of happier times gone by, Henry shuts his eyes. The weight of the silence presses in around him, so close he can almost feel its breath against his skin.

He places his hands on the soft, velour upholstery of his chair. The fingers of his right hand curl around the edge of his seat and brush against a loose swathe of material dangling beneath. Henry grabs hold of it and gives it a quick, firm tug. There's a tearing sound, then one more tug and the swatch of velour comes away in his palm.

He runs the material between his fingers. It's good as new, protected from wear on the underside of the seat. He slips it into his trouser pocket, and with a final, lingering glance at his surroundings, he gets up to leave.

Back in the foyer, the woman behind the counter looks up as he approaches. 'How was your trip down memory lane, dearie? Full of happy recollections, I hope?'

'It was wonderful, thank you,' Henry replies. 'The ballroom hasn't changed one iota since the last time I was here. Maybe it's because the world's evolving at such a pace, but there's something very comforting about the way certain places carry on regardless. Happily, the Tower Ballroom is one of them.'

He's already moving towards the exit when the woman speaks again:

'Do you know, I had a lady say something very similar a couple of weeks back. Nice woman, she was. About your age, I'd say. She said she worked in Blackpool when she was a lass and often used to visit the Tower Ballroom on her afternoons off. She said she used to get quite hypnotised by it all. It warms your heart to hear stories like that. The loyalty of some people to come back after so many years, just to see if the inside of the ballroom's still the same! She went all the way up to the balcony. I think she must have spent a good half-hour up there by herself.'

Henry spins on his heel and stares at the woman for far longer than is reasonably polite. Logically, he knows that the person she's just described could be any one of the millions who've visited the ballroom over the years.

And yet...

He shifts his gaze to the calendar hanging on the far side of the counter wall. It's March 2nd, 1968. A couple of weeks earlier would have been twenty years exactly since he and Francine first met, right here in this very building...

'I don't suppose the lady gave you her name, did she?' he asks, trying – and no doubt, failing – to sound as impartial as possible to her eventual response. In reality, he realises he must look like a kid on Christmas Day.

The woman lays her magazine on the counter, and begins to toy with a large, gold locket dangling around her neck. 'Actually, as it happens, she did. I asked her just as she was leaving, when I told her how nice it had been to meet her. I think she said her name was Franny, Francie... something like that.'

'Francine?' Henry cries, lurching gracelessly towards her. 'Could it have been Francine?'

'Yes, that's it! Pretty little name, isn't it? A pretty name for a pretty lady.'

Henry feels the blood drain from his face.

'Is anything wrong, my sweet?'

Floored, his mind racing, Henry shakes his head.

The woman – who in the course of their ensuing conversation introduces herself as Connie Shelby – offers him a glass of water. Henry gladly accepts, then proceeds to fire an exhaustive barrage of questions at the poor woman, the majority of which she's wholly unequipped to answer.

Francine (the Francine who'd stood exactly where he is standing now, just a couple of weeks earlier) hadn't given her last name. She hadn't revealed where she was currently living or working. She'd come alone, and hadn't mentioned anything of note about her present circumstances at all, as far as Connie could recall:

'Now that I come to think of it,' she confesses, 'aside from telling me she used to spend time here as a lass, she was quite vague overall. When all's said and done, I'd say I know as much about her as I do you.'

Henry asks if she can at least tell him if the Francine she'd spoken to had had a northern accent, specifically from Sheffield.

Connie shrugs. 'Nearly everyone around these parts has a northern accent, so I can't say I took much notice. Although if she'd had an obviously *different* accent – a "southern" accent like yours, for example – then *that* I might have remembered.'

As much as Henry wills Connie to provide him with something more conclusive, he's none the less certain that this is his Francine. Every fibre of his being tells him so.

He asks her for a pen, a sheet of paper and an envelope which she locates for him in a drawer beneath the counter. He then drafts the most wildly optimistic note he's ever written. Addressed to Francine, it includes his contact details (both at home and those of the school) and begs her – should his letter ever reach her – to please get in touch.

He ends the note the only way he knows how:

> *I hope you're well and happy, and I'm so sorry for not writing as I'd promised. I made a terrible mistake, Francine. I swear I never meant to hurt you.*
> *Please reply, if you can. I'd be truly humbled to have the chance to explain things to you.*
> *Yours,*
> *Henry Applebee*

On the front of the envelope he writes, STRICTLY PRIVATE AND CONFIDENTIAL: FOR THE ATTENTION OF FRANCINE KEELEY, and underneath in brackets, (*Please*

hold at the Tower Ballroom Box Office for as long as necessary).
Just for good measure, on the back of the envelope he prints
his name and telephone number in large, legible letters.

The only thing left to do now is pray.

From the way Connie's eyes are twinkling, Henry can tell
she's enthralled (and no doubt titillated) to play such a key
role in the proceedings. 'Leave it with me,' she says, winking.
'If the lady comes back, I'll make sure she gets your letter,
don't you worry.'

Henry thanks her over and over. He knows there's no guarantee that Francine will return – or that Connie will be on
duty to recognise her if she does. *But there's a chance.* An
infinitesimal chance, perhaps, but it's more than he's had to
go on to date, and he's determined not to let it pass him by.

He shakes Connie's hand and walks away from the ballroom
as he walked away twenty years earlier, in an absolute dream.

For the remainder of the morning, Henry wanders the
streets in a giddy, euphoric daze. In the new, hope-filled
shadow of the Tower, it's as though the entire past two decades
have been magically erased.

She went back, he tells himself. *Francine went back.*

Everywhere he turns he sees a flash of power-blue coat;
he smells the scent of jasmine mingling with the aromas of
rock candy, incense sticks, and sea-salt; if he concentrates hard
enough, he's sure he can hear Francine's laughter floating past
his ear. He looks into the face of every woman he passes, but
they're not her... They don't have her lightness. They don't
have her joy. Not one has the big band melody of Francine's
eyes.

He continues onwards, an urgency about him now, walking faster and faster without any clear idea where he's headed. He enters Stanley Park and comes upon a group of hippies in headbands and bell-bottom jeans. On the blanket laid out on the grass before them is a sprawling array of homemade jewellery.

'You want something for your girlfriend?' one of them asks him in a dreamy voice.

She holds up a handful of brightly coloured beads, strung together into necklaces, long and delicate. 'No two are the same,' she says, smiling. 'Aren't they beautiful?'

Henry shakes his head. He circles back to the promenade and leans against the railings. His gaze sweeps inland, searching. The pavement on either side of him is brimming with locals and tourists. Pale imitations. Stand-ins. A million different expressions of humanity except the one he seeks.

He's so close. *So close*. He can feel it.

He scours the horizon, willing her to appear.

'Francine,' he murmurs under his breath, '*I'm right here. Where are you?*'

19

Esprit de Corps

DECEMBER 6: *EN ROUTE*

Henry

'Henry,' Travis said when Henry had finished speaking, 'this story is absolutely *killing* me.'

Ariel glanced across the aisle and smiled.

'What?' he asked, turning to face her. 'Don't tell me you're not feeling it, too.'

'Oh I'm feeling it. I just think it's nice that you are.'

'You mean because I'm a *guy*?' he cried. 'What kind of sexist bull is that?'

Ariel stared at him in amazement. 'Of course it's not because you're a guy!' She bit her lip, and for a second, Henry thought she might actually burst out laughing. 'Honestly, I just think it shows you have heart, that's all. It's cool. I like it.'

Travis's face relaxed, then a moment later, cracked into a

smile. 'Oh. Great! I mean – it's good to know we're on the same page.'

Henry watched them in silence. There was an undeniable *frisson* percolating beneath his companions' repartee. Whether *they* were aware of it or not, it was clear as a bell to him.

'I'm sorry, Henry.' Ariel threw Travis a quick, sidelong glance. 'We both are. Please don't stop. What happened to your letter? Did you ever hear from Connie?'

'Well,' he replied, 'that was certainly the dream.'

Ariel's face fell.

'But you didn't give up,' Travis said with customary eagerness. 'No way would you have done that.'

'No,' Henry replied. 'But there also wasn't a whole lot I could do under the circumstances except return to work and be patient. So that's exactly what I did. I resisted the urge to call for as long as possible, but in the end I couldn't bear the suspense any longer. I managed to get Connie on the phone and she was as kind and friendly as ever, but my letter was right there behind the counter – exactly where I'd left it.

'I called her every few months after that. But the answer was always the same. I just couldn't stop wondering what might have happened if I'd passed by the Tower Ballroom two weeks earlier. I was sure the timing of Francine's visit must mean something. Or perhaps it was only a cruel coincidence. Maybe some things were just not meant to be.'

Henry felt the deflation washing over him all over again. 'In time, my resignation deepened, and as the years slid by, I was forced to accept how high the odds were stacked against me ever seeing Francine again.'

'Is that when you stopped looking?'

Ariel's eyes, Henry noted, bore no trace of reproach, just a vague inflection of stubbornness; a refusal, perhaps, to believe him capable of letting Francine slip away.

'Yes,' he replied. 'In a way...'

'And you never met anyone else?'

This time, it was Travis who had asked the question.

Henry turned to peruse the fresh coating of snowflakes crystallising on the carriage window. 'A woman called Vivienne came into my life in my mid-forties. By then, everyone assumed I would never marry. There had been girlfriends over the years, though no one you could call serious, and sooner or later, the relationships always fizzled out. But Vivienne wasn't like the others. She was French, and already twice divorced when we met. I saw her as a breath of fresh air; a free-thinking, modern woman who had no burning desire to marry again. She also made it clear that she didn't want children, so in her opinion, there was no compelling reason to tie ourselves down.

'Vivienne was a teacher, like me. We spent the holidays in her converted farmhouse just outside Poitiers, and eventually set up home in London. I assumed we'd stay together indefinitely, but I was wrong. As we neared our retirement, she announced one morning over coffee that she was leaving me. Her plan was to return to France – *alone*. It was all settled. She'd be gone before the week was out.'

Henry shook his head. 'It didn't make any sense. And then she told me: "You know as well as I do that I'm not the person you wished to grow old with. I'm sorry, Henri. *C'est fini.*"

'We parted amicably, and for that I'm grateful, but I missed her none the less. I missed her honesty. I missed her courage for making me face up to a situation I'd long since tried to forget.'

'Did you never marry after that, Henry? What about Francine? What if she felt exactly the same way you did, only she didn't know how to find you?'

Ariel's eyes were so full of fire, Henry hardly knew what to say next.

Before he could reply there was a loud creak, a long expulsion of air from the brakes, and finally, just when he'd convinced himself they'd still be there come nightfall, the train was once more on the move.

A tentative cheer went up from a group of passengers-turned-opportunistic-revellers further down the carriage. Their optimism was rewarded by an announcement from the guard confirming that the electrical fault had been rectified, and they could now resume their journey at last.

The train gathered speed, racing along the tracks with a renewed burst of vigour. Henry was heartened to see the snow easing off, the sky ahead starting to clear. Before long, they rocketed past two lone wind turbines rotating their three-armed spokes to the heavens. Beyond them, the train cut through a mysterious forest, then abruptly – majestically! – the sea. White-crested waves breaking on a distant shore. A tumble of multicoloured cottages overlooking a river. A heady onrush of water entering the sea's colossal, foaming mouth.

The sliding door to their carriage opened, and through it came their steward carrying a fresh round of drinks. Henry asked if he could have a cup of tea. He had yet to answer

Ariel's question. Just a drink, he just needed a warm drink to soothe his throat before finishing his tale...

'I dream about Francine often,' he said, once the steward had taken his leave. 'It's the strangest thing. The dreams seem to grow more vivid as time goes by. Perhaps that's what they mean by the elderly regressing to childhood, only I'm regressing to when I was twenty, to the period I would most like to revisit if I had my time again. Sometimes, I actually believe I can feel Francine and I drawing closer together, pulled along by that fine, gold thread.'

His eyes were shining now, bright as tin.

'I never married. After Vivienne, I didn't live with anyone again. The only exception was Devlin. After his wife passed away, my niece, Amy, thought it would be a good idea for us to keep an eye on each other, so he moved into my spare room for the last two years of his life.

'It was wonderful; just like old times, only with denture cream and magnifying glasses and walking sticks thrown in. Devlin had been living the high life for years, and his heart was deteriorating, but he was still bossing me around, and I was still laughing at his jokes and buying him the occasional packet of cigarettes under duress. There were days where he drove me to distraction, but then he'd look at me and grin, and say, "Come on, Henry, lighten up! At least when I annoy you I'm consistent! Better the Devlin you know, eh?"

'We even crawled up to Parliament Hill once or twice to look for UFOs, though never after nine o'clock. Two old fossils roaming the streets by themselves aren't safe anywhere in

London after dark. It was a shame, really. We had as much right to be out on the roads as anyone else.'

Henry's smile slipped sorrowfully from his face. 'When Devlin's heart finally gave way I thought my world had come to an end. I bought a puppy to ease the loneliness. I did endless crossword puzzles to keep myself mentally alert. A few months ago, I began a writing project to give some focus to my day. Despite all the pain and heartache, life settled. It began to find its rhythm once again.

'And then, eight days ago, I received a phone call from Amy. She'd been reading a newspaper interview with the author of a mystery novel set in Blackpool in the 1940s. According to the article, the author's mother had worked as a waitress at the Shore Hotel. She'd even used her mother's maiden name for her protagonist. That name was Keeley. Her mother's Christian name, the article said, was Francine.

'My niece would never have connected any of this to me if I hadn't told her about Francine shortly after Vivienne returned to France. They'd been very fond of one another, and Amy was struggling to understand why our relationship had fallen apart. She asked me if I had loved Vivienne and I answered yes, absolutely, in my way, but I had only truly loved one woman my entire life, and that was a long way behind me now.

'Amy pressed me on the subject, and eventually I gave in and told her everything I've recounted to you today.'

'Holy *crap*, Henry.' Travis clapped his hand to his mouth. 'Sorry, guys, I didn't mean to butt in again, but *seriously*, this is one hell of a rollercoaster journey!'

Henry nodded. 'Yes, I suppose it is!'

'How did you feel when you got Amy's phone call?' Ariel asked. 'It must have literally blown your mind!'

'Well,' he replied, 'it certainly left me reeling. Francine's happiness had always been of paramount importance to me, so it gave me some comfort to learn that presumably she'd married and had a daughter. But there was no further information about her in the article, and Amy was sceptical about what might be gained from trying to make contact with her now. When I finally picked myself up off the floor, I told her I had no choice in the matter. I'd been waiting for this moment for sixty-five years!

'In the end, she agreed to help me track down Francine's daughter. She was able to locate her website quite easily, as it turned out. That's how we traced her to Edinburgh, where she's scheduled to give a talk to promote her debut novel tonight.'

'*That's* why you're going to Edinburgh? To meet Francine's daughter?' Ariel cried. Her face was all wide eyes and wonder, easily the most animated Henry had seen it.

'Yes, well, assuming the train isn't taken hostage by bank robbers, or abducted by aliens, neither of which possibility would surprise me the rate *we're* going,' he replied.

He was starting to feel slightly flushed himself. He wondered if he were simply feeding off the enthusiasm of his two youthful companions. Either that, or he was developing a fever – as far as he could tell, the symptoms were the same.

'Does she know you're going?' Ariel asked, a little more cautiously. 'It's just... who will you tell her you are?'

Henry shook his head. 'She's not expecting me, no. I thought it would be best to approach her in person at the end of her talk. As for who I am, I'll tell her the truth. I'll introduce myself as an old friend of her mother's and then make my enquiries about Francine. After all this time, I'm really in no position to have any expectations beyond that.'

He gave a deep exhalation. 'Anyway, thank you! Thank you both for the *esprit de corps*!'

Travis looked confused. 'Es-pree... ?'

'It means *camaraderie*,' Henry clarified with a smile. 'An old-fashioned notion, perhaps, but there you are.'

Travis reached his arm across the aisle and shook Henry's hand. 'You're one cool guy, Henry. I think what you're doing is awesome. I wish you the very best, I really do.'

Henry blinked. 'I'm not sure about cool or awesome. Love is love, Travis. That's all there is to it.'

The world sped up around them and the sea crept once more into view. It teased from afar until the train swerved to meet it, and all that separated the two was a narrow hill dotted with grazing cows.

They crossed over a river via a long, stone bridge and pulled at last into Berwick-upon-Tweed. Henry watched a Highland Terrier and its owner alight from their carriage. His thoughts turned immediately to Banjo... With any luck, he was behaving himself at the Papadopouloses' house next door, and staying well clear of their chickens.

On the final leg to Edinburgh Waverley, Henry noted a solitary fishing vessel bobbing on the horizon. A cliff wearing a crown of yellow gorse rose up. Tapered off. Fell away. More cliffs appeared; the hollowed out remains of an ancient dwelling; a flock of sheep, their woolly rumps daubed with red circular markings like miniature crop circle tattoos. And then, as quietly as it had appeared, the sea departed for the final time and the train curved inwards on the homeward stretch to the Scottish capital.

Henry checked his watch. *Almost four o'clock*. The book talk was at seven-thirty. It had been a long, and in many ways, tumultuous day, but there was only one word to describe how he was feeling now.

Ready.

Part Three
SECRETS

20

Decaf Americano

Frank

Frank Carmichael was sitting alone, his back to the wall, in an airy café on the Mound. His right hand was busy scooping up two poached eggs, American-style, with a fork. His left lay relaxed and inert on the glass covered table top.

Captured between glass and wood, preserved like century-old flowers, were a collection of postcards of famous dancers and film stars, past and present: Nureyev and Brando, smouldering in peaked biker caps; Meryl Streep, haunted and haunting as *The French Lieutenant's Woman*; a fresh-faced, pixie-jawed DiCaprio. Frank ran his eyes over the glittering assembly of expertly lit faces, silently namechecking them as he ate. He prided himself on knowing every single one, including the younger generation, whose youthful eyes blazed bright with

253

longing, with bare-naked ambition. Their secret: an unwavering belief that the world was theirs for the asking. And boy, were they fearless about reaching out and asking for it!

He'd been like that himself, once. And he'd had the talent to back it up, too. Never in all his years on the celebrity circuit had he considered being a lookalike a second-rate profession; it took just as much discipline, technical know-how and stamina as it did to be the real thing. Sadly, a few bad apples would occasionally tarnish the legitimacy of the job, devaluing what he'd toiled for decades to perfect. To do it well took dedication and meticulous attention to detail, and Frank had been nothing if not painstakingly committed to getting it right.

The modest hotel in Morningside where he'd checked in earlier that morning didn't have much in the way of a communal area – not one you'd actually want to pass any amount of time in, anyway – so he'd spent most of the day ambling through the Old Town, across to the Georgian squares of the New Town, eventually continuing through Broughton and Canonmills, all the way to the botanical gardens. From there he'd retraced his steps to his present location high on a hill, so he could take it all in: the entire urban sweep of it. He'd covered quite some ground, but walking had always been his favourite means of staying in shape...

City walking, Travis! That's the best way to get a workout when you're on the road! It's no different from a metal ball whizzing around a pinball machine: all you gotta do is plough straight ahead, double back if you need to, and not get yourself in a twist if you take the occasional wrong turn.

Frank narrowed his eyes and tried to remember the last time he'd performed in Edinburgh. If he stuck to the same well-trodden paths it was as though he'd been here just yesterday. He loved that about returning to places he'd visited before: the sense of belonging, of temporary citizenship that comes from knowing the location of the nearest drugstore; where to grab a coffee and a decent bite to eat late at night.

Back in the day, the threat of harassment had been one of the downsides of getting out late after a gig. One time, a group of youths had trailed him, eventually cornering him in the supermarket car park of a sad-ass town he'd long since tried to forget. Most people were supportive of his appearance; others found it cool to be cruel, their jibes hackneyed, uttered – almost without exception – for show. He still couldn't say to this day what might have happened if an off-duty police officer hadn't driven by on his way home and told them to move it along.

Frank finished his eggs, pushed his plate to one side and cast an appreciative eye over the historic city unspooling before him. He wondered whether he might move up here, far away from London's constantly escalating cost of living, street crime and lung-choking traffic pollution, or whether such a definitive move would mean he'd be missing out on too many work opportunities down south.

One thing he knew for certain: Long Island was *history*. It wasn't that he didn't have happy memories of his years spent on the East Coast when he and his sister, Clare, were kids. It was the idea of retreating, moving backwards, *regressing* – even if just in a purely geographical sense – that bothered him. Of course, if he could get a regular performance slot – a *residency*! – like Elvis had had at the Las Vegas Hilton, now *that* would be a different story altogether!

Frank rubbed his thumb along the curve of his chin and chuckled. He may have struggled to redefine himself over the better part of the last ten years, but he wasn't so far gone that he couldn't see the absurdity in such a ludicrously optimistic suggestion as *that*.

'Waitress? When you have a minute, please?'

He raised his hand and beckoned to the young woman (Polish? Hungarian?) who was taking orders with consummate efficiency around the room.

She swung her *L'Oréaled* ponytail over her shoulder and threw him an enquiring glance.

'Any chance I could get another coffee?' Frank said with a friendly shake of his cup.

'Sure thing. Coming right over.'

She'd been cute with him when he first took his seat and asked him straight out if he was famous. Frank beamed, felt the erstwhile glow of recognition spreading over his cheeks, and said no, he was a singer, but no one a youngster like herself was likely to have heard of.

That hadn't happened in quite some time, actually.

He dropped his hand to his stomach and adjusted the waistband of his jeans. Back at the hotel he'd left his suit for the following evening's performance hanging on the wardrobe door, so he'd remember to press it.

Frank sighed. *What a waste.*

Now that he was performing *'as himself'*, his stage clothes were so bland, so depressingly conventional compared to the show-stopping outfits he'd worn when he was at the height of his success...

Occasionally, waiting backstage in a poky, makeshift dressing room littered with cigarette butts and empty convenience food packaging, he'd stand in front of the mirror, close his eyes and remember, just for a second, how it had felt to be dressed as him, *The King*:

First, the malleable veneer of the jumpsuit which yielded to the touch, facilitating every gyration, every impromptu lunge. The lookalikes' jumpsuits were made of polyester gabardine because it was softer. Lighter. Cheaper in every respect. After ten minutes on stage the fabric would start to heat up and steam against his skin like an *o-shibori* hand towel. But not once had he considered his outfit to be mediocre; it always felt silky smooth beneath his fingers. And while most people thought the jumpsuits were white, they weren't; they were *ivory*. Elvis's were made of impeccably woven Italian wool flown in from Milan. They'd mix it with a gabardine blend so there'd be some give, so they'd hug the topography of his body like a finely tailored Savile Row suit, robust enough to accommodate entire solar systems of glittering rhinestones. The Napoleonic collar (stiffened with costume boning!) used to brush against Frank's neck and chin, tickling the lobes of his ears, framing his face perfectly; that's why Elvis himself had liked them so much.

Finally, the belt. Metal or macramé, it didn't make much difference; at the end of the day, Frank had loved them all...

'Hello, Frank. Sorry I'm late. I've had a bit of business to deal with.'

Frank snapped his attention back into the room. His agent, Ray Maloney, was lowering himself into the chair on the opposite side of the table.

'Hi Ray. Nice of you to show up! How ya doing?'

Ray responded with a noncommittal grunt and turned his attention to the drinks menu. He was conspicuously tanned despite the season, his rugged features glistening with sweat and unnaturally set, like those of a man steeling himself for a discussion he'd rather not be having.

'If I didn't know you so well, Ray-boy, I'd think I was on the verge of being stood up,' Frank said with a grin. 'I swear I'm never as over-caffeinated as I am when I'm waiting for you to show up to one of our meetings.'

A motorbike zoomed past the café window travelling much too quickly around the bend in his opinion, but Ray didn't seem to notice. Instead, he began to bounce his knee up and down so vigorously under the table, Frank could feel the vibration in his coffee cup.

'Hey, buddy? Did you change your coffee habit since I last saw you? In all the years I've known you, it's been decaf all the way. Did someone slip you the hard stuff while you weren't looking?'

'I'm fine, Frank,' Ray replied. He avoided Frank's gaze and motioned politely to the waitress.

'Yes, sir,' she said, materialising in an instant at his side. 'What can I get you?'

'I'd like a decaf Americano – large – with hot milk on the side, please. Frank, anything else for you?'

Frank gestured to his recently delivered third cappuccino.

'Gee, I don't know, Ray. How 'bout a chamomile tea?' He threw the waitress a good-natured smile. 'Just kidding. I'm good, thanks.'

He waited for her to leave, then crossed his forearms and planted them firmly on the table. 'So, do you think it might be easier if you just told me what's weighing so heavily on your mind?'

Ray puffed out his cheeks. 'Sorry, Frank. Is it that obvious?'

'Come on, give me some credit! We go back thirty years, you and I. I know every single expression in your repertoire, and this one's priceless! You look like you're about to face your execution.'

Ray pressed his lips so tightly together, Frank was convinced he must be trying to curb a mounting wave of acid reflux. 'You're right,' he said at last. 'You know me too well. There *is* something I need to tell you.'

Frank's stomach dropped. *Crap. This didn't sound good.*

He lowered his hands to his knees and focused on the air moving in and out of his nostrils. He knew the drill well enough, by now. He had to relax (and *fast!*), otherwise his body might just seize up altogether...

It was always the way. Oftentimes – when he wanted something really, really badly – the intensity of his desire was so great, it was as though his very being closed in on itself until no eyelet, no opening of any kind remained for whatever it was he was yearning for to come in. He'd force himself to stay focused on his goal, while simultaneously already tasting his defeat. Occasionally, the pain became so unbearable, he figured it was easier to just not want anything at all...

'On second thoughts,' he said, 'if it's bad news then maybe it's best if you don't tell me right now. Tomorrow night is kind of a big deal for me, you know? I just need to know what time I can get in to the venue for a soundcheck. It's my first gig since... well, you know better than anyone how long it's been... and I want it all to be perfect. I always do, you know that. 'Course, if I've jumped the gun or –' Frank's face fell, his train of thought suddenly derailed by a brand-new prospect entirely – 'Holy Mother of God, Ray, you're not *sick* or anything, are you?'

'Frank –'

'I'm serious! You've been a terrific agent and an even better friend. Just be honest with me on this one, would ya?'

'Jesus, Frank!'

'What? What is it? What's the matter?'

'Listen to me! The show's been cancelled, okay?'

'*Cancelled?*' Frank slumped against his chair like a broken puppet. He felt as though he'd just taken a bullet. 'What are you talking about? It's tomorrow night! How can they cancel a performance today when they've already been promoting it for weeks?'

Ray rubbed his hand over his forehead. In a low voice he said, 'Look, it's not exactly the *show* they've cancelled, it's *you*. They've got someone else in – it was all very last-minute – the guy's a friend of the owner's, some kind of local hot-shot. It was obviously a favour. I've been on the phone with them all morning, but there was nothing I could do to change their minds. I'm sorry.'

Frank stared at Ray in disbelief. 'You're *sorry*? Are you

yanking my chain? This is my *life*, Ray! This is what I do! This is *all* I've ever known how to do! What goddamn right do they have to do this to me with only twenty-four hours' notice? What right, Ray? You tell me that!'

Ray glanced apologetically around the room. Frank's voice had soared, his tone becoming increasingly more strident with each successive word.

'Frank, just listen to me for a second. They're going to pay you fifty per cent minimum of what they would have paid if the gig had gone ahead. I'm trying to argue for full recompense, that's why I was late getting here today. Contractually, I should be able to get them up to seventy-five, but I'm shooting for the full hundred. They don't want any trouble. I have a lot of other artists on my books. They're going to want to keep me sweet.'

'Keep *you* sweet? What about me? Don't I count for anything?'

Frank reined in his voice and spoke through gritted teeth. An acute awareness of how he appeared in public had long since been ingrained in him over the years. No one respects a scene-maker. The last thing he wanted was for anyone to think he lacked class.

'Of course you count for something, Frank! I told you, it's nothing personal. He just had his hands tied with this other act. Seems like a promise was made somewhere along the line that he can't go back on, yadda, yadda, yadda. What can I say? They fucked up. It's as simple as that.'

Frank felt his life force begin to wane as the full impact of Ray's words gradually hit home. This wasn't just any old show; this was his way of maintaining his tenuous foothold on the overcrowded (and in his opinion, too easily derided) lounge circuit, all the while keeping his dignity intact in the process.

'I don't understand. I travelled all the way up here like some numbskull. For Chrissakes, I have my nephew arriving tomorrow specifically to see me sing! I can't let him down, Ray. Please, you gotta get them to change their minds. Do whatever you have to, just this once. Do it for Travis. I'm begging you, Ray. Please.'

Fresh pinpricks of sweat had begun to surface on the dome of Ray's brow. He flicked the clasp of his Rolex open and shut – his go-to move whenever he was trying to gain time, or in this instance, his composure.

'Your nephew'll understand, Frank. Travis is a musician. He'll understand better than anyone how this kind of thing can happen. It's disappointing, I agree, but do yourself a favour: take the money and let this one go.'

Frank stared mournfully into the grainy depths of his coffee cup, a deep V forming between his eyes. 'Like I said, I don't want to let him down. I want Travis to see that his Uncle Frank is still good for something on his own terms. It's not about the money. It's just so *humiliating*, don't you see? I may not be at the top of my game anymore, but I still have a voice, Ray. Goddammit, I have my own voice.'

Later that evening, as he was downing his second vodka and tonic in the crowded bar of Ray's fancy hotel, a text message pinged through on his phone: Hey uncle F just wanted to say how psyched I am about the show tomorrow. See u when I get in! T.

Frank stared at the letters, at the innocent, well-meaning intent hovering behind the words. A ripple of laughter filtered over from a group of clean-cut businessmen standing to his left. Someone was celebrating a deal, toasting some corporate roasting or other. Maybe just admiring a pretty girl.

He felt his shoulders crunch beneath his shirt. A dull ache was building behind his eyes, and there was a palpable weightiness to his skin.

Slowly, he tapped out a response. Succinct. Just a nip of denial: Sounds great, kiddo! I'm psyched about it too. F.

He dropped his phone back into his pocket and took a long, restorative gulp of the transparent liquid in his glass. Raising his forefinger into the air, he twirled it around, signalling to the barman to bring him another. In his hand, the last of the ice cubes clinked and swirled, drawing him in, keeping him company until they dissolved, inevitably, from view; gone, but not forgotten.

21

Cloudburst on a Midnight Shore

EDINBURGH, DECEMBER 6: *ARRIVAL*

Henry

Henry hung his suit jacket on the back of the chair next to the desk, slipped off his black Derby shoes and laid his body neatly on the bed. Soon, when his breathing regulated again, he would put them back on, smooth down his hair in the bathroom mirror and venture downstairs.

Three hundred and fifty miles, give or take, separated Kentish Town and the Old Town hotel where he found himself now. And somewhere along the way, his appetite had mysteriously frittered away. Instinct dictated that he should eat something, but he couldn't stomach the idea of anything more elaborate than a warm drink and a toasted teacake. He hadn't even been tempted to join the lively group of fellow guests enjoying high tea in the lounge when he'd arrived. All he'd wanted was the lift, and beyond it, the quiet oasis of his room.

'Would you like me to see you to your hotel?' Ariel asked, as they climbed down onto the platform at Edinburgh Waverley. 'Just to make sure you settle in all right? It would be no trouble.'

Henry smiled, thanked her for her kindness, and declined, graciously. She was young. She didn't need the responsibility of a lovelorn old man hanging like an albatross around her neck. *No*, he told himself, *she's been considerate enough already. The important thing is that I'm here. I've arrived! I'm unequiv- ocally, exactly where I'm meant to be.*

'Okay, well I'll call you tomorrow at your hotel,' she said. 'To see how you got on. I'll be thinking of you in the meantime.'

'Thank you,' he replied. 'And I'll be thinking of you. I suspect one way or another we'll both have a story to tell when next we speak.'

Ariel leaned in towards him and gave him a quick peck on the cheek. 'For luck, Aircraftman Applebee,' she said, then she spun round on her heel and she and her wheelie bag were gone, the fringes of her multicoloured scarf trailing behind her as she disappeared up the crowded station walkway.

After a token cucumber sandwich and a cup of loose leaf tea in the lounge, Henry passed by the concierge and asked if he could order him a cab for seven o'clock. Now that he was here – *now that it was all finally happening!* – it felt nothing short of surreal to think that he was just one cab ride away from an encounter which could potentially reshape his life.

'Don't go blowing it out of proportion,' he cautioned himself. 'You'll give yourself a heart attack! Keep a sense of perspective. And breathe.'

Back in his room, Henry opened his suitcase on the bed. He removed Francine's butterfly hair clip from the elasticated pocket running down the side and tucked it into his inside jacket pocket. He left the remainder of his precious store of items in the case for now. Whatever relevance – if any – they might have for the days ahead, a pronounced, inner urging told him to keep the silver hair clip close at hand.

Henry glanced around the room to check there was nothing he'd left behind. The digital alarm clock by the bed was flashing '12:00' over and over, the numbers an urgent, fire engine red. He lowered himself onto the edge of the bed and closed his eyes. The prospect of meeting Francine's very own flesh and blood suddenly struck him as an event of unquantifiable significance.

He pulled the *Evening Standard* article from the bottom of his suitcase and stared at her daughter's face.

The possibility – no matter how remote – that Francine herself might be there to watch her speak, was too staggering a notion, too cherished a dream for him to even entertain.

At a quarter past seven, Henry's taxi dropped him on a brightly lit stretch of road in Stockbridge, the north-westerly neighbourhood where the talk was scheduled to take place. A line of people were already trailing along the pavement outside the bookshop, chatting and shuffling their feet back and forth to keep warm. With no obvious alternate means of gaining entry, Henry made his way towards them and joined the back of the queue.

Overhead, the sky was a brooding, moonless black. Henry lowered his gaze and cast a critical eye over his appearance. Thankfully, his dove-grey suit had been salvageable, and he'd given his shoes another quick wipe with a damp flannel at the hotel. He scanned his eyes over his fellow attendees in their puffy winter jackets and jeans. He wondered whether he may have overshot the mark in terms of dress code, but the fact remained it was a peach of an outfit, and he wouldn't have had it any other way.

He straightened his tie and uttered a series of polite 'good evening's to the newcomers who joined the queue behind him. The line seemed to be moving quickly enough, but as he drew nearer to the entrance, Henry was startled to see a young woman with a clipboard and pen waiting in the open doorway.

'Hello,' she said, as each new person filed past. 'May I take your name please?'

As far as Henry could tell, only those whose names appeared on the young woman's list were being granted entry.

His heart froze.

Then, as the space in front of him cleared, Henry saw the notice hanging in the shop window:

TONIGHT!

An Evening with Local Author **E. M. Hope**

to discuss her debut novel *Cloudburst on a Midnight Shore*

Reading followed by Q&A commences at 7:30 p.m.

PLEASE NOTE: THIS EVENT IS NOW <u>SOLD OUT</u>

Henry stared at the words 'SOLD OUT' with the twin

emotions of horror and incredulity. The event was *ticketed*?

He turned to the young woman standing sentry in the doorway. When Amy had found details of the talk on the inter-whatsit, it had said nothing at all about needing to buy a ticket! Surely, he hadn't travelled all this way only to be turned away at the door?

'I'm very sorry, sir,' the young woman said, 'but as you can see, it's only a wee shop. And with the author being local, it's proven to be a very popular event. It's generally the case, I'm afraid.'

'But on my niece's computer it said nothing about needing to buy a ticket!' Henry protested. 'If it had, I would have purchased one!'

'That was obviously a very unfortunate error, sir, for which I can only apologise. Our author events have always been ticketed, as I say, because we only have wee premises. There are strict fire regulations limiting our capacity, and right now we're full to bursting.'

'What do you suggest I do?' Henry asked in a tone of deepening despair. Bells of panic were now ringing in his ears. He could feel the desperation taking hold of him, manifesting itself in a barely suppressed whine. 'I've travelled all the way from London for this! It's rather important to me, you see. For personal reasons.'

The young woman *aahed* sympathetically. 'Are you a friend of the author's?'

Henry cleared his throat. 'Well no. Not exactly. It's a little complicated...'

As their conversation continued, Henry became aware of

quiet mumblings of discontent issuing forth from the handful of people still huddled on the pavement behind him.

'I'm sorry, sir,' the young woman said, 'could I ask you to step aside for a moment, just so I can let the rest of the ticketholders inside? The talk is due to start shortly and I don't want to keep everyone else waiting.'

Henry took a reluctant step backwards and watched as one by one, the lucky recipients of what may as well have been Willy Wonka's Golden Tickets gave their names and made their way inside.

He moved around to the front of the shop and peered through the window. In deference to the season, the entire shop front had been strung with garlands of twinkling fairy lights. Henry had always been a sucker for Christmas lights, or illuminations of any kind, for that matter. Occasionally, at this time of year, he liked to sit in his living room with the lamps off and the curtains open so he could watch the coloured lights dancing and flickering in the windows of the houses up and down his road. During the two years Devlin had lived with him, they'd enjoyed the spectacle together, a bumper tin of Quality Street balanced on a footstool between them. Henry still kept the Toffee Pennies to one side, partly because they got stuck in his dentures something awful, but more importantly because they'd been Devlin's favourite sweets.

He shuffled an inch closer to the window. Inside the shop a shifting sea of people were moving to take their seats. And just beyond them, hovering at the back of the room, was a woman he recognised at once as Francine's daughter.

Henry raised his hand and pressed it against the glass. She

looked just like her photograph in the newspaper, only perhaps a little less self-assured in the flesh. It was *beyond* maddening... To be stuck outside on the pavement, no more than a few metres away from her!

He wondered whether it would cause a terrible kerfuffle if he simply launched himself through the door like an uninvited wedding guest, but decided not to risk it – getting arrested would hardly be conducive to the matter at hand.

Henry kept his eyes pinned firmly to the scene before him, as though at any moment a velvet curtain might descend and sweep it all away. Finally, after what seemed like an eternity, the young woman with the clipboard called him over.

'Sir, there have been no cancellations at all, I'm afraid. I can't let you in just now, but if you'd be willing to come back in an hour, you'd be more than welcome to come in for the signing. I'm sure you'd like to get a copy of Ms Hope's novel, signed with a personal dedication?'

Henry gave a weak nod.

'Lovely! That way you can at least get to meet her in person. In the meantime, there's a nice wee pub on the corner. Perhaps you could wait in there out of the cold?'

The girl flashed him a toothy smile and switched the '*Open*' sign on the door to '*Closed*'. As Henry turned to leave, the door swung to behind him, sending an ignominious backdraft of icy cold air whooshing down his neck. With his heart yo-yoing all the way from his chest to the tips of his freshly polished shoes, Henry had no option but to walk away.

* * *

He found a seat near a frosted glass window, a pale gold Glenmorangie in his hand, a packet of cashews lying open, but as yet untouched, on the table. Scotch whisky wasn't his usual tipple, but at this point he was past caring. The barman (who'd greeted him rather unexpectedly with 'Evening, soldier') asked him what he liked. When Henry replied, 'Peaches,' the barman tapped his finger knowingly on the side of his nose and recommended a faintly floral, ten-year-old single malt 'to chase away the chill'.

Henry sipped his whisky and surveyed his temporary refuge. The place was homely, at least; all oak wood and exposed beams and good, strong lighting so you didn't have to peer at your drink through a haze. The clientele were largely on the older side, but Henry still felt positively ancient by comparison.

The last time he'd found himself in a pub he'd been with Devlin, the night of Devlin's eighty-third birthday. As usual, wherever Devlin was concerned, the night had not passed without incident. Thirty minutes in, his denture cream came loose, sending his top set of teeth slithering from his mouth and landing with a loud *splosh!* in his pint of Guinness. They'd suffered similar fates numerous times at home, culminating in one catastrophic episode where they'd dropped like a cheap fairground ornament onto the bathroom tiles and promptly cracked in two. Devlin picked them up, dusted them off and stuck them back together with superglue.

His birthday, however, was the first time he'd lost his teeth in public. Henry and Devlin laughed so hard, a pair of Dutch honeymooners came over and asked if they could join them for a *shelfie*. They raised their glasses to the camera and howled with laughter, while Devlin – holding his dentures aloft – yelled, 'Alas, poor Yorick! I knew the toothless bugger well!'

Henry smiled to himself. That was the same night he and Devlin had first started calling themselves *The Monochrome Men*. They'd coined the name off-the-cuff, intending it as a tongue-in-cheek commentary on the unsung, superhero status of senior citizen tailoring. Green, brown or beige, the regulation uniform of the elderly (inevitably: dull, earthy shades of muted monochrome) contained a potent camouflage all its own. People scanned over them all the time with scarcely a second glance. They didn't stop to read the small print, rewarding though it might be, and Dutch honeymooners aside, very few took the time to say hello.

Henry gazed around the room and noted that there were only a handful of couples in the pub tonight. The rest were groups of friends, or solitary drinkers like the man sitting on a stool directly across from him, his back rounded, his elbows weighing heavily on the bar. The man wore the hardy self-possession of late middle-age; Henry put him in his late-fifties or early-sixties. He was staring intently into the bottom of his glass, his gaze shifting every so often from his drink to his mobile phone lying alongside it.

Ah, Henry surmised, *another lost soul with an appointment he doesn't want to miss!*

At a quarter to eight the man finished his drink, pulled on his overcoat and strode towards the door. He gave Henry a courteous nod as he passed, and Henry – flattered to have been acknowledged at all – nodded back. Something about the man's striking physiognomy struck him as vaguely familiar. He was just debating whether he'd seen him on the television when the man suddenly stopped, turned around, and doubled back towards him.

'Excuse me,' he said in a broad American accent, 'would you happen to know the quickest way on foot to George Street?'

'Oh,' Henry replied, 'I'm afraid I'm only visiting. Like you, by the sounds of it. I came here by taxi, so any directions I might give you would be highly suspect at best. Rather like the blind leading the blind.'

The man slid his hands into the pockets of his overcoat and smiled. 'I've never really been convinced by that saying, have you? I mean, blind or not, there's safety in numbers. Just having someone else to lean on makes all the difference, if you ask me.'

'You're right!' Henry cried. 'I'd never thought of it like that! In fact, that would make quite a good Mantra of the Day!'

'Sorry?'

Henry held up his glass. 'Here's to having someone to lean on. Though alas, I'm afraid I still couldn't direct you to George Street...'

The man flashed him another amiable smile. He pulled a pair of dark glasses from his pocket and rather enigmatically (and unnecessarily, Henry thought) slipped them onto his face. 'You take care and have a good night, now.'

'And the same to you,' he replied.

* * *

When the time finally arrived for Henry to return to the bookshop, he found several audience members already spilling out onto the pavement. He bowed his head and inched past them through the now open doorway.

Francine's daughter was at the back of the shop, sitting off to one side on the arm of a dark plum leather sofa. Henry drew to a stop a short distance away and waited while she signed copies of her book and chatted to an enthusiastic group of readers. He scanned the assemblage of faces drifting past him, but the one he was most anxious to locate was nowhere to be seen.

Settling himself on a folding chair, Henry took the opportunity to study the only person present who now mattered to him. Like her mother, Francine's daughter had light brown hair which she wore tied back from her face in a low ponytail. There was a familiar radiance to her eyes, but her mouth was wider, perhaps a little harder set. And she was taller than Francine, as far as Henry could remember. But then how could he be sure of anything any more? He'd clung so doggedly to his fading image of Francine that at this point, it was in danger of morphing into the most perfect picture of a human being that had ever existed.

Henry waited until finally, after a nod from the young woman with the clipboard, Francine's daughter rose from the sofa and walked towards him.

'Hello,' she said, holding out her hand, 'I'm Eve Marie Hope. Were you waiting to speak with me?'

Henry clambered to his feet. 'I was, yes! I'm Henry Applebee. From Kentish Town. It's a pleasure to meet you.'

He took Eve Marie's hand in his own and searched her face

for the merest hint of recognition, but there was nothing. Not even a flicker.

He took a deep breath and continued: 'I'm an old friend of your mother's. She was Francine Keeley when we met, but that was a very long time ago now. 1948, if you can believe it.'

A humungous pressure lifted from Henry's chest as he uttered Francine's name. The sensation was so pronounced, he wondered for the second time that day if he were going to swoon. He loosened his grip on Eve Marie's hand and dropped his right hand to meet his left on the handle of his walking stick. Two seconds later, he took a faltering step backwards and promptly sat down.

Eve Marie pulled up a chair alongside him. 'It's good to meet you, Henry. 1948, you say? My mother must have been so young! Would you mind if I asked where you met her?'

'Not at all. I'd just returned to England after serving in the Far East and was a couple of days away from demob. Your mother and I met in Blackpool, at the Tower Ballroom. In fact –' he fumbled for the square of tissue paper in his jacket pocket – 'she was wearing this in her hair at the time.'

'Oh my goodness!' Eve Marie stared at the butterfly clip in Henry's palm. After a moment's hesitation, she reached out her hand to touch it, but at the final instant pulled away.

Henry wondered if he'd inadvertently said or done something to unsettle her. He glanced over her shoulder and saw that a bearded man (the only other person present wearing an actual suit and tie!) was making his way over to join them.

'Hello, darling.' The man placed his hand on Eve Marie's shoulder and gave Henry a quizzical stare. 'Is everything okay?'

Eve Marie swivelled round in her seat. 'Callum! Yes, everything's fine. It's just been an emotional evening, that's all.' She turned back to Henry and smiled. 'Henry, this is my husband, Callum. Callum, this is Henry Applebee. Henry is an old friend of my mother's.'

'Oh, that's great!' He held out his hand. 'It's very good of you to come, Henry.'

Henry gave Callum's hand a firm shake. In the brief pause that followed, he sensed a vague air of awkwardness rising up between them. He prayed Callum's arrival didn't mean that his time with Eve Marie would be over before it had barely begun. There was still so much to say, but the situation called for diplomacy; a modicum of delicacy, at least...

'Evie, we'll need to get going pretty soon I'm afraid,' Callum said. 'The others are already at the bar having a drink.'

'The others?'

Callum's face took on a decidedly sheepish grin. 'I wasn't supposed to tell you, but I'm taking you to a surprise dinner for having completed your first book talk. You did such a great job, hon. I'm proud of you.'

He bent down and kissed Eve Marie tenderly on the lips.

Eve Marie threw Henry a quick, apologetic glance. 'Oh, that's so nice of them. I'll be right with you, Cal. Just give me a moment with Henry, would you? I'll meet you outside in a sec.'

Callum bade Henry goodbye and joined the last of the audience members drifting towards the exit. Henry returned Francine's hair clip to his jacket pocket. A thick knot of anxiety was already forming in his throat at the realisation that his time with Eve Marie was drawing to such an unforeseen and premature close.

'Henry, I'm sorry to have to abandon you like this.' She pushed back her chair and stood up. 'It's something of a big night for me, and I don't want to be rude and let my friends down – they've had to put up with so much from me over the years. Perhaps we could meet again?'

'Absolutely,' Henry replied, 'I'd like that very much! I live in London, but I'm staying at a hotel in the Old Town for a few days. To tell you the truth –' he gave a small, self-conscious cough – 'I travelled up this morning with the express purpose of seeing you.'

Eve Marie raised her eyebrows. 'You did? Well in that case, why don't I come and pick you up at your hotel in the morning? You can come back to the house and we can have a cup of tea and a chat without being disturbed. Would that be convenient?'

Henry gripped the handle of his walking stick and rose to join her. Miraculously, he'd had the foresight to pick up one of the hotel's business cards on his way out the door, just in case – God forbid! – his mind gave way and he forgot where he was staying. He pulled the card from his coat pocket and pressed it into Eve Marie's palm.

'That would be wonderful! If you're sure it's not too much trouble, here's where you'll find me.'

'No trouble at all, Henry. I'll be with you by nine-thirty. Will that suit?'

Henry beamed. 'To a T.'

* * *

The taxi that ferried Henry back to his hotel dropped him under a shaft of light shining down from a brass lamp in the outer porch. He lingered a moment on the pavement and breathed in the newly exhilarating night air.

To his left, a chorus of voices filtered out from the hotel bar. To his right, the lounge was almost deserted apart from a middle-aged couple, dressed up to the nines, waiting, he assumed, for someone to join them before heading out. Henry raised his stick and greeted them with a friendly salute.

He was already halfway up the short flight of steps to the front door when he was struck by an overwhelming impulse to turn round.

Henry stopped, glanced instinctively behind him.

Leaning against a lamp post on the opposite side of the road, his arms crossed in front of his chest, a heartrending smile upon his face, was Devlin. A hazy, semi-transparent version of Devlin, perhaps – one that Henry knew no one else could see – but it was Devlin none the less, young and handsome and vital, just the way he liked to remember him.

A feeling of intense lightness rippled through Henry's body. Its touch blanketed him from head to toe, cushioning his heart, his mind, his ailing bones. At first, the origin of the sensation eluded him, but then Henry recognised it for what it was: a dizzying, life-affirming breath of pure, unconditional love.

Devlin made no attempt to speak or move; he simply stood, grinning affectionately, his irrepressible smile never wavering for an instant. Henry found himself grinning back, and with an unexpected diffidence, he acknowledged Devlin's presence with a nod.

A series of raps on one of the hotel's upper windows caused Henry to turn his head. A small child was tapping her fingers insistently against the glass. Henry opened his mouth, saw her wave. He was on the verge of waving back when her mother swept up behind her, and laughing, carried her away.

When Henry turned once more towards the lamp post, Devlin was nowhere to be seen. Just a single metal bottle top, tossed playfully by the breeze, traversed the length of the pavement, rising and falling at intervals, weightless, unbounded; graceful as a pebble skimming the surface of a mountain lake.

Henry lowered his head.

Deep inside his chest, his heart quivered.

Slowly, he continued up the steps of his hotel. There was no reason in the world, he realised later, why Devlin's appearance should have surprised him. He knew his brother well enough to understand that it was just his way of showing he was with him.

No matter what the following day might bring, Devlin wanted Henry to know that he was not alone.

22

Brand-new World

EDINBURGH, DECEMBER 6: *ARRIVAL*

Ariel

It was the all-encompassing aura of mystery that struck her first, the very air marinated in history and dark deeds and the spilt blood of ancient clans. According to one section of Travis's guidebook (which he'd pointed out with great enthusiasm during the final push into Edinburgh Waverley) there were entire *streets* buried underground like sewers.

Ariel stared in wonder at the epic magnitude of her surroundings. On all sides a warren of eerie wynds and tortuous closes funnelled off into the darkness, and – she was sure of it – the perverse brilliance of Miss Jean Brodie strode among the shadows like a ghost. Now that she was here, she was determined to soak it all in: the rawness; the bleakness; the bone-numbing cold. Edinburgh rose like the

ends of the earth, the tartan-hooded pinnacle of the world.
You couldn't see Wales, or even England for that matter,
for dust.

She braced herself for adventure and felt instantly at home.

Within an hour of her arrival, she'd bought a foldout map
of the city centre and was out wandering the streets. With the
wind gnawing at her cheeks, she clambered over the well-
trodden cobbles of the Royal Mile until she reached the
Esplanade, splayed out like an asphalt carpet at the base of
Edinburgh Castle. Rising skyward out of the treacly darkness,
the castle stopped her dead in her tracks, causing her to utter
a long, spontaneous '*Wow*' of appreciation.

She glanced down at her map and spun a full three hundred
and sixty degrees on her heels. To the north, the multicoloured
lights of the Winter Wonderland fairground in East Princes
Street Gardens; to the east, the curvature of the Royal Mile
along which she'd just passed; to the south, the inky rooftops
of the Edinburgh suburbs; and finally, the floodlit castle itself,
anchored at the summit, fiercely surveying all.

Ariel stood lost in the grandeur of Castlehill and tried to
remember if Estelle had ever talked about coming to Scotland
herself, but there had been no mention of it as far as she
could recall. She flipped open her canvas bag and pulled out
her phone. Right on cue, a brand-new message from
Tumbleweed popped into view.

'Hi, Tee.' She smiled and opened the message up. Staring
back at her was a black and white photograph of an old-
fashioned chimney sweep, his clothes plain and threadbare,
his iconic circular brush propped against his shoulder like a

spindly umbrella. Her smile gave way to a puzzled frown. *What was Tumbleweed trying to tell her this time?*

She chewed the side of her lip and scoured the photograph for clues. The man's face was soot-splattered, resigned, but behind the sheen of his button-black eyes she thought she detected a faint, underlying ray of optimism. *William Blake*, she thought suddenly. *Hadn't they studied* The Chimney Sweeper *poem at school?*

Ariel sighed. All she could remember was something about a boy who'd dreamed of coffins and angels, and his belief, on waking, that everything would be all right. She lingered a while longer over the image, then closed the message down. For now, it would have to remain one more Highland mystery to add to the pile.

She gazed out over the Edinburgh rooftops and breathed in the crisp December air. *I'll come and see you,* she'd written in her brief email exchange with Eve Marie. *I'll stay somewhere central and come by your house on December 7, like you asked. I'll be with you around midday, if that's okay?*

She had made no mention of the package she would be bringing from Estelle.

'Too bloody right!' Tumbleweed hollered down the phone when she told him. 'Why should *she* be the one with all the information? At least this way you'll have a secret of your own. Un*less*,' he said slowly, 'she already *knows* Estelle had something she wanted you to give her?'

'Fuck me,' he added after a beat. 'This thing gets weirder by the minute.'

Ariel held up her phone and took a landscape photograph

of the castle. Despite the murkiness of the conditions, she managed to capture an exceptionally kick-ass shot.

'*Nice*,' she muttered under her breath. She wondered if Tumbleweed would interpret it as closed off, overly guarded. *People can make mistakes,* Henry had told her earlier that afternoon. *Someone could get hurt... it would be a terrible shame for something to be misinterpreted...* The fingers of her right hand hovered mid-air. Taken at face value, wasn't it just proof that she'd safely reached her destination?

She touched her index finger to the screen and tapped Send.

At the north parapet wall, she stared into the distance towards what her map told her were the far-off waters of the Firth of Forth. As she followed the horizon eastwards to Leith, her phone trilled loudly in her hand.

'Hello?' she answered with a start.

'Call it a giant fuck-up,' said a voice she didn't immediately recognise, 'because that's what it is. Uncle Frank got dropped from his gig, only he didn't tell me until I arrived. Meanwhile, his agent had to leave town to put out a fire somewhere else, so I've been walking around for a couple hours trying to come up with a Plan B. D'you have a pen? We're going to a new place now. It's in the New Town, just behind George Street. Table in the name of Farlan. Booked for 8.15.'

Ariel arrived early to discover that Travis had chosen a cosily lit restaurant with an exposed-brick interior laid out over two floors. A waiter greeted her just inside the doorway and ushered her down a spiral staircase from the smaller dining space at ground level, to an unexpectedly large and labyrinthine area underground.

She followed him through a stone arch to a table next to an old, decorative fireplace. A candle, wedged into the neck of an empty wine bottle, flickered moodily in the centre of the table. She chose a seat facing the staircase and sat down.

Behind her was a stage set up with percussion, keyboard, and various other musical paraphernalia, though there was no sign of any actual musicians. Her eyes rested momentarily on the drum kit. A few years earlier, Isaac had built his own homemade version using a collection of sweet and biscuit tins and a pair of chopsticks from the takeaway down the road. The noise was horrendous, but he soon gave it up when Linus agreed to sign him up for surf lessons instead.

'Hey!' a voice rang out from the stairway. 'You found it all right, then?'

Ariel turned to see Travis making his way down the spiral staircase. She felt a fluttering in her stomach, which surprised her, and which she decided must just be nervousness at the prospect of seeing her wing man, Frank, again after so many years.

Immediately behind him, a slightly less sprightly pair of legs dropped into view. She stood up, exchanged smiles with Travis, and peered past his shoulders. Frank, dressed in a navy blue suit, overcoat and a pair of dark glasses, emerged with a *film noir* gravitas from the shadows.

'Frank!' She stepped forwards to meet him and gave him a warm hug hello. He'd brought the cold inside with him, she could feel it against her cheek, buried like a stowaway deep in the soft, woollen fibres of his coat.

'Ariel!' Frank slipped off his glasses and held her out at arm's length. 'Look at you! All grown up! I have to admit I may not have known it was you if Travis hadn't told me you were going to be here. I never forget a face, but you had your hair in pigtails the last time I saw you. Now you're what, eighteen?'

A faint roll of alcohol drifted from his mouth as he spoke.

Ariel nodded. 'I wasn't sure you'd even remember me after all this time.'

'Of course I do! Those few weeks Cyn and I spent in Oystermouth were a blast!'

He took off his coat and sat down at the table. Travis did likewise before excusing himself to go upstairs and make a call.

'Order for me, would you, Uncle Frank? You know I'll eat just about anything aside from anchovies and olives. And get something to drink, too. We need to celebrate your reunion with Ariel.'

Travis draped his leather jacket over the back of his chair and retraced his steps up the spiral staircase. Ariel glanced down and saw his phone poking out of his jacket pocket. She opened her mouth to say something, but when she looked back in his direction, he was gone.

'So, you met my nephew on the train?' Frank said cheerfully. He was sitting with his hands clasped loosely in front of him. His eyes, clearly visible now, were bloodshot, and there was a slight puffiness to his face. The overall effect wasn't pronounced enough to be considered bloated, but Ariel guessed it was moving tentatively in that direction.

She swallowed a mouthful of water and answered his question with a nod. The ice cubes bumped against her teeth, causing a sharp twinge of sensitivity. She pressed her hand to her lips and groaned.

'Well I'm glad of it,' Frank continued. 'Travis is a good kid, though I don't get to see as much of him as I'd like.'

'It's been such a weird day,' she replied. 'Weird good, I mean. I couldn't believe it when I found out you were Travis's uncle.'

Frank plucked a piece of lint from his sleeve and placed his cupped palms back on the table. Ariel saw that there was a slight tremor to his fingers, an uncharacteristic suggestion of sadness in the downward arc of his eyes. She wanted to say something, ask him if he was okay, but she was afraid it would come out all wrong, like she were somehow being disloyal, or indiscreet.

She filled his glass with water and nudged it towards him.

'Travis told me about your mom and the reason you're here in Edinburgh,' Frank said gently. 'I'm sorry, kid. That must have been tough on you and your dad and your younger –' He paused. 'Was it a brother or a sister in the end?'

'A brother. His name's Isaac. He's ten now.'

'Ten!' Frank shook his head. 'Boy, time flies.'

'It's been hard, but we're getting on with things. It's what Estelle would have wanted. And she'd be made up to know you were here with me today. She always used to say how you and Cynthia brought a touch of glamour to the house.'

Frank grinned, and suddenly there they were, the famous cheekbones were back. 'She did, did she? That was nice of her.'

And then, as swiftly as it had appeared, the grin was gone. 'Cyn and I aren't together any more, though. She left me for someone else a few years back. Took the whole Priscilla thing a step too far, if you ask me. The guy wasn't her karate instructor, he was her chiropractor, but it was close enough. Anyway, it doesn't matter who it was, I thought we'd be together forever, you know? So her leaving me was always going to hurt.'

Frank brushed his fingers along the underside of his chin. 'Cyn was like sunlight, I just couldn't hold on to her. I guess whatever was left between us after our double act broke up just wasn't strong enough for me to convince her to stick around.'

'I'm sorry,' Ariel said. 'But I can't believe you haven't met anyone else. Everyone was crazy about you the summer you came to stay.'

Frank pressed both hands to his face, and without any prior warning, he suddenly let out an enormous, stifled sob.

'Oh my God,' she cried. 'Frank, are you okay?'

Frank's shoulders began to shake. He nodded his head, but when he lowered his hands to the table, there were tears running down his cheeks. 'I'm so sorry, Ariel. You don't see me for a decade, and the first thing I go and do is burst into tears. How mortifying! You must think I'm a total sap!'

'Of course I don't,' she said softly. She pulled a tissue from her bag and handed it to him. 'Is it... because of Cynthia?'

Frank groaned and wiped his eyes. 'The thing is, in my heart of hearts, I *know* she wasn't right for me. She was much too flighty. She wasn't *The One*. It's just so hard, you know? When the person you love doesn't appreciate you. I'd have given her the world, if I could. I'm just way too soft for my own good, Ariel. That's my problem.'

'You don't have a problem, Frank. You're kind. And you're amazing! Any woman would be lucky to have you.'

Frank's eyes filled with gratitude, his features suspended somewhere in the vast, open wastelands between heartache and a smile. 'Well, it's nice of you to say so.' He raised the tissue to his face and blew his nose. 'Right now, if I'm honest, I'm holding out for Jennifer Lopez.'

Ariel laughed, and to her relief, Frank did, too. He moved his hand involuntarily to the top of his head. When he'd sat down she saw that he was starting to thin on top, just at the crown. It was a small circle of bare scalp, no bigger than the diameter of a two pound coin, but at least he'd resisted the temptation to maintain his famous quiff to disguise it. He told her later that a former Jerry Lee Lewis lookalike had insisted on keeping his signature hairdo long after his performance days were over, spraying the bejesus out of it despite the fact it was so fine, you could damn near see daylight through it. Frank's hair was impressively thick for the most part, and still dark, with just a whisper of grey blossoming at the temples. He wore it in a side parting, neatly brushed back from his face. Ariel couldn't help wondering if that was what Elvis would have looked like if he were still alive today.

288

'Do you miss performing as Elvis?' she asked. 'Or were you glad to give it all up in the end?'

Frank took a deep inhalation of breath and admitted it was a question he didn't always answer truthfully. The stock response he rolled out to his peers in the entertainment business was that he'd been more than happy to move on. He'd say that he had quit while he was still at the top of his game, before things started to slide:

'No judgement, Ariel, but cruise ship engagements and third-rate clubs where the storeroom doubles up as a dressing room just weren't for me. And you know, some of the so-called tribute acts who get booked today just don't have the range to do the job properly. I saw a Michael Jackson lookalike a couple of years ago who made me hang my head in shame. All he did for his entire set was grab his crotch and shout "woo hoo" and "cha'mone" over a tinny backing track. You could hear the squeak of his shoes during the *Billie Jean* moonwalk segment from the street.'

Ariel laughed. She couldn't help herself. But then Frank's expression changed.

'The thing is, Ariel, it's all a lie. I didn't quit while I was ahead. I kept holding on, the way I tried to hold on to Cyn and failed. It was terrifying. I'd been impersonating Elvis for so long, he was ingrained in my DNA. It sounds crazy, but when I was him, I knew who I was. I had self-respect. A *purpose*. And I liked excelling at something. I liked looking in the mirror and knowing I was doing exactly what I was put on this planet to do.

'When I was forced to give that up I honestly didn't know

if there would be anything – or anyone – on the other side. After thirty plus years on the celebrity circuit pretending to be someone else, I didn't have the faintest idea who the real Frank Carmichael was.'

Ariel stared into Frank's mournful eyes. For a second, she was terrified she'd embarrass them both and cry. 'We're such a pair of weirdos,' she said at last. 'But at least we're owning it.'

Frank's forehead wrinkled into a frown. 'Hey, people aren't still calling you that, are they?'

Ariel looked at him in surprise. 'You actually remember me *telling* you that?'

'Damn right, I do! I felt bad for you. Weird's something I've been called my whole life – and fine, you could argue that looking the way *I* do, I was asking for it – but hell, you should never say that to a *child*.'

She almost flung her arms around him. 'Do you know how much it meant to me?' she said instead. 'The fact that you noticed how lonely I was? At the time, I never really admitted how shitty it felt, but things are better now. I found my tribe.'

'*Good*,' Frank replied, 'I'm glad. Anyway, it's not about being weird or not being weird. At the end of the day, all you can do is be you.'

Ariel smiled. 'I wish Estelle were with us. She'd have loved to hear you say that.' She lowered her eyes.

'I'm sorry, kid. You miss her a lot, don't you?'

She nodded. 'All this time I've been trying to replace her, for Linus's sake, and for Isaac's. But I can't replace her. No one can. And now someone new has arrived at home and everything's changed. I don't know where I fit in any more. I'm just drifting... It's scary, Frank. Half the time, I don't know who I am, any more than you do.'

Frank reached across the table and squeezed her hand. 'Oh, hallelujah!' he cried. He raised his eyes to Travis, who was at last making his way back to join them. 'The wanderer returns! Did you just call the whole of the Edinburgh phone book, Travis?'

'Sorry, guys. I had to ring my friend Curtis in New York. Today's his birthday.'

Frank shook his head. 'Well, I hope for your sake you've got one helluva favourable calling plan to dial overseas for that long.'

Ariel flicked her eyes to the mobile phone poking out of the pocket of Travis's jacket, which was still draped over the back of his chair, but she said nothing.

'God, I'm *starved*,' he said, sitting down. 'So what's everyone eating?'

By the time the band took their places on stage, Ariel was convinced she was having an out-of-body experience. Twenty-four hours earlier, she'd been holed up in a dingy basement in Finsbury Park, watching a film of cheese congeal on an abandoned pizza. The night before that she was at home in Oystermouth, climbing her bedroom walls as they closed in around her, though now that she'd gained some distance from them, it seemed less like they'd wanted to suffocate her, and more like they were trying to squeeze her out.

Tonight, she was at the other end of the country with Frank

and Travis. She smiled at each of them in turn, then glanced over her shoulder just as the saxophonist tapped a 'One, two' on his microphone.

'Ladies and gentlemen,' he cooed, 'we have a very special guest in the house tonight from the United States. A hugely talented performer we'd like to invite to join us on stage –'

Frank dropped his cutlery onto his plate and shot Travis a look of utter disbelief. 'So *that's* why you chose this place! I don't know how you do it! You've been in Edinburgh for all of a few hours and you've already secured yourself a gig? Do you even have your sax with you?'

Behind them, the musician's voice rose: '... so please put your hands together for a legendary vocalist, Mr Frank Carmichael!'

'*Me?*' Frank cried.

He twisted round in his seat. There was a polite ripple of applause, a few whoops, and one enthusiastic 'Yeah!' from a guy in a fedora who'd been caning shots of tequila in the corner.

'Give it up, everybody, for Frank Carmichael! Come on up, Frank!'

Frank rose mechanically to his feet. His chest and shoulders visibly expanded, his entire being metamorphosing before Ariel's eyes. With one well-practised movement, he buttoned up his jacket and pulled down the cuffs of his shirt to reveal a pair of shiny onyx cufflinks. He walked the short distance to the stage and spent a moment or two conferring with the band. When he turned back round to address the audience, microphone in hand, she saw that every last trace of shock had melted from his face. In its place was a radiant aura of belonging – the exact same glow she remembered in the charismatic, confident Frank of old.

'Good evening!' Frank announced to the room. 'It's a pleasure to have the opportunity to sing for you tonight.'

The percussionist counted in the beat to a song Ariel didn't recognise. Travis leaned across the table and told her it was Billie Holiday's *Comes Love*, one of Frank's favourites.

'How did you do it?' she asked. She slid over to Frank's seat so she could get a better view of the stage. 'It's why you went upstairs, wasn't it? I saw you didn't even have your phone with you.'

Travis grinned. 'Well spotted. And yes, guilty as charged.'

'So... ?'

'So the jazz world's not as big as you might think. When Uncle Frank came clean about being dropped from his gig I could see how devastated he was, especially since I'd travelled all the way up here to see him perform. I told him there was nothing to apologise for and made some excuse about wanting to go out for an hour or two by myself, just to get the lay of the land and stretch my legs after being stuck all day on a train.

'Long story short, I took my guidebook and raced around a string of venues until I wound up at this one. I gave them my best marketing pitch on Uncle Frank and said he was only in town for a couple of days, so it was a one-shot deal. The manager told me their house band would have to agree to it before they'd let him get up on stage – which is fair enough – so I snuck upstairs right after we got here to meet them.

'I had to drop a few names, but I guess I got lucky. I told them to be sure and let me know if they're ever over in the States – that way I can return the favour.' Travis tipped his head towards the stage. 'He's killing it, isn't he? Uncle Frank's always had such a fantastic tone.'

Ariel turned and saw the unmistakeable glimmer of contentment in the pools of light dancing in Frank's eyes.

'He's great. *Really* great.' She nudged Travis's elbow and felt a sliver of electricity shoot up her arm. 'He's lucky to have you,' she added quickly. 'You know that, right? I'm sure your dad would be proud of you for what you did tonight.'

Travis was gazing at her the exact same way he'd looked at her on the train – like he was making a study of her, soaking up every last detail.

Ariel held her breath.

'Maybe he'd be proud,' he replied with a faraway smile. 'Maybe not. But I didn't do it for him. I did it for Uncle Frank.'

Forty minutes later, a euphoric Frank reclaimed his place at the table. Travis rose to meet him, and Frank – his face flushed with emotion – pressed his forehead tenderly against Travis's brow and gave him a long, wordless hug.

It was well past midnight when they exited the restaurant draped with Christmas streamers the waiting staff handed to them as they left. The brightly coloured swirls of corrugated paper dangled from their necks like Hawaiian leis, catching and fluttering in the soft, night breeze.

Ariel dug around in her bag for her phone. 'I have to take a photo of you both. At least then I can show Linus what I've been up to. He'll get such a kick out of seeing you again, Frank.'

As she activated the screen, an incomprehensible tally of notifications – none of which had been there when she'd arrived at the restaurant just a few hours earlier – flashed up to greet her:

Twelve missed calls...

An unspecified number of voice messages...

Nine new texts...

A blast of air stung her cheeks like a cool, sharp slap to the face. She scrolled through the messages and saw that they were mainly from Linus, with a few from Tumbleweed, and one, unexpectedly, from Rosemary, which she ignored for now. The contents told her little overall, the gist both vague and chilling in its brevity: ARIEL, CALL HOME NOW.

'Shit,' she muttered under her breath.

'Is everything okay?' Travis edged towards her, his woollen beanie pulled low over his forehead like a tea cosy. His eyes, just visible beneath it, were scouring the length of the street for a taxi.

'I'm not sure.' She tugged nervously at her lip. 'I think something may have happened at home.'

A nauseating cocktail of guilt and fear began to pour through her insides. Her thoughts were already ricocheting from one terrifying scenario to another when her phone rang in her hand.

'Tee?' she said, answering on the second ring. 'What is it? What's happened?'

'Fuck, where were you, Ariel? Didn't you hear your phone ringing?'

'I'm sorry... I can't have had any reception. I was underground, listening to jazz. With friends,' she added in a weak voice.

There was a momentary silence on the other end of the line.

'What friends? You don't have any friends in Edinburgh. You only just arrived.'

She dropped her gaze to the ground.

'There's been an accident,' Tumbleweed continued. His voice was softer now. 'It's Isaac.'

'*Isaac?*' At the sound of her brother's name, Ariel's legs buckled. 'Oh my God! What happened?'

'He was at Mumbles pier on his bike. When he left for home, a group of boys were waiting for him and his friends outside the arcade. One of Isaac's mates got pushed off his bike and they started laying into him. Isaac went ballistic and cycled after them down the promenade. The group out front were quick, really quick, but Isaac wouldn't stop. He kept pedalling straight across the road. He didn't see the car coming, Ariel. He was riding too fast.'

Ariel's hand flew to her mouth. '*Please,*' she whispered, 'please tell me he's okay.'

Tumbleweed paused. 'He's got a broken leg, a broken collarbone and two broken ribs. The side of his face is pretty bashed up, and it's going to take a while for the bones to mend, but he's going to make it, Ariel. Isaac's going to be okay.'

Behind her, a ripple of laughter floated out from the restaurant doorway and a group of girls burst onto the pavement, hugging each other, calling out their goodbyes.

'Thank you,' she mouthed into the darkness. 'Thank you for keeping him safe.'

'I know what you're thinking,' Tumbleweed went on, 'but it wouldn't have made a scrap of difference if you'd been at home or not, so don't go beating yourself up about not being there for him when it happened.'

Ariel felt her legs begin to shake. 'How do you know all this, Tee? Did someone call you?'

'Your dad tracked me down when you didn't respond to any of his messages. He asked me to put you on the phone. I'm sorry, but when he said there'd been an accident, I had no choice but to come clean.'

'It's okay,' she said quickly. *He's going to kill me.* 'You did the right thing.' She bit her lip. 'Out of curiosity, what did you tell him?'

Tumbleweed groaned. 'Some bullshit about a school friend at Edinburgh uni asking if you'd go up and see her. I said it was boyfriend trouble – you know, girl stuff – otherwise I'd have tagged along myself. Load of bollocks, but it was all I could come up with on the spot. I said you were probably just out somewhere where you couldn't hear your phone. At least that part was true.'

Ariel let out a long, deep exhalation. 'I'm sorry you had to lie for me, but thank you. You're a really good friend. The best. I'll make everything right, I promise. I'll tell Linus everything just as soon as I've met with Eve Marie.'

'It's fine,' Tumbleweed mumbled. 'We're friends, right? You'd have done the same for me. Hey,' he said, his tone suddenly lifting, 'did you see the picture I sent you earlier?'

'Which one? The chimney sweep?'

'Yeah. I thought you should know it's a symbol of good luck, that's all.'

Frank and Travis told her not to worry; the important thing was that Isaac was going to be okay.

As Travis redoubled his efforts to flag down a taxi, she listened to her final voice message from home:

'Your brother's stable and doing as well as can be expected. He wants you to bring him an extra big present, from Edinburgh, it would seem... You know, pet, you and me and Isaac, we're all we've got now. We need to look out for one another, don't we? Just look after yourself, that's all I ask. Isaac's at Morriston Hospital paediatric ward. Give him a call in the morning. I know he'd appreciate hearing your voice.'

I'm really sorry u couldn't get hold of me, she texted back. I'll call Isaac first thing. Please don't worry about me in the meantime. Everything's fine. I promise x x

The message from Rosemary, sent at ten minutes to midnight, was the only one left unread on her phone.

Hello Ariel. Rosie here. Isaac's a wonder & will bounce back so don't u go thinking u need to hop on the 1st train home. Do whatever it is u went to Edinburgh to do & then come home. What can I tell u? I have a nose for this sort of thing. Love R xxx

Ariel sighed. Why did it *always* feel like Rosemary was shining a spotlight into her brain?

'Let's go, kid,' Frank said. He stepped gingerly towards her.

'It's too cold to hang about here any longer. I think we should start walking.'

She dropped her phone back into her bag and slipped her hand into the pocket of her jeans. Way down at the bottom, something small and hard and plastic brushed against her fingers. At first she couldn't place it, then she remembered: a lifetime ago – or so it seemed – Henry had offered her an Everton mint on the train.

Henry.

Suddenly, all she wanted was to hear his voice, calm and assured and wise, but it was much too late to call him now. Besides, his day had been turbulent enough already.

She followed Frank and Travis onto the busy thoroughfare of George Street, where Travis succeeded at last in attracting the attention of a passing cab. He opened the car door and swept his arm out with a flourish.

'After you, m'lady.' He lowered his hand and held it lightly to her back. 'Remember, tomorrow's another day.'

Ariel shivered. The unexpected intimacy of his breath felt warm and heady against her ear.

'Thank you,' she replied.

She focused her gaze on the interior of the taxi cab and stepped inside.

Travis slid into the empty seat beside her. His hand touched briefly against hers, lingered there for a second or two, then catching himself, he moved it to his lap.

'Everything'll be fine,' he said, with a reassuring smile. 'You'll see. In a few hours' time the sun's going to rise on a brand-new world.'

23

The London Airman

CRAMOND, EDINBURGH, DECEMBER 7: *D-DAY*

Henry

Henry found himself in a tranquil living room presided over by an enormous gilt mirror which lay propped, rather magnificently, above the fireplace. Whether it was a genuine antique, or one of those modern affairs hoping to pass itself off as one, he couldn't tell. In any event, it gave the optical illusion of doubling the size of the space, while simultaneously filling the room with refracted winter light.

Behind him was a wall entirely covered with books. Randomly interspersed amongst them were the occasional vase and small wooden carving. Henry's knowledge of interior design consisted for the most part of snippets gleaned from the Sunday colour supplements. Nevertheless, he knew enough to appreciate that Eve Marie's home was cosy and relaxed; more serendipitous flea market finds than fancy consumerism.

In the corner nearest the bay window (and adjacent to a cheerfully rotund Christmas tree) was a display cabinet containing additional eclectic curiosities: a Toby jug; a gaudily painted ceramic elephant; a stone Buddha; a silver paper-weight in the shape of a woman's shoe. Henry lingered over this last item, his eyes making a careful study of the rounded toe, the arch of the heel, the bright sheen of metal moulded to the contours of an imaginary woman's foot. He tried to remember why something so unusual should strike him as so familiar. *Of course!* he realised with a start. *It was the same one he'd seen on the windowsill in Francine's bedroom! He was certain of it!*

Henry managed to tear his gaze away long enough to spot a collection of framed photographs on the shelf immediately above it. He pressed his hands to his knees and had to employ a Herculean effort of will not to get up and examine them more closely. A quite violent and irrational fear of who or what the photos might – or might not – contain swept over him, dominating his thoughts entirely until the sound of approaching footsteps caused him to divert his attention to the living room door.

Eve Marie was making her way towards him, a tray of tea and biscuits in her hands. She placed the tray on the coffee table, handed him a mug, and settled herself across from him in a plump, red chair.

This is it, Henry told himself. *She's sitting right across from you. DO NOT BACK DOWN NOW!*

Unsurprisingly, perhaps – given his preoccupation with not appearing crass or overeager – the drive to Cramond had revealed absolutely nothing. His conversation with Eve Marie had comprised almost exclusively of casual chit-chat. It was only as they drew closer to Eve Marie's home that she began to quiz him further on the particulars of his meeting with Francine. Henry obliged her by answering everything she wanted to know, all the while dancing around the one question burning brightest in his mind: *where would he find Francine today?*

He resolved to broach the subject just as soon as he and Eve Marie were seated inside, but before he could do so, she posed a question of her own, the directness of which took him somewhat by surprise.

'I'd like to ask you something, Henry. Why did you never get in touch with my mother again after you returned to London in February '48?'

Henry's eyes drifted to the silver paperweight in the display cabinet, to the collection of photographs, their subjects tantalisingly obscured from view.

'Well, there was a misunderstanding, you see. A terrible misunderstanding...'

His voice trailed off. His spirits sank. Could he possibly feel any more of a fool?

'If you don't mind,' Eve Marie continued, 'I'd be interested to hear the details. I'd like to understand what happened, if I can.'

She was smiling, but there was a keenness behind her eyes; the same unyielding proclivity to the truth that Henry had witnessed so many years before in the intensity of Francine's gaze.

'Of course,' he replied at once. 'I'll tell you everything you need to know.'

Henry felt his heart crumble. He placed his mug on the coffee table, cleared his throat, and slowly, as he always knew he would be called to do, he took a deep breath and began…

From his and Francine's initial encounter at the Tower Ballroom, to the incident on the Kirkham train; his chance meeting with Sturridge nearly a decade later, and his eventual return to Blackpool in 1968. Henry left nothing out, and as he reached the relevant touchpoints in his story, he removed from a brown paper bag at his side all but one of the items he'd so painstakingly preserved over the years: the silver butterfly hair clip; the paper napkin from Fortescue's café; the uniform cap that Francine had waved like a trophy above her head; a small swatch of dark red velour. One by one, he laid them out in an orderly line on the table for Eve Marie to see.

Finally, Henry explained how Amy had stumbled across Eve Marie's interview in the newspaper; how they'd tracked her down; and how he knew, no matter what the outcome, that he absolutely had to travel to Scotland to meet her.

'And what is it that you want now, Henry?' Eve Marie's voice was impassive, her features all but impossible to read.

'I'd like to tell her how sorry I am,' he replied. 'I'd like to ask forgiveness of the only woman I have ever truly loved – your mother, Francine Keeley.'

A flicker of emotion passed at last over Eve Marie's face.

Henry was still struggling to interpret it when he suddenly became aware of a presence in the room – a presence so powerful, it seemed to permeate every corner, inhabiting every nook and cranny of the suspended space between them. *Silence*, he mused, *can be the loudest sound in the world when it's the very last thing you're hoping to hear.*

As Henry watched and waited, its roar echoed against the walls, compressing his lungs, filling his body with an inexplicable dread.

Eve Marie got up from her chair and walked to the window. She stood with her back towards him, her hands pressed to her cheeks. Henry didn't dare guess what sentiments she might be experiencing, but when she turned back around to face him her features were once again composed.

'I have something to tell you, Henry,' she said, 'and I suspect it will come as quite a shock, but I want you to know that from everything you've told me, there's no doubt in my mind about who you are. No doubt whatsoever.'

Henry swallowed. Whatever Eve Marie was about to say next, he was convinced his entire future happiness was hanging precariously by a thread. 'Go on.'

'The evening my mother spent with you at her flat in Blackpool, she fell pregnant with your child. The question of it being yours can of course be scientifically validated, but as I said, given everything I know, there's no doubt in my mind about the child's paternity.'

Henry opened his mouth, but not a single sound came out. Not a gasp. Not a whisper. Nothing.

He shifted his gaze to the mirror above the fireplace. He

tried to absorb the magnitude of Eve Marie's words, but the cool, sacred symphony of silence had already slipped inside him, weaving a cobweb around his heart, making the blood rush like a windstorm in his ears.

Eve Marie gave him a moment to compose himself before continuing: 'As you know, my mother was nineteen. I have no idea where she found the courage to face it all alone, but even though the baby wasn't planned, it was hers, and it was yours, Henry. Taboo or not, nothing and no one was going to make her give it up. Her biggest concern was how you'd react to the news, but as fate would have it, that was a conversation the two of you would never have.'

Henry lowered his head. *The guilt. The unimaginable consequences of what he had done. He was sure he'd never, ever get over it.*

'It was my fault,' he said quietly. 'All of it.'

Eve Marie made no attempt to contradict him, but when he looked into her face he found an unexpected trace of compassion in her eyes.

'You understand now why I asked why you never got in touch with my mother again after you returned to London. She told me you'd promised to write to her as soon as you were home. When your letter didn't come she invented all sorts of excuses for your silence. Jenny tried to persuade her to forget you. She told her you'd used her. That men like you were all the same. But Francine insisted you were different. She'd never met a boy like you before, she said.

'By the time the summer season was underway, her pregnancy was starting to show. She handed in her notice at the

Shore Hotel and moved out of her flat, leaving word with the landlady to be sure and forward any post to her mother's house in Sheffield.'

'So she *did* go back to Sheffield!' Henry cried.

Eve Marie nodded. 'I don't know if she mentioned it, but her father had been killed some years earlier in the Sheffield Blitz. From everything she told me about him, it was probably just as well; he was deeply religious, and probably wouldn't have been too happy to see his only daughter turning up on his doorstep pregnant and unwed. But like I said, my mother was determined to keep her baby. And so, Henry, in November 1948, Francine gave birth to your son.'

A small cry, no louder than an infant's mewl, escaped Henry's mouth. He placed his hands, which were now trembling uncontrollably, to his lips. He could barely take it in. The whole idea was monstrous. *Inconceivable!* Eighty-five years on the planet, and thanks to his own rashness and stupidity, not one of them had been spent in the role he never imagined for a minute might be his – as a father to his and Francine's son!

'She must have despised the very thought of me,' he said heavily. 'Forgive me, Eve Marie, I have so many questions, I don't know where to begin.'

Eve Marie made her way back to the armchair and sat down. She seemed to be waiting for Henry to continue, but when all further attempts at articulation failed him, she began speaking once again:

'It's true that from what my mother told me, things weren't exactly easy; everyone was so unforgiving of girls in her situation back then. But her mother rallied round and agreed to take her in. After she had the baby, a neighbour encouraged her to train as a typist, and she was eventually taken on by a small accountancy firm – a job she supplemented by wait-ressing in a local café at weekends.'

'I could have helped,' Henry cut in. 'I *would* have helped, of course, if only I'd known...' His voice drifted away, his gaze sinking miserably to the ground.

Eve Marie paused. 'For what it's worth, I know she thought about you a lot in those early days. My mother loved you, Henry, I'm sure you know that. But you'd disappeared from her life without a trace. In the end, you must realise how unlikely it seemed that you'd do as you'd once promised, and get in touch.'

'Yes,' he replied in a hollow voice. 'I understand.'

He clasped his hands in his lap and waited for what he knew must surely be coming next.

'She was twenty-five when she met my father, Bill. He was a Scotsman who'd relocated to Sheffield for a job at the Tinsley Wire steel works. He was a good man, and he was prepared to adopt your son as his own – in name and deed – and that meant more to Francine than you can imagine. Her child would be legitimate. He'd be able to hold his head up high.'

'They were married?'

'Yes, in the spring of 1955. I came along three years later. As far as I was aware, we were a united, happy family like any other. I couldn't honestly say what secret feelings my mother may have harboured for you, Henry. But if she still thought about you, she would never have spoken of it openly. Not to us, anyway.'

Eve Marie's gaze fell upon the swatch of red velour on the coffee table. 'There is one thing I *can* tell you, though,' she said suddenly, 'and that is that she did visit Blackpool in the spring of 1968.'

'She did?' Henry said, his spirits lifting. 'You're sure?'

'Absolutely. Jenny stayed on there after she got married. She and my mother fell out of touch for a while, but after they reconnected Jenny invited her to visit one weekend while her husband was away. I remember my mother being unusually distracted in the days leading up to her trip. I asked her what was wrong, and she said she was just nervous and excited at the prospect of seeing her old friend again after so many years. She was calmer when she came home, though how she'd spent her time while she was there, she didn't say.'

Henry nodded. There was so much to take in, and yet still so many things he had yet to say...

'Francine's objective was to protect me, Henry,' Eve Marie said gently. 'That's how I know everything I've told you today. When I turned sixteen she told me all about you, as a kind of warning, I suppose. It was a mother's prerogative. She didn't want me to fall victim to a similar fate.'

'So last night,' Henry ventured, 'when we spoke at the bookshop, you knew who I was?'

'Not immediately, no; although by the time we parted I was fairly certain it was you. You see the one thing she never told me was your name. When she spoke about you she referred to you only as "the London airman". The closest I ever got to discovering your identity was your initials a few years later, but that's a whole other story. Of course, if she'd known the truth about what happened that night on the Kirkham train – and how desperate you were to find her – things may have turned out very differently.'

Henry was unable to stand the suspense a second longer. He'd listened to every word Eve Marie had said, but one crucial question had yet to be addressed:

'Where is she, Eve Marie? I didn't come here to make trouble, and I'll always be grateful to your father for taking such good care of Francine and my –' he faltered, the word catching in his throat – 'my son... but I have to see her. Assuming she'll allow it, of course.'

As the words left his mouth, Henry saw the grim spectre of grief rise up in Eve Marie's face. He tried to ignore it, but with every passing second it seemed to grow bolder, more real, more defined.

'No,' he mumbled at last.

'I'm so sorry, Henry.'

Henry reached his hand towards the objects lying on the table, straightening them, letting his fingertips brush across them, as though their very proximity contained the power to resurrect what he now knew was lost to him for good.

'When?'

'A long time ago. There was a car accident. My mother was forty-nine. My father, who was sitting beside her, was fifty-three. They were on their way to see me. So you see, Henry, like you, I understand everything there is to know about guilt – I've been living with it for over half my life. If my actions hadn't forced them to make that journey, they'd probably still be alive today.'

Celia Reynolds

Eve Marie got up and walked to the display cabinet by the window. She took out a photograph in a rosewood frame, brought it back to the sofa and placed it in Henry's quivering hands.

'This is my parents, my half-brother and me on holiday in Brighton in 1963. He was fifteen, I was five. I have many more, of course, but this was the first family holiday I remember. It was magical. One of my happiest memories as a child.'

Henry stared at the carefree family portrait laid out before him. It hardly seemed possible; for the first time in sixty-five years, here he was gazing into Francine's smiling face.

Her peaches and cream complexion was bronzed and glowing, her light brown hair styled into a lustrous bob. She must have been thirty-five when the photo was taken, her appearance being naturally less girlish than he recalled. And yet still her liquid blue eyes had the power to floor him.

Francine was leaning against a bench, her hands resting on her young daughter's shoulders. To her left was Bill, an agreeable looking man with a receding hairline, his own hand looped around the curve of Francine's waist. To her right was a gangly teenage boy, his arms folded casually in front of him. In the distance, the Palace Pier unfurled out to sea, frozen in time. Inexplicably, Henry's son had turned his face towards it, as though some sudden noise or movement – some merry seaside distraction – had caught his attention at the very moment the camera shutter was released. The teenager was grinning broadly, his profile strong and smooth and perfect against a jazzy turquoise sky. It was, unmistakeably, Henry's own profile. He just prayed his son had been blessed with Francine's eyes.

Henry traced his fingertips over the outline of Francine's face, his vision so blurred from the pooling tears, he could barely make out the intricacies of it any more.

Slowly, he moved his fingers aside and held his hand an inch above the glass. Later, when he was once again alone, he wondered whether it had been out of shyness that he hadn't dared touch his son's face. Maybe it was awe. All Henry knew was that in that one pivotal moment, he was overcome by the crippling realisation that he didn't *deserve* to caress the features of the innocent teenage boy, smiling and gazing in wonder at the pier. Not even in a photograph dating back fifty years.

A tear trickled down Henry's cheek and landed with a splash in the corner of the frame. He looked up at Eve Marie and tried to find the words to express the very last question he could ever have imagined asking when his journey first began:

'My son,' he said, the newness of the word confounding him once again. 'What's his name? And where will I find him?'

24

The Firth

CRAMOND, EDINBURGH, DECEMBER 7: *D-DAY*

Ariel

*R*emember, the strapline read, *as far as anyone knows, we're a normal family...*

Ariel smiled and slipped her brand-new fridge magnet into her jacket pocket. While Linus and Estelle parked the car, she and Isaac walked to the children's play area at Blackpill Lido. Looming large against the gull-flecked, grey-tipped backdrop of Swansea Bay was an angular metal construction, at least five metres high, from which thick black ropes of elastic dangled above a circular trampoline.

Isaac strained like a tethered pony, desperate to climb on board. 'I want a go! I want a go!' he cried. He gestured to the attendant standing off to one side, his heavily inked arms folded in close against the barrel of his chest, his astronaut's jaw set like stone.

'Go on, then,' Ariel said. She dug around in her purse for the fare. 'I'll wait for you here. Make sure you jump as high as you can.'

'I will!' Isaac replied. 'Higher than the moon!'

She lifted her six-year-old brother onto the edge of the trampoline. The attendant gave her a flirty wink which turned her a violent shade of red. He began to attach a series of straps and harnesses around Isaac's waist, legs, and arms. Isaac watched the buckles slot and snap together, then he raised his head and called out to the approaching figures of Linus and Estelle.

'Mam! Dad! Come and watch! I'm going to make a record bounce for the whole of Blackpill to see!'

The attendant grinned and tugged on the overhead ropes. Isaac rocketed upwards, his legs dangling like human bunting. His hands – balled into fists – punched the air in delight.

'I'm flying!' he screamed. 'Higher! Higher!'

As he made his descent, the attendant caught him by the waist, and with biceps flexing, propelled him back into the air. Isaac stretched his arms and legs as wide as they'd go. He soared, spreadeagled, starfished, to the salty sky.

Ariel's laughter was swallowed by the shouts of the children splashing around in the paddling area nearby. She held up her phone and took an action shot of her brother mid-flight, suspended high above the trampoline.

'You did it!' she cried. 'You did it, Isaac! You were almost on the moon!'

The alarm clock buzzed so loudly, the sound hurt Ariel's ears.

She flung out her arm and fumbled with the buttons until she found the one marked OFF. A triptych of red deer nuzzled their way into focus, their enormous branched antlers defying gravity on the wall ahead. She pushed her hair back from her face and stared up at the ceiling. Where *was* she? Oh yes... An overheated, but otherwise comfortable B&B, just south of Edinburgh city centre...

Warily, she closed her eyes. The dream from which the alarm had wrenched her had been a happy one overall. But then time bent and fractured, and what started out so innocently had culminated in a nightmarish loop of Isaac hurtling to the ground amidst a tangle of twisted bicycle metal and ominously spinning wheels.

'Oh no.'

Ariel sat up and wiped the sleep from the corners of her eyes. She reached towards the bedside table for her phone.

'Hello, can I speak with Isaac Bliss, please?'

Pause.

'Yes, he was admitted last night. It's his sister calling.'

There was a blast of elevator music while the hospital put her on hold. She heard three short beeps and finally Isaac's voice – hesitant, slightly awed – on the other end of the line.

'Hello? Ariel?'

'Isaac! I'm so happy to hear your voice! Tumbleweed told me what happened and I feel terrible for you. Are you okay? What did the doctor say? Are you in a lot of pain?'

'I'm all right,' Isaac replied. 'I'm hurting all over, but the doctor said I was lucky. He said I must have flown sideways off my bike, but I don't remember much about it. I think I was too angry.'

'Oh Isaac, I'm really sorry. Were you able to get any sleep?'

'A bit. But I had some really mad dreams.'

'Really? That's weird! So did I.'

She paused, the distance hanging heavy and unfamiliar between them. 'I was so worried about you,' she continued after a beat. 'I know you feel rubbish right now, but it was very brave of you to stand up for your friend like that. It can't have been easy.'

'I didn't do anything,' he replied. 'Not really.'

'Of course you did! I'd say "give yourself a break" if it wasn't so inappropriate under the circumstances.'

She waited for laughter, a *ha ha very funny* at the very least, but neither came. Instead, the line whooshed and hummed with the steady reverberation of Isaac's breathing.

'Are you sure you're okay?' she said. 'You seem quiet... If something were bothering you – anything at all – you would tell me, wouldn't you?'

'I'm fine,' he replied, in a thoroughly unconvincing voice.

'You don't *sound* fine.'

There was a loaded pause.

'Lee's glasses got smashed. He's short-sighted and he couldn't ride his bike home after 'cos his mam says he's not allowed to ride without his glasses on. It's the second time he's broken them this year.'

'Oh. I didn't know that. But your whole body got smashed. I think that's worse, don't you?'

'I s'pose.'

Ariel tried a little harder to sound cheerful. 'Everything's going to be fine, you know. I promise.'

'You don't know that.' Isaac's voice was almost unbearably forlorn. 'The thing is, the others would never have gone after Lee in the first place if he hadn't been with me.'

Ariel stared at her reflection in the mirror opposite the bed. For one awful moment, she wondered if her brother was suffering from concussion.

'What are you talking about, Isaac?'

'Lee... I told Dad he's being bullied, but it's not him they're bullying, it's me. I lied, Ariel. They only went after him because he's my friend. They pushed him off his bike and kicked him and everything. All he was doing was trying to stick up for me.'

A deep frown spread across Ariel's forehead. Isaac had never said a word about being bullied before. He'd never so much as come home with a scratch on his face or a tear in his clothes, and now *this*?

'Hang on a minute,' she said. 'Who's been bullying you? And why?'

Isaac began to cry. 'The boy from yesterday. His name's Hard Boy Harry. He says the reason Mam died was because she was a witch. He says in the old days people would have thrown stones at her and burned her on a bonfire. I told him he's a liar. Just because she worked in a shop selling books about runes and druids and stuff didn't make her a witch. But he said God took her away from us because she was wicked. I told him it's not true. *None* of it! But he said Mam's gone to hell where she belongs. He says we should be glad she's dead. I miss her so much. I can't... stand... to hear it... any longer, Ariel...'

Isaac's voice trailed away, his words punctuated by breathy, convulsive sobs.

Ariel scrambled from the bed and paced furiously around the narrow confines of the room. 'Isaac, just listen to me for a minute, that's the biggest load of *crap* I've ever heard! That boy should never, *ever* have spoken to you like that. How long has this been going on?'

'I don't know. I don't remember. A while.'

'Why didn't you say something?'

'I don't know, Ariel. I thought maybe it would make things worse.'

'*No,*' she cried with mounting defiance. 'It would have made things *right!*'

Waves of anger pulsed through her body. She raised her eyes to the ceiling and tried desperately to channel Estelle.

'Isaac,' she said, in a considerably softer voice, 'you do know that you've done nothing whatsoever to deserve this, don't you? No one with half a *brain* would ever say anything as vile and hurtful as that to someone who's just lost their mam.'

'I know,' Isaac mumbled, 'but Lee told me that Harry doesn't have a mam either. He said she ran off and left him alone with his dad and his two brothers. They never see her any more. His dad's even taken away all the photos they had of her in the house, like she never existed. I've got a picture of Mam by my bed. We've got pictures of her all over the place. I thought maybe that's why Harry's so mean to me, because I don't have a mam either. Maybe the reason he hates me so much is because I remind him of himself.'

Ariel closed her eyes. 'Isaac, when did you get to be so smart?'

'I dunno,' he replied with a loud sniff. 'I didn't feel very smart last night when I was lying in a heap in the middle of the road.'

The corners of her mouth rose despite herself. 'Well I still wish you'd told us instead of bottling it all up inside. Just promise me you won't worry about it any more, okay? The school will take care of it now. In the meantime, all the nastiness and the name-calling is going to stop.'

Isaac gave another loud sniff. 'Okay. What about you?'

'Me?' she asked, surprised. 'What do you mean? I'm fine.'

'Are you coming back?'

'Of course I'm coming back!' she replied. 'Why would you ask me that?'

Isaac hesitated. 'Because Dad told me you went to Scotland, not England. And then last night I dreamt you'd run away. When you come home will you tell me what you've gone there to do?'

At twelve minutes to midday the number 41 bus dropped Ariel in Cramond, a quiet, picturesque suburb which seemed to act as a racing ground for blustery gusts of wind tearing inland from the nearby Firth of Forth.

She coiled her multicoloured scarf around her neck, and per Eve Marie's instructions turned off the main road into a long, downward-sloping side-street. Contrary to her expectations, the houses on either side of the road were almost chalet-like in appearance – wide and airy, with steeply gabled slate roofs – not at all the pinched, terraced cottages she often associated with coastal locations. Ariel ran her eyes over each one individually. Roughly halfway down, she arrived at a pretty, semi-detached property fronted by a small rectangle of garden. She checked the number on the door, placed her hand on the gate and stepped inside.

In the canvas bag hanging from her shoulder, she felt Estelle's envelope nudge against her hip. Her throat was horribly dry. She searched for Henry's Everton mint in her pocket, slipped it from its wrapper and placed it on the end of her tongue. A fresh burst of minty sweetness oozed down the back of her throat. She breathed it in, then rang the door-bell and steeled herself for the proceedings to begin.

No sound came from within the house, nor was there any immediate sign through the frosted glass panel in the front door that anyone was approaching to let her in. She glanced to her right. The only visible evidence that the house was occupied was an unlit Christmas tree, decorated with a galaxy of glittering gold and silver stars, standing in the bay window.

'Come *on*,' she muttered under her breath. 'I'm here now. Where are you?'

She rang the bell again. In the resounding silence that followed, it suddenly occurred to her how ironic it would be to discover that Eve Marie Hope was some sort of deranged prankster; that after all this pretension to subterfuge, she had, in fact, been punked. She stepped towards the window and peered past the Christmas tree. In the centre of the living room was a coffee table, a plate of biscuits and two abandoned mugs. A casual displacement of the cushions on the sofa suggested that someone had been sitting there, but evidently, was now gone.

Ariel's heart sank. 'Shit.'

She wondered if there'd been a mix-up, or an accident. What if some last-minute change of plan had thrown her meeting with Eve Marie off course?

The sound of an approaching car caused her to turn her attention to the road. The driver all but raced along it, beeping the horn twice before pulling to a stop outside the house. Ariel stood with one foot planted awkwardly in a flowerbed and stared at the car open-mouthed. A moment later, a middle-aged woman climbed out of the driver's seat and threw her an apologetic glance.

'Ariel? I'm so sorry! I'm Eve Marie. Have you been waiting long?'

'That wasn't a great start, was it?' Eve Marie said as she ushered Ariel through the front door. 'But you have no idea how happy I am to see you. There's so much we have to discuss.'

Ariel downplayed the inconvenience and followed Eve Marie into the house.

'Oh wow.' Her eyes settled on an expensive looking candle on the hallway table. 'That's beautiful! It's not even lit, and it still smells exactly like Christmas.'

She continued on into the living room, and at Eve Marie's request, sat down on the sofa. She handed her coat and scarf to Eve Marie and placed her canvas shoulder bag where she could see it – and easily retrieve it – on the floor at her feet.

'You have a lovely home,' she said, in a voice so quiet and reverential, she might almost have been talking to herself.

'Thank you, Ariel.' Eve Marie gave her a warm smile. 'My husband and I have been here for quite a while now. I don't think either of us could imagine living anywhere else.'

Ariel stared at the fireplace, and then, involuntarily, at the dirty tea things on the coffee table.

'Let me just take that lot out to the kitchen,' Eve Marie said quickly. 'I'm usually far more organised than this, but well —' she shook her head. 'I'll be back in a sec.'

When she returned, she was carrying a fresh set of refreshments. Ariel studied her as she laid two new mugs and a plate of shortbread on the table. The woman Estelle had introduced to her as Mia had had short, blondish hair, but today it was back to what she presumed must be closer to its natural colour – a soft, tawny brown – and it was longer, tied in a loose ponytail worn casually to one side. She was dressed in jumper and jeans and a pair of flat leather boots. Her face was almost entirely free of make-up, but her nails, Ariel noticed, were neatly manicured and painted a fashionable shade of lavender grey.

'I remember you now,' she said. 'I remember more than I thought.' She stopped herself from saying anything further and waited, determined to let the older woman speak first.

Eve Marie sat down in a chair opposite the sofa. 'I appreciate you coming all this way,' she began. 'At first I was worried you might not come at all, but as I wrote in my letter –' she paused, shook her head once again – 'Actually, things have moved on quite a lot since then. But I'm already getting ahead of myself. I think I'd better start by explaining exactly who I am.

'In London, Estelle introduced me to you as Mia. There was a reason for that, but first you should know that Hope is my married name. My maiden name was Bliss.'

'The same surname as mine?' Ariel asked, surprised.

'Yes, just like yours. I was the second of two children. My older brother – my half-brother, to be exact – is called Linus, the same Linus who just over twenty years ago married your mother, Estelle.'

Ariel uttered a short, nervous laugh. 'I don't understand. Are you telling me you're Linus's *sister*?'

Eve Marie nodded. 'Well, half-sister, as I said. Which in turn makes me your half-aunt – if such a term even exists – though I think just plain "aunt" or "auntie" sounds less stiff.'

Ariel stared at the expression of complete and utter calm on Eve Marie's face.

WTF???

'But my whole life Linus never once mentioned anything about a sister,' she stammered. 'Why would he have kept you a secret from us all these years? It doesn't make any sense.'

'I'm afraid he had his reasons.'

Ariel gave another nervous laugh. 'What do you mean?'

'Let me ask you this,' Eve Marie replied. 'How much has Linus told you about his parents?'

Ariel shrugged. 'Only that they were killed in a car crash when he was twenty-nine. I don't really know much more about them than that. I don't even know their names. We always referred to them as Grandma and Grandad Bliss, but they almost never came up in conversation. Estelle used to tell me and Isaac not to ask questions about them, because Linus would get too upset. So we never did. The only grand-parents in my life when I was growing up were Grandma and Grandad Hooper – Estelle's parents – but they've both been dead for many years now, too.'

She scanned Eve Marie's face, trying to find some thread, some telltale physical likeness that might connect her in some way to her father. The paleness of their skin was the same, and she supposed they both had a kind of directness of expression – the wide, open quality of a face that couldn't lie – but as far as she could tell, the similarity ended there.

'I'm sorry, Eve Marie, but I still don't understand.'

Eve Marie steepled her hands beneath her chin. 'Okay, I think this will help. Linus and I had the same mother, but different fathers. What Linus didn't tell you is that he was born illegitimate. His biological father abandoned our mother after a brief love affair. Linus never met him. Never so much as knew his name.'

'Oh,' Ariel cried, 'I had no idea! No wonder he used to get so upset if Isaac or I asked questions about his parents.'

'Well you shouldn't blame yourself for *that*,' Eve Marie shot back. 'Linus was always that way.

'I'm sorry,' she added after a beat. 'I didn't mean to sound so defensive.'

Ariel saw the colour deepen in Eve Marie's cheeks.

'The truth,' Eve Marie continued, 'is that not knowing his father's identity cast a massive shadow over Linus's life. I never understood why, but he got it into his head that this mythical man was out wandering the world searching for him, and that it was only down to some bizarre twist of fate that they'd been separated in the first place. It became an obsession. Linus just couldn't accept the fact that for whatever reason, his father turned his back on him before he was even born.'

'Did he never find out who he was?'

Eve Marie shook her head. 'No matter how many times Linus asked, our mother always refused to reveal his identity. Linus's birth certificate contains nothing more than a cold, hard dash where the name of his father should have been. She told him she withheld it out of love. She was so afraid Linus would get his hopes up and one day go looking for him, only to have his heart broken in two.'

'Do you think he'd have done it?' Ariel asked. 'Gone looking for him, I mean?'

'Yes,' Eve Marie replied at once. 'I do.'

Ariel's eyes briefly fell to her canvas bag lying at her feet. 'So Bliss was *your* father's surname, not Linus's?'

'Exactly. My father's name was Bill Bliss. When he married my mother, Linus legally took his surname. They became very close over the years, though I know Linus never stopped speculating about his biological father. As he got older, he built a kind of wall around the subject and refused to let anyone else in. He became very adept at internalising things – at least, that's how it seemed to me. After that, he kept his thoughts on the matter firmly to himself.'

Ariel ran her hand over her forehead in an attempt to process everything Eve Marie was saying. 'Okay,' she said slowly, 'so basically, what you're telling me is that Linus never got over the fact that his real father abandoned him. Then, despite gaining a stepfather who cared for him like his own – until Linus lost him, too – he remained –' she stopped, corrected herself – '*remains* traumatised by the event even now. But what about you? What I don't understand is why you'd completely disappear from Linus's life?'

Eve Marie sighed. 'Because after my parents died I discovered something I believed held a clue to the identity of Linus's father. Except instead of giving it to him, I told him what I'd found and then deliberately threw it away.'

'Why would you do that?!' Ariel cried.

'I'm sorry.' Eve Marie fiddled with a thread poking out from the sleeve of her jumper. 'This was always going to be the hardest part. It's why I invited you here in person – so I can explain.'

Ariel's stomach began to churn. She reached her hand to the floor and tugged her bag an inch closer to her heel. 'Go ahead,' she said. 'I'm listening.'

Eve Marie nodded. 'The year my parents were killed, I was a first year English Literature student at Edinburgh University. We'd moved here as a family from Sheffield several years earlier, though Linus was already living in London by then. I missed him like crazy when he left, but he was always very attentive about staying in touch. He'd send me mix tapes and books, and funny little postcards from places he'd been.

'The night of the accident I was at a student party in town. I was suffering from my first real dose of teenage heartache, and I was out of my mind, desperate for anything that might numb the pain. I'd never experimented with drugs before that. I was so naïve, I couldn't even tell you what I took in all, only that I said yes to whatever was offered to me until it achieved the desired effect.

'The last thing I remember was falling unconscious in a stairwell. When my friends couldn't wake me they made two phone calls – one to the ambulance service, the other to my parents. Mum and Dad were on their way to the hospital to see me when their car skidded on an icy stretch of road and smashed headfirst into a tree.

'I regained consciousness to the news that both of them had been killed on impact. It was like a never-ending nightmare; every time I woke, it was always to the same horror, the same altered universe where nothing was as it should be.'

'Eve Marie, I'm so sorry,' Ariel said softly. 'I know the pain of losing someone you love, but for it to happen like that...'

Eve Marie nodded once again. 'From then on, it was just Linus and me. He was devastated, but he never once blamed me. He stood by me and helped put things in order. It was only when he had to return to London that I was alone to face the consequences of what I had done. During the day – whenever I could get my act together to attend class – I continued with my degree. And at night I'd get wasted and spend hours sifting through my parents' belongings, searching for pieces of who knew what.

'I found my mother's diary in a shoe box stuffed full of vintage gloves at the back of her wardrobe. The diary itself didn't surprise me – she'd kept one every year without fail for as long as I could remember – but she always tossed the old ones out at the start of each new year. I was curious why she'd chosen to keep this one. I opened the cover and checked the date. The year was 1948. I leafed through the pages until I arrived at February, the month I knew she must have met Linus's father. I found what I was looking for, leaned back against the foot of the bed and began to read.

'It was all there, everything she'd once told me, all laid out in her rounded, girlish handwriting. I was sure if I persevered I'd discover the man's name, but the only reference I could find in the handful of pages I looked through were his initials. Everywhere else she'd used the same anonymous codename: "the London airman".

'I closed the diary and put it to one side. My plan was to give it to Linus during his next visit home, that way he could make the discovery for himself. But the following weekend when he came up to Edinburgh we had a huge fight. He'd been hearing rumours about me, and he was furious. He read me the riot act, said that if I was hoping to kill myself and join our parents in their graves I was going the right way about it. And in that one moment of insanity, I hated him; I was that far gone. I accused him of spying on me, then I grabbed my mother's diary from the dresser in the kitchen and waved it in his face, telling him it held a clue to his father's identity. Linus reached out to take it from me and I ran. I turned and ran as fast as I could from the house. He didn't even have a chance to hold it in his hands.'

'Where did you go?' Ariel asked. As the words left her mouth, she realised the location hardly made a difference; she already knew the story didn't end well.

'The house I was living in back then was our old family home here in Cramond,' Eve Marie replied, 'a little further down by the causeway. I ran to the edge of the firth and threw the diary as far into the distance as I could.

'When Linus found out what I'd done he said he'd never forgive me. Neither of us knew – or would ever know – whether the remainder of the diary went on to reveal his father's full identity. I couldn't even tell him the man's initials. I'd only seen them once, and it was as though the shock of what happened between us wiped them right out of my head. That was it as far as Linus was concerned. He said he never wanted to see me again.'

'You mean he just *abandoned* you?' Ariel cried. 'You were all he had left in the world! How could he turn his back on you when you were so obviously in need of help?'

To her surprise, Eve Marie shook her head and smiled. 'No, Linus is far more complex than that. He may have said he never wanted to see me again, but he still cared about me. He arranged for me to attend a private rehab clinic here in Edinburgh. He took care of the cost himself, and in return, they sent him regular reports on my progress. He was grieving just as much as I was, only in his case, the pain was heightened by the fact that he'd already lost one parent before he was even born. I'm sure he started dreaming about finding his biological father all over again, except I'd now ruined that chance for good.'

Eve Marie got up from her seat and walked to the fireplace. She flicked a switch and the wooden logs burst into a mass of bright, flickering flames.

'So Linus went back to London,' Ariel said slowly. 'And then when he married Estelle he moved to Wales, while you stayed here?'

'Exactly.'

Eve Marie stared at her reflection in the mirror, then turned and made her way back to her chair. 'When he knew I was sober and back on track with my degree, he no longer felt any obligation towards me. I was an adult, and I had money and a roof over my head. I know from mutual friends that he kept tabs on how I was doing, but Linus is stubborn. I don't know what else may have been going on for him at the time, but when he said he would never forgive me and didn't want me in his life, he meant it.'

'Estelle,' Ariel said at length. 'How much of all this did she know?'

Eve Marie smiled. 'Estelle knew everything. She reached out to me one day without Linus knowing. The idea of two estranged siblings – or orphans, in our case – was unthinkable to her.'

'That's because it *is* unthinkable.' Ariel tugged at her sleeves. 'I'm sorry, I don't mean to sound judgemental, but I could *never* cut Isaac out of my life like that. No matter what he did to me.'

Eve Marie held her gaze. 'Families are complicated, Ariel. Relationships are never black and white. It's hard to understand if you haven't experienced it first-hand, but when there are that many raw emotions involved, things sometimes escalate... Neither Linus nor I stopped caring about the other – I really believe that – but *someone* has to make the first move.

I could give you a hundred examples of all the times I wanted to reach out to him, my wedding day being just one of them. I made sure he knew about that.'

'Why didn't he come?' Ariel cried. 'I don't understand.'

Eve Marie's smile widened. 'It turns out there was a pretty significant arrival in his life on that day eighteen years ago: *you*.'

'Oh.'

'Don't be too hard on him,' she continued. 'When I sold my parents' house, he refused to take a penny. He told our solicitor he wanted it all to go to me. In the end, Estelle and I kept in touch in secret – sporadically, as I mentioned in my letter – but at least it gave me the opportunity to hear about your lives, even if I wasn't able to participate in them directly.'

London, Ariel thought at once. *A last-minute surprise organised by Estelle. Linus unavoidably detained at home and unable to come with them...*

'What about when we met before?' she asked. 'Did Estelle arrange that, too, so Linus would never know?'

'Yes. It was the first and only time I saw you all in the flesh. She introduced me as Mia – a name nobody else has ever called me – just in case Linus asked any questions about who you'd met. But I understand he never did ask. Linus never suspected a thing.'

Eve Marie's face fell. 'In the final email I received from Estelle she said nothing about being ill. But this year, nothing came from her at all. I tried calling her mobile, but the number had been disconnected. My sixth sense told me the rest.

'When I found her obituary online I was in pieces. Estelle

was one of the few people who knew I was writing a novel inspired by stories my mother told me from her youth. The last time we emailed, we agreed that if my book ever saw the light of day, it would be the perfect opportunity for me to visit you all in Oystermouth. It was her dream to bring the family together again at last.'

Eve Marie stood up and walked to a cardboard box lying on the floor next to the bookcase. She reached in, pulled out a shiny new paperback and placed it in Ariel's hands.

Ariel read the title out loud: '*Cloudburst on a Midnight Shore.*'

She opened the cover and turned to the book's dedication:

> ~ *In memory of my parents, Bill and Francine,*
> *for Callum, with love always,*
> *and for Linus, that it may lead us to a brand-new shore*
> ~

Ariel stared at the neatly italicised words. She was still trying to process everything Eve Marie had said during the course of their extraordinary conversation, when one name leaped emphatically from the page, the name of a woman whose story had so moved her on the train journey from London less than twenty-four hours earlier.

'Francine?' she said, looking up. 'Your mother's name was Francine?'

Eve Marie nodded. 'Her maiden name was Keeley. Francine Keeley was my mother and your grandmother. Linus – the son she had illegitimately – was fathered by the man I understand you met for the first time yesterday, Henry Applebee.'

Ariel gasped. Like the pieces of a Rubik's Cube slotting magically into place, it all made sense at last. Henry hadn't told her the name of the author whose book talk he'd been planning to attend the previous evening. And she, in turn, hadn't mentioned the name of the woman she was coming to visit at Estelle's request. Now, it was clear not only that they were one and the same person, but that Ariel and Henry's paths had, from the very beginning, been inextricably inter-twined...

'A year ago I looked up *"E.M.H., Cramond, Edinburgh"* online, but I found nothing that could have led me to you. Definitely not the website that Henry's niece found, anyway. I stopped looking after that,' she said.

Eve Marie smiled. 'That's hardly surprising. I never had much interest in social media until now; I was far too absorbed in writing and editing my book. It was my agent who encouraged me to establish an online presence in the weeks leading up to publication. My website has been live for less than a month. Henry's timing – in that instance, at least – was impeccable.'

'Oh,' Ariel said, 'I see.'

A myriad thoughts and emotions came hurtling towards her, each vying for her attention until one surfaced sharper and more poignant than all the rest. It was even more pressing than the existence of the suddenly forgotten package lying in the canvas bag at her feet.

'Henry!' she cried. 'Henry came here hoping to see Francine!'

'Yes,' Eve Marie replied, 'I'm afraid that was his intention. Based on what he told me at the bookshop, I suspected who he might be, though after all this time I almost didn't dare believe it. I invited him here this morning and we had a long, illuminating conversation. He knows everything, Ariel. About Francine. About Linus. About Isaac and you. As you can imagine, it was quite a lot for a man of his age to take in.'

'I have to see him,' she said, jumping to her feet.

Eve Marie's book slithered from her lap and landed with a soft thud on the carpet. She bent down, picked it up and placed it on the coffee table, the very same coffee table where Henry had left his empty mug just a couple of hours earlier.

'Where did he go, Eve Marie? Not back to London, I hope?'

Eve Marie shook her head. 'No, don't worry. Henry hasn't left yet. There was still something important he wanted to do.'

25

Between the Cracks

EDINBURGH, DÉCEMBER 7

Henry

The long, winding road through the trees was still and hushed and sacred as the hallowed graves recumbent at the end of it. Henry arrived at the summit where the road gave way to a large, oval clearing. Further ahead, the formidable expanse of the cemetery was clearly visible, a ghostly township unto itself, fanning outwards as far as the eye could see.

To his left was a sturdy looking cottage which he assumed must be home to the cemetery's caretaker. A band of grass wrapped around its base like a verdant moat, and a thin trail of wispy white smoke rose in broken puffs from the chimney.

Beyond the cottage, built into a stone recess with a roughly hewn trough beneath, was an outside tap. It dripped intermittently as Henry made his way towards it, despite the entreaty of a metal plaque nailed into the mossy stonework overhead. Henry leaned in close to read it. Some of the words had blackened over time, while a fringe of ivy draped its leafy arm across the corner of the sign, obscuring a small portion of the text:

> ITORS TO THE CEMETERY ARE WELCOME
>
> O USE THIS FAUCET FOR THEIR FLOWERS.
>
> LEASE REMEMBER TO TURN OFF AFTER USE.
>
> THANK YOU

Henry removed the coloured wrapping paper from his pot of winter violets, scrunched it up and tucked it into his coat pocket. He opened the tap fully and let the water flow over the soil until it began to seep out of the perforated holes at the bottom of the container. A thin stream trickled down his hand and along the inside of his sleeve. He shook his arm, closed the tap as tightly as he was able, then turned and wove his way towards the garden of graves.

'As long as you approach from the main central pathway, you should have no trouble at all in finding her,' Eve Marie had said.

Henry stepped onto the path and cast a respectful glance to either side of him. Some of the older graves had cracked and sunk like under-baked cakes in the middle; others were wilfully overgrown. The remainder lay cheek by jowl in long, orderly lines, straight and neat as dominoes. He continued onwards, counting the designated number of rows as he walked, and turned in to his left, carefully negotiating the placement of his feet until he arrived at last at Francine's sleeping angel.

Henry stood in silence to regard it. It was surprisingly small, as angels on gravestones go; probably not much longer than his forearm. And yet he sensed at once how it radiated a profoundly peaceful presence. The angel was reclining on its side in perfect alignment across the top of Francine's head-stone, its hands tucked in under its cheek, hair and robes flowing freely over its body, wings folded behind it.

He placed his stick on the ground and stooped to arrange his violets at the head of the grave. First, he cleared a small, round space in the gravel with his fingers. When he was satis-fied he'd made enough room, he pushed the stones flush against the bottom of the container. There were no other flowers present, he noted; just a pale pink ceramic vase half-filled with rainwater, and a few errant shoots peeping up here and there, displaced, presumably, from a nearby grave.

'I'll be taking some holly and a seasonal flower arrange-ment to my parents' graves on Christmas Eve,' Eve Marie told him. 'My mother, especially, would have appreciated that. It was always her favourite time of year.'

Henry stepped back to assess his work. The spray of indigo petals, with their leaves of dark, succulent green, looked so vibrant, so alive against the flat, mackerel grey of the head-stone, as though they'd been created for this one moment alone, their divine purpose gloriously, rapturously fulfilled. He paused for a minute to admire them, then he slipped his brown paper bag from his pocket and took out his uniform cap.

Should I wear it? he wondered. The thought passed fleetingly through his mind, but it seemed maudlin, somehow – exactly the kind of sentimental gesture that Davy Hardcastle (who last he'd heard was living a life of ageing hedonism in the Costa del Sol) would say made him look like a complete and utter arse.

Henry held it, instead, to his chest, his fingers pressed for comfort, for stability, to the rough, blue cloth. A stray thread, gilded by the afternoon light, fell from its surface and floated to the edge of the grave. He watched it settle onto the gravel, then straightening his shoulders, he moored his gaze to the anchor of Francine's name.

'Hello, Francine. It's me, Henry.'

His voice sounded so small and thin amongst the vast repository of dust and bones; a place where weeds flourished between the cracks; where all was attended by an inevitable crumbling, a final settling, a crisp and eerie calm.

He rocked lightly on his feet. 'I came to tell you that I'm sorry. Whatever you may have thought of me, however it must have looked, the truth is, I'm still in love with you.'

Henry closed his eyes and stood, cap in hand, a lone figure among the graves. Outwardly, he was as decrepit as the wildest graves themselves, his face marred with lines, his rheumy eyes fighting back the pain that trickled through the cracks in his tired, wounded heart. And yet on the inside, he knew that in

337

some enduring corner of his being he was at once a boy, a teenager, a man. He was every age he had ever been, transcending definition. He was Henry Applebee, brimming still, with love.

Henry couldn't be certain how long these thoughts absorbed him, but in time, he stooped down once again and made a further indentation in the gravel, this time at the near end of the grave. When the stones had been sufficiently swept aside, he picked up his paper bag and reached inside it for a second time.

What he withdrew was a brightly coloured picture postcard. On the front was a photograph of Blackpool Pleasure Beach, its famous wooden rollercoaster dipping and arching against a cobalt blue horizon. He'd bought it in March 1968, the very same day he'd discovered that Francine had returned to the Tower Ballroom just a couple of weeks before him. He'd sat on a bench on the seafront and filled it with fragments of remembered conversations – things she'd said to him, that he'd said to her – isolated phrases, confidences, meaningless now to anyone who might stumble upon them but him. Henry laid the postcard flat on the powdery soil and covered it over with gravel until no visible trace remained. The words had long since been committed to memory; the card itself would disintegrate quickly enough with the winter rain.

He returned his cap to his bag and made his way back to the clearing. He walked to a bench and sat down for a final view of the grounds, of the benevolent angel slumbering on Francine's grave.

The thud of a door being pulled to behind him caused

Henry to turn his head. The cemetery caretaker ambled towards him, a bright yellow thermos in his hand.

'Yeh'll be stiff as a board sitting out here in the cold!' the man said. 'A nice hot coffee'll warm yeh up. I've added a wee dram of whisky, just to chase the gremlins away.'

He threw Henry a lopsided grin and handed him a paper cup which he filled to the brim with a strong, dark liquid, as rich and invigorating as the inside of a Lyons Corner House. 'If yeh need anything, my name's Douglas. We'll be closing at four today, or thereabouts. If yeh're not gone by then, I'll come and shoo yeh away.'

'Thank you,' Henry said. He took a sip of coffee and smiled. 'You're very kind.'

Douglas tipped his head towards the graves. 'Aye, they'll not appreciate us here after sundown. They'd want us home and in the warm, that much I can guarantee.' He pulled a set of keys from his trouser pocket and pointed to a nearby van. 'Off to do my rounds!'

Henry raised his hand and gave him a comradely wave.

When he turned back to face the graves Henry was surprised to see a girl with long, wavy hair making her way along the central pathway. She held up her hand, counted off the rows as he had done, and began to pick her way between the gravestones until she was standing where Henry had stood, directly in front of Francine's angel.

The girl bent forwards at the waist – he assumed so she could better read the inscription on the headstone. Seconds later she spun round, one hand pressed to her hip, the other held flat above her eyes, as though to shield them from an invisible sun.

'Henry!' she cried. 'It's Ariel! Where are you?'

Henry supported his weight with his stick and raised himself to his feet. 'Here!' he called back. 'I'm over here!'

At the sight of his granddaughter's face, Henry's heart broke its moorings and floated into the sky, high overhead, like a carefree Chinese lantern. His immediate instinct was to run to her, the way he and Devlin used to race to the top of Parliament Hill, but his legs were powerless beneath him. He gripped the handle of his stick and waited while she retraced her steps through the graves. She was back on the pathway in an instant. From there, she ran to the clearing and arrived flushed and breathless at his bench.

Ariel threw her arms around Henry's neck and held him as though she would never let him go. He felt his body weaken; felt certain, in fact, that he might be in danger of toppling over, of losing his senses altogether, but the firmness of her grasp kept him upright on his feet.

Henry closed his eyes. Try as he might, he couldn't remember the last time anyone had hugged him.

Moira Macclesfield, a former ambulance driver who now worked in his local corner shop, had once given him a polite *air-hug-pat-on-the-back-combo* when he told her that the 'Two-for-one Senior Citizen Discount Day' (an initiative of her own devising) had revolutionised his life.

But this was something else entirely.

Holding his granddaughter in his arms, Henry realised he'd forgotten what it felt like to melt so completely into another person's embrace. The gentle brush of hair against his cheek. The flow of breath beside his ear. Above all, that most tender and generous of human connections: the reassuring warmth of another, supporting him, raising him up so that he did not stand alone.

'I'm so sorry about Francine,' Ariel said softly. 'But I'm happier than you can ever know to have found you, and I know Linus and Isaac will be, too.'

She was holding him so tightly that Henry could scarcely conceive of letting her go.

He kept his eyes closed a moment longer. Relinquishing his grip at last, he took a step backwards and stared into Ariel's face. 'I never expected any of this. I just wanted to see her, just once more.' Henry's vision blurred. 'It almost doesn't seem right that an old man like myself should be given so much, just when I thought everything had been lost for good.'

Ariel's arms had fallen to her sides, her gaze locked on his. 'Honestly, I didn't expect any of it either. It feels a little bit like it's happening to someone else.'

She laughed then. A laugh of incredulity. A laugh, Henry suspected, of release.

She raised her hand to her mouth, as though the sound of laughter had taken her by surprise.

Her eyes were as wide and full as his.

'I know it's been a shock, but please don't go back to London just yet. Come with me to Eve Marie's. She's waiting for us outside in her car, and I still need to give her the envelope from Estelle. It's what I came here to do, only now I think I finally understand what it contains.'

Henry shifted his gaze in the direction of Francine's sleeping angel. *This is our granddaughter,* he mused. *Can you believe it?*

'Grandad?'

Henry started.

Ariel slid her hand through his arm. 'If you're ready, we should probably get going. You're family now. It would mean the world to me if you could be there with me when she opens it.'

26

Pie and Mash

EDINBURGH, DECEMBER 7

Travis

Travis was feeling strangely distracted. Like a returning melody, his thoughts ebbed and flowed, circling in a dizzying refrain to Ariel, and by association, to Henry, the old man who'd had the *chutzpah* never to give up on love.

Time and again during the course of the morning, he'd found himself drifting. The understated beauty of Ariel's face had imprinted itself on his retinas, so that wherever he looked, there it was: her otherworldliness, projecting back at him.

His friend JP – a half French, half Chicagoan bartender he knew in New York – would doubtless call it *recherché*.

'Translation, please,' Travis said the first time JP used it.

'Look it up, man. I've never been able to find a satisfying English equivalent.'

'Seriously? I thought you were fluent?!'

JP shrugged and threw him a look of calculated insouciance. 'You're such a ball-breaker, Travis. You know that?'

Travis grinned. 'Yup.'

JP placed a wine glass on the counter and slid it towards him. 'So in *my* world, *recherché* isn't obvious like, say, a cocktail; it's never gonna hit you over the head with the first sip. It's more like a fine wine; you might need to work a little harder to appreciate it, but once you get it, everything else tastes like shit.'

Travis had understood instinctively what JP meant, though this was the first time he'd experienced it in the flesh.

Ariel's face floated before him, hijacking his thoughts once again. He tried (and failed) to dim it. *Get a grip*, he told himself. *You're leaving in a few days!*

But it was too late, and he knew it. He'd seen the resolve behind her eyes. She wasn't half as lost as she thought. And whether *she* was aware of it or not, it was obvious to him that Ariel had way more strength, and way more clarity of purpose than she realised.

The floaty, wheeling sensation in his brain persisted. He'd just have to go with it. In the meantime, he figured he may as well get started on the task he'd set himself the day he boarded his plane from JFK.

'I got an email from home overnight,' he announced. 'Mom sends her love. And she wants to know when she's next going to see you.'

He expected Frank to reply, but his uncle just smiled and gave an evasive, De Niro-esque shrug.

They'd spent the early part of the day climbing to the top of Arthur's Seat, or at least, as close to the top as Frank's adult-onset acrophobia would allow. He told Travis he'd never suffered from the affliction in his youth; it was a new shade to his character, which along with the proliferation of nose and ear hair – and the inability to sleep past eight a.m., even after a late-night show – had caught him unawares. Frank had almost made it to the top – all he had to do was negotiate the final bend – when he froze just metres from the craggy summit. Cursing his paralysing inability to move either forwards or backwards, he lowered himself to the ground, his back pressed against the grass verge, his heels digging into the path to steady himself, and urged Travis to continue on without him.

'I once climbed all the way up in full Elvis regalia for a photo shoot and I didn't so much as blink at the notion of it,' Frank said, shaking his head during their eventual, somewhat laboured descent.

'What was different that time?' Travis asked. 'And don't tell me it's just because you were younger.'

'I couldn't tell you. Cyn was with me that day. As I recall, I was more concerned about her. She was in her Priscilla clothes and had to take three steps for every one of mine. I learned a long time ago that the easiest way to forget your own cares is to have someone else's to worry about. Putting her welfare first came naturally to me. I guess it stopped me from being self-absorbed.'

Travis stifled a snort. 'Pity she didn't give a thought to *your* welfare when she dumped you for that massage therapist.'

He glanced at Frank out of the corner of his eye, saw him wince. He wondered if he should apologise, but Frank kept his eyes fixed on the path ahead and continued to plant one foot in front of the other until he felt confident enough to let go of Travis's arm.

'I told you before,' Frank said stoically, 'the guy was her chiropractor. She had a minor vertebrae displacement. The thing had been niggling her for months.'

'Right. Whatever.'

Travis flipped his gaze to the horizon. Thin runnels of blood began to throb at his temples. He wished his uncle had never got involved with her. Travis had met her once, the one and only time she and Frank visited New York together. Frank had organised a dinner for a group of friends at a Greek restaurant in Hell's Kitchen. Travis felt the heat burning up off the sidewalk as he climbed the steps from the subway to go meet them. It was July, a total sweatbox of an evening, the air so thick and humid, it was like wading naked through soup. The first thing he noticed about Cynthia were the tresses of liquorice-black hair clinging to her shoulder blades, curling round to the hollow dip at the base of her throat where drops of sweat had begun to pool. And yet the heat didn't seem to bother her; if anything, it enhanced her. She gazed around the room, sheathed in one of those flesh-coloured strapless dresses he'd once seen on an actress during the TV broadcast of the Emmys.

She started making eyes at him the minute he sat down.

Frank, who was next to her, was lost in conversation with the couple sitting on the opposite side of the table. *How could he be so oblivious?* Travis asked himself. Maybe his uncle had developed some sort of superhuman immunity where Cynthia was concerned. Or maybe he was just far too trusting for his own good?

Travis looked away, but he could feel Cynthia's gaze burning into him. Later, when he got up to go to the rest room, Cynthia followed. He heard the click of her stilettos on the limestone floor as she scooted up behind him and caught him – casually – by the arm. In a narrow, dimly lit corridor lined with crooked pictures of the Acropolis, Cynthia pressed her body against his own. Her breath was warm, and smelled faintly of taramasalata. Her hand slid to his waist, then meandered downwards and clamped itself, buttress-like, around his crotch. Travis couldn't believe it; Cynthia was gorgeous. And he was just a regular college kid. *What the fuck was she doing messing around with him?*

He tried to override his reflex physiological reactions by telling himself he didn't need this forty-something celebrity lookalike running her tongue over his earlobe, offering herself up like a cannolo on a plate; especially not when she was supposed to be in love with Frank – a man Travis worshipped – sitting just ten feet away on the other side of the restaurant door.

And yet.

Despite himself.

Stuff happened...

They kissed, right there in the semi-darkness listening to the sound of a moth's wings battering against an upturned light. Every so often the shouts of waiters and the clattering of plates filtered out from the kitchen on the other side of the wall. Travis was gone, all right. The taste of mint on her lips from her half-drunk Watermelon Mojito. The scent of vanilla on her skin. Her entire body a masterwork of curves. He was mere seconds away from being lost on the road to hell when the door to the restaurant swung open, and a woman wearing a sour expression of disapproval loomed nightmarishly into view.

Travis broke away, took several moments to compose himself – alone – in the rest room. When he rejoined the others at the table, Cynthia looked over at him and smiled. Her arm was draped around Frank's shoulder, her posture proprietary, as though she were a hunter, and the man beside her a freshly butchered hunk of meat.

And Frank – Frank, who so clearly suspected nothing of what had just transpired – gave Travis a look of such profound affection, such overwhelming joy at seeing his nephew again after so many months, that Travis knew he must surely die of guilt.

By one o'clock they found themselves three-quarters of the way along the Royal Mile. On Frank's recommendation, they took a left and made their way to a minimalist café at the southern end of George IV Bridge. Frank told Travis he remembered the place from his previous visits to the city, and insisted he order the speciality of the house: venison pie and mash.

Travis tucked into his food and kept one eye trained on Frank. Beneath the bright, peppy lighting his uncle's eyes had taken on a raw, red-rimmed quality, and his hands – when they weren't fluttering about his person as he spoke – had imperceptibly begun to shake.

'Hey, what do you say we just stick to water today, if that's all right with you?' Travis said in a deliberately matter-of-fact voice.

'What's up, kid? Did you overdo it on the Rioja last night or something?' Frank leaned across the table and speared a forkful of Travis's pie. 'I'd've thought the Carmichael powers of recuperation would've kicked in by now.'

Travis scooped a hefty mound of mashed potato into his mouth and laid his cutlery on his plate. 'So listen... I was just wondering... what're your plans, Uncle Frank? If the lounge work doesn't pan out here the way you'd hoped, would you consider coming back to the States? I mean – seriously, just between you and me – is everything all right?'

Frank looked up from his food, his eyebrows arched in surprise. 'Did your mom put you up to this? Or was it Travis Sr. – the world expert on how to realise your dreams? Because I can guarantee whichever one it was is hardly qualified to comment on my career.'

To his credit, Travis noted that there was nothing bitter or antagonistic about his uncle's tone; if anything, he thought he sounded pretty chilled under the circumstances.

'Come on, you know me better than that,' he replied. 'Neither one of them put me up to anything. As it happens, they don't know the half of it. They think you're doing just fine.'

'Well that's probably because I *am* doing just fine.'

Travis rolled his eyes.

'Hey! What's with the attitude?' Frank cried.

'Sorry, Uncle Frank, it's just... if you can't be honest with me, then who can you be honest with?'

Celia Reynolds

This time, Frank's expression darkened, his mouth pinching at the corners, his eyebrows dipping sharply over narrowed eyes, but Travis knew it was too late to put the brakes on now. 'Look,' he said gently, 'I know you're struggling to get work. You told me so yourself, and I've witnessed it first-hand since I've been in the UK. Maybe it's time to start over, closer to home? You could get a place near me in the city, or anywhere else for that matter. It's not as though you'd be back in Long Island, or – crap, I don't know – beating a retreat to Florida in search of a retirement condo. We could hang out. I've got a lot of contacts of my own now. I could easily hook you up with some of them?'

'I'm disappointed in you, Travis,' Frank said flatly.

Travis flinched. *There it was. The D word.* 'Yeah, well, you wouldn't be the first man in the family to say that.'

Frank shook his head. 'That wasn't what I meant, and you know it. I couldn't be prouder of you for the choices you've made. But you're a musician. And you're smart. I thought you'd be able to empathise a little more with my situation.'

Travis pushed away his plate and leaned his forearms on the table. 'I *do* empathise with you. I'm not saying you should necessarily give up what you love... I'm just wondering what's here for you now? I mean, are you happy with the way things are going, Uncle Frank? *Honestly?*'

A wall of silence dropped like a guillotine between them; the kind of climactic interlude that cleaves the air in two and leaves you wondering which side you're going to be left standing on, assuming you're still standing at all.

'I've been living outside the U.S. for almost forty years now,'

Frank replied. 'London is my home. If I came back to the States I'd have to start all over again. Do you have any idea how hard that would be for a man of my age? In case you hadn't noticed, the world looks a lot different when you're sixty-something than it does when you're twenty-six.'

'*Horseshit,*' Travis cried. 'The world looks a lot different when you have the right attitude, no matter what your age.'

'Hey, Travis, give me a break, would ya?'

'Give yourself a break, Uncle Frank!'

Travis slumped against his chair. 'I'm sorry... it's just that I know what you're capable of, remember? You were on *fire* last night because you were with real talented musicians, not some second-rate cabaret outfit with about as much stage presence as a clapped out karaoke machine. You *know* you're better than that. You write your own music, for fuck's sake! When are you going to get to perform that?'

Against all expectations to the contrary, Frank's face adopted a mellow, dignified smile. 'I'm trying, Travis. The fact is, somewhere along the way people stopped believing in me.'

Travis shook his head. 'I don't buy that. I think you just stopped believing in yourself.'

Frank took a swig of water from a glass tumbler on the table and was quiet. Travis waited, but when it looked like Frank had no intention of breaking his silence, he picked up his knife and fork, pulled his plate back towards him and continued to work away at his lunch.

'This wasn't what I aspired to be, you know,' Frank said after a while.

Travis stopped chewing mid-mouthful. 'It wasn't?'

'Hell, no. When I was a kid I dreamed of becoming a furniture maker. Or a sculptor. At any rate, I wanted to work with my hands. The way I saw it, being able to stand back and admire something you'd fashioned out of thin air had to be the greatest way of justifying a day's work. It was a skill, and there was honour in that. But there was no guarantee of money, and as far as your grandparents were concerned those kinds of vocations were hobbies – something you did in the garage as a break from the office job, or the teaching job, or whatever else paid your wage from nine to five. I can't say I blamed them. It's not as if I had any God-given talent for it. I think I was more in love with the idea of craftsmanship than anything else.'

'So what happened?'

'I entered a talent contest for a bet. And in the process, discovered I had a backhanded gift for music... I didn't win any prizes, but one of the organisers took me aside after it was all over and asked me if anyone had ever told me I looked and sounded like a young Elvis. Back then I had braces on my teeth and was real skinny. I thought he was just yanking my chain. But you'd be amazed how that one little grain of a compliment got me thinking. One throwaway remark from someone I figured knew what he was talking about, and I started to see myself in a whole new light.'

Frank's eyes glimmered as he spoke. 'We all want to find our rightful place in the world, Travis. And it doesn't matter if you're President of the United States, or a guy making cabinets in a workshop in Hoboken – it's knowing you're doing your bit that counts. So I guess what I'm saying is that I'm lucky. As unlikely as it may have seemed at the time, I found a skill. I found my place in the world. And you know what? It felt pretty damn amazing.'

'I get it, Uncle Frank, I really do,' Travis said softly. 'But life doesn't stand still, no matter what we think. Things evolve, and it's up to us to evolve with them. The question is, what happens now?'

'Now I'm adapting to the times, is all. Maybe some things you can't do forever. I'm finding a new fit for what I have to offer. I'm not done here. I have more to give, kid. You just need to have a little faith.'

Travis smiled to himself. *You just need to have a little faith.* Those were the exact same words he'd used himself with Travis Sr.

They finished the rest of their meal, for the most part, in silence. Travis didn't tell Frank how pissed Travis Sr. was about Travis supposedly 'running out on a crisis' to fly to Europe. The whole thing was ridiculous. Superstorm Sandy may have hit the East Coast just days before he left, but there was no way he'd have turned his back on his parents if the immediate area around their home hadn't got off relatively lightly. *Anyway, don't you worry*, his mom wrote in her email. *I told him, 'Travis has his own life now. He's making a good, honest living. And I'm proud of him.'*

'Did you hear from Ariel today?' Frank asked as they were waiting for the check. 'If not, you should call her and see how she's doing. She's a nice kid, and she's grown up into a real nice young lady. It's a shame you're flying home in a couple of days.'

Travis flicked his gaze upwards, caught the twinkle in his uncle's eyes. 'Meaning?'

'*Meaning*,' Frank replied, 'it's a shame you're flying home in a couple of days.'

'Uh-huh.' He suppressed a smile and wondered if the Ariel-sized bubble floating above his head had been visible to Frank for the entire duration of the morning.

'Yes,' Frank said. 'It has.'

Travis burst out laughing. 'What are you talking about?'

'That puppy-dog look on your face. It's been there the whole damn day. Don't think you can pull the wool over *my* eyes. I'm a crooner, remember? I know loved-up when I see it.'

Travis felt as though the floor had just slid from under him. 'So anyway,' he said, his eyes settling somewhere in the middle-distance, 'since you ask... Ariel and I traded messages earlier. She sounded okay. She was on her way to her meeting. Said she'd check in with me later.' He paused and met Frank's gaze. 'You know, maybe you should consider taking a break in the New Year? Get out of London for a while? You could go back to Oystermouth. I'm sure Ariel and her family would love to see you.'

Frank raked his fingers through his hair, pursed his lips. 'I don't know, Travis. I'm sure Ariel and her dad have enough on their plates already. And besides, now that I come to think of it, that was when I first suspected Cyn was fooling around on me. She was forever hanging up the phone whenever I walked into the room. Guys used to swarm around her like flies.' He lowered his eyes. 'I guess some hurt more than others.'

Travis nodded and looked away. There wasn't a trace of malice in Frank's voice. No veiled accusation or inference of any kind to suggest that he knew. And yet somehow, the worst part of all was Travis's hunch that Frank would probably have forgiven him if he did.

'That's life,' Frank added with a shrug. 'We all have our demons to contend with. I'll think about it. As ideas go, it might not be the worst you've ever had, kiddo.'

27

The Colour of Caviar

CRAMOND, EDINBURGH, DECEMBER 7

Ariel

The mid-afternoon light was already starting to wane as Ariel and Henry made their way back up the path towards Eve Marie's house. Ariel helped Henry into the hallway where he took off his coat and hung it alongside his stick on a wooden stand just inside the front door. He wasn't wearing a suit today. Instead, he was dressed in a brown V-neck jumper, a white check shirt, and a maroon tie. There was a small hole in the elbow of his right sleeve, she noticed; a tiny road sign of neglect which she guessed he'd have patched up in an instant, had he been aware of it.

'Well, here we are,' Eve Marie said. 'Back where we started! Is everyone all right?'

Before either of them could answer, they heard the sound

of a phone ringing somewhere at the back of the house.

Eve Marie frowned. 'Probably a cold caller. I'll hang up if it is. Make yourselves at home in the living room. I'll be back in a sec.'

Ariel and Henry seated themselves side by side on the sofa. 'I thought it was only defenceless pensioners who got cold calls,' Henry whispered in Ariel's ear. 'Drives me crackers. Most of the time I pretend I'm the butler. I tell them I have the newspapers to iron. Then I cut them off.'

'Nice one,' she replied. 'I'll have to remember that.'

A shiver trickled down the back of her spine as she spoke. She glanced slowly around the room. *Mam?*

The air stilled.

Ariel froze. *Is that you?*

Henry's weight shifted and settled beside her. She opened her canvas bag and placed Estelle's envelope in the centre of the coffee table. Her mother's words, emblazoned across it, suddenly looked so mundane, so perfunctory – as though she'd been compiling a To Do list, not one of the final written instructions she would ever compose.

Ariel caught at the word, mulled it over in her mind. Com-pose. *Verb*: *To make or produce by combining parts or elements; to set in order, or at rest.* Wasn't that exactly what they were doing here today?

'Penny for your thoughts?' Henry asked in a low voice. He leaned in and nudged his hand against her knee.

'Actually,' she replied, 'I'm hoping that after everything that's happened, this final gesture doesn't feel like an afterthought. Not when it was so obviously meaningful to Estelle.'

'It won't. You've come all this way, just as your mother asked you to do. Whatever happens from here on in, we're partners now. In it to the bittersweet end.'

'Partners,' she echoed. 'That sounds great.'

Henry's skin smelled of shaving cream and soap suds. His cheeks were still red from the cold, the grooves of his finger-tips lightly ingrained with soil.

He hadn't said much at all during the drive back from the cemetery.

'You're sure everything's all right?' he asked.

Ariel nodded. 'My dad's going to flip when he finds out about all this. He's been dreaming of meeting you his entire life.'

'Flip?' Henry said in a startled voice. 'Is that good or bad?'

'Good,' she said, smiling. 'It's definitely good.'

Eve Marie appeared in the doorway and busied herself with reigniting the fire and switching on the garlands of pale yellow lights draped around the Christmas tree.

The room shrugged off its shadows and glowed.

Ariel shifted her gaze to the envelope. 'Go ahead. Open it,' she said, when Eve Marie had finally sat down. 'I'm sorry it's taken me so long to give it to you.' She moved it closer to Eve Marie's side of the coffee table and gave her an encouraging nod.

Without any further ado, Eve Marie pulled the envelope towards her, flipped it over and tugged on the adhesive strip running along its back. She balanced the package on her knee and peered down into its wide, yawning mouth. A small V, like the calyx of a rose petal, formed between her eyes. She laid the envelope flat on her lap and slid her hand inside.

What revealed itself, inch by inch, was a prodigious tome

of a book, its cover an intense, midnight blue. An inky cuttle-fish blue. A blue the colour of caviar. There was nothing printed on the outside, just a short, handwritten message pinned to the top right-hand corner with a paper clip.

Eve Marie slipped on a pair of glasses and read the note out loud:

Dear Mia,
This slightly unconventional scrapbook was to be my gift
to you on the publication of your novel. It's pretty much
a random snapshot of everything that's gone before. Forgive
the inevitable cliché, but the future is yours to write…
  Keep smiling, and please – take care of Linus for me.
  With much love,
  Estelle x

'Oh!' Eve Marie cried. She placed the note to one side and opened the book's cover. The spine cracked like a starting pistol and a semitransparent sheet of ivory paper fluttered briefly upwards before rippling back into place. She lifted it up and flipped it over. On an otherwise empty page beneath were four handwritten words: The Book of Bliss.

'Henry, you'd better take a look at this.' Eve Marie glanced at him over the rim of her glasses. 'Estelle addressed it to me, but I think it's going to mean just as much to you.'

Ariel felt her palms begin to sweat. She moved around to the armchair so that Eve Marie could take her place next to Henry on the sofa. Henry's body creaked forwards, his lips parting, his mouth falling open to form a perfect letter O.

It began with a key held in place by two strips of Sellotape. Beside it, a photograph of a beaming Linus and Estelle leaning against the counter of their newly leased shop.

Wispy locks of baby hair, sewn onto the page with thick, red wool followed. Then:

Christening cards and seashells.

Sprigs of dried gorse from the cliffs over Langland Bay.

Fairground tickets; train tickets to London.

A collage of a castle overlooking a crimson meadow.

Rhinestones – a whole sprinkling of them – swept up like forgotten treasure from an attic floor.

A plastic sheriff's badge; the rubber wheel from a toy truck.

Valentine cards.

Photos of candle-extinguishings, cake-demolishings. With each consecutive turn of the page, the powerful scents of patchouli and sweet orange drifted like threads of incense into the room.

'It's incredible. A living, breathing tapestry of life!' Eve Marie cried.

'Of a family's life,' Henry added. His grey eyes were wide, unblinking. 'I can't believe how much I've missed. And yet here it all is; like a dream I never remembered having!'

Ariel watched as one by one, the pages turned. The collage she'd made herself using handfuls of red geranium petals gathered up from the back lawn after a summer storm. On the following page was a photograph she'd taken with the Olympus of Isaac learning to ride a bike. Estelle clearly hadn't paid much attention to chronology, because alongside it was a picture of Ariel, not much older than four or five, peering out of a tent and waving. She remembered the tent well – she remembered playing inside it for hours and hours – but she didn't remember the photograph. She couldn't say for sure at what, or to whom, she was waving.

'Traveller's blood.' She looked up at Eve Marie and Henry and smiled. 'Estelle told me once that way back, there was a troupe of travelling performers on her side of the family, though I don't know what she was basing it on – I never saw any photographic evidence. Maybe it was just an urban family myth. Either way, I definitely remember her being very attached to that tent.'

'Do you still have it?' Eve Marie asked.

Ariel shrugged. 'I'm not sure. It probably got stuffed away in a cupboard somewhere. I doubt she'd have given it away.'

The whimsical – sometimes banal, often nonsensical – pieces of family life that Estelle had chosen to preserve had been gathered together with such care and attention, offset here and there with random doodles and annotations. Ariel wondered if Linus had any knowledge at all of its existence. Maybe he'd known about it all along, without realising for whom it was secretly intended?

She stared around the room, searching for signs of her mother's invisible presence. *I'm sorry,* she said, silently. *I'm sorry I thought you were more interested in the business than you were in us. I didn't understand. I'm sorry –*

Henry raised his head. *Penny for your thoughts?* his glance seemed to ask her once again.

Ariel met his gaze. 'Are you okay?' she mouthed.

'Right as rain,' Henry mouthed back.

She leaned to one side and picked up the discarded envelope from the floor. It felt so light and airy now that its contents had finally been set free. She toyed with it for a moment in her lap, running its fluted edges between her fingers, smoothing the paper flat against her knees until for no apparent reason, she was seized by an overwhelming impulse to turn the envelope on its side and look inside.

The first thing that popped into her head was a Russian matryoshka: a doll within a doll within a doll...

Ariel flicked her eyes to the sofa. Eve Marie and Henry were both still sitting with heads bent, poring over Estelle's book. She held her breath and reached her hand towards a plain white envelope lying – until now undetected – at the bottom. Nudging it discreetly with her forefinger, she saw that there was just one name written on it: *her own.*

Ariel caught the envelope between her fingers, fished it out and slipped it into the back pocket of her jeans.

The touch of it alone was enough to send her reeling.

Mam?

A soft throb of longing pulsed against her skin. She tucked her hands beneath her thighs. Slowly, the contents of Estelle's book receded into a benign haze. All she could think about was the envelope in her pocket. *What was inside it? What, in the end, had her mother wanted to say?*

The question was mind-bending, monumental. Ariel willed herself to be patient. To *wait*. Whatever it contained, there would, she told herself, be time to read it later; time alone in private, before she finally turned for home.

28

Pas de Deux

OYSTERMOUTH, WALES: *CHRISTMAS*

Linus and Henry

When the call came through, Linus was sitting behind the counter gazing at a sodden trail of pedestrians as they scurried, heads bowed, hats and hair askew, up the winding Newton Road. Dogged, near horizontal spikes of rain, tossed like darts across the gusting bay, fell sharply against the window. The noise was so loud, so relentless, he very nearly didn't hear the phone at all.

He pressed his finger to his ear. 'Ariel?'

'Yes, it's me. Can you hear me?'

Her words kept coming, tumbling through the ether in one long, delirious rush, exactly the way they'd done when she was a child.

'Slow down!' he cried. 'I can't make head or tail of what you're saying!'

King's Cross he caught. Then *love affair. Betrayal. Alive.*

Finally, the message hit home: his father – an eighty-five-year-old ex-serviceman and former language teacher from north London – had been discovered travelling halfway across the country on a London to Edinburgh train.

'His name's Henry,' Ariel kept repeating. 'Your father's name is Henry Applebee.'

'*Henry.*' The word slipped momentously from Linus's lips. His eyes skimmed past the window and settled amongst the overladen shelves. 'Henry Applebee,' he murmured, his voice laced with awe. 'What a brilliant name.'

'He didn't know about you,' Ariel went on. 'You'll have to hear him tell it to you for himself.'

Linus paused. 'Is he coming home with you?'

'He'll come – very soon – but not right away. I hope that's okay?'

Linus nodded. If he'd correctly followed what his daughter was trying to tell him, Henry wanted to go home to Kentish Town. Collect his dog and a change of clothes.

'Where is he now?' he managed at last.

Ariel called out to someone in the background.

'Evie?' The word left Linus's mouth and dropped, unnoticed, into the void. Every aborted attempt at reconciliation – all the half-finished letters, the unwritten birthday cards, the telephone numbers dialled only in part – came hurtling back towards him. 'Jesus, I'm a bloody fool.'

'Henry's gone,' Ariel blurted into the phone.

'What?'

'A couple of minutes ago. I think he wanted to give you some time to process everything. He's taken a taxi back to his hotel to get ready for his return journey home.'

'He left? Already?' Linus brushed a stray speck of dust from the countertop. 'Right, pet,' he said, comprehending nothing, 'I understand.'

'I wish I'd known,' Ariel said in a reproving voice. 'I wish you'd told me about it all instead of shutting me out.'

He cradled his forehead in his hand. 'Shutting you out was never my intention, pet, Mam knew that. It's a shoddy excuse, but families are –'

'Complicated,' Ariel chimed. 'I know. It's the second time today I've heard that.'

Linus was silent. Something was rising in his chest; something that felt thrillingly like hope. 'Ariel, what's he like?'

Ariel paused. 'I'm not sure I can put him into words. You'll see soon enough.'

He gave a short, nervous laugh.

'Are you all right?'

Linus nodded vigorously into the phone. 'I'm grand. I think Henry was right, though. I probably do need some time to get used to it all before hearing his voice for the very first time.'

'Great,' Ariel replied. 'In the meantime, there's someone else here who wants to talk to you. Hang on. DON'T GO ANYWHERE! I'll just put her on.'

* * *

Henry's eventual arrival was organised for the week before Christmas, when the Swansea air hung thick with the lure of Happy Hour and four o'clock pints.

In the centre of town hordes of office workers wearing Santa hats and light-up reindeer antlers swarmed like drunken dockers into the pubs. People were predisposed to be cheerful, and mass frivolity was already spilling out onto every pavement like the pools of vomit which would inevitably follow, in some forgotten corner, under cover of darkness, once the drinking reached its peak.

On hearing the news, Rosemary told Linus she'd be vacating the attic room for a couple of weeks to spend the holidays with her sister in Tunbridge Wells:

'I'll be off the day before your father arrives, so there'll be no problem with giving him my room. I hope he's okay to walk up all the stairs, but once he's there I'll make sure it's left nice and tidy. I've cleared out a couple of drawers and half the wardrobe. And I'll do another smudging ceremony before I go. It's time to welcome new energy into the house. New energy, and new blood.'

Linus pressed his palms together in front of his chest. 'Thank you, Rosie. You're one in a million.'

'Yes,' she replied with a wink. 'I know.'

The day itself arrived in unimpressive fashion, with sky the colour of putty, and air that was fat with damp. It drizzled intermittently as seagulls swooped over the bay, diving and circling in wide, eager loops, hunting for scraps, their outstretched wings slicing like seaplanes through the mist.

Linus parked the car in town and walked with Ariel through the train station entrance. He'd been up since dawn. He'd barely slept for days.

He pinned his gaze to the monitor. 'The London train's on time,' he muttered. 'Good. Good.'

They positioned themselves a short distance from the electronic gates. 'Is everything okay?' Ariel asked. 'You look like you're about to heave.'

Linus's stomach rose vertiginously to his throat. 'Thank you. That makes me feel so much better.'

'It's all right,' she said, laughing. 'Really. I know how much this means to you.'

Linus clenched and unclenched his fists. His nerves were hopelessly frayed. 'Actually,' he confessed, 'I do feel a bit sick.'

Ariel needled him with her soft, clear eyes. 'Nerves are totally understandable. Anyway, I'm sure you and Henry are both feeling exactly the same way.'

'Thanks, pet.' He gave her a weak smile. 'Big day, I guess.'

His spine, neck and arms locked and stiffened. He felt as awkward as a schoolboy in a pair of short trousers and Sunday best tie, his hair pressed flat as a swimming cap against his skull, a pair of sensible Clarks lace-ups on his feet. As it was, he'd shaved and put on a clean shirt. He'd even stopped by the barbers so that the mutinous mass of hair (which normally dangled around his face like a pair of badly hung curtains) now assumed some recognisable semblance of style.

He gazed past the barriers and scanned the stream of passengers filtering towards them from the London train. He wiped a film of perspiration from his brow. There may be eight million people in London, but he still couldn't get his head around the fact that for two full decades, he and his father had been living in exactly the same place...

'Jesus Christ.'

'You really need to calm down.' Ariel elbowed him in the ribs. 'You look great! Nervous, but great.'

Linus stared into the distance. 'It's the waiting that's killing me. It's God-awful.'

He watched the last of the crowds disperse until only a solitary elderly gentleman and his dog remained. Henry approached the gate, a walking stick and Banjo's lead in one hand, a small brown suitcase in the other.

'Henry!' Ariel shot her arm into the air and waved. 'We're over here!'

Henry cast an expectant glance in their direction.

A bolt of energy spiralled through Linus's body as Henry passed through the barrier, and continued walking until he was standing directly in front of them. Linus stared at the tufts of feathery white hair smoothed back along the rim of Henry's cap; at the sagging half-moons of skin beneath his eyes; at the slow, steady pulsing of his neck. And in one fell swoop, the fantasy he'd been playing out for decades was over.

Tension drained from his body, sweeping with it every last remnant of the imaginary figure he'd been carrying with him for so long.

The smile all but exploded out of him.

'Hello, Dad.'

Henry peered back through the lightly smudged lenses of his glasses. He placed his suitcase on the ground, raised his hand and laid it on Linus's shoulder.

'Hello, Linus,' he replied. 'I *knew* it! I *knew* you'd have your mother's eyes!'

Within twenty-four hours of his arrival in Oystermouth, Henry had coined a brand-new Mantra of the Day: *If our time on earth is little more than a flyby, there's no point wasting a second of it on things we can't change.*

He lingered inside the entrance to the shop and marvelled at the brimming shelves and crowded display tables mushrooming upwards from the shiny parquet floor. 'It's wonderful!' he cried. 'All of it! Just wonderful!'

Linus circled around him, sweeping stray volumes aside, straightening piles of books that to Henry's eye had looked perfectly fine as they were. 'Welcome to *Bliss Books*,' he said, with a rather endearing smile. 'It's probably the one instance when I've been grateful for my adoptive surname. *Applebee Books* has a lovely ring to it, but it's maybe not quite so fitting for the area of specialisation I had in mind.'

Henry's eyes glistened in the arcs of light elbowing in through the shopfront window. A shy, proverbial *pas de deux* was unfolding between them – he could feel it as clearly as the shooting pains in his right knee. He hadn't stolen glances at anyone like this for years! And yet here they were, acting like some sort of courting couple, trailing at each other's heels. The very prospect filled him with a near overwhelming sense of joy. He cast a furtive glance at his son's benign demeanour.

Youthful impetuosity. Stubbornness. Barefaced pride...
Whatever name you gave it, Henry saw now that the very
flaw that bound them together had led them both to turn
their backs on a woman they loved...

'I am proud of it,' Linus replied, slipping behind the counter.
'It hasn't always been easy, though. Bookshops are facing so
many challenges, especially the small independents like *Bliss
Books.*'

Henry roused himself from his thoughts and gave Linus a
sympathetic nod. 'It sounds nothing short of criminal. Where's
it going to end? They'll be closing record shops next!'

He wiped the lenses of his glasses on his shirt end so that
he might better peruse the stacks. He wondered whether they
had anything in their burgeoning second-hand section in
French. He'd never read a book of the kind sold at *Bliss Books*
in another language, and it occurred to him that it might be
an excellent way of expanding his vocabulary.

He traced his finger along the shelf nearest to him and made
a mental note to bring it up later in his stay. He was equally
keen to explore the *UFOs/Unexplained Phenomena* section, and
with something of an unaccustomed thrill, he suspected he'd
be among open minds as far as that subject was concerned.

'Anyway, I'm sure there'll always be folks who like to feel
the weight of a book in their hands rather than an electronic
screen,' Linus mused. He gave a hopeful scratch of his head.
'We'll muddle through. In a world gone mad for technology,
I'm going to trust that books, like art, will never truly go out
of style. With any luck, those will be the things that people
gravitate towards when we're all living in sterile pods and

driving cars through the sky. Maybe that's when bookshops like this one will have a renaissance –'

His voice trailed off, his gaze plummeting to the floor.

'What is it?' Henry asked in alarm. He made his way to the counter and wondered if it would be acceptable to take hold of his son's arm. 'Where did you go?'

'Oh, it's nothing,' Linus replied with a wistful smile. 'It's just something Estelle used to say about the world speeding up, that's all. She said no matter what, she'd still be here, keeping everything ticking along, putting everyone's neuroses into perspective. She liked to joke that she was a Renaissance woman, always one step ahead of the curve. And she was certainly that, and more besides.'

On Christmas morning Henry woke with a start at dawn. He opened and closed his eyes three times in a row, just to establish his surroundings were truly real.

'If anyone up there's listening,' he whispered, 'PLEASE don't let this be a dream.'

A smear of light refracted against the eaves, casting watery shadows along the walls. Henry turned his head to the window. Tiny crystals of hoarfrost had formed a fine white crust on the pane. In Kentish Town, it was often the wail of passing sirens that greeted him when he woke. Here, it was the *thump thump* of a bird hopping heavy-footed across the roof.

The air creaked. Everything smelled fresh, and coastal cool.

He raised himself up on his pillow and drew the promise of the day deep into his lungs. 'Today,' he announced, 'will be unlike any day of my life so far.'

The way it had been, years ago: *The Perry Como Christmas Album* playing on a loop in the background; Devlin handing out cognac and cigars to the men; cherry brandy and selection boxes to the girls. There'd be singing and card-playing; everyone growing louder and brighter and blowsier, none more so than Devlin himself sitting with his wife, Kathleen, on his knee, his customary Black Russian cocktail in his hand.

Amy, a child still, playing with her toys on the rug.

Henry, folded in amongst them, tapping his toes in time with the music, smiling, looking on.

'Happy Christmas, Devlin,' he whispered.

He tied a festive red ribbon around Banjo's neck and made his way downstairs.

'FYI, Linus says no presents,' Ariel told him a few days before his arrival. 'I think he's worried it'll put too much pressure on everyone. He's trying to keep things casual.'

'Casual!' Henry cried. 'After sixty-five years?!'

The sound of her laughter echoed down the line. 'I know… It's because he's nervous. Humour him. It's what I do all the time.'

'Fine,' he replied. 'It's your house. Your rules. *No presents*.'

Which, being the fervent traditionalist that he was, he then immediately ignored.

'You're giving me *Banjo?*' Isaac cried midway through Christmas morning. He'd been discharged from hospital in time for the holidays and was sitting with his legs stretched out on the sofa, a living art installation of plaster and bandages and slings. 'Grandad, that's *amazing*, but won't you be lonely without him in London?'

Henry threw Linus a quick, sidelong glance. 'Well,' he began, 'the truth is, his needs are growing, and I'm not sure my constitution is sufficiently athletic enough to handle them. So in the spirit of co-parenting, I thought we could give him the best of both worlds. In London he'll have me, and the Heath. And when we're here – assuming you'll have us back, of course – he'll be all yours. He'll enjoy having seagulls to chase after, not to mention someone with a young pair of legs who can keep up with him. Once your cast is off, that is.'

'Dad, we've only just found you,' Linus said. 'You'll always be welcome here.'

Henry turned to him and smiled.

'And anyway,' Linus went on, 'it's not as if we haven't got any catching up to do.'

'A word of warning,' Isaac cut in, when he caught Henry's eye. 'He *seems* quiet enough, but if you get him onto a subject he's passionate about, my dad can talk for Wales.'

Henry's gift to Linus were his (still ongoing) 'recollections', with the bulk of what he'd written to date neatly collated in the recently completed *Notebook #1*.

Linus's eyes immediately misted over. 'Honestly, I don't know what to say.'

'No need to say anything,' Henry replied. 'Just bear in mind that your memory gets a little slippery when you get to my age. The things I've written are the things I couldn't forget. I never imagined anyone might actually *read* any of it, so I dare say some parts may not make much sense. But you can ask me anything. I'll tell you whatever you need to know.'

Linus held the notebook in his hand. 'It's perfect, thank

you! I'll start reading it tonight.' He opened the cover and gave Henry a quizzical stare. 'Oh, you've given it a title? *Henry Applebee: Monochrome Man?*'

'The explanation's inside,' Henry answered brightly. 'It's all there, in black and white...'

He found Ariel buttoning up her coat in the kitchen. Her canvas shoulder bag was lying nearby on the countertop, and as he walked towards her, she opened it up and dropped in a bottle of water and her phone.

Henry spotted a plain white envelope poking out from the inside pocket. He'd first seen her with it the day he arrived, but he hadn't wanted to pry and ask who it was from.

'Are you going out?' he said. 'Now? Alone?'

She coiled her multicoloured scarf around her neck and smiled. 'Yes, just for a bit. It's tradition – well, actually, it's something Estelle liked to do after lunch, but the light's better in the morning. I thought I'd go down to Mumbles Head and take some photos. I won't be long.'

Henry's hand fluttered to his cardigan pocket and the gift he'd been waiting all morning to give to her once he finally got her on her own.

'Why don't you come with me?' she asked. 'We could take Banjo along for a walk?'

Henry shook his head. 'No, no, I wouldn't want to hold you up. And Banjo's been out for a run already.'

His eyes drifted to the half-dozen empty wrappers from the bumper tin of Quality Street he'd brought with him from home. Brushing them to one side, he pulled a stool out from behind the breakfast bar and attempted to hike himself onto it without breaking a hip.

'I expect you'll want to be making plans now, anyway,' Henry said casually. He reached for a Toffee Penny and twirled it round in his fingers. 'For the future, I mean. Nothing like a bit of sea air to stimulate the mind.'

Ariel shrugged. 'I wish it was that easy.' She tugged at the ends of her coat sleeves. 'There doesn't seem to be an instruction manual for that. At least, not one that seems to make any sense to me.'

'Ah well,' Henry replied, 'as far as I can tell, I don't think there ever has been. Life would be dull as dishwater if we knew every single destination before we'd even set off. Although in your case, I think you probably have a pretty good idea of where it is you'd like to end up.'

She opened her mouth to speak, but Henry waved his hand. The Toffee Penny flew from between his fingers, sailed through the air with a series of flamboyant cartwheels, and against all bets to the contrary, made a perfect landing back inside the tin.

'Nice one!' Ariel said with a smile.

Henry tapped his hand against the countertop. 'Anyhow,' he resumed, 'even if you didn't have the faintest idea about *any* of it, the important thing to remember is that you're not alone. I'd play my opening move, if I were you. Pick a road and see where it takes you. You can always cross to another one if it doesn't work out. Meanwhile, if you don't mind me delaying you for just a minute, I wanted to give you this.'

Henry pulled a small box from his cardigan pocket and placed it on the counter between them.

'Henry! I thought we weren't doing presents!' Ariel cried.

'Really?' He shook his head. 'Oh no... I don't remember ever agreeing to *that*.'

Ariel drew the box towards her and tugged on the shiny gold ribbon which – after something of a struggle – he'd finally managed to secure in a semi-respectable bow. Nestled inside, wrapped in a square of pale blue tissue paper, was a silver hair clip, a pearl and diamanté butterfly perched on its tip. The butterfly's wings were spread high and wide, as though it had just that moment alighted, or conversely, was preparing itself for flight.

'Whether it's coming or going depends on your perspective,' Henry said. 'Like most things in life, it all comes down to how you choose to view it.'

Ariel gasped. 'It's beautiful! But you know I can't take it. It has way too much meaning for you. It wouldn't be right.'

She placed the clip in her palm and held it out in front of her, as though the pale December rays filtering through the kitchen window might somehow coax the butterfly to life.

Henry covered her hand with his own and pressed her palm shut. 'Your grandmother wouldn't want it to be buried away in a musty old suitcase any longer. It's far too pretty for that.' He released his grip and watched her fingers slowly uncurl. 'I think it's time to take it out into the world and let it breathe, don't you?'

Ariel faltered. 'Ye-es... But what about Eve Marie? It was her mother's. If it goes to anyone, shouldn't it go to her?'

'Perhaps,' Henry conceded. 'But I know for a fact that she's more than happy for it to pass to you. She can tell you so herself when she and Callum arrive next week for New Year.'

Ariel walked to Henry's side of the breakfast bar and gave him what he had now come to recognise as one of her long, inimitable hugs. 'In that case,' she said, 'thank you. I'll take excellent care of it, I promise.'

She gathered a section of hair from the side of her head and pinned it behind her ear. 'Can I tell you something?'

Henry stared open-mouthed at her transformation. 'Of course,' he replied, when he'd composed himself. 'You can tell me anything.'

Ariel swallowed. 'It's about our day together... when it was just you and me and Travis on the train. It's weird to think about it now after everything that's happened, but the fact is, even if all that connected us in the end was that one journey, I'd still have wanted to find a way to keep you in my life.'

A smile so broad, so ebullient radiated across Henry's face that for a second he thought his cheeks might split in two. He reached out and squeezed Ariel's hand, then remembered he hadn't yet given her the second part of her gift.

'I almost forgot!' he said, sliding his brand-new notebook out of his trouser pocket. 'I jotted something down this morning that I thought you might like to read.'

'You're still writing?' she said. 'Since you've been in Oystermouth?'

'Yes!' Henry cleared his throat. 'Though it's barely more than a few paragraphs for now. It's more of an extended Mantra of the Day, really... In any event, you'll need to give it back to me when you've finished. The story isn't quite over yet, you see.'

A thin rectangle of light slanted in through the window, illuminating Ariel's face, causing the butterfly's wings to shimmer. She gave the notebook a curious stare, then she unbuttoned her coat, settled herself on the stool next to Henry, and began to read.

29

Notebook #2

OYSTERMOUTH, WALES: *CHRISTMAS*

Henry

There's the truth we tell others, and then, when the curtains are closed and we think no one's watching, there's the truth we tell ourselves. This is the second of those, the most potent truth of all.

*

As a boy, I thought that if I didn't make my imprint on the world I'd be a nobody all my life; living in the shadows, too afraid to find out who I was. But one day I put on a uniform and discovered I might be someone after all.

*

And it was marvellous. The world hollered! Life opened up before me like a rare, exotic dream.

*

Celia Reynolds

When I came home I fell in love with a girl in a powder-blue coat. She was far too good for me, but I couldn't see it at the time. When I knew I'd lost her I told myself someone else would come along. I thought: maybe not a waitress. I thought: maybe someone better; someone who'd lived a bigger life. My mother would never have approved of her anyway, I told myself. She would have wanted more for me. But it was a lie.

*

Francine caught snowflakes in her eyelashes. Her spirit spun circles around the room while she was sitting spell-bound in her seat. She embraced both the dance, and the stillness in between. And she did it all without any help from me.

*

It's the simple things that matter in the end. As simple as sitting on a balcony, in perfect harmony, watching dancers twirl beneath.

*

My name is Henry Arthur Applebee. I'm eighty-five and counting, a father, and a grandfather to boot.

The world, as I've witnessed it, veers constantly. At once creation and calamity. A miracle and a marvel. A sliver of glass to the heart. An invitation to never stop being amazed. It doesn't stop calling. Not if we're willing to listen. The secret is to grab it by the coat tails, hold on to our hats and –

(to be continued...)

30

A Stranger Smile

UPPER WEST SIDE, NEW YORK: *FIVE MONTHS LATER*

Travis

It was Travis's favourite kind of New York morning: dazzlingly incandescent, the crystalline sky so unerringly blue and the quality of the light so bright, it almost pierced your eyes.

After three months touring the West Coast, he was finally back east. He'd planned the day ahead as a reunion of sorts. The moving pieces had taken forever to come together, but he knew if he kept his spirits high and his intentions crystal-clear, that they would. He'd caught the red-eye from LAX and landed that morning at sunrise. And now he was home, and he'd never felt so happy – or so nervous – in his life.

He headed north along Broadway towards the intersection with West Ninety-First Street and let the warm, May air ripple

381

through his shirt sleeves, through the lazy rough-and-tumble of his hair. Earlier, he'd passed a street vendor hawking prints of the Manhattan skyline; another selling pretzels and coconut juice from a cart. 'Hey, how's it going?' he called out to them. 'Beautiful day!'

He drew it in – the suck and yell and vigour of it – and slowly breathed it out. As far as he was concerned, New York would always be more than a temporary docking station. It was where he felt his limbs take root in the very asphalt of the sidewalks, his arteries entwining with the metropolis's beating heart, pumping his body with the life-blood of the city itself. He knew its concentrated surge of immensity wasn't for everyone, but for him it was a panacea, as natural and vital as a baby drawing sustenance from its mother's breast.

A few weeks after he'd flown home from London, a package addressed to *Mr Travis Farlan, Esq.* arrived at his East Village apartment. The handwriting across the front had an elegant, old-world quality to it – bold, forward-sloping letters which looped in on themselves with lavish sweeps of the pen. He flipped the envelope over and found the sender's name printed in capital letters in the top left-hand corner: ***HENRY APPLEBEE, KENTISH TOWN.***

Travis weighed the envelope in his hand, gauged the heft of it. Not so light, not so heavy; its contents flat and pliable. He tore open a corner and wriggled his finger inside. Paper. Maybe a couple of inches' worth. Carefully, he eased the envelope fully open. What awaited him was a thick bundle of sheet music. *Vintage* sheet music.

Jazz.

A piece of writing paper, folded neatly in two down the middle, sailed in gentle undulations to the floor.

Dear Travis,

Hello! If you're reading this letter then it means the British (and indeed, American) postal services haven't fallen into total disarray and my parcel has safely reached you. I hope it finds you well? I enjoyed meeting you on our train journey to Scotland and trust that now you're home again your saxophone playing is keeping you on your toes.

I don't know if the enclosed may be of interest, but my brother, Devlin, had many wonderful quirks, not least of all collecting and cataloguing sheet music when he himself was incapable of playing a single note. Not that that matters a jot, of course. The truth is, in music, as in everything else, Devlin always had impeccable taste.

The samples included here are a small selection of some of his favourites. My spare room is filled with boxes of them, and my niece won't even look at them; she says they're dust magnets and a fire hazard to boot. (A harsh assessment, in my opinion. For all anyone knows, I might be sitting on a goldmine! Next time you're in London you're welcome to come by and take a look for yourself.)

Anyhow, I'm sure Devlin would feel happy (and vindicated!) to know that a handful had found their way to a fellow jazz fan, and one living in New York – a city he always dreamed of visiting – at that.

Well, Happy New Year to you, Travis! Happy New Year!!!

*By the way, when Ariel gave me your address she asked
me to be sure and say 'hello' to you. (She talks about you
often, as it happens, but don't let on you heard that from
me.) I dare say you youngsters have your own ways of
staying in touch. For my part, I still find that ink and paper
do the job as well as anything else.*

Must dash now to get this in the post.

Sending you all good wishes across the miles.

Your friend,

Henry

A huge smile spread over Travis's face as he refolded the
letter and placed it to one side. He took the stack of sheet
music in his hands and began to thumb through each piece
individually. The sheer artistry of their illustrated covers was
nothing short of awesome. Most were in pretty good condition
overall, with only a couple speckled here and there with
yellowish-brown stains and the occasional fleck of mild disin-
tegration. Typically, vintage sheet music wasn't so difficult to
come by as perhaps Henry thought; provided it wasn't auto-
graphed, you could usually pick up samples online for less
than five bucks apiece.

But that, Travis acknowledged, was hardly the point.

An overwhelming surge of warmth at Henry's impromptu
act of kindness seized hold of him. He would write to him!
He'd go out that very afternoon and buy a postcard, or better,
a notecard – something cool and classy and timeless, like
Henry himself; something with a picture of old New York on
the front! He'd send his thanks old-school, through the mail,

to assure Henry that his brother's precious heirlooms had found a safe and happy home.

He crossed over West Ninetieth Street and headed directly for *Carmine's,* just a few blocks north of the tearoom where his mom had worked when he was a kid. The waiting staff greeted him with a smile and directed him to a large, circular table upstairs. He faltered as he made his approach and saw that his parents – all bustle and efficiency and pressed pastels – were already in their seats.

'Hey, Travis,' Clare cried, 'welcome back! This was such a great idea! It's been way too long since we've all got together like this!'

Travis kissed his mom on the cheek and sat down. 'Hi Dad,' he said, leaning forwards to catch Travis Sr.'s eye.

'Hello, Travis. Nice choice of restaurant. Even if it did mean us travelling all the way to the Upper West Side.'

Travis smiled. Let that one go.

'How was California?' Clare asked.

'Oh, you know... sunny. Busy. Actually, it's nice to be home again and settled in one place.'

'*Ugh*, don't talk to *us* about busy! Your dad and I have hardly had a minute to ourselves since you left. But it's all good. We're feeling quite reborn!'

From the copious emails she'd sent to him while he was on the road, Travis learned that in the aftermath of Superstorm Sandy, his parents were both in the throes of some sort of social and ethical renaissance. Their new neighbours, the Vines, had encouraged them to get involved in a

385

string of local initiatives, including a voluntary educational facility which provided older members of the community with basic computer training, so they didn't feel marginalised and out of touch. They'd even invited them to assist with a crowdfunded arts and theatre project for underprivileged kids.

Such an unexpected burst of altruism had, it seemed, inadvertently given Travis Sr. a whole new lease of life.

'We're overseeing an afterschool programme for kids who want to learn to sing or play an instrument,' he said, waving his hand at a waiter and ordering a cold beer. 'When you're not gallivanting on tour on the other side of the country, you might like to drop by one day and help out.'

Travis balled his hands into fists under the table. *Unfuckingbelievable! Here was his father trying to pitch him on a music initiative!*

He took a deep breath and managed to avoid the temptation to throw out a rejoinder; some acerbic quip on the hypocrisy of Travis Sr.'s almost laughable, self-aggrandising change of tune.

'We can't afford to pay,' Travis Sr. continued, 'but –'

'Dad,' Travis cut in, 'it sounds fantastic. I'd love to.' He met his father's gaze and held it. *Fast.* 'Just tell me where and when. I'll be there. I'm sure I can convince some friends to come along, too.'

Travis Sr. pressed his pale, wiry lips into a closed-mouth smile and nodded. It was a wordless response, but, Travis figured, if that was his idea of an olive branch, he wasn't too proud to reach out and grab it.

He tossed a stray curl of hair out of his eyes and willed his father to say something nice. Just *once*. He wondered what it must have felt like for him to watch his son thrive in the pursuit of his dream. Travis wasn't exactly a *millionaire*, and he had no tangible career trajectory ahead of him at all, in the traditional sense. And yet fundamentally, he was happy. Surely, that counted for *something*?

'So,' Clare said, tapping him pointedly on the arm, 'who's this new lady friend Frank's bringing along with him today? He never even mentioned her name until recently. It sounds like she's quite a bit younger than he is. Is she someone you met while you were over in the UK?'

Travis plucked a breadstick from a basket on the table and casually snapped it in two. 'Actually,' he replied, 'it's kind of a long story.'

His mom rolled her eyes. 'Can't you just tell us the *short* version?'

He chuckled and tipped his head towards the stairway. 'Here's Uncle Frank now. He can tell you himself.'

Frank, looking trim and resplendent in an eggplant-coloured shirt and dark chinos, glided into view at the top of the stairs. On his arm was a pretty, petite, auburn-haired woman around twenty years his junior. She had a camera slung low around her neck and was sporting a wide-eyed expression which seemed to err more on the side of wonder than intimidation. Frank paused a short distance from their table to chat with one of the waiters. As he spoke, the woman raised her hand and brushed a piece of lint from the collar of Frank's shirt – a subtle gesture, Travis noted, laced with understated intimacy. When Frank turned back to face her, she winked at him and squeezed his arm.

'Hey, baby sis!' Frank called out a second later. He strode towards their table, gave Clare a warm kiss hello, then pumped Travis Sr.'s hand and greeted Travis with a long, heartfelt hug. 'Everyone, this is Rosemary De Marco, Rosie to her friends. Rosie, this is my sister Clare, her husband Travis Sr., and their charming, dissolute son Travis, the musician.'

'Hiya,' Rosemary said. She beamed happily around the table. 'It's so nice to finally meet you all! I've heard such a lot about you.'

Travis glanced sidelong at his mom. The words *Wish we could say the same about you* hovered like a storm cloud above her head, though you'd never have guessed it from the beatific expression on her face. She stood up to shake Rosemary's hand and insisted on her husband changing seats so the two women could sit together.

Rosemary wasn't the only piece of news Frank had to share today, Travis knew that much. But he'd let him get to that in his own time.

He slipped his phone out of his pocket and checked it for messages under the table. A steady stream of lunchtime arrivals were making their way up the stairs. Travis raised his head and scanned their faces as they passed by. Considering he'd slept less than an hour on the plane, he should probably have been hallucinating by now, but the sheer excitement of being here had well and truly kicked in, and the happy, nervous feeling in his stomach was rapidly intensifying.

He switched his cell to vibrate and slid it into the pocket

of his jeans. When he turned his attention back to the table he saw that the spotlight was firmly on Rosemary, who at Clare's urging was preparing to regale them all with the story of how she and Frank had met:

'One way or another,' Rosemary began, 'I'm convinced Frank and I were destined to cross paths. We didn't know it, but we already had a connection: we'd both rented the same attic room in Oystermouth – which for those of you who don't know it is what I like to call "Swansea adjacent" in South Wales. It blew me sideways when I found out. Travis here –' she gave an appreciative nod in Travis's direction – 'had a chance meeting with the owner's daughter, Ariel... who knew Frank... and from that moment on, the distance between us started to shrink. There was just one degree of separation between us. Or was it two?'

Travis grinned at Frank across the table. If Rosemary's opening monologue was anything to go by, her story was shaping up to be spectacularly colourful and convoluted.

'Anyway,' she continued, 'there was a change in circumstances, so I agreed to vacate the room by the middle of February. Meanwhile, Frank visited Oystermouth a few weeks before I moved out, only I wasn't there – I was in London attending a course.' She turned to Frank and smiled. 'We were like ships passing in the night.'

Frank held out his hand and skimmed it like a catamaran across the table.

'Ten days later, I had to go back to London for a job interview. It finished earlier than I was expecting, so I went and sat on a bench in Green Park, but it was freezing. Then it started to tip down with rain. I walked through the West End until I arrived in Covent Garden. By now, all I wanted was to be somewhere warm and dry, and suddenly there I was, standing in the doorway of a bar about halfway between the market and the Strand. The place seemed nicely done out – sort of cosy and sophisticated. And while part of me hesitated, a voice in my head told me to stop being an idiot and go inside.

'So I did. I walked straight up to the bar and ordered a glass of pinot noir –'

'Tell them about the movie!' Frank cut in. 'The Paul Giamatti one! The one about the wine!'

'Oh, okay.' Rosemary turned back to the table and smiled. '*So*, there's a scene in the movie *Sideways* where Paul Giamatti tells the woman he's interested in why he's such a fan of pinot. He says something about it being a grape that needs contin-uous care and attention; one that only the most patient growers can coax into its fullest expression... It was very poetic. Admittedly, he made it sound like a bit of a hard slog, but with the right amount of luck and determination, it was worth it in the end. And I thought: that sounds a lot like love, really, doesn't it?'

She paused briefly – and somewhat theatrically – for breath.

'At that point,' she resumed, 'I turned and saw that there was only one other customer in the whole place, a very distin-guished looking man sitting in a booth by the window. What struck me was his expression – I can only describe it as *luminous*. I smiled – I couldn't help myself, it just sprang out of me – and he smiled back. And all I remember thinking was, *Please God, if you're listening, please don't let me get my heel caught in my skirt when I get up and look a fool. Because I swear, I've never wanted to look less like a fool in my entire life.'*

Travis flicked his eyes back to Frank. He'd never seen his uncle look at Cynthia the way he was looking at Rosemary now. This was way bigger than love (if that was even possible). Frank had a kind of magnetic glow about him, but more than that, he actually looked *peaceful*.

'It was then,' Rosemary went on, 'that I started to feel a bit unnerved, the way you do when your sixth sense tells you that something momentous is about to happen, and there's nothing you or anyone else can do to stop it. *Like it was written*. I actually started to tremble. I was on the verge of paying my bill when I heard someone say –'

'Excuse me,' Frank interjected, 'if you're not waiting for anyone, would you like to join me at my table? It's a beautiful day, don't you think?'

Rosemary beamed at him. 'In fact, it was *pouring* down outside, but there was Frank standing right next to me, so I said, "Yes, I'd love to." Just like that. I hadn't accepted an invitation to join a man for a drink in twenty years, not since I met my ex-husband, who wouldn't know luminosity and sophistication if they waltzed up behind him on a scooter and smacked his arse. The only thing I knew was that I had to say yes. That this was it. *This was my moment.* Frank just had that look about him. Like he was carved out of magic dust.'

To Travis's amazement, Rosemary actually started to blush.

'And that was it. When it was time for me to leave Frank flagged down a cab to take me to Paddington, and when I got home he called me and we carried on talking. We've been together ever since. It's funny, isn't it, how your life can be transformed in an instant, just by turning around on a bar stool and seeing a stranger smile?'

Rosemary reached for a breadstick and was quiet at last. The whole time she'd been talking Frank kept his hand in the small of her back, as though she were some rare, precious creature who might at any moment take fright at her surroundings and fly away.

He leaned in tenderly and kissed her.

'Hey, guys, all the best to you!' Travis cried. He raised his glass in a toast and gazed cheerfully around the table. He assumed his parents – who were both sitting bolt upright in some sort of mummified silence – would follow suit. Instead, Travis Sr. shot his brother-in-law a confused glance.

'I'm sorry, Frank, but I have to ask... Why exactly was it such a beautiful day?'

'*Honey!*' Travis's mom wagged her head in horror. 'Don't be so rude!'

'Clare, I'm not *being* rude. I don't mean to sound coy or facetious, but if there was the mother of all rainstorms outside, I'm just curious, that's all. What was it that put Frank in such a good mood?'

Frank stared at him open-mouthed, then slapped his hand on his thigh and burst into loud peals of laughter. 'Seriously, I don't know whether you're the least romantic man on the planet, or just the most astute, but you're right, I *had* had some good news just before Rosie walked in that afternoon. That's why I was there in the first place, for a minor – if admittedly, premature – celebration. And if it hadn't been for my good humour, I may never have found the courage to approach her at all. So I guess as Rosie says herself, something about the circumstances of that day just conspired to bring us together.'

Travis groaned. He couldn't take his uncle pussyfooting around the subject a moment longer. '*So?* Did you get the job or not, Uncle Frank?'

Frank smoothed his fingers over his perfectly coiffed hair and grinned. 'You're looking at the brand-new star of the West End stage! Well, technically speaking we're debuting in Manchester. But with any luck, we'll be transferred to the West End if the show plays well to audiences outside London.'

Clare's face lit up like a Fourth of July parade. 'The West End? *Frank!* That's *terrific!*'

'Terrific, yes, but it was more a question of me being in the right place at the right time, if I'm being absolutely honest with you,' he replied.

'You're much too modest,' Rosemary said with a shy smile. She kissed Frank on the cheek. 'You earned it. You know that, don't you? The cream always rises to the top, as my mother likes to say.'

'Well, this *is* a surprise.' Travis Sr.'s tone suddenly shifted gear from neutral to mildly interested. 'What's the show about? Is it anything we might have heard of?'

Frank hiked himself up a little taller in his seat. 'It's a brand-new commission about a group of former celebrity

393

lookalikes and what happens to them after their careers are deemed to be over. It's called *Famous Last Words*. It's actually a commentary on celebrity culture as a whole – very topical – and the score has some wonderful original songs in it, too. The day I met Rosie I'd just had my second call-back and was feeling quietly optimistic. There was a huge amount of interest in my role, but deep down, I knew they'd never find anyone as perfect for it as me.'

Travis Sr. held out his hand. 'Congratulations, Frank. Sincere congratulations, indeed.'

Frank waved his brother-in-law's hand aside, grabbed him by the shoulders and pulled him in for a bear hug. 'Thanks, bud. I gotta say I owe Ray big time for this. He worked his ass off to get me an audition, especially considering I don't have the formal acting credentials of most of the cast members – though in a way, you could say I've been prepping for this role my entire life... We start rehearsals next week, that's why Rosie and I decided to slot in a quick trip to the U.S. now, because once the show starts previewing – all being well – I'm not going to have any free time to travel for a while.' He looked over at Clare and winked. 'You'll have to watch this space to see if we make it to Broadway.'

Travis waited for Frank to finish speaking. When he caught his uncle's eye, he gave him a private look of recognition he knew Frank alone would understand.

It didn't matter that something could go awry. The financial backing could fall through; the show's run might be cut short and never actually make it to the West End at all.

Or not... At the end of the day, Frank always told him to

take what life throws at you and get on with it. *Just put yourself out there, Travis, and give it your best shot!*

Travis grinned and gave him a hearty thumbs-up. 'That's awesome, Uncle Frank! It might even be the surprise smash of the season! I mean, *fuck* – sorry, Mom – but an unconventional concept didn't hurt *Book of Mormon*. Why shouldn't a bunch of renegade celebrity impersonators have just as much luck?'

There was still one empty seat at the table, and as the backslapping and glass-clinking drew to a close, Travis finally spotted a girl with a canvas bag slung diagonally over her body making her way across the room. She paused for a moment to catch her breath, her hands resting on her hips, her wavy hair piled high on her head in a casually messy bun. Her eyes were shining, her normally pale skin warmed by a bronze sheen of colour on her cheeks, across the ridge of her forehead, along the subtle upsweep of her nose.

'Hey!' he called out to her.

'Hi!' she replied. 'I'm so sorry I'm late!' She locked eyes with his and gave him a truly spectacular smile. 'I really wanted to get here early,' she said in an apologetic voice, 'but I got wrapped up in something and completely lost track of time.'

Four pairs of eyes turned expectantly to greet her.

Frank was already on his feet.

Travis felt his heart – happy, nervous – swelling inside of him. He waited while she hugged everyone, saying her hellos, then he pulled back the spare seat alongside him, and grinning broadly, gestured to Ariel to sit down.

31

The City

UNION SQUARE, NEW YORK: *A FEW HOURS EARLIER*

Ariel

> 'The first time it happened, you were five years old. It was
> summer and you were playing in the tent in the back
> garden. The tent was second-hand and musty, but that
> didn't bother you. You saw only the perfect doll's house
> angles of its sloping roof, the tautness of its mustard walls,
> the crisp brown grass beneath your feet.
>
> Later, when we were...'

'"... sitting making daisy chains in the shade,"' Ariel read out
loud, '"you told me what had happened."'

She paused, lowered Estelle's letter to her lap and looked
up. Twenty blocks or so away, holding sway over the horizon,
was the Empire State Building, the undisputed queen of the

Midtown skyline. She'd lost count of the number of times she'd read Estelle's letter over the past few months, but she'd never before been sitting anywhere even remotely as exhilarating as this.

"'You'd closed the canvas ties and shut yourself inside to make a hidey-hole,'" she continued. "'The air was stiff with heat, but when...'"

'... you raised your hands to your face they were cold and clammy. Beads of light shimmered in front of your eyes. You reached out, trying to catch the pretty coloured discs spinning around you. You didn't feel like Ariel any more, especially when you began to sink towards the ground. But you weren't afraid. You swung your hands behind your back and groped along the damp, hollow space between your shoulder blades. "Wings!" you cried. "Please let me have wings so I can fly!"

By the time I found you, you were lying semiconscious on the floor of the tent, your arms splayed out like a teddy bear's at your sides. You were always running, always bumping your head on door handles or half-open drawers. I was so worried, but you just turned your head to me and smiled. "Mam, I'm an angel! All I'm missing now are my wings."

I picked you up and carried you upstairs to the kitchen. Sweat was trickling down the back of my neck from the fright, but you were calm and content as can be. "Mam," you whispered, "can I tell you a secret?" I leaned over the sink, still cradling you in my arms. "Of course you can, poppet." I didn't know what you were going to say. I was just relieved you were okay. You slid your arms around my neck, curled your fingers through my hair, and said: "This is the best day of my life, you know."'

Ariel smiled and slid the letter back inside its envelope. She didn't read the rest. She could already recite the entire thing by heart, if she needed to. She tucked it safely inside her canvas bag and took out her journal and a pen.

'Are you an actress?' a woman's voice asked nearby.

She raised her head and saw a slim, grey-haired lady aged anywhere from fifty to a hundred, dressed in a black roll-neck jumper, tapered black trousers and black suede pumps. The woman looked at her kindly and smiled. 'I was sitting on that bench over there and I saw you talking to yourself. Thought maybe you were running through your lines?'

'No, I'm not an actress. I'm a student,' Ariel replied. 'I was just reading something out loud. From my mother.'

'A student!' The woman tilted her head to one side. 'I don't think I've ever stopped being one of those. Seems to me like there's something new to learn every day! Still, with that pretty accent of yours, I bet you'd do a fabulous turn on the stage.'

Ariel laughed. 'I don't know about that. My dream is to be a photographer... so I can tell people's stories with pictures. My dad thinks it's hilarious when my best friend and I message photos to each other. He says it's a cop-out if we're not using words. But I keep telling him: photographs aren't about silence. They're about giving things a voice.'

'Well *said*, young lady!'

The woman shifted her gaze and threw an admiring glance at her hair. 'Oh, what a beautiful hair clip! I don't think I've ever seen anything so precious!'

Ariel touched her hand to her head. 'Thank you! It was my grandmother's. She was wearing it the first time my grandfather laid eyes on her. I've been a bit nervous about using it, just in case I lose it, but he told me it was time to take it out into the world and let it breathe. So here it is.'

'Good for you, honey! Show it some of our fine Manhattan air!' The woman waved a bony hand in the direction of Ariel's journal. 'Well, I'd better let you get on. Looks like there's something you're waiting to say. Bye, sweetie.'

Ariel gave her a bemused smile. 'Bye...'

She waited for the woman to leave, then glanced into the distance and contemplated the Empire State Building once more. By the time her month in New York was over, she'd be nineteen – the exact same age Francine was when she and Henry met. She wondered what her grandmother would have made of it had she had the chance to visit New York for herself. Brooklyn... Harlem... Long Island... She'd spent the last couple of weeks racing around all over the place. She'd even taken the ferry to Staten Island so she could photograph the famous skyline from the deck.

She'd wandered around art galleries and photography galleries until she was so overstimulated by the brilliance of it all, she could hardly see straight. Afterwards, she'd sit in Bryant Park, near the New York Public Library, or rattle around on an orange plastic seat on the subway until the images untangled and settled in her brain. Ariel smiled to herself.

Francine would probably have kicked off her shoes and danced through the streets...

She opened her journal and turned to a blank page. *Write to me,* Estelle's letter said. *I won't be far away. Remember, you can write to me whenever you like.*

She pressed her pen to the page:

Tuesday, May 21: Travis arrived back home today.

Ariel stopped and stared at what she'd just written. The word 'home' had flowed so naturally from her pen, but this was his city, not hers. She lived over three thousand miles away. Maybe she was just imagining things? Maybe the quick, nervous kiss he'd given her when she'd opened the door to him that morning had been nothing more than a friendly greeting? But if that was the case, then why did it feel so great?

Hi! she'd said. *Welcome home.* He'd given her one of those enormous, impossible-to-ignore smiles of his, and then he'd leaned in close and kissed her.

And just what were they supposed to do now?

The future, Henry always liked to remind her, *can take you anywhere.* And if it could take *her* anywhere, then maybe it could take Travis and his sax anywhere, too?

She took a deep breath and turned her attention back to the page:

He arranged for me to have keys to his apartment while he was in California, though his place wasn't exactly empty while he was away. Friends dropped by looking for him every now and then. Sometimes it was musicians. Other times it was people living in his building. I don't know if he specifically asked them to check in on me (he'd never admit it if he did), but they all smiled and said they liked my accent, and a few even offered to show me around. It's worked out great. I haven't been lonely at all.

As for the city, I never imagined I'd visit a place so famous for its skyscrapers and mile high billboards and be blown away, of all things, by the trees. It's like they're from another age, they're almost preternaturally green!

And the air smells different. It's no better or worse than home, just different. I'm seriously thinking of bottling some up in a jam jar and taking it back for Isaac, though I don't know if he'll be able to get a sense of it. It might just evaporate the minute he takes the lid off, and he'll look at me with those huge, questioning eyes and ask if I've turned into a New York crazy while I've been away.

The light is different, too. It's as though there are no filters on the sky, it just pours straight through, like it's flowing from another dimension. Some days are as grey as home, only here the grey is fierce and uncompromising – like the giant steel girders you see in those famous black and white photographs of New York. Then other days it softens, and when the cloud cover lifts it's the pale, mercurial grey of Henry's eyes.

I've taken way too many pictures to send to Tumbleweed, so I'm saving them all up to show him when I get home. Last night he sent me one of him and his other half, Simon.

Celia Reynolds

They've been together for a couple of months now, though I don't think that'll come as a surprise to you. I'm pretty sure you'd picked up on it long ago.

Yesterday, I got lost in Central Park trying to find Bethesda fountain. Do you remember when we watched Angels in America *together on DVD? You said it must be wonderful to sit right there by the water and just soak up the atmosphere and think. And I was curious. I wanted to see it for myself.*

I'd been walking around for ages trying to work out where I was. I bumped into an Indian couple in the Ramble pointing out a red-tailed hawk to their son. He started giggling and bouncing up and down in his buggy, just like Isaac used to do, so I stopped and looked up at the trees, but I couldn't see a hawk, or a nest, just a single yellow balloon caught way up in the branches like a fallen sun.

I walked past the boating lake, onto a curving path. I turned a corner and came across a lady kneeling in the shrubbery. She was wearing a tangerine-coloured headscarf which she'd knotted at the back of her head like a factory worker from an old wartime movie. I thought she must be a gardener, so I stopped and asked her if I was going in the right direction for the fountain.

She stared all around her and seemed really confused, then she shook her head and mouthed a single word: 'No.' It wasn't even loud enough to be a whisper. Her lips rounded like a perfect letter O, the way I'd seen Henry's once do, only his face had been filled with wonder. The lady in the shrubbery seemed motivated more by despair.

I wanted so badly to reassure her, so I said, 'Please don't worry. I'm sure I'll find it. Thank you!'

I started to walk away, but I could feel her eyes following me. I felt terrible for having disturbed her. I thought maybe she didn't work in the park after all. Perhaps it was just a hobby, or a form of therapy? Maybe she was damaged or unwell. I had so many questions. Most of all, I wanted to know how she managed to get by.

In the end, the conclusion I came to was that whatever the millions of stories that made up her life, all that mattered to her on that sunny afternoon were the flowers and plants she was tending. She'd borrowed a quiet corner of New York's most iconic urban park for herself, and it gave her pleasure, and I was glad.

I found the fountain eventually. I sat in the shade and gazed at it for ages, and you were right. It was amazing! Before I left I circled around the base and photographed the angel from every possible angle. I don't think I managed to get a good shot of its face, though. One day, I'll go back and try and capture the look of determination in its eyes.

Now I'm sitting on a bench in Union Square. On my way in, I passed a homeless man with a cardboard sign saying, IF YOU GIMME YOUR CHANGE I'LL TELL YOU A JOKE. I gave him a dollar and do you know what he said to me? 'A dollar don't even buy a cup of New York coffee no more. Ain't that the funniest thing you ever heard?'

So I went up to the café at Barnes & Noble and bought him the biggest coffee I could find. He let me take his picture for that.

Celia Reynolds

When I go home I'll be back on the fast-track study programme Mr Deacons put me on in January. I told him I want to finish the final year of my A-levels and then see. Sometimes the idea of university scares me (I'm still trying to work out why), but Henry says there's nothing unusual about that – the most rewarding things in life often do. He's even offered to help Linus with the tuition fees. Linus nearly burst into tears when Henry told him, but Henry said that considering he didn't have the chance to do it for Linus, the least he can do is help Isaac and me.

Ariel paused, then pressed her pen to the page once again:

I wish you could have met him. He's the most incredible human being. He said he wants to spend more time with us given that he could be 'gone for a burton' at any time. And then he told me I should give myself a month here to think about what I want, and that when I go home, 'I'll know.'

I wonder a lot about what you'd say if you were here. Sometimes, I think I can feel you near me, but I can't be sure it's you. I keep your letter for when I need to hear your voice, and I keep it for Isaac, like you asked, so that when he needs it he can read it, too.

Most of what you wrote about, I don't remember. I don't remember fainting in the tent and telling you I thought I was an angel. I don't even know if it's true? But it doesn't matter. Even if it was nothing more than a beautiful vision that filled your dreams at the end, when things weren't so clear for you any more, it still makes me smile because it came from you.

Ariel raised her head. A short distance away, someone was waving at her with what looked, quite possibly, like New York's most appreciative smile.

Guess what… The homeless man across the square just grinned and waved his shoe at me, so I raised my journal and gave him a little wave back.

She flicked her eyes to her phone and saw the time. '*Crap.*'
She dug her hand into her bag and pulled out her map of the New York subway. '14 Street – Union Square,' she said, locating the stop with her forefinger and tracing the line north to the Upper West Side.
She slid the map back inside her bag and picked up her pen.

I have to finish now, but I'll write again soon, I promise.

Ariel paused, one last time.

I miss you, Mam. Every single day. Please just don't worry about us, okay? We're good. I'm good.
I love you.

She placed her journal inside her canvas bag, slung it across her body and set off in the direction of the subway. On the

Celia Reynolds

road beyond the square, horns beeped intermittently, traffic whizzed by. She passed beneath the sheltering overhang of trees and glanced overhead. Through layers of tangled green, she caught flashes of a luscious, blue sky.

A breeze stirred the leaves; the breath of the city, and of the billowed bay back home. The fine Manhattan air lifted, whispering and crackling inside her. Ariel drew to a stop and smiled. *Henry was right:* the world was calling. She could hear it.

406

Epilogue

BLACKPOOL, EIGHTEEN MONTHS (AND COUNTING) LATER

Henry

Henry teeters on the edge of a wide, sparsely populated promenade. It's November, and he's barely finished buttoning up his coat when a mischievous gust of sea air blows in over the water and tweaks the peak of his flat cap. The force threatens to whisk it off his head entirely, but he manages to reach up and grab it before it spirals away, spinning like a herringboned frisbee into the boundless blue beyond.

'Are you sure you'll be all right by yourself?' Linus asks. He leans across the empty passenger seat of the car Henry has just vacated and extends him a now familiar glance.

Henry watches the shifting prism of anxiety and encouragement, reverence and doubt which flash in quick succession over Linus's face. In all its profound complexity, he has, over the course of the past, thrilling twenty-three months, come

407

to acknowledge his son's expression as simply this: the undreamed of embodiment of deep, filial love.

'No need to worry,' Henry assures him. He blinks several times in deference to a surprisingly effulgent, mid-morning glare. 'You know me – I'll be right as rain!'

'Okay, Dad, if you're sure. I'll come back for you a little later. Go slowly, now.'

'At my age,' Henry quips, 'is there any other way?'

Linus laughs and prepares to drive away. Henry hears the low, guttural growl of the ignition. Sees his son's attention shift to the road ahead. Shuffling to the edge of the kerb, he raises a knobbly finger and raps three times on the windscreen. 'Linus?'

Linus rolls down the window and leans across the passenger seat once again. 'Everything okay? Did you forget something?'

'No,' Henry mumbles, 'I didn't forget anything. I just wanted to say thank you. For the trip. For the wonderful company. And well, for everything really.' He feels a quickening in his chest, a faint, but none the less discernible *tick tick tick*.

'Pleasure's all mine,' Linus replies with a wink. 'But don't thank me too soon. I've still got the business to sort out first. We're not heading home just yet.'

'Yes,' Henry says, 'I hope it all goes smoothly. Make sure you grab us a bargain or two. Let the book-pulping factory wait!'

A smile – wide, open, brimful with affection – graces his son's face.

I love you, Henry thinks. *I love you so much.*

'Bye, Dad.'

'Bye, son!'

Linus toots the horn and slowly drives away.

Alone on the esplanade, Henry checks his watch. He estimates he has at least a couple of hours, by which time Linus should have completed his work in nearby Lytham-St-Annes. Though he'd be loath to admit it to anyone but himself, Henry has never before experienced such elation at hearing the (regrettable) news of a second-hand bookshop closing down. After all, it was Linus's decision to drive up and evaluate their stock in person that prompted him to organise the trip north in the first place, and Henry wasted no time at all in suggesting he tag along for the ride:

'It'll be the perfect opportunity for a road trip,' he told him. 'Father and son together!'

As for Lytham-St-Annes' proximity to Blackpool, *that* – it went without saying – was nothing more than a happy coincidence...

Henry takes a step backwards and observes the Tower through narrowed eyes. He feels strangely disorientated. From here, at least, nothing is how he remembers it. Where the magnificent grand entranceway once stood facing the shore, there is now only a rough blockade of monochrome boarding. The wooden panels – which have been painted a deep russet red (the same colour as the Tower itself) – stand in closed ranks, tight and impenetrable as a human police cordon. The unforeseen transformation takes Henry's breath away, and for one awful moment he worries he might not be able to get inside after all.

His gaze climbs to the top of the spire. The pinnacle soars

with brassy confidence, steadfast and heroic, extending ever higher to the clear November sky. Henry's brain clinks and whirs. The Tower can't possibly be closed...

There must be another way?

He tries to remember the phrase, the motto of some kind stumbled upon in Eve Marie's book. It belonged to the Anstruther clan as he recalls. *Periissem ni periissem*, that was it!

'*I would have perished had I not persisted.*'

Henry smiles triumphantly to himself. Now *that's* what he calls a Mantra of the Day!

He crosses the road, and with slow, shuffling steps begins to inch his way around the perimeter of the building. Walking isn't as easy as it used to be. He knows where he wants to go, knows exactly what his body should be doing to get him there, but it's been maddeningly disobedient of late. His lips press together in concentration as he turns first one corner, then another, until finally, immediately ahead of him, the brand-new entranceway muscles into view.

'You can't be serious,' Henry cries. He comes to a stop and casts a disconsolate glance at his shadow stretched out on the ground before him. 'What in the name of all that's sacred have they done?'

The Tower's new entrance is bland. Automated. Modern in the extreme. Henry stares at it once again, half hoping to discover he's mistaken. It isn't the same. How could it be? It doesn't have half the glamour or panache of the original entrance, but he sets off towards it none the less, his eyes trained with dogged determination on the rhythmically sliding doors.

With a tenuous grip on his walking stick, Henry steps inside. From behind a nondescript counter a shiny young woman looks over at him and smiles. He reciprocates, asks how he can access the Tower Ballroom. Round he goes, following her directions through a noisy neon pathway of slot machines and flashing lights until he arrives at last at the place he remembers, on the opposite side of the building where the original booth once stood.

The familiar staircase unfurls before him. Henry stands and stares at it in awe.

Inset at intervals into the mahogany, red-brick walls turquoise marble cherubs gather and whisper in merry pairs. Bracing himself for the climb, he takes a determined step towards them. He's barely advanced more than a few inches when a woman with cropped silver hair and large, hooped earrings crosses in front of him.

Henry draws to a halt and notices that she's trailing a small carry-on suitcase in her wake.

'Will you be wanting the lift?' she calls out in a friendly tone, her question delivered in a flat, local drawl.

Henry turns and suddenly, he sees it; the possibility of there being a lift hadn't even crossed his mind!

'My dance stuff,' she says, pointing to her case. 'I'd take the stairs if I didn't have to bring a change of clothes. You have to be able to move freely and smoothly for all the turns and spins.'

'Oh, I don't doubt it!' Henry says, making his way towards her. 'I don't doubt it at all!'

The lift doors shut behind them and up they go in calm,

easy silence. The woman gets out one floor below him, at dance floor level, but Henry remains where he is and continues all the way to the fifth floor.

When the doors open again, Henry emerges into the Tower's upper foyer. A panoramic sweep of enormous windows dominates the foreground, framing between them the intractable sea, and the long-limbed North Pier, and all of life below. He hesitates, thinks perhaps he should take a minute or two to admire the view. But then, from beyond the double doors he hears the sound of the Wurlitzer organ. Henry's heart leaps. *Eighty-seven and counting, and the music moves him still!*

The shooting pains in his legs melt away, swept from his body by a powerful tidal wave of adrenaline. Henry manoeuvres himself towards the dance hall with a remarkable resurgence of dexterity. Through the doors he goes, and there it is! *There it is!*

The first thing he sees is the inscription engraved in the stonework above the stage: BID ME DISCOURSE, I WILL ENCHANT THINE EAR...

Henry climbs the short flight of stairs to the upper balcony. Most of the other spectators are one tier below, scattered along the edges in twos and threes, but Henry holds his course and heads directly for his place in the balcony's front row.

He rests his stick against the barrier and slips off his cap. He will, he decides, keep his coat buttoned all the way to his chest for now. Tucked into the collar is a paisley scarf – a birthday present from Ariel – a splendid, wholly unapologetic carnival of colour, fringed at the edges, about as far away from monochrome as one could possibly go.

412

'You look so handsome!' she said the first time he wore it. 'Like Anthony Hopkins and Paul Newman all rolled into one!'

Henry runs his hand along its silken folds, presses the fabric against his neck. It's deathly cold. He doesn't remember it ever being this cold in here before, but judging by the rosy faces of the dozen or so couples on the dance floor, no one else seems to be bothered by the chill.

He settles into his chair and peers over the barrier. Seated on the periphery of the dance floor is a woman with an elaborate, feathered fan. Henry follows her gaze and sees that she's looking not at the dance floor itself, but at a distant doorway. When the door opens, the woman raises the fan above her head and beckons to the silver-haired lady from the lift who sails through in a pair of buckled dance shoes, and a dress that floats like candy floss about her legs.

Henry smiles and turns his attention upwards – to the intricate array of murals on the ceiling, to the clusters of quietly glitzy crystal chandeliers. (No sign of the glitter balls today.)

The famous Wurlitzer organ is where it always was, directly ahead, centre stage.

'Plus ça change,' he says, glancing with a chuckle at his seat, 'plus c'est la même... "*chaise*"!'

Effortlessly, the rhythm changes and a Lilac Waltz fills the room. Way off in the corner, a young man in his early twenties takes to the floor with an older gentleman of indeterminate age. The older man has a sallow complexion and thin, wispy hair. The young man is lithe and light on his feet, enviably graceful, with dainty hips and finely-tapered

413

hands. The older man does his best to keep up, but he's neither as mobile, nor as precise in his movements as his youthful companion.

They are, Henry notes with interest, the only male couple on the dance floor – something which had been strictly prohibited back in the day. He taps his foot in time with the music as the pair glide and turn, turn and glide, looping in endless circles through a rotating tureen of bodies, blending into one, lifting almost, into the air. He loses himself so completely in his surroundings, he very nearly misses the voice ringing out just inches from his ear.

Henry swivels in his seat, glances behind him.

All he can make out are empty chairs, the upholstery faded and worn, occasional rips in the fabric crudely covered over with strips of adhesive red tape. He shakes his head. *Is it possible,* he wonders, *that the voice spoke his name?*

Henry turns once more to the dance floor. For some time, all he does is watch and listen. He draws the cool, dank air into his lungs. Feels the music reverberate behind his ribcage. And then, with the music thrumming a melody against his sternum, he opens his eyes wide and understands instinctively what he is being asked to do.

Resting his hand palm upwards on the empty seat beside him, Henry closes his eyes. All at once, as though she'd been sitting next to him the entire time, he feels the weight of Francine's hand in his. He holds his breath, careful not to grip her fingers too tightly for fear the sensation might slip away. But it does not slip away; it grows stronger, more defined.

Slowly, he caresses the back of her hand with his thumb.

'Francine?'

'Yes, Henry.'

A shiver, nimble as quicksilver, shoots along his spine. 'Is it really you?'

'Of course it's me,' she answers playfully. 'Who were you expecting? Rita Hayworth?'

Henry's face erupts into a euphoric smile. 'I –' He pauses, catches the scent of jasmine floating in the air. 'Would you like to dance?'

'Yes,' she cries. 'Yes! I'd love to.'

At the sound of her voice he falters, afraid he'll forget the steps, afraid he'll spoil it all again by messing up. But somewhere deep inside him an uncontrollable urge to move forwards – to step freely, *boldly!* into the spotlight that's been waiting for him all this time – grabs him by the shoulders and presses him onwards.

Decades slide from his body. Like snow-melt.

Henry's free hand begins to shake. *It's okay,* he tells himself. *I won't be alone. I'll be with Francine.* How difficult can it be, for heaven's sake? Even if he falls flat on his face, gets trampled to the ground by life, by the burden of expectation, by the rollicking, runaway rollercoaster of love, isn't that a chance he's prepared to take?

'I must warn you, though,' he says quickly, 'I'm not much of a dancer. It's the mu –'

'*Shhh…*' Francine squeezes his hand. 'Come on, nobody's watching us. Just follow me. It's this way.'

Henry opens his eyes and sees her face at last. He wants to embrace her, to tell her everything he's been holding inside him for so long, but she's already on her feet. As she leads him from his seat, a lock of hair tumbles against her cheek.

She laughs, not bothering to brush it away.

Together on the dance floor, Henry and Francine spin round and round, their feet barely skimming the ground, the rush of air cool and sharp and exhilarating against Henry's skin. On they dance, until everything in Henry's immediate line of vision begins to dissolve in a kaleidoscopic blur of colour and glittering luminescence. Spheres of light leap and whirl before him. There is, he realises with a start, such an overwhelming surfeit of beauty in this moment that for a second, he's convinced he can feel his heart cry out and bend beneath the very weight of it.

He shuts his eyes. Utters a silent prayer:

Don't wake up. Don't wake up. Don't wake up.

The music roars. Henry's heart sings.

He isn't shaking any more. Instead, it's as though his entire body, from tip to toe, is vibrating. With one hand resting in the curve of Francine's back, the other entwined with hers, Henry draws a thin inhalation of air into his nostrils. When he exhales, for the very last time, his breath is steady, and certain, and deep. Around him, as the colours slowly intensify, the variegated spectacle of all that has been, and all that is, rises up. Melts away. Transforms.

And still, they dance.

Acknowledgements

Heartfelt thanks, first and foremost, to my wonderful agent and wing woman, Rebecca Ritchie, for believing in me, for taking such good care of me, and for quite simply, being a dream come true.

A huge hug of gratitude to everyone at HarperCollins who has embraced this book so warmly, especially Kimberley Young for taking a chance, and my big-hearted editor, Charlotte Ledger, whose guidance and enthusiasm led me back to the coalface and encouraged me to give the story a bright new pair of wings. Thank you, too, to Sophie Burks, for consistently helpful and attentive editorial insights, and to my copyeditor, Laura Evans, for having such a keen eye.

To my friends Samantha Wakefield, Sarah Duggan, Michael De Lucia, and Lindy Shufflebotham – thank you for your mighty and tireless support, good-humoured pep talks, and for keeping me smiling and sane, no matter what. And to my friend (and dedicated dream chaser!), Sonja Vilsmeier, I have to add to the above a rallying cry of *Fortune favours the brave!* My world wouldn't be the same without any one of you. You are all heroes.

I am grateful to Maggie Hamand of the *Complete Creative Writing Course* for her expertise and for giving me crucial feedback on a very early draft. Additional thanks to Faber Academy for their valuable comments on a significantly reworked later one...

A special (musical) note of gratitude to Laurie Lewis, whose generosity in sharing his knowledge of jazz was instrumental (pun intended!) in bringing the jazz references to life.

Warm thanks, also, to Ian Johnstone, for his very helpful and timely writerly advice.

I am indebted to the following people for their friendship, positivity, and world-class encouragement: Todd Huntley – who, in addition to being a brilliant human being, created a genuine 'pivotal moment' by giving me the tickets that set the wheels in motion; Shelley Atkin – a human dynamo, whose awesomeness knows no bounds; Jeff Rowland – greetings to tutta la famiglia (ci sentiamo, va bene?); and the lovely Lynne Davies, Gareth Davies, and the entire Mumbles Coffee crew – thank you with all my heart for cheering me on with epic smiles and such great coffee.

I am lucky to have had the support of Michael Forero (photographs!), Kristen Francis, Samantha Russell, Barbara Thalhammer, Mick Passeri, Stuart Baldwin, Emma Evans, Jo Warring, Hayley Morgan, and Alyson Mellin. And for 360 degrees of wisdom I am indebted to Jacqui Bastock, and the exceptional Dawn Brown.

Blockbuster-sized thanks to everyone who was part of the Fox family – for the laughter, and for still rooting for me after all this time.

I am humbly grateful to the London Library – a place of magic, where the early drafts of this novel were written.

Lastly, to Joy Reynolds, thank you so much for never doubting me.

This book would not have come into being without the encouragement and support of my sister, Caroline, and my father, Brian. They are no longer here to read it, but somewhere, perhaps, they're smiling at me and waving. For this, and for so much more, I'm forever grateful.